Mark Munger

S0-FPG-795

Muckraker: a Novel Noir

By Mark Munger

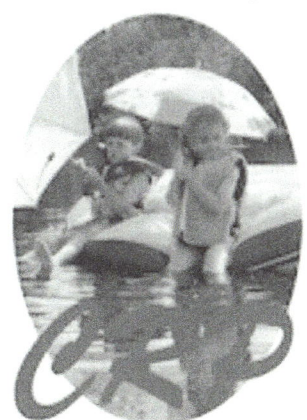

www.cloquetriverpress.com

First Edition
Copyright 2023, Mark Munger

All rights reserved, including the right to reproduce this book or any portions thereof, in any form, except for brief quotations embodied in articles and reviews without written permission from the publisher. The opinions, observations, and historical references herein are those of the author alone.

This story is fiction. Places, names, characters, organizations, or incidents depicted in this work are products of the author's imagination. Any reference to "real" people, places, organizations, or events, living or dead, past or present, is made to facilitate the fictional tale.

ISBN 978-1-7324434-4-0
Library of Congress Control Number 2023914671
Edited by Scibendi
Find out more at: www.cloquetriverpress.com
Email the author at: cloquetriverpress@yahoo.com

ACKNOWLEDGMENTS

I would like to thank the following individuals who served as readers for this project: Vicky Hubert, Ken Hubert, Mark Rubin, Fred Friedman, John Simon, Eric Hylden, and Hanna Erpestad.

Without these dedicated friends devoting their time and effort to reading the manuscript, the content and flow of this tale might be vastly different and—more than likely—vastly inferior.

A word of thanks to my wife, René, who also pre-read this book. Many days and nights have been lost to family while I type away at the keyboard, struggle with revisions, or sleep in my chair because I've been up at five in the morning working on this book. Her patience through the duration of this project is much appreciated.

                    Mark Munger
                    2023
                    Duluth, Minnesota

Dedicated to the writers, poets, and journalists of the world who have given their lives for truth.

PROLOGUE
Minneapolis, Minnesota
Christmas Eve 1931

The man eased his temperamental 1924 Oakland as close to the curb on Bloomington Avenue as poor snowplowing by Minneapolis teamsters would allow. Earlier in the day, Bill Anderson—the Farmer Labor Mayor of Minneapolis—had cajoled and berated and threatened city plow truck drivers to "Clear the streets boys or start looking for other work!"

The man turned off the key to the Oakland, sat silently behind the steering wheel, and contemplated the waning day. He'd been out that morning, shoveling the sidewalk in front of the upstairs duplex that his family rented. Now, it was near dusk. Wispy clouds of little consequence floated above the gritty, coal-heated city. Despite fires raging in the furnaces of the city's homes, businesses, and factories—the heating plants spewing clouds of black smoke and foul expressions of burning anthracite into the crisp winter air—the man breathed deeply. After holding his breath for a moment, he exhaled and reached across the Oakland's front passenger seat and retrieved a brown paper sack containing cheap cuts of lamb and beef purchased at Greene's Butcher Shop on South Chicago. His family would eat well, if inexpensively, on the lamb shanks, beef brisket, and chuck roast crammed into the sack by Emil Greene, the proprietor of the neighborhood's only butcher shop. The man grabbed a second paper bag containing modest holiday gifts wrapped and addressed to his two children and his wife. He struggled with the awkward weight of the presents and groceries as he straightened to his full height and exited the Oakland.

A southbound streetcar, its lights swaying in time to the clickity-clack of the coach, rumbled down the middle of the avenue. A handful of passengers sat inside the streetcar. Many of the trolley riders had packages—likely from Dayton's or other storefronts lining Hennepin Avenue in downtown—stowed on empty seats.

"Damned holidays," the man cursed, using his right overshoe to close the driver's-side door.

Though he was a Socialist, he was also a believer. The driver of the Oakland was not a Communist, not an atheist Marxist hell-bent-for leather to upend the American republic and replace it with a Soviet-style dictatorship. His politics were in line with the Democratic Socialism of Norman Thomas, Eugene Debs, and Margaret Sanger. His outcry wasn't because he didn't celebrate Christmas or appreciate the symbolism of gift giving. His angst came from the fact that, as the owner of a progressive weekly newspaper, his wallet was empty and his savings were insufficient to make next month's rent. As he stood on the sidewalk, his freshly polished black Oxfords covered by rubber overshoes—the boots' black metal buckles undone—the man's attention was drawn to five-year-old Marjorie, his eldest child. It was Christmas Eve. Marjorie greeted her father with childish expectancy. Silhouetted in the warm glow of electric light, the girl left the front door open to reveal an interior staircase leading to the family's upstairs apartment. It was below freezing. Marjorie shook like a leaf as she waited for her father. Her tiny form was covered only by a thin brown shift against winter's cold, as she impatiently tapped a stockinged foot against the unyielding boards of the covered porch.

"Daddy, come inside," the girl urged. "You'll catch cold standing out in the street."

The man smiled and nodded, fully intending to answer his daughter, but he found his attention drawn to the streetcar. There was nothing extraordinary about the trolley's journey. But its departure revealed an elegant Cadillac Fleetwood—the sedan's ebony hood polished to luminescence and reflecting light from an adjacent streetlamp—across the snow-dusted thoroughfare. Though the big motorcar crept along Bloomington Avenue with its headlights off, the reporter recognized the Cadillac and felt his chest tighten. He was about to scuttle up the stairs and into the duplex when the rear passenger-side window of the Cadillac rolled down to reveal the muzzle of a Thompson submachine gun.

> # BOOK ONE: THE PEN

"The pen is mightier than the sword."
Edward Bulver-Lytton
(1839)

CHAPTER ONE
Oak Ridge, Minnesota
1917

Donny Swanson wasn't naturally gifted when it came to athletics. He was tall, gangly, and awkward in movement. His grades at Oak Ridge High School were average, with one exception: In Miss Almquist's newswriting class, Donny turned in a performance worthy of Mark Twain. His subtle wit and cleverly drawn send-ups of the farmers, shopkeepers, would-be debutantes, and star athletes of the town surprisingly passed muster when it came to Miss Almquist—an overbearing dowager whose casual orneriness ensured her unmarried status.

Certainly, there were times when the teacher—who was also the faculty advisor for *The Trumpet*, the school's newspaper—clamped down on Donny's muckraking. "No, we cannot run this article about the Farmer's Cooperative Elevator the way you've written it," she might say, while smiling inwardly—the crack in her stern demeanor hidden from scrutiny—at the boy's cleverness. "You make a valid point about the need for the elevator to stand up to eastern interests that control the railroads and the flour mills. But you need not humiliate a local business in the process. The owners are our neighbors and our friends, and they will surely take offense."

"Yes, Miss Almquist. I'll edit the piece and see if I can't get my message across in a less demeaning manner."

Hilda Almquist, despite an outwardly rigid aspect and bearing, was in fact a Bull Mooser, a Progressive who had voted for Teddy Roosevelt in the 1912 election. Steeped in the tenets of Populism and the Grange movement, Hilda concealed her support for Donny's Nonpartisan League leanings. She didn't wish to be discharged by the less-than-progressive citizens dominating the Oak Ridge School Board for encouraging sedition. Her savings at the Farmer's Cooperative Trust Bank in Alexandria were meager, wholly insufficient to see her through a termination of work if she was forced to seek a new position in another district. *No,* she thought, as she studied the typewritten bombs thrown by young Donny, *that I cannot do. Better to keep my views to myself and continue on here, in this town, mentoring young minds.*

"Town" is a generous term when applied to Oak Ridge, Minnesota, circa 1917. Other than the school, the tiny crossroads consisted of the Farmer's Cooperative grain elevator, the First State Bank of Oak Ridge, a post office, Walter's Grocery, Seed, and Hardware store, Emma's Diner, a single church, a silent movie theater, the public library, and a smattering of bungalows housing most of Oak Ridge's one hundred and seventy-five inhabitants. In addition to the bungalows, a half-dozen classic Victorian homes—some constructed of brick, some featuring clapboard siding, but all boasting covered porches—lined Lincoln Street, the only paved thoroughfare in town. Miss Almquist rented a room and took her meals in a six-bedroom, three-fireplaced Goliath that had once been home to a Democratic state senator, the election of whom was regarded as something of a mistake by the town. The palatial three-story was inhabited by Miss Almquist and the family of Theodore Walters, the owner of the town's grocery, seed, and hardware store. Theodore ran a tight ship when it came to his wife, Elmira, and their two teenage daughters, Elizabeth and Nanette, such that Miss Almquist hardly knew others shared the home with her. In addition to being the wealthiest man in Oak Ridge, Walters was also an elder in All Saints Missouri Synod Lutheran church of Oak Ridge, the only house of worship for ten miles. The combination of possessing a fat bank account and personal piety made the overweight bald-as-an-egg shopkeeper the de-facto mayor of the mayor-less unincorporated town.

Oak Ridge possessed no city hall, no dry goods shop, and no place to nurse a beer or down a shot of hard liquor. Even before the advent of Prohibition, Oak Ridge was dry. There had been no bar, no saloon, and no liquor store to be found in the town prior to the Volstead Act. The perpetually parched nature of Oak Ridge society was due to the anti-alcohol predilections of the Missouri Synod Lutheran settlers, who claimed the place once the Dakota were rounded up and shuffled off to reservations. Thirsty men (and women of little virtue) who wanted something stronger than lemonade or coffee to buck them up against the rigors of prairie life were perpetually unable to find liquid solace in the town.

The Swanson farm was located two miles from Oak Ridge. Each day after school, Donny's path led him west on a single-lane gravel track that dead-ended at a slanting, leaking-like-a-sieve farmhouse. The Swanson place—a one-hundred-and-sixty-acre parcel homesteaded by Donny's maternal grandfather, Oscar Johnson—was tucked against the east bank of the Pomme de Terre River, a slow, meandering trickle that amounted to little more than a source of water for the thirty Swanson dairy cows grazing brittle grass. Fishing the Pomme de Terre, something Donny did during hot, humid summers on the prairie, was more about sneaking away from chores than catching fish. At best, Donny would hook and land bullheads: ugly, whiskered, slimy creatures that only Iowans would eat. At worst, he'd catch carp: invasive rough fish Donny's mother ground up and deposited as fertilizer in the family's vegetable garden. Still, sitting on the river bank, daydreaming of a life away from the dull day-to-day sameness of the farm, gave Donny respite from chores and allowed him to fantasize about his future.

There was no question in the young man's mind that he would, once he graduated from Oak Ridge High, attend the University of Minnesota to pursue a journalism degree. That was a given. *But what then?* There was speculation in Donny's mental wanderings that, at some point, he would work for an Eastern newspaper, perhaps in Boston or Philadelphia—though his real goal was New York City. His well-practiced vision of the future included arriving in Manhattan by luxury train coach, striding boldly up pedestrian-clogged streets, waltzing into the office of the *Times* or the *Post*, and bedazzling editors with clippings from *The Trumpet* and *The Daily*—the University of Minnesota's student newspaper. Such dreams were naïve, but even cautions from Miss Almquist—gentle admonishments that Donny might have to "start at the bottom"—did not impede the boy's ardor.

In the spring of his senior year, young Donald managed, despite his general lack of athleticism, to land a position on the Oak Ridge Egrets varsity baseball team. He'd been egged on by his best friend, Ernest Winter, a rotund, slow-footed kid who played center on the football team and catcher on the baseball nine. What Ernest lacked in speed, he made up for with his bat. Ernie led the league in extra-base hits: bombing ten home runs over the fence and smacking a dozen two-baggers and a triple, despite a rain-shortened season. Ernie's goading caused Donny to dig out his old leather glove, beg his father for cleats, and give America's game a try. It turned out that, despite never having expressed an interest in sports, Donny was a natural. It didn't hurt that he was left-handed, making the coach's decision to keep the slow-throwing but accurate knuckle-baller on the team a no-brainer. Donny won all four of his starts, hit a solid .300, and even managed three stolen bases while helping the Egrets to a district championship.

Donny started the Egrets' first regional playoff game against Willmar, his confidence brimming from a seven strike-out victory over Alexandria in the district final, and promptly gave up home runs to the first three batters. It seems a cadre of Willmar fathers had scouted the Egrets game against Alexandria and noted that Donny's befuddlement of batters could be bested with patience. Instead of swinging wildly at the first offering or two—pitches that invariably skirted the strike zone—the Willmar boys heeded their fathers' advice and laid off, waiting for Donny to put one over the plate when his knuckleball failed him and he fell behind in the count.

Boom!

The third or fourth pitch Donald tossed was sent screaming over the fence. Coach Mullaney pulled Donny before Tug Evers, batting cleanup for Willmar, came to the plate. It didn't matter. Tug teed off on the reliever, Eddie Salmela, who'd just moved into the Oak Ridge school district from the Finnish enclave of New York Mills, without missing a beat. Though Tug's blast didn't clear the ballpark, the ball hit the bottom of the outfield wall and caromed away from the centerfielder before it was corralled and fired toward the infield. Tug was standing on third, out of breath, his hands on his prodigious hips, when the relay was caught by the shortstop. The final score was thirteen to zero. Donny was tagged as the losing pitcher, and that was it for the farm boy from the Pomme de Terre River: he never played organized baseball again.

True to his dreams, Donny Swanson forsook attending Concordia College in St. Paul (the Missouri Synod Lutheran School favored by his parents), despite the urging of his mother, Fawn, who believed her only child had the makings of a fine preacher. "No, Ma." Donny said when, in one last ditch plea, Fawn urged him not to go to the "U," not to throw away his family's religion to become a muckraker. "My path is clear. I'm no saint and the life of a pastor is not my calling."

    Donny dutifully returned to the Swanson farm when university classes were over for the school year. Other than insisting that his friends and family call him "Don," he was the same farm boy who'd left Oak Ridge for the big city. He wasn't transformed into an urbanized man-about-town by attending college. Don was little changed in his habits, his likes, his dislikes, or his view of the world. He milked cows twice a day; cut, raked, baled, and stacked hay in the loft of the rickety old dairy barn; and tended the twenty pigs and the dozen or so chickens providing the Swanson family sustenance. Though offered an internship with a Saint Paul newspaper—a position that paid little but promised an education in the publishing business beyond anything taught at the "U"—Don declined, cognizant that, as the only child of Gordon and Fawn Swanson, he was needed on the farm when not attending school. He adhered to the promise he'd made to his father the August he left for his freshman year, "I'll be home every summer, Pa," and he was as good as his word.

    The blond-maned, blue-eyed young man's collegiate path wasn't stellar. There were poor grades early on, some near-failures, and a slowness to realize that college was far harder—and required more determined rigor—than high school. But, with the assistance of a study group of fellow freshmen and the grounding that came from meeting his wife-to-be, Beatrice Mondale, a squarely built, blond, Norwegian girl from Elmore who boasted a quick smile and a dimpled chin (she was studying to be an elementary school teacher), Don became engaged, graduated, and secretly married Beatrice before setting off for New York City.

The newlyweds planned to live off the small dowry Beatrice had received from her maternal grandmother. Even so, the couple's elopement was a risky gambit. Don had no job waiting for him in New York City. Additionally, as the young couple waited inside St. Paul's Union Depot for the Chicago, Great Western's *Legionnaire* passenger train, Beatrice shared a bombshell with her husband.

"I'm with child," she whispered.

Beatrice's surprise announcement prompted Don to undertake an accounting as the couple waited for their train. Don's fevered assessment established that—including Beatrice's dowry, the paper bills in his wallet, and the change in his wife's coin purse—their savings amounted to less than two hundred dollars.

CHAPTER TWO
Minneapolis, Minnesota
1918

There were no clear lines of demarcation between the Swedes, Norwegians, Finns, Jews, Negroes, and Irish living in North Minneapolis.

"Hey, Kid," a skinny, tall, languid young man whispered, his hazel eyes, pale skin, and neatly cropped blond crewcut concealed in shadow as he pressed his back into the clapboard siding of Amundson's Liquor Store. "You sure this is a good idea?"

The recipient of Sigurd "Siggy" Larson's query was a short, square-shouldered, dark-featured, brown-eyed, ebony-haired Jew of approximately the same age. Abram Rosenstein, his Minnesota accent colored by his birth in and emigration from Kiev, an enclave of ancestors on both sides of the boy's heritage, scrutinized the empty street and nodded. "Your family needs to eat, right? Best way to make sure that happens is to steal from Old Man Amundson. Booze and money; plenty of both inside the store," Abram whispered. Known around the neighborhood as "Kid Rose," the leader of a gang of hooligans that made no end of trouble for genteel shop owners, compliant citizens, and religiously devout families living in his fiefdom, he'd been born into the depths of poverty of Czarist Russia, but acquired bravado, a fierce demeanor, and balls of brass as he aged into adolescence.

Larson considered his erstwhile companion, eyed the shadowy interior of the store through the plate glass window overlooking the empty street, stroked his chin with large hairless hands, and nodded.

It wasn't that Sigurd Larson was an inherently bad or stupid boy that led him to follow Kid Rose. Rather, Siggy's loyalty was born from the shared impoverishment of their childhoods and the fact that Kid Rose had once saved Siggy's life.

Sigurd Larson was twelve, and Abram Rosenstein was eleven when the boys, along with three neighborhood pals, decided to venture across the frozen Mississippi River to Nicollet Island. They followed Plymouth Avenue to the river's edge, but instead of crossing the Mississippi by bridge, the adventurers chose to reach the island by walking across river ice. Their goal was to find and fight the Warner Gang: boys whose families owned tenements and slums that, aside from De LaSalle High School, occupied every square inch of the once-monied enclave. Over time, the Warners' island domain had deteriorated in both architectural glory and median family income. To maintain their place in the hierarchy of Nicollet Island's youth, the Warner boys became as tough as nails, giving no quarter in their battles with rival gangs and often using baseball bats and pry bars to subdue anyone foolhardy enough to challenge them.

"Looks like as good a place to cross as any," Abram had said after reconnoitering the ice. Winter's scant snow had melted, though the ice had, after several nights of sub-freezing cold, regained the appearance of forming a solid bridge from the west bank of the Mississippi to the island.

Sigurd shook his head. "Are you sure it's safe?"

Another boy laughed at the Norwegian's hesitancy. "You chicken, Fish Eater?"

Abram scowled. "Knock it off, Dixon." The Kid paused and studied the frozen river again. "It looks solid."

"Why not use the bridge? Come in from the other side?" Siggy asked.

Abram shook his head. "The Warners live on this side of the island. Only slummers and poor folk live on the east side. We need to come in from the west to surprise the Warners and give those assholes the whoopings they deserve."

Dixon—a boy as tall as Larson but even skinnier, his face full of adolescent acne, his thick black hair greasy and dirty and hanging loose from beneath a filthy wool watch cap—had smiled, revealing two missing teeth. "What's got you so riled up we have to walk miles to find assholes to clobber?"

The Kid glanced at Dixon, spat, and answered, "I heard they don't like North Siders. Call us 'inbreeders.' It's enough to make me fightin' mad, I tell ya."

"Me too," Dixon agreed.

"Norskie, you ready?" the Kid asked Larson.

Siggy shrugged. "I'm game, if you are."

Their route consisted of moments of imbalance on glare ice, followed by sure-footed passage in those places where snow still clung to the river's frozen surface. "Seems at least five or six inches thick," Kid Rose said, as he led the group over a clear-as-glass section of ice. Beneath the boys, the river moved in frothy constancy toward the Gulf of Mexico, the flowing water mesmerizing the boys as they slipped forward.

Kid Rose wore battered Chippewas—hand-me-downs from his father. The soles of the boots were nearly gone; the uppers were scuffed and devoid of polish. Without warning, the Kid stopped and kneeled on one knee to tie a vagrant lace. Siggy and the others continued on.

Splash.

Larson broke through precarious ice disguised by remnant snow and disappeared.

"I've got you, Siggy!" Abram shouted, ignoring the untied lace to stand, race to the hole, and dive into the bone-chilling water.

Though it was difficult to see in the murky turbulence, Kid Rose kept his eyes open in hopes of discerning something—anything—out of the ordinary. Swimming urgently beneath the river's frozen surface, the Kid caught a flash of color. A boot, perhaps. Or an arm. Or a leg. The Kid couldn't be sure. He kicked with all his might, reached out with a mittened hand—the cold beginning to arrest his muscles—and latched onto the collar of Sigurd's jacket.

The other boys flopped onto their bellies to form a human chain. Dixon, his boots held firmly by another boy, inched toward the water's edge. "I see the Kid!" he yelled, peering into the hole. "And it looks like he's got Siggy!"

The boys never confronted the Warner Gang that day. Instead, they found aid and comfort with the Cohen family, friends of Abram's parents who lived on the island. Rosenstein, his teeth chattering, his clothes encased in ice, held up a barely conscious Sigurd Larson while knocking on the front door of the Cohens' apartment.

"Why, Abram!" Mrs. Cohen had exclaimed, recovering from the start of encountering a boy she'd last seen as a fifth grader standing soaking wet on her doorstep in the dead of winter. "Whatever happened?"

Propriety was ignored. Within seconds of the Kid's first tentative knock, Mrs. Cohen shuttled Rosenstein, Larson, and their pals inside. She commanded the soaked boys to "strip, towel off, and sit" on the living room's oak-planked floor in front of an oil stove. The kindly matron handed the hypothermic, shivering visitors scratchy wool Army blankets to preserve their dignity. The boys' sodden clothing was hung above the stove on a clothesline. Their wet boots were placed near warmth, causing steam to rise from the leather. Water dripped from hanging clothes and pooled on the hardwood floor. Mrs. Cohen had served bowls of hot chicken dumpling soup to her unexpected guests, and before the sun had set, the boys were dry, warm, and headed for home.

Crash.

The brick Abram hurled at the window of the liquor store's front door made a racket. "Come on," he urged, "old man Amundson sleeps upstairs. We need to get in and get out before he hears us."

Abram slipped his hand through the hole created by the brick, avoided jagged glass, found the skeleton key the shopkeeper kept in the lock, turned the key, and opened the door. The burglars—Larson on the cusp of eighteen and valedictorian of his graduating class, and Rosenstein, seventeen and professing a disdain for formal education—surveyed the store's interior.

"Get a move on!" Abram hissed after stepping into the liquor store and noting that Siggy remained outside on the sidewalk. "We only have a few minutes to get what we came for."

"OK," Siggy whispered before joining his friend in the store.

The boys crept forward until Kid Rose found himself in front of a cash register—a big, imposing National—and began working the keys.

Ping.

A drawer opened.

"Holy shit!"

An eruption of light caught the delinquents in the middle of their thievery.

"Hold it right there, fellas," said John Amundson, proprietor of the establishment and a veteran of the Rough

Riders' charge up San Juan Hill. The would-be criminals gaped at an old man sitting rigidly erect—like the soldier he'd once been—in an oak swivel chair not three feet away. "This here scattergun is loaded with double-ought. Don't like to think what it'll do to a couple of youngsters making bad decisions."

CHAPTER THREE
Minneapolis, Minnesota
1918

Judge Edmund Reilly sat behind his bench in a courtroom of the Hennepin County Courthouse. The big green cloth-bound minute book in which he scratched notes—his unofficial record of court hearings and trials in juvenile delinquency, probate, family disputes, and mental infirmity matters—was open. The judge's pen rested on a brass rim, black India ink dripping from its nib and pooling in the bottom of a shallow ceramic tray, as Reilly eyeballed Siggy Larson and Kid Rose. The jurist was as red-faced as a schoolgirl caught in an illicit embrace. Patches of scarlet hair slicked with tonic were combed forward to cover premature baldness: pink, nearly baby-new skin obvious in the places where hair no longer grew. Reilly rubbed an unruly ginger beard with his right hand, straightened to the apex of his potato-shaped, five-foot-six frame, adjusted his eyeglasses, and glared.

Reilly had sorely wanted to win the last election, one where he challenged an incumbent District Court judge, a "big boy" in the courthouse, in a contested race. He'd been endorsed by the Knights of Columbus, by the Minnesota Irish Barristers League, and a handful of business organizations—all for naught. Voters supported Judge Angus Dubus—the son of immigrants of uncertain lineage—and Dubus had handily bested Reilly. Losing an election he'd been deeply invested in caused Edmund Reilly's already crotchety demeanor, something fairly remarkable in a thirty-nine-year-old ex-prosecutor with a loving wife, four beautiful kids, a steady job, and a modicum of prestige, to become even less charitable. *I was the better man;* Reilly could not help but think on a daily basis. *That ambulance chaser had no business being re-elected.*

Before taking the bench, Dubus had made his mark suing the City of Minneapolis, slum lords, local businesses, and automobile and truck drivers on behalf of the evicted, the cheated, and the injured. His "David versus Goliath" persona made him beloved by immigrants and garnered him support among, of all people, working-class Catholics: folks whose natural inclinations should have been to vote for Reilly, a kinsman. But that hadn't happened, and, rather than being a judge in charge of high-profile murder, rape, and arson cases, Reilly was stuck with the dregs of county-level courtroom work where he dealt with wayward children, dysfunctional parents, grieving heirs, and the mentally infirm.

"Mr. Rosen*steen*," the diminutive judge said, intentionally mispronouncing Abram's surname. "This is your third time before me this year."

Kid Rose, normally cocky in the face of authority, kept his eyes fixed on his mud-caked, dirty, hole-filled Chippewas, the laces bedraggled and threadbare, the soles nearly worn through to his stockings. The teenager gulped and continued staring at the floor as he replied, "Yes, Your Honor."

"But you," the judge said, a hint of respect inflecting his speech when he turned toward Sigurd Larson, "are a scholar and, according to letters provided by your parents and teachers, have never been in a lick of trouble."

Siggy nodded, but kept his eyes locked on his newly polished, hand-me-down black dress shoes. "That's true, Judge."

Reilly continued to stroke intermittent red whiskers with his right hand, the fingers short, fleshy, and salmon-colored. "So, one must ask oneself, Mr. Larson: How did you come to be in cahoots with this boy?"

Larson lifted his head and cast a glance at Rosenstein. Abram was sitting as still as a frog on a lily pad, being stalked by a pike. "I guess my judgment failed me, Your Honor," Siggy replied.

Reilly guffawed. "I'd say that's an understatement, young man. You and your associate were within a whisker's breath of being cut to ribbons. And for what? A few dollars from the till? A bottle or two of cheap whiskey? Doesn't seem quite an even trade, two lives for chump change and booze, now does it?"

"No, sir," Larson whispered.

"You present a quandary, young man. You truly do."

Larson shifted nervously in his chair but did not reply.

"Says on the police report that you turn eighteen in a week."

"That's right, Your Honor."

"Maybe there's another approach I can take with you, Mr. Larson," Judge Reilly said tenuously, as if thinking aloud. "But you," the judge continued, diverting his attention to Kid Rose, "are quite another matter. No real question what society wants to see happen to you."

Abram understood his goose was cooked; that, given his propensity for crime, his ethnicity, and the fact neither of his parents were in attendance, the punishment handed out to the boys would not be equal in severity.

"I understand that Mr. Larson's parents are here," the judge said, shifting his attention again.

Elmer Larson, holding a brown felt wide-brimmed fedora nervously in work-roughened hands, stood up from a wooden pew and approached the rail, the picket functioning as the dividing line between the People and their Court. "We are, Your Honor."

Elsa Larson, Siggy's mom, sat with her eyes fixed on a black patent leather purse resting in her lap, her worn-to-the-lining green wool coat buttoned tightly across her ample bosom, pot belly, and thick thighs. She was the mother of six—Sigurd being the eldest—world-weary and done in by children who, for the most part, while they were good little Norwegian Lutherans, raised holy hell. Subservient in all ways to her husband, a mechanic for the Minneapolis Streetcar Authority, Elsa remained mute.

"Do you have anything to say on his behalf?"

Elmer Larson stared at his boots, polished as best as could be, but still oil-stained from working at the city garage. He'd come right from the night shift, eyes bleary for sleep, wearing soiled dungarees and a wrinkled long-sleeved shirt, with no chance to change into more appropriate attire or do more than dampen his face with a washcloth and comb his graying, blond hair to make himself presentable. Judge Reilly noted all of this as he waited for the tall, thin, broken-down-by-life man to reply. Unlike his instantaneously formed opinion regarding Kid Rose (which was absolute), the judge held out hope that Elmer Larson would say something to save his son.

"Sigurd is a good boy, Your Honor. As you said, he just graduated high school at the top of his class. Been trying to get him to stay away from that one," Elmer said quietly, never looking at Kid Rose, never releasing his hat to point in the Kid's direction, "but it ain't easy. We're poor folk, Your Honor, but honest as the day is long. Church goers too, the whole lot of us. The boy knows better. He's been raised better. But with six young 'uns to feed and clothe and keep an eye on, sometimes things, well, they just happen when they shouldn't. I can promise you this: you let the boy come home, he'll face consequences, and as soon as I can arrange it, he'll be back in school or working a job. No more wandering the streets, no more pulling stunts like this. You have my word."

Reilly removed his glasses and studied Siggy. "That sound fair to you, young Mr. Larson?"

The boy nodded.

"See, the thing is, Mr. Robertson over there with the big book, he's my court reporter, my stenographer. He takes down everything said in this courtroom by shorthand." The judge paused. "Nodding your head is like saying and doing nothing. You need to answer aloud, Son."

"Yes, sir," Siggy choked out. "That sounds fair."

Reilly resituated his eyeglasses, picked up his pen, dipped its nib into an ink well, and scribbled in his notebook. "One year of court probation. Payment of restitution for the broken glass to Mr. Amundson. You are to report to me the first Monday of every month by nine in the morning, sharp. Additional conditions of probation include that, within thirty days of today, you enroll in school, be working full time, or, if you're the patriotic sort, you can enlist in the military." The judge paused to catch his breath, his belly pressed tight against the bench, his face more flaming than when he'd begun his little speech. "You do understand there's a war going on, a conflict between good and evil? Don't care if you join the army, the navy, or the Marines. You'd be an asset in the fight, what with your physique and your brains." Another pause. The judge reached for a tumbler of lukewarm water, raised it, sipped elegantly, and returned the glass to its coaster. "Or you may decide to enroll in a course of study at Dunwoody or at a college. Or go to work, making an honest living like your father." The judge smiled, the gesture causing his pouchy cheeks to dance. "Understood?"

Sigurd forgot the judge's prior admonition and nodded.

"Aloud, Mr. Larson!" Reilly spat.

"Yessir. School, a job, or the military," Siggy replied with chagrin.

"Something else on your mind, young man?"

The boy nodded.

"Aloud, Mr. Larson," the judge admonished again, with lessened severity.

"Sorry, Your Honor. If I choose the military, how do I report to you?"

The jurist reflected on the question. "Ever hear of the United States mail, Mr. Larson? I'm told it's available to folks serving in the military. With free postage, no less." Reilly collected his thoughts. "You choose the military, and I'll expect a letter from you every month. One year of court probation. You're to pay one-half of the required restitution within sixty days of today. Employed, in school, or enlisted. Reporting in person to me or by letter if you choose military service. No other acts of truancy or delinquency; a spotless record over the next year. That will be the disposition of this court. Are we clear?"

"Yes, sir."

"Good." The judge finished writing, looked up from his notebook, and flashed contempt. "And you, Mr. Rosen*steen*," Reilly said tersely. "There is nothing more to be done with you in this community. You are a danger to yourself and others."

Abram Rosenstein, experienced as he was in the ways of the world, with full knowledge that society was not fair, kind, or benevolent to Jewish kids who burglarized stores, knew what was coming next.

CHAPTER FOUR
Red Wing Training School
Red Wing, Minnesota
1918

Abram sat on a wooden chair in the superintendent's office. Across the flat plain of the desk, the burled oak shiny from linseed oil, John T. Fulton, the man dictating and controlling the day-to-day lives of three hundred boys under his charge (girls had been at the institution through 1911 before being relocated to their own reformatory at Sauk Center), studied legal documents and crisply typewritten correspondence chronicling Abram Rosenstein's misadventures.

After completing his inventory of the boy's delinquency history, Fulton smiled, his brown eyes dauntingly focused behind the thick lenses of his eyeglasses, and he turned his attention to studying the young man who'd just been deposited by a Hennepin County deputy sheriff at the reformatory. "You know," Fulton said matter-of-factly, "Mr. Rosenstein, you remind me of an unfortunate boy who once spent time here." The warden stopped to gather his thoughts. "When I say 'unfortunate,' I mean that, due to his behaviors within these walls, much unsuccessful effort was extended to redirect his untoward propensities."

Kid Rose remained mute, defiance clear in his pursed lips, scornful eyes, and slouched posture.

"Unfortunately, that boy—Carl Panzram—did not leave here a better citizen. True, that was before my time, when Superintendent Whittier held sway." Fulton looked away to study wind-buffeted trees on the lawn outside the pompously configured administration building, its red sandstone construction meant to convey the atmosphere of an expensive eastern boarding school or an Ivy League college. It was early October. The maples and oaks shading the grounds were resplendent. Fulton returned his gaze to Abram, refocusing scrutiny on a boy who didn't blink, change expression, or give any hint of deference to authority. "Mr. Panzram was not made better by this place. He did not come away from his experience at the Red Wing State

Training School for Boys a better human being. He was subjected to cruel punishment that didn't modify his behavior. The administration of the lash upon Mr. Panzram's back is but one example of the cruelty inflicted upon that young man during his time within these walls."

Fulton paused to sip hot coffee, steam from the raised cup merging with dust-mote-filled beams of sunlight streaming into the office. The air was stale and tinged with a faint odor that reminded Kid Rose of his mother's mothball-filled closet. The superintendent studied Rosenstein while sipping coffee with elegance and grace. Fortified by caffeine, Fulton placed the white porcelain cup on its saucer. "You, young man, need not face such horrors. But—and here is why I wanted to spend time talking ancient history with you, Mr. Rosenstein—your personal disposition and record are strikingly similar to Mr. Panzram's. Nearly identical, in fact. And that concerns me."

For the first time during the interview, Abram Rosenstein felt regret. He was not a young man prone to self-examination; after run-ins with the law, countless truancies from whatever school he was charged to attend, and numerous excursions into alcohol and—on one occasion—opium smoked with an older crowd he was trying to emulate, Kid Rose had never regretted his incorrigibility. But now, sitting before the large-headed, amply muscled, kindly Superintendent Fulton, he felt something—a twinge of failure, perhaps, he'd never acknowledged before. "Yes, sir."

"Because of your tendency to break rules, to show little remorse for your actions, and your consistent disregard for discipline, I'm assigning you to Dartmouth House. There, you'll encounter boys who are 'toeing the line' and are exemplars of how good behavior and hard work find reward." Fulton nodded and smiled, a slender gesture that, even to a hardened delinquent like Rosenstein, displayed empathy. "Your sentence will pass quickly. You'll be a better person for having stayed the course. You'll return to *your people* a new man."

My people, Kid Rose thought. *He means the Jews. I know this place prides itself on Christian values, the use of Jesus and God and all that bullshit to tame boys like me.* Kid Rose adjusted his demeanor to evince acceptance. *I've fooled my parents for years, fooled teachers, and fooled the coppers.*

I can pull the wool over this ninny's eyes, just like all the others.

"Do you understand what I'm telling you, Mr. Rosenstein? Here, if you do what needs to be done, you'll learn a trade. Maybe farming or butchering or cooking or leatherworking or metalworking or one of our other many vocational choices." The superintendent pushed a small button atop his desk. A bell rang in another room. "Or you might choose to work on the school's newspaper, *The Riverside*. All valuable skills, Mr. Rosenstein: All tickets to a better life."

Herman Enquist, a large, bulky man, and the head counselor of Dartmouth House, knocked on the door, entered before receiving permission, and stood at rigid attention next to Abram, his ample body shadowing the boy. "Yes, Mr. Fulton?"

"Mr. Rosenstein is ready to settle in at Dartmouth House. I'm thinking he bears watching, though I'm hoping against hope he'll take our discussion to heart and not cause trouble during his time with us."

Enquist extended a bear-like paw, the palm and fingers of his right hand fully calloused, the result of being charged with tending the school's vegetable garden. "Pleased to meet you."

Kid Rose stood and extended his own small right hand, the smoothness of his palm evidence of never having done an honest day's labor. "Likewise, I'm sure."

CHAPTER FIVE
The Somme, France
September 1918

Sigurd Larson stood in a trench, a twelve-gauge Winchester pump—a weapon considered barbaric by the Germans encamped across the killing plain—held at port.

"What's happening?" Larson asked his companion, Sergeant Ernie Banes, a thin, reedy soldier from Trenton, New Jersey. Banes was no older than Larson but had been elevated to a position of authority due to cat-like quickness and an ability to kill without remorse.

Banes cradled a periscope in his hands and stared unblinkingly into the device's mirror. "Nothing. No one is stirring," he replied in a hoarse whisper. "Not even a mouse," he added with a grin.

Banes's helmet hung by its chin strap from a tree root protruding from the western berm of the Canal du Nord. The canal was an unfinished project designed to link the Oise River with the Dunkirk-Scheldt Canal near Cambrai, France. Most of the canal-in-progress had been flooded by the Germans. But in front of the American scouts and their Canadian cohort, the unfinished portion of the waterway remained dry. The eastern wall of the incomplete canal rose five feet above the undulating forested landscape and provided modest cover for the enemy. On the western bank of the uncompleted project, a fifteen-foot earthen berm protected the Allied troops.

A platoon of American doughboys had been detached from their company and inserted into the line during the Second Battle of the Somme, plugging a gap in the Canadian force caused by casualties and the Spanish flu. The remainder of Company C, 349th Infantry Regiment, 88th Division was in the rear, out of danger. The detached American platoon, which included Banes and Larson, was charged with scouting for Canadian Corps, First Division.

To the north, British troops were preparing to drive the enemy toward the Hindenburg Line. Another, larger Canadian force was assembling alongside the Brits and poised to cross the flooded canal on temporary bridges. At the southern tip of the allied spear, the American platoon and its 3,000 Canadian comrades were preparing to attack across open ground: a bold move meant to surprise the Germans.

Larson gulped, removed a soiled white handkerchief from the breast pocket of his tunic, wiped sweat from beneath the brim of his steel helmet, and nodded. "They say we'll go tonight."

Banes returned the periscope to its wooden case, leaned the case against the trench wall, retrieved his helmet, put it on his head, and considered the tremor in his companion's voice. *It's his first battle,* Banes thought, as he studied Larson's countenance, *he's untested and afraid. Hell, I've killed a half-dozen Huns and still shake like a leaf when the whistle sending us over the top blows.* "Once you get over the jitters," Banes finally whispered, "it's nothing more than running as fast as your kit allows, keeping your head down, and listening for artillery. Duck into the nearest crater when I say 'duck'. Understood?"

Larson nodded. Behind the American scouts, the Canadians were stirring. The southernmost prong of the allied attack would follow the edge of the flooded canal to where the berm ended and a peninsula of dry land pointed like an offensive middle finger at the enemy. To the north, meager German forces had gathered to face the onrushing British Tommies and other Canadian troops crossing the flooded canal on temporary, rickety, wooden bridges. The German commander had erroneously positioned the majority of his firepower in front of the small force of Canadians and Americans hunkered down behind the canal's western berm. The dry ground to be crossed by Banes, Larson, and their mates was overwatched by German infantry, artillery, armor, and the dreaded MG08; a modified Maxim machinegun firing over five hundred rounds a minute.

"You boys ready?"

Larson and Banes were so entranced by the waning dusk, the sun's fiery globe dipping behind the horizon until silhouettes of oak and beech merged with advancing night, that they failed to note the arrival of Captain Ian McLain, their adopted company commander. A grain farmer from southern Manitoba, McLain was a burly, gregarious Scot who defied regulations by growing a mustache and side whiskers while in country. He had led his fellow Canadians along a dusty path to reach the advance position occupied by the American scouts. His bleary-eyed soldiers stood—Enfields, Tommy guns, and Browning Automatic Rifles held loosely in their hands—behind the officer as he spoke.

Baines nodded.

McLain studied Larson's Winchester. "You carrying that goose gun into battle, private?"

"Yes, sir."

After Sigurd Larson chose the military option offered by Judge Reilly and enlisted in the United States Army at the armory in downtown Minneapolis, he had little opportunity for regret. He was hustled off to Camp Dodge in Johnstown, Iowa, for initial training. After completing a crash course in order, discipline, and marching, Sigurd was shipped east with fellow would-be soldiers. The nervous young men had been crammed into Pullman cars like unneeded roosters destined for the butcher. The raw recruits disembarked at Camp Sevier, South Carolina, and proceeded to learn the basic elements of modern warfare. Sig qualified—after two attempts on the rifle range—as a marksman, but he lacked confidence in his ability to select a target, squeeze the trigger of his M1917 Enfield, and place a .303 bullet in a target.

His preference was for the Winchester, a weapon assigned to him after his debarkation from the passenger ship *Manchuria* in Brest, France. Given a forward position as a scout, Larson had been offered an Enfield to replace the Winchester, the twelve-gauge being a gun commonly used by Minnesota boys to shoot mallards and pheasants. The only difference between the weapon in Larson's hands and a sporting arm was the bayonet mount attached to its barrel. Sigurd had declined the offer, finding comfort in knowing that the buckshot exploding from the Winchester gave him a better chance of hitting his target.

"I'm satisfied with the Winchester, sir," Larson replied.

"Very well, private. Just make sure you empty it on the enemy and not on a flock of French partridge," McLain said with a wink.

Dark enveloped the land. The Canadians shuffled forward; the canal's unfinished grassy berm concealing the noise of 3,000 men trudging toward destiny. Satisfied with the disbursement of his soldiers, McLain raised his right hand. The column halted. Across the dry floodplain, myriad German campfires twinkled like fireflies. A harsh wind blew in from the north. Weather arrived. Rain began to fall. Thunder boomed. Lightning flashed.

"Good," McLain whispered. "This storm will conceal us. Fan out behind those trees," he ordered, gesturing toward bushes no higher than a man's waist. "First Sergeant, get the men in battle order. We advance on my signal."

"Come on, Boys," said First Sergeant Emil Anderson, an auto mechanic from Brandon, in a stern voice. "You heard the captain."

The Americans led the way. Reaching the bushes, the Yanks flopped on their bellies behind scraggly cover. Waves of Canadians fanned out alongside the Americans. The allied troopers—nervously quiet, their bodies trembling in apprehension—claimed their assigned positions without disclosure.

"The guns will begin shortly," McLain whispered, hunkered down alongside the Americans. He glanced at his wristwatch, studying the watch's luminescent radium dial—a recent innovation that allowed him to tell time without digging into his tunic for a pocket watch.

British howitzers barked. Artillery rounds tore apart the pastoral German camp. Though Sig Larson was untested in battle, he appreciated what was happening. He'd marched past shell craters and innumerable bloated, unburied corpses of dismembered men and pack animals strewn across the French countryside. But it was not memories of dead soldiers, horses, or mules that manifested as Sigurd considered the clamorous barrage. Rather, it was the stench of rotting bodies—human and animal—that formed a vivid, lasting remembrance.

The cannonade continued. Larson realized his bladder was full. He cradled the Winchester and pressed his body into new mud. He willed his shaking hands and his racing heart toward calm by inhaling and exhaling in concise breaths. But Larson's efforts to steady his nerves had no effect on his bladder. Ashamedly and unexpectedly, his drawers dampened. Sigurd Larson's only solace was that it was too dark—and his trousers were too rain soaked—for his comrades to witness his manifested terror.

British guns pounded the German encampment for half an hour. Suddenly, the barrage stopped. Rain descended in sheets. Captain McLain drew his revolver from its holster, stood in the downpour, raised a tin whistle to his lips, and blew like holy hell.

CHAPTER SIX
North Minneapolis
1924

Kid Rose sat at the lunch counter of Goldie's Delicatessen, eating corned beef on rye slathered in mustard. The most recent edition of the *Minneapolis Daily Tribune* was propped up in front of him against a glass sugar dispenser. A hot cup of coffee sat to one side, and Goldie Cohen's award-winning coleslaw was piled next to the sandwich on the plate. The Kid was reading an article buried on the third page, one that he'd normally skim over to get to the sports and the comics. But the headline, in small font but bold type, caught his eye:

Larson to Run for County Attorney

The short, perfunctory piece contained a brief biography of Sigurd Thaddeus Larson, Assistant Minneapolis City Attorney, profiling a young man who had, in a few short years following his return from the war and his graduation from the St. Paul College of Law, become the scourge of prostitution in Minneapolis.

"Interesting," Kid Rose said, setting the half-eaten sandwich on his plate, lifting the coffee cup to his lips, and, despite the liquid being scalding, drinking heartily as he considered what he'd learned. "My old pal is entering politics!"

Abram Rosenstein's time at the reformatory had not been all peaches and cream. He was high-strung and mischievous—traits that did not endear him to Warden Fulton or Mr. Shermer, the print shop instructor in charge of Rosenstein's day-to-day life at Red Wing. The Kid was constantly, from his first day on the grounds of the youth complex to his last, getting into squabbles and engaging in fisticuffs when his point wasn't made. Abram never backed down from a dustup, even when his opponent was twice his size. He would tussle with anyone over anything if he felt it was his destiny to correct a misunderstanding or avenge a slight.

An incident toward the end of his stay at the reformatory nearly caused Warden Fulton to ship Kid Rose back to Hennepin County. It started, as most beefs involving Rosenstein did, over nothing. The Kid had secured cigarettes from another boy, trading nudie postcards—scandalous shots of a girl he knew from his neighborhood who posed in the altogether for money—for a pack of Lucky Strikes.

The altercation that landed Kid Rose in hot water began when he sought to smoke in front of Teddy Collins, a sixteen-year-old Irish kid also living in Dartmouth House. Collins had a year to go on his sentence, one also handed down by Judge Reilly after Collins beat a Minneapolis copper silly with the officer's own billy club while being arrested for shoplifting. The Irish kid wasn't just ornery: he was also a tattletale, always seeking to engender favor from staff members at the reformatory willing to listen to his revelations—and outright lies—in hopes of getting other boys in trouble and currying favor from those in charge.

"You're not supposed to be smoking," Collins said, as the pair set type for the latest edition of the *Riverside,* the school's newspaper. Kid Rose had pulled the pack of Lucky's from a rolled-up sleeve, retrieved a book of matches from a pocket, and grinned.

"What's it to you? Shermer isn't here," Kid Rose replied, striking a match, lighting a fag, and blowing smoke in Collins's face. "So, you can just fuck off."

Teddy dropped the type he was holding, straightened to his six-foot height, and glared. "What did you say, Heeb?"

It wasn't the first time a Gentile had used a slur toward Abram. The Kid had grown thick-skinned regarding casual remarks about his religion, a faith his family adhered to through weekly visits to the synagogue, but a religion Kid Rose had little appetite for. Despite Abram's apostasy, Collins's use of the term caused the Kid's blood to boil. And though he did not strike out, Rosenstein could not hold his tongue.

"That's a fine thing coming from the mouth of a Mick bastard—a kid who doesn't know who his own fucking father is."

Collins's fist connected with Kid Rose's chin and drove the Kid to the floor. Though dazed, Rosenstein grabbed Collins's legs, pulled the Irish kid onto the cement, and began flailing his arms like a windmill. Other boys in the shop stopped working, formed a circle, and shouted encouragement to the combatants.

"What's this?" Arvid Shermer, the counselor in charge of the print shop, asked, rushing inside the building from his own cigarette break. "At it again, Rosenstein?"

Two large hands—calloused and blackened by years of loading type and handling printer's ink—grabbed the collar of Rosenstein's blue denim shirt and yanked the Kid free of the fray. "This is the last straw," Shermer muttered, as he pulled Abram to his feet. "Warden Fulton is gonna ship your ass back to Hennepin County for this."

Johnny Simonson, a timid kid—freckled, blond-headed, pale-skinned, and just shy of puberty—cleared his throat. "Mr. Shermer . . ." the boy said meekly, casting a glance in Teddy's direction.

The counselor, his right hand holding fast to Kid Rose's neck, turned, and glared. "What is it?"

"Rosenstein didn't start it. Teddy sucker-punched him."

Shermer puffed out his cheeks, pondered the situation, looked at Collins, and asked, "That true?"

Teddy squirmed, lowered his eyes, and lied. "No, sir. He hit me first."

"Where?"

"Right here in print shop."

Frustration manifested on Shermer's face. "No, you idiot. I mean, where ON YOUR BODY did he hit you?"

Before Teddy could answer, Kid Rose spoke up. "That's a lie, sir. I didn't start it. I'll admit I ended up wrestling with Collins and getting in some licks, but that was after he started things."

Shermer tightened his hand on Rosenstein's neck. "I'm not talking to you, Kike. I'm asking Collins where you hit him."

"But . . ."

Without warning, Shermer raised his big left hand and slapped Kid Rose. Shermer's palm striking Rosenstein's cheek emitted a "crack" loud enough to startle the other boys. "Shut the hell up. I said I'm not talking to you."

"In the gut, sir. He hit me in the gut," Collins lied.

"Mr. Shermer," Johnny said, his voice trembling, the words nearly inaudible.

"Quiet, Simonson. I've heard enough. Rosenstein started the fracas, and it's time he got his just desserts."

Warden Fulton, not wanting to undo what he perceived to be progress in the rehabilitation of Abram Rosenstein, did not merely rely upon Shermer and Collins's version of events. He called Johnny Simonson into his office for a sit-down and, after hearing from the boy, also interviewed Abram.

"It's inconclusive at best, Arvid," the warden said as he sat behind the desk in his office addressing Arvid Shermer. "You failed to tell me that young Mr. Collins, who, as you know, has a penchant for, shall we say, 'stretching the truth,' may not only have instigated the fight. He may well have used a racial slur toward Mr. Rosenstein."

"But, Warden, you have my report. The accusations that Collins started things and insulted the Kid aren't in the paperwork."

Fulton took off his glasses and studied the counselor. "Look, Arv. I know you don't like Jewish folks. I get that you have animosity toward them. But let me pose this question: Did you ask any of the other boys how the ruckus started?"

Shermer, a short, bulky man sporting massive forearms, an inky stubble atop his head, and a clean-shaven face ending in a lantern jaw, considered lying. Though he held little respect for Fulton, a man who had, in the counselor's eyes, undone the Christian rigor instituted by Warden Whittier, Shermer believed Fulton had already made up his mind. Lying wouldn't change the outcome, and so the instructor told the truth. "I did not, sir. I thought young Collins's rendition sufficient."

Fulton smiled. "I know you did. Be that as it may, Mr. Rosenstein will serve out his last few weeks with us and be released back into the community." The warden paused before adding a final prayerful note. "One hopes he's learned his lesson."

After his release from Red Wing, Kid Rose landed a position with the *Minneapolis Jewish Times*—a weekly publication with a small but loyal following—as an assistant printer and tried to walk the straight and narrow. But his salary at the newspaper was paltry, a mere ten dollars a week, and with Prohibition in full swing, the cost of a good time, including gaining entrance to innumerable speakeasys where one could wet one's whistle, was out of reach. Still, the Kid's position with the *Times* introduced him to Jews who ran houses of prostitution, operated high-stakes gambling rooms, and partnered with Irish mobsters to smuggle liquor into Minnesota.

Four months of typesetting at the *Times* passed before Mosiah Feldman, a middle-aged man whose taste for younger women was notorious, who owned jewelry stores in Minneapolis, St. Paul, and Duluth, and who was the proprietor of innumerable whorehouses, asked young Abram if "He really wanted to spend his life elbows-deep in ink."

To this, the Kid answered, "No, sir, I do not."

"I've heard you're a good man with your fists," Mosiah said. "That you rarely back down from trouble."

Mosiah, known to friends as "Moe," had observed Abram as the men sat in a booth of an illegal gin joint two doors down from the *Times*'s office. They were enjoying the company of two fetching lasses—girls recruited by a madam working for Feldman—blond Scandinavian gals, fresh off the farm, who'd grown tired of small towns and clueless hayseeds. Agnes, the taller of the two, who was dressed modestly despite her profession and whose figure suggested androgyny, sat next to Abram, her left hand atop the young man's right thigh. Lois, shorter, more garish in attire and makeup, her blue eyes flitting and darting at every sound, movement, or entry into the speakeasy, sat on Moe's side of the booth. The girls were drinking gin. The men were sipping whiskey.

"That's the rumor," Kid Rose had answered, slightly distracted, given his manhood was being aroused by his date's attention. "To be honest, I've lost my share of fights."

"Integrity. I like that in employees," Feldman said with sincerity, conveying respect despite the difference in the men's standing.

"Employees?"

Moe laughed. "Ha! You may be quick with your fists, Rosenstein, but you're slow on the uptake. Yes, I'm offering you a job. As a doorman in one of my establishments. The one where this fine young lady, Miss Jacobson, is employed."

Agnes Jacobson blushed, removed her right hand from Abram's leg, raised her glass, and took a generous swig. Lois Gregorson—Moe's escort, who was nicknamed "Lou"—continue to watch folks enter and exit her field of vision. She was, from the lazy focus of her gaze, slowly drinking herself to oblivion, a habit that Moe Feldman was trying to discourage.

"What's it pay?"

"Fifty."

"A month?" Kid Rose asked, raising his glass, and filling his mouth with whiskey while awaiting an answer.

"A week."

Feldman's reply, one that revealed Kid Rose would be making more in a single week than he made in a month at the *Times*, caused Abram to draw booze into his nose. "You serious?" the Kid asked, after he stopped snorting and coughing.

"I never joke about business." The older man patted Lou on her arm, kissed her on her left cheek, and whispered, "Don't you think you've had enough? I don't want you passing out when we get back to your room."

Lou batted sullen, defeated, leaden empyrean eyes, nodded, and pushed her empty glass into the center of the table.

"Miss Jacobson, don't you think young Mr. Rosenstein could benefit from a tour of the establishment where you and Lou work?"

Agnes, never comfortable with small talk despite her profession, had blushed anew. Though an intelligent and able girl, after graduating from high school, she found that she could not countenance staying in Wheaton, Minnesota, marrying a local farm boy, and birthing a slew of children. "That would be nice."

"Then it's settled, Kid. Drink up."

It hadn't been his first time with a whore. Abram had visited a handful of the seedier brothels in Minneapolis and St. Paul after his release from Red Wing. But until he spent the night with Agnes Jacobson, he'd never fallen for a prostitute. He'd always kept such relationships brief, perfunctory, and cordial. Sex simply for sex—nothing more. But that night, when he accompanied Agnes to the top floor of the old

Victorian—the four tippled adventurers having been met at the establishment's front door by Delores DeRider, the brothel's hostess, and Feldman's longest-serving madam—the way Agnes moved beneath him changed how Abram viewed her. What he thought of her.

In accepting Moe's job offer, a position that required Abram to enforce the rules of the house on the occasionally unruly and often intoxicated clientele of Madam DeRider's establishment, he fully appreciated that Agnes's occupation required her to sleep with strangers—men who paid good money to see her undress, slide beneath well-used sheets, and engage in illicit conduct. But blessed with an uncanny ability to separate business from pleasure, Abram didn't let jealousy interfere with his or Agnes's work. After manning the door at the whorehouse for three years and gaining Moe's trust, Kid Rose was promoted and began bartending at a speakeasy owned by Moe and his Irish business partners.

"That connection," Kid Rose mused, putting down the *Tribune* after reflecting on his work as a bouncer for Feldman, something the Kid put behind him after he connected with the Irish mob, "was a gift from God." Abram hadn't suddenly become pious. His comment was but an acknowledgement that Fate, since leaving Red Wing, had blessed him with a lucrative occupation and a fine companion—one whom, though he loved, he'd never marry.

Abram saved his money and bought a bungalow in St. Paul near St. Catherine's Women's College. Despite their nefarious lives, Agnes's being that of a former prostitute working as a receptionist at an insurance agency and Abram's being that of a valued member of an Irish bootlegging ring, the couple lived discretely in an enclave of Catholic respectability. Neighbors waved to the lovebirds whenever the pair was out and about, conversed politely with them, and generally left the Rosensteins to themselves on the assumption that they were a young, married—but unfortunately childless—Jewish couple. The fact that Agnes attended services at St. Mark's Lutheran church, riding the streetcar from Highland Park to West Seventh to receive the grace she required as a God-fearing Lutheran farm girl, did not deter the neighborly assumption that Agnes was Jewish.

Kid Rose drained coffee from his cup while his mind churned. He did not hold it against his friend that Sigurd Larson had received deferential treatment from Judge Reilly. *It wasn't Siggy's fault. He's not responsible for me spending time in Red Wing.* The Kid gathered his newspaper, left cash for the bill and the tip, walked to the front door, and stood by the coat rack, intent upon removing his slicker and hat before venturing out to confront a late summer downpour. As he reached for his coat, the Kid stopped short to ponder the divergent paths he and his friend had taken. *Besides, Siggy suffered far more being sent to France than I did being shipped off to the reformatory.* His reflection over, the Kid dressed, opened the diner's heavy front door, and confronted the storm.

Abram was meeting James "Slim" Harris, an Irishman orchestrating the importation of Canadian whiskey, Jamaican rum, and English gin into Minnesota from Ontario under the protection and scrutiny of Irish mobster Ian "Stuffy" McNulty. Details concerning the next shipment of illegal liquor should have preoccupied Abram's thoughts, but he couldn't shake the newspaper's headline.

My old friend—the war hero—running for office, Abram thought as he walked through pelting rain. *That's not a bad equation; one filled with opportunity. I know things about Siggy—things his handlers, his wife, and his supporters would not want splashed across the front page. I can use history to my advantage.*

Rosenstein arrived at the warehouse. *I <u>could</u> share what I know with Slim and Stuffy,* he mused, opening a heavy door to enter the high-ceilinged industrial space as rainwater dripped from his slicker and hat. *But I won't. Such information is delicate, a winning hand to be savored and revealed only when necessary. I'll keep what I know to myself,* the gangster concluded, *though if Siggy won't play ball, some unsavory stories about his past might find a reporter's ear.*

CHAPTER SEVEN
Minneapolis, Minnesota
1924

Sigurd Thaddeus Larson limped his way onto the stage in front of the Farmer Labor gathering. The Party's endorsement convention was being held in the ballroom of the Curtis Hotel, a palatial mecca for weary travelers occupying an entire block of downtown Minneapolis. Larson straightened to his six-foot-three height and placed his mahogany cane—the implement's head made of polished African elephant tusk—before adjusting the podium's microphone.

"THANK YOU, MINNEAPOLIS!" Larson boomed, the broad smile on his face genuine despite the phantom pain in his left leg—the one that had been amputated after the Somme—and residual aches in his low back and left thigh, the collective aftermath of being hit dead on by a German mortar round.

The Americans and the Canadians had quickly breached the eastern dike of the waterless canal. The enemy's faint initial resistance was not due to the hubris of the allied assault: the panicked retreat of the Huns was the product of Canadian and British divisions further to the north advancing over temporary bridges and turning the German's right flank. With the enemy in disarray, the Yanks had swept across dry ground in the company of their Canadian mates, crossing open ground virtually unscathed only to face stubborn, reconstituted German units anchored in forest.

"Damn, this fighting is hot," Siggy muttered, as he and Banes raced forward. Dawn arrived. The storm abated. The sky cleared. Emergent daylight afforded clear targets for German rifles and machine guns.

"It is. Keep your noggin' down, private!" Banes admonished.

Larson lowered his head, his steel helmet filthy with splattered mud, and nervously quipped, "OK, sarge. I don't wanna add another hole to this mug . . ."

The Minnesotan had taken out three German soldiers—all point blank kills. Gone was the fear that had caused Larson to wet himself. Terror had been replaced by a rush of adrenaline that obviated any sense of caution.

A mortar round landed nearby. Banes and Larson dove behind a fallen beech, the ancient tree shorn at its base, ending a century of providing cool repose for French lovers. A drumbeat of bullets thudded against decaying wood. Detritus of dirt, leaves, splinters, bone, flesh, and shredded clothing fell from the sky. "We need to get the hell out of here," Banes urged.

Larson nodded. He had two shells left in the Winchester, though there were more in his bandolier. "Agreed. You say when."

Another mortar round whooshed overhead but landed behind the Americans. Banes took it as a sign that the Huns were refining their aim. "Now, you blockheaded Norwegian. We go now."

It had been, as it turned out, a miscalculation on Banes's part, an error that the rest of the Yank platoon seized upon as gospel. The doughboys sprang from cover, and, using beech and oak trees to shield them, sprinted toward the entrenched Germans protecting the road to Cambrai. "Let's take that fucking road and cut their supply line, boys!" Banes had shouted above the din, as he and his mates surged forward, each man firing and reloading his weapon as quickly as possible. Sigurd Larson held his fire. He had only two grenades and the two rounds left in the Winchester and he didn't want to stop to reload. The sky lightened to reveal a Hun machine gun nest mowing down attacking Americans and Canadians. Larson reached for his utility belt and freed a grenade. With the enemy gunners concentrating fire elsewhere, he moved forward, tree by scarred tree, until he could hear the enemy conversing in German. Calm under fire, Larson stopped, methodically pulled the pin on the grenade, stood up, and tossed it toward the enemy gun emplacement.

As Sigurd addressed convention delegates, the Great Depression had not yet arrived to cripple the United States' economy. Even so, financial hardship and wealth disparity were major themes in the Farmer Labor Party's (FLP's) platform.

"They say," Larson continued, "we have no right to demand fairness in wages, mortgage rates, transportation costs, or farm prices." Sigurd boomed his version of a political gospel in a voice so deep and resonant that he did not need amplification to fill the cavernous room. "They—the Eastern bankers and lawyers and politicians wearing hundred-dollar suits and silk ties," he continued, raising his voice to a crescendo, "say that we, all of us—the farmers, factory workers, construction laborers, housewives, teachers, and those who find themselves, through no fault of their own, unemployed or unable to work—should be happy with our lot in life." He reached out with his right hand, grasped a tumbler of cold water, lifted the glass, drank greedily, and slammed the empty tumbler against the wooden surface of the podium for affect. "As my Norwegian immigrant grandfather would say, *'Tull!'* Because we have ladies present, I'll not translate for fear of offending. But understand this: If I'm elected Hennepin County Attorney, I'll do my very best to be fair-handed and open-minded. I'll curry no favor from the Bully Boys; I'll take no campaign contributions from corporations, rich men, or those who control the levers of power. As your county attorney, I'll root out corruption and crime and illegality, no matter who is behind such violations of the law." Before uttering the final sentence of his carefully written speech, Sigurd Larson paused, looked over the crowd, and, for a brief moment, remembered the aftermath of his time on the Somme.

Over forty thousand Brits, together with uncounted numbers of their allies, suffered amputations during the Great War.

Canadian medics found Larson and Banes in a crater left by a mortar round. Banes had been spared serious injury. But Larson's left leg was mutilated. His back and left hip were riddled with shrapnel. His uniform was blood soaked, and his appearance was that of a soldier who was most assuredly dead.

Medics carried Sigurd by stretcher to the nearest field hospital. Once his left leg was removed, the jagged wound was cleaned and hastily sutured in a gruesome tent facility known as a "chopping block." After the largest pieces of shrapnel and dirt, wood, and rock were excised from his ancillary wounds, the patient had been taken by truck to a medical facility near Amiens. Additional intervention stabilized Larson's condition before he was loaded onto an ambulance bound for LeHavre. He had waited in the French port for a day—in and out of consciousness, delirious with fever caused by infection—before being placed on a transport ship filled with other wounded destined for Dover. In England, he was loaded by medics manning an aid facility adjacent to the Dover-to-London rail line onto a converted baggage car bound for Roehampton Hospital. At the hospital, Sigurd endured successive debridements of his stump. The surgeons and nurses at Roehampton had mastered the craft of rebuilding war-shattered human beings to the point that, when Larson was discharged with an articulating American Leg (an improvement over the staple of prosthetics, the Anglesey leg), he was ambulatory, aided by the elegant ivory-headed cane gifted him by Sergeant Banes. The sergeant had returned to combat duty in France, while Larson had been discharged from the army and sent home.

  Sigurd was subsequently awarded the Silver Star and other Canadian and French medals. He was recommended for, but did not receive, the Medal of Honor. Larson's grenade had destroyed the enemy machine gun emplacement and cleared the way for allied troops to overrun the Huns. Sig Larson was a hero, a man celebrated as such in local newspapers when he returned home to resume his education, first at the University of Minnesota and then at the St. Paul College of Law, where he took night courses while working a full shift at the local Ford assembly plant. He quit the Ford job during his last year of law school to accept an internship with the Minneapolis City Attorney's office. Sig's past transgressions, including the aborted break-in of a liquor store, were things hidden, secrets kept. He hoped his service to his nation, his choice to give his all for his country, would allow the ghosts of the past to remain muted and out of view.

The ache where Sigurd's prosthetic leg joined remnant flesh was perpetual. As the candidate geared up for his summation, his final argument to the delegates who held his fate in their collective hands, he grimaced, bit the inside of his cheek, and nodded. "I make this pledge to you, ladies, and gentlemen. I'll always be in the trenches with you. I'll never turn my back on you, just as I never turned my back on my duty to this nation. I also promise that I'll never curry favor with those whose mission in life is to abuse you and keep you down. This is my solemn, sacred vow."

The crowd rose in unison to its feet. Thunderous applause erupted, followed by a call for a voice vote endorsing the young veteran. The only other Farmer Laborite seeking the post was Eustice Potter. Potter was the right-hand man of Arthur C. Townley. His loyalty to Townley's quixotic quest, a quest that failed when Townley refused to abandon his agrarian vision of reform, doomed Potter's bid. After being endorsed by acclamation, Sigurd left the stage, relying upon the cane to provide stability, though steadfastly refusing to display a limp as he descended from the dais to shake hands.

Out of the corner of his eye, Larson spied a man he did not wish to acknowledge. The dreaded audience member, considerably shorter and broader of shoulder than Sigurd, waved energetically as the newly endorsed candidate worked the room.

"Hello, Siggy!" Kid Rose shouted, when Larson finally came within earshot. "Congratulations on your endorsement!" the rum-runner added, extending his right hand.

Newspaper photographers had followed the candidate through the crowd, popping snapshots of the next Hennepin County Attorney. Sigurd Larson's election was considered a foregone conclusion, given that the Democrats were not endorsing a candidate and given that the Republican nominee, George Gurthwood, was being investigated for tax fraud.

When Abram reached for Sigurd's hand, the lawyer's political instincts, his knowledge of the businesses Kid Rose had migrated to after leaving Red Wing, and the rumor that the Kid lived in sin with a former prostitute, compelled Larson to ignore his old friend and exit the building without acknowledging the man's presence.

CHAPTER EIGHT
1924

The candidate was uncomfortable. Though he had been born and raised near Negro neighborhoods, Sigurd Larson had experienced little interaction with folks whose complexions were significantly darker than his own.

He was seated in the meeting room of the Phyllis Wheatley Settlement House, surrounded by profoundly un-Scandinavian faces, people who hoped he had something enlightening to say about race and poverty. The make-up of the crowd made Larson fidgety. But despite his significant angst, Sig feigned calm as he listened to Ethel Ray—the first Negro female police officer in Minneapolis—speak in glowing terms about Larson's brief tenure as an Assistant Minneapolis City Attorney.

"Mr. Larson, while neither steeped in our traditions nor immersed in our collective values, has never, to my knowledge, targeted the Negro during his public service," Miss Ray began. "And I must say, given my experience in Duluth as a young woman, that is a valuable trait in a man charged with overseeing the even-handed application of justice."

Ethel was twenty years old when the unthinkable—at least in Minnesota, a state that prided itself on its acceptance of immigrants and a state that saw significant blood spilled by the First Minnesota at Gettysburg—occurred. Three Negro circus workers were hanged by an enraged mob four blocks from Miss Ray's home in Duluth. Rabid white men dragged the unfortunate Negroes from the Duluth jail. Taciturn police officers stood idly by as four thousand white Duluthians lynched Elias Clayton, Elmer Jackson, and Isaac McGhie for the alleged rape of a white woman, a crime that, in truth, never took place.

At birth, Ethel Ray had been one of only two hundred Negroes living in Duluth. In time, the city's "Colored" population—as it was deemed by polite society—grew. With an increased Negro presence, overt racism became commonplace. Discriminatory anger was brought to a fever pitch when Negro men (and their families) migrated from

Ohio, Michigan, Indiana, and Illinois to accept jobs in the newly built United States Steel plant located in the far-western neighborhood of Gary-New Duluth.

"Them Niggers took our jobs," was a common refrain uttered by the city's working-class white men. Bill Ray, Ethel's father, tried to shelter his children from the burgeoning acidity of the times. But untoward discourse and insults were routinely heard by Duluthians of Color as they tried to live their lives in a place inhospitable as to both its social and physical climates. A year after the lynchings, Ethel attended a meeting of the Duluth chapter of the NAACP, where she heard W.E.B. Dubois speak about the horrific events of June 15th, 1920. DuBois made such an impression on Ethel that she approached the noted luminary and initiated a friendship that ended only upon DuBois's death.

Ethel Ray's ties to the great Negro orator and thinker led her to accept a job with the Urban League in Kansas City. Later, based upon stellar skills honed as a stenographer for the Minnesota legislature (she was an official recorder during hearings held to investigate the 1918 Cloquet Fire), Ethel moved to New York City to work for the Urban League's magazine, *Opportunity.* Through her association with the Harlem Renaissance, Ethel Ray attained further enlightenment: listening to and engaging with the great Negro dissenters of the day allowed Ethel to hone her political instincts and attain critical acuity.

As a Minneapolis police officer, Ethel interacted with Sigurd Larson when he prosecuted cases for the Minneapolis City Attorney's Office. Larson made a name for himself—not by targeting prostitutes, many of whom were immigrant women or women of Color hoping to stave off poverty by selling their bodies—but by taking on the madams and brothel owners who ran the sin industry. Larson's approach, his attempt to "cut off the head of the snake," as he put it, was to pursue those who profited from female enslavement, rather than arrest and prosecute women thrown into degradation by circumstances beyond their control. Sigurd's empathy caught Ethel's attention. They were not friends but were acquainted sufficiently such that when Larson announced his campaign to become Hennepin County Attorney, Ethel Ray signed on as an enthusiastic supporter and arranged for Sigurd to speak at the Phyllis Wheatley Settlement House, where she'd once been employed.

The House, after its new building was erected on Aldrich Avenue, provided a place of residence for Negro college students who could not find lodging in the segregated dormitories at the University of Minnesota. The House was also a temporary sanctuary for Negro speakers, authors, and cultural icons visiting Minneapolis, because those men and women, no matter their intellect, education, or worth, were universally turned away by the city's better hotels. It was at the Phyllis Wheatley House where issues of race and discrimination were discussed and solutions sought, all within the hearing of Miss Ray. Ethel took that informal knowledge and training with her onto the streets as a police officer, and when she noticed Larson's even-handed approach to dealing with "ladies of the evening," she determined that Candidate Larson should address her community on its own turf.

"I've worked with Mr. Larson in his role as misdemeanor prosecutor," Miss Ray continued. The settlement house was packed with skeptics; every chair in the place was occupied. The room was bursting at its seams, the dressed-for-church-crowd overflowing onto the sidewalk. "He is, while not especially versed in our troubles and our travails, a man of integrity, a man of unscrupulous morality."

Ethel stopped and smiled demurely at Sigurd, who sat on a simple wooden folding chair. Ethel Ray stood to the fullness of her modest height at a lectern, addressing the audience without a microphone. Larson's omnipresent cane leaned against the wall. The candidate intended to make his way from the chair to the lectern without relying upon the cane, an iffy proposition given that his low back was spasming. *These people want a demonstration of strength against adversity,* he thought as he returned Miss Ray's smile. *Theirs is not an easy lot despite the notion that tolerance and "good will toward man" is said to prevail throughout the state. Such sentimentality may be applicable between white folks of differing ethnicities and differing stations in life, but has little application to the Negro, the Indian, or the Chinaman living among us.*

"He has been upright, honest, and fair-minded as a prosecuting attorney. Before that, he gave his all in France in defense of liberty. He has persevered, and he will, if given the chance, be a model reformer and supporter of our cause." Ethel Ray nodded, looked out into the faces of the crowd, and let her remarks take hold. "I give you, Mr. Sigurd Larson: the next Hennepin County Attorney!"

Despite Sig's unease, his remarks were well received. After rousing applause, the candidate mouthed a "thank you" to Ethel, and bowing to necessity, he used his cane for balance to leave the stage and shake hands with newly won supporters. Larson performed his obligatory duties and then made his way toward a waiting sedan with his campaign manager, Emmitt Eldridge—a mountain of a man, an ex-heavyweight boxer who'd once lost a title fight to Jess Willard and who made other human beings seem impotent. Outside, Sig's driver, Buster Tibbs, a thin, narrow-faced Negro who'd grown up in Columbia, South Carolina, exited a green Ford Model L Touring car, opened its doors and ushered Larson and Eldridge inside.

Tibbs closed the rear doors, slid onto the driver's seat behind the steering wheel, and slammed his door shut. "Where to, Boss?"

Larson was about to instruct Tibbs to take him home, where he hoped Amelia, his wife, had supper waiting. But before Sig could reply, a black Cadillac Fleetwood roared up the street, stopped, and blocked the Ford's path. A man Larson did not want to encounter leaped from the Caddie, dodged traffic, and advanced toward the Ford with upraised hands. Kid Rose stopped outside the Ford's rear passenger-side window and rapped on the glass. Reluctantly, Sigurd Larson rolled down the window.

"*Mister County Attorney*," Abram Rosenstein said impishly. "I finally caught up with you!" The Kid's smile widened before he continued. "Might I have a word with you in private?"

"You want me to deal with him?" Emmitt Eldridge asked.

"No, I'll handle it," Larson said, opening the door and stepping out into the cool dusk of early autumn. The lawyer steadied himself with his cane before confronting Rosenstein. "What do you want, Abram?"

The Kid smiled. "I've been trying to schedule a meeting with you," he said, "but your secretary keeps giving me the cold shoulder."

"I'm a busy man."

"Ha! And you think I'm not?"

Sigurd Larson had kept his distance from his old friend but had, out of deference to their shared history, looked the other way as Kid Rose grew bolder and bolder while working with the Irish mob to satisfy thirsty Minnesotans. By the time Larson began chasing whorehouse owners, pimps, and madams, Kid Rose had migrated to smuggling and was no longer involved in prostitution. Nevertheless, word came to Larson from time to time that the Minneapolis police or Hennepin County deputies were about to arrest the Kid for violating the Volstead Act, the legislation that installed Prohibition as a reality of American life. Pursuit of such allegations by local law enforcement, given the dirt Rosenstein had on Larson, was conveniently swept under the rug by the assistant city attorney. The newly constituted Federal Bureau of Investigation—and zealous Treasury men like Elliot Ness—presented a thornier problem.

Trades were made. Nefarious bargains were consummated that might ruin Sig's political aspirations if the attorney's efforts on behalf of his old friend saw daylight. But Larson had amassed incriminating information concerning Jerome Cunningham, the FBI agent supervising Prohibition cases in Minnesota, including evidence of Cunningham's preference for underage hookers, to keep Kid Rose out of federal custody.

"It's not wise for me to be seen in public with you," Larson muttered.

Kid Rose smiled, displaying pearly teeth. "I need a favor," he whispered.

"How's that?"

"One of your detectives stumbled onto a dead girl in a brothel."

"Why the concern? From what I know, you're out of *that* game."

Rosenstein leaned in. "True. But the whorehouse in question is Moe Feldman's, and as you know, I owe Moe a great deal."

"So?"

"He finds himself in a bit of a mess."

"Why? Who's gonna mourn the passing of an anonymous working girl?" Sig asked, immediately ashamed of his callousness.

"The deceased wasn't a whore. And she was hardly 'anonymous'. . ."

"How's that?"

"The stiff in question was Councilman Miller's daughter."

"Goddamn it!"

CHAPTER NINE
1924

It wasn't just that Abram Rosenstein had the police files, court minutes, and original transcript of the juvenile court hearing held in front of Judge Edmund Reilly.

If that was all the Kid had on me, I could easily ride out the storm and be elected county attorney, Sig thought, as he sat on the back patio of the home he'd bought before marrying Amelia. *A minor legal scrape, like getting caught as a teenager trying to steal booze and cash, wouldn't derail my ambitions. The public would understand and forgive one childish indiscretion.*

But, as Larson sipped his second gin and tonic of the evening, the giddy success of his time at the Phyllis Wheatley House was overcome by his old friend's unscripted appearance—and the bootlegger's revelation that a young girl, the daughter of a Minneapolis city councilman, had died in a filthy tenement—bringing melancholia. News regarding the teenager's sudden passing, the result of being raised Catholic and frantic with guilt to obtain an abortion, could not be easily contained.

He knew the cop who had discovered the body. Though Detective Newhouse was rumored to be in Kid Rose's pocket, the leverage such knowledge might hold over Moe Feldman, and, by guilty association, Abram Rosenstein, was something the attorney couldn't chance. Upon hearing the news from Kid Rose, Sigurd had debated calling Newhouse to encourage the relocation of the dead girl's body <u>before</u> the coroner was on the scene. On the ride home from his appearance before the Negroes, and against his better judgment, Sig had ordered Buster Tibbs to stop the Ford at a pay phone on a dimly lighted side street. Larson reached Newhouse at the whorehouse. At the end of their short conversation, the detective had assured the future county attorney that the girl's body would not be found on Moe Feldman's property when the coroner arrived.

"What's eating you, dear?" Amelia Larson asked upon wandering onto the cool cement of the home's rear patio.

The house and grounds were secluded by stately oaks planted by the home's original owner, a grain miller who'd built the expansive house for his new bride in the late 1880s when Minneapolis was truly the Mill City.

"Just work, Am'. Just work."

Amelia Salveson Larson was a waif-like woman of narrow chest, absent hips, and slender build. Despite her girlish lines, pregnancy was obvious in the woman's profile. Given Amelia's slight configuration, her abdomen extended straight out from her navel, compromising her ability to walk. "Well, do you think having a second gin and tonic is the answer?"

Amelia's father, Elliot Salveson, a Methodist preacher overseeing the faithful in Stillwater, had championed Minnesota Congressman Volstead's Prohibition agenda. His wife Uriah, Amelia's mother, fully supported Elliot Salveson's bid to remove demon rum as a major cause of family discord in Minnesota. Mrs. Salveson had grown up with an alcoholic father, a man who routinely beat Uriah and her two sisters. As a result of familial trauma, Uriah was an ardent and vehement teetotaler, though her daughter and only child wasn't a saint when it came to alcohol. On special occasions, such as Christmas or her birthday, Am' was not above enjoying a glass of red wine—generally cheap stuff, not top shelf, and sweet. Despite her modest imbibing, as Sigurd sought higher office and entered the rugged arena of Minnesota politics, Amelia believed her beloved was improvidently relying upon alcohol to steady his jangled nerves.

There were also the recurrent nightmares. Once a week, sometimes more frequently, Sigurd became agitated while sleeping, often screaming out in the middle of the night as he subconsciously recounted his wartime experiences, including the moment he was almost blown to bits by a German mortar round.

Amelia understood Sigurd had been through inexplicable hell, even though her husband did not talk about his experiences, his time in France, his wounds, or his long and difficult rehabilitation. Not to his friends, not to his wife, and certainly not in public. Such things were kept locked inside the staid, often brooding, and sometimes contradictorily cheerful man Amelia had come to love and to marry.

"No. But it does dull one's senses and make it easier to relax after a long day at work," Sigurd finally replied.

"The pot roast will be ready soon," Amelia said, taking a seat next to her husband as the sky fell to black, the twinkling lights of homes and streetlamps accenting evening's descent.

Though he appreciated his wife's perceptions and presence, Sig was absent from the conversation. He was unsettled by the indisputable truth that Councilman Cyrus Miller's daughter had died alone, bleeding out after a botched abortion at the hands of an unlicensed hack. The anonymous butcher had packed up his or her surgical equipment and eliminated any evidence of having been present at Moe Feldman's establishment before disappearing. Because of Abram's disclosure and the details of the girl's inglorious passing that Larson had learned from Detective Newhouse, the lawyer could not focus on his lovely wife.

Amelia Salveson had worked as a waitress at the Minneapolis Club, a hoity-toity private retreat for prominent men, where Sigurd Larson took lunch twice a week. Despite Amelia's handsome face bearing evidence of a cleft lip—the defect having been surgically repaired—it was instant infatuation on Sig's part.

Amelia, always wary of romance given her innate fear of rejection, eventually migrated toward affection, the woman's acquiescence beginning as a cautious meander that blossomed into adoration. In time, the couple's accelerating path toward intimacy required Sigurd to approach Pastor Salveson and ask the preacher for his daughter's hand. Given the lawyer's reputation as an honest, hard-working, and dedicated public servant and war hero, Pastor Salveson had—despite the disparity in ages between Sig and Am'—consented to the union.

Amelia detected discord coloring her husband's mood and understood his need for privacy. She removed her milky white hand from her husband's wrist, stood, and smoothed her maternity smock. "Just go easy on the gin, OK? I don't want you nodding off during dinner," she cautioned, retreating into the house.

Sigurd nodded and went back to mulling over his predicament. *If I hadn't fallen in with the Kid during our childhood, I wouldn't be in this pickle.* The lawyer drained his cocktail, stood up, and shuffled to a nearby wooden picnic table without aid of his cane. He opened a crystal decanter, poured an ample shot of gin, capped the container, topped off the drink with tonic, and returned to his chair, where he settled himself. Between sips of his drink, the lawyer contemplated the still waters of Lake Calhoun and a bank of evening fog wafting over the lake. In the ebony sky above the fog-cloaked lake, a waxing crescent moon—Earth's closest celestial neighbor in the second of its seven phases—cast mustard light. Rowboats, sculls, and canoes had been put away for the season. No pedestrians walked the graveled path skirting the shoreline. Larson found himself bathed in silence, save for interruptions of quietude occasioned by random car horns, train whistles, the clacking of trolley wheels, and the muffled voices of neighbors. "Three drinks won't put me to sleep," Sigurd mused. "And a third gin and tonic might just make things clearer!"

The Kid had long ago advised Sig that he was in possession of the original records concerning their failed burglary. That news, in the context of the lawyer's heroism, was unimportant. But there was more, much more, to Abram Rosenstein's hold on the strait-laced Norwegian.

First, there was the fact Kid Rose had risked his own life to save Sig from drowning. Then there were the street fights and brawls, after which more than a few young toughs bested by Larson required medical attention. Such dustups were routinely instigated by Abram's mouth and required his imposing friend to beat down all comers. That youthful history wasn't public knowledge, though it was preserved in the memories of Kid Rose and his associates. At Abram's say-so, witnesses to Sig Larson's wayward adolescence could be brought to bear, though for the time being, such voices were quelled by the Kid's demands of loyalty.

But sadly, there is more . . . Sigurd thought as he fingered his drink glass *. . . there is Helen Golden . . .*

Helen was Abram's cousin. Sig was eighteen and about to ship out to France when, home on leave from basic training,

Abram introduced Siggy to his maternal cousin. Helen was a black-haired, dark-skinned, exotic, well-proportioned gal with a propensity for French kissing. Larson had thought, before the deed was done, that she was eighteen—if not older—given her poise and physical maturity. It was only later, as Sigurd and the Kid walked home, that Abram had disclosed his cousin's true age.

"What? No way!" Sig had protested.

The Kid shook his head and smiled. "Sorry, pal, but she's only fifteen—just starting ninth grade."

Larson had grown quiet as the pair walked the darkened street. "Why the hell didn't you say something?"

Kid Rose chuckled. "It's not like she's a virgin." The two friends slowed their pace as they hashed out the evening's events. "Besides, even I've enjoyed her favors a time or two."

Sigurd placed his right hand on Rosenstein's left shoulder to stop him. "You slept with her?"

"Don't be crass," Abram said through a broad smile, shrugging free. "We're first cousins. We only messed around above the waist. But you gotta admit, she has great tits!"

"God, I'm so stupid. What if she ends up pregnant? What the hell do I do then?"

"Well, you're a good Lutheran boy," Abram had replied as the boys resumed walking. "Pray she doesn't."

Whether the prayers worked or whether Sig was simply lucky, Helen Golden did not turn up pregnant on the Larsons' front porch, accompanied by an angry father demanding marriage. Instead, not long after Sigurd's illicit coupling with the girl, the Golden family had relocated to Illinois. Neighborhood scuttlebutt was that Helen's folks hoped that by changing their daughter's peer group, the young girl's reputation might be rehabilitated.

Regardless of whether Miss Golden's sudden departure for Oak Park accomplished the rejuvenation of her social standing, the fact that Sigurd Larson—the FLP's endorsed candidate for Hennepin County Attorney—had committed statutory rape, if revealed, was not something that Larson's ambition could recover from. The prosecutor's long-ago encounter with Abram Rosenstein's cousin was the most devastating secret troubling Sig as he listened to the intermittent sounds of the city, breathed in the pungent odor of rotting leaves littering the backyard, and polished off his third gin and tonic.

CHAPTER TEN
1924

Detective Derrick Newhouse, sitting on the edge of his unmade bed, pulled hard on a pewter flask. The cop's claustrophobic apartment was a third-story walk-up in the attic of an old Victorian. The flat had a single window set high on an end wall beneath the eaves. It was night, and the only illumination in the space came from an electric lamp on a nightstand next to the bed.

Newhouse's flask contained Canadian whiskey mixed with opium. The addition of the narcotic rendered the concoction "laudanum," an elixir once found in patent medicines. Newhouse routinely bought opium from Jerome Washington, a Negro musician the detective had once arrested for selling the drug. Unable to endure the stomach ulcers and severe depression that made him miserable, Newhouse had reached an accord with the drug-dealing-saxophonist, which had resulted in all traces of Washington's arrest disappearing in return for access to a perpetual supply of high-quality opium. But on the evening in question, the opium in Newhouse's flask hadn't been provided by Washington. The narcotic being enjoyed by the detective had been a gift, along with a quart of rotgut whiskey, from Kid Rose.

The tincture of opium and the smuggled whiskey were partial payment for Newhouse's assistance in concealing the true circumstances of Susanne Miller's death. A wad of sawbucks, discreetly handed to the cop by one of Rosenstein's men, was further inducement for Newhouse to make any problems caused by the Miller girl's untimely death disappear. Finally, to ensure Newhouse kept his big yap shut, Moe Feldman had thrown in a night with his youngest, freshest working girl, a forlorn and mopey teenager who plied her trade in the very building where Susanne Miller met her unfortunate end. The fact that the detective ended up "doing the nasty" a few doors down from where a young Catholic girl bled to death from a botched abortion didn't seem to bother Derrick Newhouse in the least.

I've struck gold, Newhouse thought. *The fact Larson knows about this mess is icing on the cake. A future card to be played, if and when the time is right.*

After Larson's telephone call to the whorehouse, the detective had moved the girl's corpse into the basement of the tenement before sanitizing the crime scene. Newhouse used elbow grease, hot water, soap, and bleach to scrub away the blood and misery afflicting the tawdry room where Susanne Miller died. After ensuring the flat was spotless, Newhouse covered the unfortunate girl's corpse in a blanket, dragged the stiffening body from the basement, and dumped what remained of Susanne Margaret Miller in a nearby alley. Upon completing his untoward task, Newhouse returned to the whorehouse to spend the night with the young woman Kid Rose had offered up as final payment for the detective's troubles.

Gretchen Holmgren, an unspoiled innocent with shoulder-length golden hair, muted hazel eyes, and a squarely configured shape, had run away from an uninspired life in Redwood Falls. Evangeline Potts, a former madam prowling the seedier reaches of the Twin Cities in search of wayward girls, found the homeless, disheveled, hungry teenager panhandling for change in downtown Minneapolis and stopped to inventory Gretchen's figure, face, and earning potential as spring drizzle devolved into deluge.

Miss Potts brought Gretchen to the former madam's well-appointed apartment, where the girl shed her wet rags and bathed in a claw-footed tub filled with excoriating hot water. Following her bath, Gretchen was provided with fancy undergarments and freshly laundered clothes. After dressing and combing her hair, the girl devoured mountains of home-cooked food served by the smiling, seemingly kind Evangeline. A bond formed between the women that allowed Miss Potts to nudge Miss Holmgren toward a new occupation. The transition from farm girl to prostitute had been swift: within a month's time, Gretchen Holmgren lost her virginity and was sleeping with strangers for money.

After the gratis romp in Gretchen's bed, Derrick Newhouse had returned to his attic apartment. *I've had better,* the detective thought, as he climbed a narrow, steep staircase towards sleep. *But at least I know she's clean and unlikely to give me the clap, which is why I'll see her again on my own dime.* Though Newhouse was jaded by—and depressed from—what he'd witnessed over his ten-year career as a detective, he was untroubled by the fact that he'd slept with a girl young enough to be his daughter. *It's her choice to do what she does.* In a similar fashion, Newhouse had refused to condemn himself for his role in covering up the truth regarding the Miller girl's death.

Susanne Miller's father was a big-shot Minneapolis city councilor rumored to be in line for mayor. Photographs of Susanne's glamorous mother—together with companion articles highlighting her many charitable causes—frequently splashed across the society pages of Twin Cities newspapers. Given her lineage, Susanne Miller's passing had been news. But the circumstances of her demise, including the fact that her partially clad body had been discovered in an alley in a dangerous neighborhood, signs of the attempted abortion clear despite Newhouse's efforts to obfuscate such evidence, never saw print. Cyrus and Madeline Miller did everything in their considerable power to preserve their daughter's secrets, if only to ensure Susanne received a proper Catholic burial.

"What's done is done," Newhouse muttered as he set the flask on the nightstand, removed his shoes, trousers, button-down shirt, and stockings, pulled back the bedspread and sheets, and slid beneath soiled linen wearing a white ribbed undershirt and matching boxers. Snuggled in warmth, the cop retrieved his flask, took a final draw, capped the now-empty container, and returned it to the nightstand. "No one will ever know the truth," Newhouse whispered, as he turned off the light and fell into an impenetrable, opium-induced slumber.

CHAPTER ELEVEN
Polo Grounds, Manhattan Borough 1925

"The Giants are ripe for the picking," Stanley Prescott, managing editor of the *Brooklyn Observer,* said as he drank warm tap beer from a waxed paper cup in a bleacher seat at the Polo Grounds. "Shouldn't be much of a challenge for the Flock to take them down."

Don Swanson nodded at the bald, slouch-shouldered figure with a slight paunch—the man's belly accentuated by bracers—who was his boss, before reflecting on his life.

Swanson—despite being in fine physical shape from daily walks to and from the apartment that he and Beatrice and their infant daughter, Marjorie, shared in Brooklyn more than a mile away from the newspaper's offices—was tired: bone weary and exhausted because the baby would not sleep. Every night, the little girl, born a month early—making her undersized and fidgety—cried and cried and cried, necessitating Don's escape to the living room's davenport, where he covered his ears with a pillow in an attempt to secure rest.

Marjorie's malady was first ruled to be colic. Then Doc Bayer, the neighborhood's general practitioner whose office was nearby and who Don came to believe cut his medical degree out of the back of a magazine, deemed Beatrice's modest bosom insufficient for nursing. The doctor's off-the-cuff diagnosis required Don to spend a portion of his twenty-five-dollar-a-week salary on milk purchased from a grocery store around the corner from the cooperative apartment that Don and Bea sublet in the Finnish enclave of *Alku Toinen* ("Second Beginning").

Don had fortuitously encountered his old baseball teammate, Eddie Salmela, outside the *Observer's* office—where Don had stopped to apply for a reporter's position after being turned down by New York City's more prestigious dailies. Eddie was living amongst his kindred and working as a teamster—delivering block ice throughout Brooklyn. The two-bedroom apartment Eddie knew to be available, a cooperative flat owned by a Finnish bachelor on a sojourn to Finland in search of a bride, was clean, tidy, and boasted hot and cold running water; an improvement over the dump Don and Beatrice had rented in East Harlem after arriving from Minnesota.

The pregnancy Beatrice revealed before boarding the train from Minnesota to New York, a hope that ended in a miscarriage, had loomed large. After experiencing unexpected loss, Bea was convinced she'd never carry an infant to term, never know the breadth and depth of maternal love. But upon discovering the cessation of her monthly three years after the miscarriage and upon Don finding work as a newspaper reporter (after having spent time as a day laborer on the East River waterfront), the second pregnancy took, continued to fulfillment, and ended with Marjorie's birth.

"Buck Wheat," Stanley Prescott observed, as Brooklyn's left fielder strode to the plate, "is due."

Wheat's real first name was Zachariah, but he was known by a plethora of nicknames, which was also true of the Brooklyn Nine itself, officially known as the Brooklyn Base Ball Club. Most often, the team was referred to—in newspapers throughout the five boroughs—as the "Robins" or "The Flock" or, less frequently, the "Dodgers": a moniker based upon Brooklyn residents' collective ability to avoid death by streetcar.

The *nom de plume* most often attached to the Robins' slender, right-throwing, left-batting star outfielder was "Buck," though "Zach" or "Zack" also appeared in print. The '25 season would see Buck Wheat carry a .359 batting average, smash fourteen homers, and come to bat six hundred and sixteen times, all of which caused Stanley Prescott to predict that the Missourian would unload on the Giant pitcher.

Don Swanson smiled and remembered back to his own playing days. Though he'd been a Johnny-come-lately to baseball, he saw, in the windup and the follow-through of the Giant's hurler, the hallmarks of disaster. "You're right. Bucky will crush the first pitch this bum throws near the plate."

Don napped on the trolley ride home after the game, despite the jarring and jolting of the car as it crossed the Brooklyn Bridge above the East River. He napped easily, even with the commotion, because sleep was difficult to come by in the family's apartment, what with the baby's incessant bawling and his wife's nervous apprehension that, despite Doc Bayer's reassurances that Marjorie was "out of the woods," infantile death seemed to lurk around every corner.

"Hey," Stanley asked, as Don tried to catch forty winks. "How's your exposé on the Borough President coming?"

The boss's inquiry roused Don from the edges of a dream, a hazy scenario about tossing a no-hitter in the state championship, an occurrence that had never transpired in his brief baseball career. "I'm about done. Pretty sure the last piece of the puzzle will fall into place tomorrow, when I interview the building inspector."

Stanley nodded and shifted his eyes to watch rusty brown water. The East River's surface was being jostled by a steady breeze blowing in from the Atlantic. "It needs to be in print sooner than later. Time is of the essence, what with Foley about to launch his campaign for mayor."

"No need to worry, Boss," Don said, stifling a yawn. "It'll be in the hands of the copy editor by tomorrow night."

"Good. If the Democrats think they can pull a fast one on the people of this city by throwing a turd against the wall in hopes it sticks, well, they've got another thing coming!"

It was difficult for Don to control his political bias when talking with Stanley. Like Miss Almquist, his old high school English teacher, Stanley was a reform-minded Bull Mooser. Don's time around radical Finns had edged him closer and closer to Socialism. However, with a sickly child and a morose wife living in a sublet apartment and their lodging only secure until Oskar Langevin returned from Finland with his new wife, Swanson needed the reporter job. He needed to stockpile money so he could find another place for his family to live. Instead of engaging his boss, Don nodded, looked across the river toward the hurly-burly of his home borough, and smiled at the notion he'd called Buck Wheat's dinger exactly so. The first pitch thrown in the vicinity of home plate had been crushed by the Missourian.

Buck Wheat's bomb had cleared the Polo Grounds' fence by a mile, paving the way for a Brooklyn victory.

CHAPTER TWELVE
1925

Don Swanson slurped tarry coffee and waited. He was, by nature, an impatient man, not one to sit idly by waiting for the next turn of life, the next adventure, large or small in scope and importance. Hanson's Café served its coffee strong and piping hot—exactly as Fawn Inga Swanson—Don's mother—had brewed and offered it to family and guests back in Oak Ridge, Minnesota. The breakfasts at the café were served with business-like curtness by Gustav Hanson's fraternal twin daughters—Emma and Jean—who were stouter than heifers. The meals reminded Don of his maternal grandmother's kitchen, where stacks of thin, eggy Norwegian pancakes, mounds of thick-sliced, home-cured bacon, and piles of freshly cut and fried potatoes and onions routinely crowded the table. But whereas Grandma Erma served hearty breakfasts with smiles and love, none of that Old World charm could be found in the Hanson twins. The girls were always in a hurry, rarely chit-chatting or interacting with customers frequenting the ten-table, four-stool postcard of a café run by Gustav Hanson with grumpy efficiency.

"I'll have the special," Don said, looking up from the cardboard menu he held in his gangly hands, after greeting the thoroughly ordinary Jean Hanson with a smile.

The girl nodded, took the menu from Don with precision, walked across the room, deposited the menu in a box next to the wait station, and continued with assured certainty to place Don's order with Gustav, the only person allowed to cook in his café. In less than five minutes, a steamy plate of corned beef hash, three sunny-side-up eggs, and rye toast was placed in front of Don. The girl eyed him up one side and down the other, asking without a hint of politeness, "More coffee?"

"Sure."

Jean Hanson poured coffee from a stainless-steel pot into Don's cup, the cup's rim discolored but unchipped and unmarred despite the rough and tumble of cafeteria life. She glanced at the menu resting on the table across from Swanson. "Still waiting?"

Don chewed hash and nodded.

"I'll leave the menu," the teenager said, and moved off.

Don was nearly finished eating when Pete O'Brien, a red-haired, white-complected, crimson-faced, fully freckled leprechaun of a man—who also happened to be the Chief Building Inspector for the Borough of Brooklyn—opened the café's windowless front door and stepped inside. He spotted Don, waved, crossed the diner, removed his overcoat, hung the coat on a hook, and claimed a seat at the reporter's table. "How's the special?" O'Brien asked, glancing at the nearly empty plate in front of Swanson.

"Good. Hash is done just right."

Jean Hanson approached, wiped grease from her hands on what had once been a clean white apron, and scrutinized the building inspector with an attention that Don believed beyond the girl's native capabilities. "What'll ya have, Mr. O'Brien?" she asked, her inflection evincing coyness.

O'Brien took in the plump, pock-marked face of the teenager—her complexion a victim of the departed acne caused by working long hours in a café—smiled, and thought, *Honey, you're not fat: You're just generously proportioned!* But given that he had no reason to insult a child, O'Brien refrained from commenting on the girl's appearance and simply replied, "The special. And coffee, black. And a glass of prune juice, as well."

Jean leaned in to retrieve the menu. Her left breast, its subtle curvature discernible beneath the girl's starched white blouse and brassiere, nudged O'Brien's forearm as she reached. The girl blushed, snatched the menu, and retreated with haste.

"She's smitten with you," Don observed.

"She's a child. And, even if she was older, she's not my type. I like my women thin, sassy, dark haired, and Irish."

Swanson smiled. "How's the Borough doing these days?"

Jean reappeared with a porcelain cup, a matching saucer, and a coffee pot. She placed the cup and saucer in front of the building inspector, and poured coffee until it neared the cup's brim. She smiled and, without repeating her earlier suggestion of intimacy, left the pot on the table.

"Once she sheds some of that girlish weight, she'll be a decent catch," Don noted, slurping the last of his coffee from the bottom of his cup. As the waitress had failed to attend to him, he lifted the pot and poured himself a second cup.

"Like I said, not my type."

"And the Borough?" Don repeated.

"Clever how you avoid the direct and seek to find out what it is you want to know by relying upon the oblique."

"I'm a reporter. I'd rather have you tell me your story than drag it out of you."

"Bah! You're just another angler of scoops looking for a big catch."

Don let out a laugh. "Still, you called me, remember?"

O'Brien's food arrived. The building official sipped the prune juice before dousing his eggs and hash with salt and pepper. He slid a fork under the hash and raised the food to his mouth but stopped short of consummating his first taste of breakfast. "I didn't call to share anything about President Foley with you, that's for certain, friend," O'Brien noted dryly, his fork full of food still poised in the air.

The disclosure caught Don off guard.

"That surprises you?"

"I was told you wanted to talk about scandals involving Foley. Kickbacks from dock and warehouse owners, bribes involving unions, and a money trail leading back to the White Hand—the sorts of revelations that might undo a man."

O'Brien smiled, opened his mouth, drew in the hash, chewed, set down his fork, picked up his cup, and gulped coffee. "I have no such information." The redhead paused, looked directly at Don with blazingly indigo eyes, scratched his nose with the index finger of his left hand, and lowered his voice. "But I <u>do</u> have something to tell you, Boyo."

The Irish in the man was as clear as if he'd just stepped off the boat from Cratelow in County Cork, the hometown of grandparents who'd arrived in Brooklyn at the height of the Famine. Though he was the second generation of O'Briens born in Brooklyn, the building inspector's ancestral lilt had not been lost to assimilation.

"I'm listening."

O'Brien considered the quiet confidence etched upon Donald Swanson's face before whispering a reply. "The message I've been asked to deliver is simply this: 'Stop'."

CHAPTER THIRTEEN
December 24th
1925

Beatrice Swanson looked up from the front page of *The New York Times,* preferring the paper over *The Brooklyn Observer*—the newspaper her husband worked for—because the *Times* covered all five boroughs, the state of New York, the nation, and the world, whereas the *Observer* confined its reportage to events and goings on within Brooklyn. "I see that Mayor Hylan is on his way out," she remarked, lifting her eyes to study Don and their daughter, Marjorie contentedly sucking milk from a glass bottle while cradled in her father's arms. "Says here that, after losing his bid for renomination by the Democrats to Jimmy Walker, Hylan intends to resign a day before his term expires." She paused, pondered the information, and asked, "Why do you suppose that is?"

Don adjusted Marjorie as he rocked back and forth, back and forth, in an oak platform rocker—the girl's soft, auburn hair cut short, her brown eyes closed in contentment—and nodded. "Simple. He worked for the elevated railway before becoming a lawyer. He's entitled to a pension if he resigns before his term as mayor ends."

"Tricky man."

"Thick-headed dullard is more like it." Don looked at his wife, her face so fair and pretty, her demure hazel eyes and blond hair—twisted into a thick, waist-long braid—betraying her Scandinavian heritage, before continuing. "He gave that speech, the one calling Rockefeller an octopus," he added. Don knew full well that Hylan had stolen the "octopus" reference from muckraker Ida Tarbell, a writer who spent her career uncovering the secrets, corruption, and un-Christianlike behavior behind John D. Rockefeller's accumulation of wealth. "And beyond extending the subway system and keeping the five-cent fare in place, he's done nothing noteworthy since being elected."

"Has he really been all that bad?"

Don nodded. "He has. He's just another Tammany Hall stooge. A low-talent, slow-thinking anti-progressive who claims to be something he's not. But the Democrats haven't only won the hearts and minds of their Irish cronies, they've managed to steal the votes of the Coloreds as well. Damn shame that folks who won their right to vote because Lincoln and the Republicans stood up to the South now ally themselves with tricksters who don't give a damn about the Darkies."

Beatrice, who preferred the term "Negroes," ignored her husband's slur, and went back to reading the article. "Where do you think he'll end up?"

Don stood, pulled the nipple from his sleeping daughter's mouth, carried the child across the room in his right arm, placed the empty bottle on an end table, and settled Marjorie in her bassinette. The girl slept like the dead, snoring loud enough to bring a smile to her mother's lips.

"She's out like a light."

"Damn good thing we got to the bottom of her crying jags. Damn good thing you and I can finally get a decent night's sleep."

"True, my dear, along with snuggling and some other things . . ."

He'd fallen in love with Beatrice the first time he'd seen her walk across the lawn in front of Pillsbury Hall on the University of Minnesota campus. With her blond hair braided into a rope of shimmering gold, square yet feminine build, and the most alive pewter eyes Don had ever encountered, she was perkily cute. But when they were introduced through mutual friends—another couple who knew the two lonely students and thought Don and Bea might hit it off— and had a chance to spend time in a local eatery, talking and getting acquainted with their friends as mutual support, it was Bea's intellect, her grasp of modern life, and her interest in politics that compelled Don to ask her out. She readily accepted, and they saw D.W. Griffith's *Intolerance: Love's Struggle Through the Ages* on their first date.

Bea found herself captivated by the tall, young, energetic, and politically savvy aspiring newspaper man with the ready smile and steady, silent strength built from years of farm work. She agreed to that first date, despite a mutual friend, Adeline Buffington, cautioning Bea that, in all things related to women, Donald Swanson was slow on the uptake. Their first foray toward romance had been holding hands during the Griffith film while a pianist accompanied flickering black and white images on the screen. When Don left Bea at the front stoop of her dormitory after the movie, they shook hands, bid each other goodnight, and left things unsettled. But it wasn't long, despite Don Swanson's reticence and slow-footed ways, that they became an item and then a couple, their drive toward intimacy fueled by hormones that overcame the reporter-in-the-making's native shyness. They became secretly engaged—not wanting to cause a fuss or face unanswerable inquisitions from parents—during the summer between Don's junior and senior years at the university. Beatrice, two years behind Don in her studies, accepted his proposal given on one knee along the shore of Lake of the Isles. Upon Don's graduation from college, the couple eloped, and Bea accompanied her new husband to New York City, abandoning her dream of attaining the rarest of all achievements for a Minnesota farm girl born in the early 20th century: a college degree.

He smiled at her reference to the consummation of their love that had taken place the prior evening. He had learned to be a slow and patient lover, to listen, and to understand Bea's needs and requisites, though not every coupling between them was successful. But more often than not, the two came to an accord—a place of mutual satisfaction—that left them sated. Theirs, however, was not a union merely sustained by physicality. Their life together, including raising their daughter in a sublet apartment surrounded by Finns, had more depth, strength, and resilience to it than simple sensual compatibility.

God, she is so striking, looking at me through those dainty eyeglasses, Don Swanson thought.

Embarrassed by the untoward images his wife's comment conjured, Don refocused and addressed Bea's question about Mayor Hylan's future. "Given the power of the Irish in this borough, despite his loss to another Tammany man, he's likely destined for some cushy government job."

"Such as?"

Don shook his head. "Don't know for certain. Maybe as a manager in the elevated railway system, maybe something to do with the law."

"City attorney?"

Don resumed sitting in the rocker, guffawed, and stretched his legs. "He's not smart enough for that. He spent his legal career arguing minor disputes in municipal court."

"What then?"

Don smiled quixotically. "Well, he's dumb enough to be a judge . . ."

Behind the easy banter, Don was apprehensive. His visit with O'Brien and the final word uttered by the building inspector had left him with an upset stomach and a splitting headache. For several months after that disturbing conversation, he steered clear of investigating Foley. But Stanley Prescott had grown impatient and had insisted that Don get to the bottom of rumors concerning Foley's ties to the White Hand.

It was Christmas Eve. The Swanson family planned to attend the late-night service at Trinity Norwegian Lutheran Church. But before the Swansons endured another of Pastor Bergstrom's circuitous sermons and a night of the parents fighting sleep and their daughter gulping milk from a bottle to fend off fidgeting, Don had another appointment to keep.

"I need to meet a fellow," was all he said, as he left the rocking chair. He walked across the living room, donned his threadbare winter coat, slipped galoshes over freshly polished-for-church brown loafers, placed a fedora atop his blond crew-cut, and grabbed his briefcase—the brown leather satchel containing pencils, notepads, scrawled recollections from other interviews, and hastily written tips concerning Borough President Foley. "I'll be back before eight."

"What about supper? I made pea soup with the last of the ham. It's your favorite."

He nodded. "It certainly is. You must be talking to our Finnish neighbors about their eating habits! Keep it warm. I'll have some when I return."

In the back of his mind, Swanson calculated the risk he was taking by meeting with Paddy Maloney, the right-hand man to Richard Lonegan—the head of the White Hand gang. They were the thugs who controlled the Brooklyn Harbor but were on the cusp of losing their hold on the waterfront to "wine-drinking Dagos"—as Foley had recently confided to a reporter from the *Times*. The days of Irish ascendency were ending. Italian Mafioso were consolidating power across the five boroughs. It had been suggested to Don that Paddy Maloney held information about the current situation—including knowledge of where the bodies, both political and corporeal, were buried—that would be of interest to voters. *It's a gamble,* Swanson thought, as he stepped toward the door, *to believe an Irishman might turn on one of his own. But it's the only lead I have, and it's the only shot I have of keeping my job.*

Beatrice knew better than to ask where her husband was off to or who he was meeting with. The work of a muckraker, the business of uncovering and distilling the secrets and sins of those holding power in the style of Lincoln Steffens—her husband's hero—would not be shared with the woman of the house. Her duty, as she saw it, was to support Don's efforts to uncover dishonesty and illegality among the political and financial elites. She had realized, after her husband came home one evening with a black eye and a goose egg on his noggin, that such work could be, and often was, dangerous. Yet, fortitude was the essence of her companion, something as innate and inbred as his Nordic stubbornness and his steady empathy and easy kindness. She could not object. She did not object. "Just be careful. You have a daughter who needs you."

Don unlocked and opened the heavy oak door to the third-floor hallway, stopped, turned around, retreated across the hardwood floor, stooped from height, pecked his wife again on the cheek, and grinned. "You know I will, dear. It's time we started thinking about a brother or sister for Marjorie."

CHAPTER FOURTEEN
Christmas Eve
1925

It was a short walk from the Swanson flat in the Finnish cooperative building to the Dublin Social Club. It was not yet five in the afternoon, though the sun had set. A wintery chill rattled Don's bones. A fierce Quebecoise wind threatened to steal the reporter's fedora as he trudged near-empty streets. He was apprehensive about his sit-down with Paddy Maloney. *I very might well end up like Phillips,* Don thought, as he tipped his hat to a couple herding two young children—a boy appearing to be about ten and the girl, a bit younger—in their Sunday best toward what Swanson could only assume was a Christmas Eve service at a local church. No words were said, no greetings emitted, as he passed the family and they passed him.

His internal reference was to David Graham Phillips, an investigative reporter Don idolized and sought to emulate, a writer for *Cosmopolitan* who had, in 1906, written an article entitled "The Treason of the Senate" about United States senators being bought, sold, and moved about like pawns in a never-ending game of political chess. *That's the kind of dope I want to uncover and write about,* Don thought, as the rubber soles of his overshoes—redundant, as there was no snow in the air and no melt on the sidewalk—slapped cement. *Plus,* he continued to muse, *like Upton Sinclair, Phillips wrote novels.* Don stopped, adjusted the brown calf-leather satchel hanging from his left shoulder, and pondered his chosen profession and his current position with the *Observer* in context.

The term "muckraker" had been coined by President Teddy Roosevelt to note his displeasure with journalists who actually—heaven forbid—chose to do their jobs by reporting scandals and conflicts of interest among America's power brokers. In the case of Upton Sinclair, that meant going undercover to reveal the nasty truth about Chicago's meat-packing industry.

As Don resumed walking, Sinclair's clandestine infiltration of a slaughterhouse to write a series of exposés that resulted in the groundbreaking novel, *The Jungle,* came to mind and caused Don to examine his intentions and hopes. *Using fiction to reveal the unholy lives of industrial workers was a magnificent vehicle for enlightening the public,* Don thought. *Eventually, I'd like to use fiction to get my point across.*

Don's mental ramblings carried with them the realization that it was not David Graham Phillips' attacks on politicians that made him a target: it was his use of a thinly concealed character in a novel, *The Fashionable Adventures of Joshua Craig,* that caused an unhinged reader to believe the story's protagonist was a portrayal of the maniac's beloved sister. Fitzhugh Goldsborough, the deranged man in question, shot Phillips dead, and then, as if on stage in the closing act of an opera, put a bullet in his own brain. *Words matter,* Don mused, as he arrived at the windowless front entrance door of the Dublin Social Club.

The Club served as the nerve center for controlling the Brooklyn waterfront at the behest of Richard Lonergan, brother-in-law to the martyred Bill Lovett. Lovett had led the White Hand Gang until Sicilian assassin Willie "Two Knife" Alteri ended Lovett's reign with a meat cleaver. *When Lonergan says "jump," Maloney asks "How high?"* Don thought, as he contemplated whether to open the door and enter the building.

"Shit," he muttered, weighing how much he valued keeping his job for a paltry wage. As he stood in the cold, the night complete in its descent, streetlamps illuming the sidewalk, he groped with morality and mortality. After momentary reflection, he shrugged, muttered "Ah, hell," and entered the building.

Electric fixtures emitted hazy ethereal light against a tobacco fog as Don crossed the threshold and was stopped by a bulldog of a man. The bouncer's closely shorn hair was bright red. His complexion was as rosy as a baby's buttocks. The man's biceps were distinct, despite his arms being covered by a raggedy tweed jacket. The bouncer's trousers were too short for his stumpy legs and were not of the same color, pattern, or fabric as the jacket. "State your business, Mister."

The Irishman's face was disrupted by a nasty scar, likely the result of an untoward encounter with a knife. The fact that the blade had missed the bulldog's jugular was likely the only reason he was still among the living.

"Donald Swanson, reporter from the *Observer*. Here for a meeting with Mr. Maloney," he managed with *faux* aplomb.

The bouncer grunted, nodded, and barked, "Wait here," before turning and walking toward the back of the tavern. The narrow room was occupied by a half-dozen working men sipping stout or whiskey in violation of Prohibition. The political power of their benefactor ensured that their illegalities were without consequence. No police officers—most coppers patrolling Brooklyn were Irish Catholics, some of whom were kin to higher-ups in the White Hand—dared disturb the patrons of the club.

Don noted the heavy scent of booze, cigars, and sweat wafting in the still air of the speakeasy, while shifting nervously on the soles of his overshoes. Absentmindedly, he listened to steam escaping from the tavern's radiators while admiring oil paintings depicting fetchingly naked women hanging on the wall behind the bar. The sound of the barkeep washing glasses and the murmur of disparaging comments from customers affronted by the unscripted appearance of a stranger joined the noise of radiating steam as he patiently waited for the bouncer.

The bulldog returned with two black-headed, powerfully built men. "Follow us," he grunted. "Boss wants to see you in the office."

It was at that moment that Don Swanson had a choice to make. Follow the thugs—who, from the looks of things, had built steely muscle by unloading freight on the waterfront, and likely have an unpleasant session with their boss—or turn tail and run.

A smart man, a man valuing his wife and daughter, would do just that. But his job was on the line. Stanley Prescott had made it clear the reporter was on a short leash, given his failure to place an article about President Foley's unscrupulous behavior in the hands of the copy editor. *I fail here, and Stanley will probably show me the door.* Swanson nodded and followed the men. As he walked, stiff legged and mute—like a condemned prisoner on his way to Old Sparky—Don passed a pair of Irishmen playing billiards but the rough-looking patrons didn't adjourn their game or acknowledge the group walking silently toward the back of the tavern. Don and his escort stopped at a closed door. The bulldog rapped knuckles against oak, his muted announcement evincing a deftness belaying his bulk.

"Come in."

The bouncer opened the door and gestured for Swanson to enter.

Paddy Maloney was not behind the desk. A small, beady-eyed man in his early fifties with no hair on his shiny head sat in Maloney's chair. The man nodded, smiled in an unappealing manner, and bade the reporter to sit. Don complied. The sleek wooden surface of the desk was as neat as a pin. Pencils, pens, an inkwell, and stacks of paperwork were precisely arranged. To Don's eyes, it appeared that Paddy Maloney was a fastidious man.

"So good of you to visit on such short notice." The man looked intently at the reporter, smiled the same, wickedly confusing smile, turned to Swanson's escorts, and said, "You may leave." The thugs left. "I'm sorry," the man said, after the door closed. "I forgot we haven't met. I'm Michael O'Leary, Mr. Maloney's assistant." O'Leary tapped his right index finger on an ink blotter before continuing. "Here's the thing, Mr. Swanson," O'Leary said. "We've heard rumors, disturbing whispers about your intentions regarding President Foley."

Shit. I knew this was a mistake. He's not about to spill the beans on Foley's illegal activities, bribes, or any other skeletons in the man's closet. Don cleared his throat, clutched his briefcase, and answered, "I don't understand, Mr. O'Leary. I thought your boss invited me here to share information."

The Irishman's mouth curved into a disingenuous smile. "Subterfuge, Mr. Swanson. An excuse for me to meet you and take your measure."

"And?"

"Here's the thing, Don. May I call you 'Don'? Seems far less formal. In return, you may call me 'Mike'."

"Don's fine."

"So, Don. What I wanted to tell you personally, so there's no misunderstanding between us, is that you must, as you were forewarned, stop snooping around President Foley or anyone or anything connected to the man."

Don's ire rose. Despite the apprehension that had gripped him upon entering Maloney's inner sanctum, O'Leary's demand that he cease investigating Foley, a man who, might—with the help of the Democratic Party and the Colored vote—become mayor of New York City, caused the muckraker's dander to rise. "It's my job, sir, to find the truth."

"Ha! The truth? That, my young friend, is something to consider in context. Truth can be this or it can be that. It is, in my considerable experience, a very fungible commodity."

"Not where I come from."

"Ah, yes. You're a Minnesota farm boy, as I recall. Raised on a convoluted Lutheran notion of unrequited grace, something we Catholics don't subscribe to. Let me tell you, Sodbuster, as straight as I can: if you don't extend your hand and shake mine, promising to end your investigation into President Foley—his past, his current activities, and his associates—well then, *Don*, you will have to accept responsibility for what befalls you."

Don's face flared. "Is that a threat? You know I can't agree to leave Foley alone. It's my job to go where the scuttlebutt leads me. Whatever the results, whatever the consequences."

O'Leary's enigmatic smile turned into a frown. "Suit yourself. MR. HANRATTY!"

Hanratty—the bulldog—and his two companions returned. Don stood, visibly shaken by O'Leary's threat, and the fact, despite being physically fit, he was no match for three men. Disguising his trepidation, the reporter mustered up bravado: "If any harm comes to me, O'Leary ..."

"Tsk, tsk, *Don*. Addressing me by my surname when I offered you the privilege of conversing as familiars, as equals ..." A smirk emerged across the man's wide, cherubic face. "Boys," Michael O'Leary said to his men, "I think we need to teach this farmer's son from Minnesota some Brooklyn manners."

CHAPTER FIFTEEN
December
1925

"Shit."

Don Swanson sat up in a hospital bed, his right leg elevated and poised in midair by a system of pulleys and ropes meant to facilitate the healing of fractures to the tibia and fibula just above the ankle where Gerry Hanratty had stomped on the reporter's leg, shattering the bones while Don writhed on cold asphalt in the alley behind the Dublin Social Club. Don's head was bandaged, concealing a nasty cut at the hair line–a wound opened when another tough working for Michael O'Leary gave the Minnesotan his comeuppance with brass knuckles. The cut would leave a visible scar, one that would remind the reporter of his encounter with men protecting the image and legacies of Richard Lonergan and President Foley. There were also three broken teeth that, once Don was released from Brooklyn Hospital, would require dental work. Don had also suffered two broken ribs: the fractures caused by a third man kicking the defenseless reporter as he moaned, groaned, and twisted on the pavement. There was no medical intervention available for the ribs; they would have to heal on their own.

"We can't afford this," Don muttered, ignoring his wife, and staring out windows casting beams of sunlight into the cavernous hospital. Despite the spirited holiday season—normally a time of uncontrolled celebration and chaos leading to the full occupancy of New York hospitals—Don found himself alone on the ward. "Ruined. We're ruined."

A copper walking his beat on Christmas morning had discovered the unconscious reporter. Don's disappearance had been reported by Beatrice, though her frantic disclosure to the police had not generated urgency, given it was not uncommon for husbands or boyfriends in the Big Apple to disappear into alcohol or into the arms of a lover over the holidays. Beatrice had enlisted Mrs. Maki from the apartment next door to watch Marjorie, while Bea visited the nearest police precinct and filed a missing person's report.

When the sergeant at the intake desk informed Bea that nothing could be done until a day or two later because, "You know, ma'am, it's Christmas, and we're short staffed," Beatrice had set out to find Don on her own. She was deeply concerned, given that her husband had failed to return home in time for Christmas Eve service, a brush-off that was out of character for the man. With the police unwilling to act, Bea had commenced an urgent search, an unscripted effort that led nowhere.

Beatrice was finally telephoned, once Don's wallet was inventoried at Brooklyn Hospital by an emergency room nurse. Bea was given no forewarning, the nurse matter-of-factly reporting, "Ma'am, your husband is undergoing surgery for multiple injuries. It would be best if you'd come quickly." The news had sent Beatrice into a tizzy. A neighbor, Mrs. Maki, agreed to keep Marjorie overnight, and a very distraught Beatrice arrived at Brooklyn Hospital breathless, harried, panicked, and just in time to see her unconscious husband being wheeled onto the ward on a gurney to recover from surgery.

Bea had departed from the hospital before Don came out of his ether-induced fog. She was not able to return to the hospital again that day, having no one to watch Marjorie, as the Makis were leaving town to visit relatives in Ohio for the holidays. The following morning, a kindly Finn woman living a floor below the Swansons—Miss Harju, a spinster Bea did not know, but someone Mrs. Maki assured her was a fine caretaker of children—had agreed to babysit.

Bea had returned to the hospital to find her husband sweating, swearing, distraught, and in severe pain, because the morphine being administered did not begin to touch his agony.

"Goddamn it!"

"Darling, please watch your language."

Don sat up in his narrow hospital bed, crisp white linen sheets drawn tight across his chest, and grimaced. "I can't help it, Bea. My stupidity, my drive to expose Foley, has accomplished our complete and utter ruin."

Bea, who was sitting on the edge of her husband's hospital bed, placed the exquisite fingers of her left hand, the tiny diamond and gold of her engagement ring, and the simple, matching wedding band glimmering beneath the hospital lighting before asking, "Is it really so bad as all that?"

Don reached up with his right hand and, with jagged pain from the fractured ribs making him wince, retrieved a tumbler of ice water, shakily raised it to his mouth, and drained it. "We're nearly tapped out. Worse than that, Stanley sent word, after I came out of my stupor, that I was done. Sacked. He fired me as I lay broken and bloody in a hospital bed after trying to satisfy his demands."

Beatrice patted her husband's wrist and nodded. "There are other jobs," she whispered. "You can look for something once you're up and around."

Don shook his head. "Doctor says it'll be at least two months before I can walk without crutches. The ankle bones were so shattered, they had a devil of a time putting them back together. Had to install a steel plate and screws to hold things in place."

"Really? I've never heard of such a thing!"

Don removed his wife's fingers and raised his right hand to itch his chin. He hadn't shaved. The beginnings of a beard chafed his palm, as he considered a reply. Moments passed as the two sat in silence, with no other patients yet on the ward. That would change when an automobile accident involving two motor cars landed a family of four—and the drunk driver who blew a stop sign and caused the wreck—in the emergency room. Sadly, the youngest victim of the accident would die on the operating table. The drunk and the other three victims would survive and eventually join Don Swanson on the ward. A compassionate nurse had given Don a heads' up that his time of privacy and silent reflection was about to end.

"Doc Waters, the orthopedic man who did the surgery, checked the fracture by X-ray before the operation, saw what needed to be done, went in, installed hardware, and then checked his work by taking another film."

Bea folded her hands across her lap, her baby roll, the consequence of carrying and birthing Marjorie present as a reminder she was no longer the firmly constituted, virginal girl Don Swanson had taken a shine to from across the plush lawn of the University of Minnesota campus. A look of concern slipped into Bea's attitude. She was trying her best to remain unmoved by the state of their finances, but, having been alerted to the fact her husband had no job and knowing full well their savings held, at best, a month's rent and a few weeks of groceries, Beatrice found it nearly impossible to remain stoic.

"That, as you can well imagine, along with the costs of the other care and interventions my beating required, will total, my dear, thousands of dollars. Thousands we do not have."

A tear formed in Bea's left eye. *This cannot happen. I cannot cry. He is broken, both in body and spirit. Jesus, Blessed Savior, help me find residual strength to put on a good show.* "We will manage, dear," Bea whispered as a singular tear fell like a rare gem onto the sleeve of her white, linen blouse. "We always have."

While she waited for Don to reply, to reassure her that she was right, that he would find a way to pay the hospital and the doctor, another reality crept into Beatrice's mind as she looked out a window and watched thick, lazy, slow-dancing snowflakes descend and blanket the soiled city. *He cannot be told,* she thought, her hands coming together in a tight, viselike grip atop the blue frayed wool of her skirt. *It would be too much for him to deal with.*

The Finn, Oskar Langevin, from whom they were subletting their apartment was apparently quite a catch in the eyes of the single women of Tampere. A letter from Finland had arrived advising the Swansons that Oskar and his new wife, Estera, formerly Estera Nurminen, would be sailing for New York City on January 15th.

I know this is short notice, Oskar had written, *but I must insist that your family vacate the premises no later than January 20th so that my new wife and I can be assured of lodging when we arrive.*

Beatrice could not bear the upset that such a revelation would cause her downtrodden husband. She'd formed a plan, carefully constructing and deconstructing a narrative in her mind that she would, at the appropriate time, share with Don.

After receiving Langevin's letter and the news of her husband's injuries, Bea had sent a telegram to her parents in Elmore, Minnesota. Her curt message laid bare the dire circumstances in which her family found itself. Despite having eloped, despite having chosen to throw away her own career as an elementary school teacher—something her mother, Angeline, had hoped and prayed would come to pass even after Bea's unsanctioned marriage—Beatrice Mondale Swanson had remained in touch with her parents and, over time, the wounds caused by her elopement had healed. The Mondales were not rich but, given Albert's frugalness and the fact the family owned some of the best farmland in Faribault County, Bea's folks were positioned to help the struggling young couple and the Mondales only grandchild. There were no children other than Bea, a circumstance that dictated she was, even in disgrace, the apple of her parents' eyes.

The Mondales' telegraphed reply, when asked if they could provide Don and Bea and the infant Marjorie with a temporary place to stay and a modest loan to prevent bankruptcy, was simple and direct. *We will help,* Bea's mother had promised at the end of her telegraphed remonstration. But those words were not shared by Beatrice with her stricken husband as she sat on the edge of his bed in Brooklyn Hospital. *That news can wait. Now is not the time to tell Don we are going home.*

CHAPTER SIXTEEN
St. Paul, Minnesota
January 1926

Everett Remington Cooper, a slender man of meager height with curly white hair and a freshly barbered face, stood before a double-hung window in his office on the eleventh floor of the Minnesota Building overlooking Cedar Street, watching a scuffle between a St. Paul cop and a drunk. The patrolman won the tussle and deposited the sot in the back seat of a black Ford Model A station wagon displaying St. Paul Police Department emblems. As the drunk continued to thrash, the cop's partner, a guy built like an ice box, reached into the back seat, whacked the unfortunate soul with his billy club, and made it clear that more blows would follow if the drunkard didn't settle down. After gaining compliance, St. Paul's finest jumped into the Ford, slammed the doors, hit the siren, and roared off.

The excitement over, Cooper returned to his modest maple desk. The writing surface was piled high with paperwork and notepads full of quotations from interviews he and Ellis Beckett, the only other reporter at the *St. Paul Truthsayer*, had conducted. A mountain of words scribbled by the two men was precariously stacked and in danger of spilling onto the room's polished terrazzo floor.

"Just another day in Irish paradise," Cooper mused, picking up a notebook. "Huh. I've been neglecting this story," he muttered as he read Beckett's account of a sit-down with a disgruntled associate of Hennepin County Attorney Larson. "Best do some more digging. Get some collateral verification regarding the man's past indiscretions before we move forward." Cooper paused to consider a salient reality: that his newspaper had endorsed Larson for the office of county attorney. *He deserves some time to get his house in order, to work on reform before he's caught up in scandal. That's the least I can do for the man.*

"Mr. Cooper," a female voice called out from behind the closed office door, "mail's here."

"Thanks, Alice," the newspaperman replied to Mrs. Alice Sullivan, the *Truthsayer's* secretary, receptionist, and bookkeeper.

Alice Sullivan was the granddaughter of Irish immigrants who'd arrived in St. Paul in the late 1870s. She was also the daughter of a well-known Democratic operative and his poet wife. Her finest attribute was an ability to keep everything discussed at the newspaper confidential. And, despite her familial connection to the Democratic Party, Mrs. Sullivan was a proud Farmer Laborite—as was her husband Eddie: a delivery truck driver and a loyal member of the Teamsters.

"I'll be out in a second," Cooper added. *Best examine this information and see if we can't get our new man or woman, whoever that turns out to be, to dig a bit deeper. It's salacious gossip, to be sure, hinting at scandals involving the dead daughter of a Minneapolis city councilman, the Irish mob, and the state's most notorious rum-runner.*

Cooper paused to consider the chance he was taking by hiring another reporter. *Money is tight. Damn tight. Alice, the old skinflint, is against it. But there're more stories out there than two reporters can cover. I must take the chance, even if it sinks us.* The editor left Beckett's notebook upside down on his desk, stood, walked to the door, and opened it. "Let's have that mail, Mrs. Sullivan."

Alice—plump, attractive, and perpetually cheerful—retrieved a stack of envelopes from her desk, walked to the doorway, and extended the packet. "There are a few letters replying to the 'reporter wanted' ad you placed in *The New York Times,*" she said, with edge. As the paper's financial gatekeeper, Alice was cognizant of the *Truthsayer's* hand-to-mouth existence. She had not been supportive of her boss casting a wide net, including placing an expensive want-ad in the *Times*, in his search for a new reporter. She had also asserted that there were local writers—men and women who'd grown up during the muckraking times of the early 1900s, who'd sharpened their investigative and journalistic teeth in the styles of Lincoln Steffens, Ida Tarbell, and David Graham Phillips—looking for work. "There are five responses," she continued, stifling her urge to protest hiring another sailor to board a sinking ship. "Four letters and a telegram. Only the telegram references the sort of credentials you're looking for."

"I trust your judgment, Mrs. Sullivan. Draft rejection letters to the other four, and I'll have a look-see at the telegram."

Alice nodded, sifted through the envelopes, removed the letters of application she deemed unacceptable, and handed the remaining mail to her boss. "I'll get right on it, Mr. Cooper."

Everett nodded and accepted the stack of mail and the telegram from Mrs. Sullivan before retreating into his office.

CHAPTER SEVENTEEN
January 1926

"**This** is a mighty fast train," Donald Swanson observed, as the coach he and his family were riding in sped over steel rails and creosoted ties.

"That's for certain," Beatrice said softly, staring out the finger-smudged window next to her seat while pressing her sleeping daughter to her chest. "But they say Burlington Northern's *Empire Builder* can hit one hundred miles an hour," she added. "That would make this train's pace seem turtle-like!"

Don smiled and noted that Marjorie was finally settled after the long trip from New York City to Chicago. The child, now ten months old, had spent much of the first leg of the journey bawling at the top of her lungs, despite her mother's best efforts to calm her. *It's a miracle the head conductor didn't give us the boot,* Don thought, returning his gaze to the slumbering Wisconsin landscape. Vague outlines of snow-covered morainic hills and somber, dormant fields and second-growth forests devoid of leaves zipped past, the blackness of waning night punctuated by pinprick glows of kerosene lanterns carried by farmers undertaking morning chores.

Don had been taken aback when he'd received a telephone call from Everett Remington Cooper a few days after his discharge from Brooklyn Hospital. Don was familiar with Cooper's reputation for uncovering and exposing lies and conflicts and dirty dealings in Minnesota, but he was truly surprised when the editor called him long distance, out of the blue, to chat.

Stanley Prescott had been as good as his word. After the White Hand's minions had pummeled Don to the point of a long and very expensive hospital stay, meaning that the reporter was unable to complete his investigation into President Foley's untoward activities, the *Observer's* editor had cut Don loose. Worse than the termination itself was the fact that Prescott dismissed Don in a hastily scrawled note delivered to the broken man's hospital bedside by a mutual friend. Prescott had neither the guts nor the decency to personally deliver the fatal blow. *Sacked by a third-party messenger,* Don had mused before sharing the news with Bea. *The wormy cad!*

What Donald Swanson did not know was that Stanley Prescott was also a victim.

After Gerry Hanratty and his goons had beaten Don to within an inch of his life, Prescott had, at first, every intention of visiting Don and assuring him that, despite his failure to get the goods on Foley, the young Minnesotan still had a job. But on a Monday afternoon, as Stanley Prescott's seven-year-old daughter Evelyn walked home with friends from school, she was accosted by strangers and had been abducted. When a blue Dodge Town Car pulled up in front of the Prescott home hours later, as evening cloaked the city, young Evelyn had leaped from the car and into the waiting arms of her sobbing mother. The car's license plates had been blackened with grease, and the abductors' identities were concealed by masks. Stanley, the affronted father, had rushed after the Dodge, spewing threats, recriminations, and assorted curses at the kidnappers as the vehicle sped off into the night.

But the kidnapping of his daughter wasn't the sole event that had forced Stanley's hand. That action, as alarming as it had been, was merely a first salvo. The real cause of Prescott's decision to fire Swanson was the envelope Evelyn had handed Stanley upon returning home after her ordeal. Inside the manila parcel were photographs of the child walking to and from school, of Stanley entering and leaving his office, and of his wife, Ionia, shopping at Magnuson's Grocery Store. A single, simple, and precisely penciled sentence scrawled on brown freezer paper accompanied the pictures: *No one in your family will be safe until you stop poking your nose where it don't belong.* The message was clear. Despite the declining power of the White Hand, the editor's family was in danger. Consequently, Stanley Prescott made the unilateral decision to back off from the paper's inquiries into President Foley's unseemly associations, which meant Donald Swanson was expendable.

Don had returned to his family's apartment in the Finnish cooperative building downhearted, jobless, and broke. It was only when he was sitting on the davenport, his head in his hands, tears falling from his eyes like faint summer rain, that Beatrice broached their future.

"We can start over," Bea had said, her fingers softly caressing the base of Don's neck. "Think of this as not the end, but as a new beginning."

Don wagged his head like a mistreated dog, looked into his wife's gray tending-to-blue eyes, and sobbed. "I have no job. We have no savings to speak of, no way to pay the hospital bill. Nothing for rent or groceries. How can you say that this is the beginning when, dear heart, it's quite clearly the end?"

It was then that Bea revealed a second untoward blow. "I don't want to alarm you further, but there is more we must talk about . . ."

Don wiped away tears with the sleeve of his shirt. "What is it?"

Beatrice could think of nothing to say that would lessen the blow, so she unhesitatingly shared the additional, untoward news. "Langevin is on his way home from Finland. We're to vacate the apartment by Monday."

"Shit." Tears began anew.

"I know you're a proud and stubborn man when it comes to accepting help," Bea had asserted with firmness, building up courage to reveal the steps she'd taken to save them. "But, as you were otherwise occupied, I took it upon myself to reach out."

"To whom? Who have you asked for help? Surely not my parents. They don't have a pot to piss in now that farm prices are in the toilet. Dad can't even pay the bank for the bridge loan he took out to tide them over. Surely not them."

Bea shook her head.

"Then who?"

She retrieved papers from an end table next to the couch and handed a telegram to her husband.

MRS. BEATRICE SWANSON:
    I WAS INTRIGUED BY YOUR INQUIRY CONCERNING YOUR HUSBAND'S SEARCH FOR EMPLOYMENT. I AM FAMILIAR WITH HIS RESUME AND WORK FOR THE *BROOKLYN OBSERVER* AND HAVE TAKEN THE LIBERTY OF CONTACTING HIS EDITOR, STANLEY PRESCOTT, WHO HAS GIVEN DONALD A GLOWING RECOMMENDATION.

I UNDERSTAND THAT DONALD IS PRESENTLY INDISPOSED. I WOULD APPRECIATE YOUR PROVIDING ME WITH A TELEPHONE NUMBER SO THAT I MAY CONTACT YOUR HUSBAND IN A WEEK OR SO. YOU MAY CALL ME COLLECT AT THE ABOVE-LISTED NUMBER TO RELAY THE CONTACT INFORMATION.
    SINCERELY,
    EVERETT REMINGTON COOPER
    EDITOR
    ST. PAUL TRUTHSAYER

"But . . ."

In anticipation that Don would have questions concerning the costs of moving, train tickets, and the repayment of their debts, Beatrice had handed her husband a second telegram.

Donald had studied the message from Beatrice's mother. When he'd finished reading, Don handed the second telegram to his wife, looked across the room to the crib where Marjorie slept, and shook his head. "I can't . . ."

Bea had touched her right index finger to her husband's lips. "But you can," she whispered. "You've done everything humanly possible to provide for us. You've worked hard, honorably, and for little pay, trying to expose sin and corruption and avarice and evil in the world. It's time to take your talents home. There, too, men of power, manipulation, and exploitation await discovery and revelation. You can do your good work in St. Paul for the *Truthsayer* as well as you did in Brooklyn for the *Observer*."

She had lowered her finger and stared unblinkingly, her position firm, her decision final. "Donald Swanson: we are going home, and that is that."

The call from Everett Remington Cooper had gone well. A salary of twenty dollars a week was agreed upon. Don was to start his new job on May first. After receiving confirmation that the Swanson family was returning to Minnesota, Beatrice's parents wired a money order for five hundred dollars, enough to pay coach train fares for three and a down payment toward the debt due Brooklyn Hospital. It was settled: the Swansons would stay with the Mondales until the end of April, an interval that would allow Don to fully heal and Bea's parents to become acquainted with their only grandchild.

Aboard the *Legionnaire,* Don reflected on the travails and burdens he'd left behind. Beatrice placed the sleeping Marjorie on a velvet-covered seat in front of them, situating the child's head on a pillow provided by the conductor, who had, while handing Bea the pillow, remarked, "How well behaved your child is!", a comment that caused Don to chuckle. After assuring herself that the child would sleep as the train rumbled on, Bea placed her right hand on her husband's left wrist and whispered, "It's nice we're going home, right?"

"Yes." From the tone of her voice, Don guessed that Beatrice had more to reveal. But rather than engage, tired of speculating about the future, he asked no questions.

Bea nodded. The declination and extension of her handsome head seemed to signal she was summoning up the courage to relate additional news; perhaps some final, unwelcome snippet of information she felt compelled to air, now that Marjorie was asleep. After moments of silence, Bea turned in her seat, kissed Don on the cheek, found his ear, and whispered to the man she would, come hell or high water, always stand by.

"I'm pregnant."

CHAPTER EIGHTEEN
Elmore, Minnesota
April 1926

The Swanson family disembarked from the *Legionnaire* at the Union Depot in St. Paul, but their journey by rail was not over. To conclude their trek back to Minnesota, Don, Bea, and Marjorie boarded a third train. The plush, clean, and pristine Pullman coaches the Swansons had enjoyed from New York to Chicago, and from Chicago to St. Paul, were replaced by dingy passenger cars of the nearly insolvent Minneapolis and St. Louis Railway, a rail line that had been abused by regulators during the Great War when the United States Railroad Administration operated the company. That was the downside to buying tickets on the southwestern leg of the M&SL's system, being transported in coaches that had seen better days. The plus side was that the family's sojourn by rail would end in Sherburn, Minnesota, the Sherburn depot being only an hour's drive from the Mondale homestead.

"Lovely to see you, dear," Angeline Mondale said, hugging her daughter while casting a recriminating look at her son-in-law.

"You as well, Mother," Bea said softly, noting the rigidity of Angeline's gaze toward Don, a look magnified in the impenetrable attitude of her father.

Bea created distance and reached out to Don, who was holding Marjorie as he struggled to balance on wooden crutches. The child seemed content and fully alert to the strangeness of the landscape and the unfamiliar people who'd come to greet her. Marjorie didn't cry or squirm as Bea took the child from Don.

"What a beautiful bundle of joy!" Angeline gushed upon first holding her granddaughter. "See here, Albert. She has your eyes!"

Angeline's enthusiasm softened Albert's steely exterior. "She does indeed," the farmer replied, suppressing pride. Albert Mondale was a simple yet intelligent man. He had not been enamored with the choice his only child had made in running off without so much as a "goodbye" to New

York City—a den of sinfulness that was, in Albert's rigid view of the world, akin to Sodom and Gomorrah. Despite his disdain for Donald Swanson and the dire circumstances Albert believed his son-in-law had brought upon his young family, the farmer offered his right hand.

"Pleased to meet you, sir," Don mumbled, releasing the grip on his crutch to reciprocate.

The men ended their greeting. Albert took a slight step back and nodded. "You've got a good handshake there. Must've worked some in your time."

"Don grew up on a farm. In western Minnesota," Bea interjected.

"That so?"

"It is, sir. My folks—who've hit hard times lately what with drought and bank rates and freight charges and such—farm a quarter-section near Oak Ridge."

"Never heard of it." The edges of Albert's opposition softened further as the men found common ground.

"Few folks have. It's near Alexandria."

"Heard of it. Never been."

While the men engaged in verbal fencing, the women gushed and cooed over the baby.

"My folks milk a couple dozen Holsteins, raise a few pigs and chickens," Don added. "The farm's on the Pomme de Terre. Not much of a river, I'll admit, but pretty."

Albert lifted a suitcase in each calloused hand and walked toward an Oakland four-door sedan. "No trunk. We'll have to make room on the rear seat," he grunted, setting the suitcases on dry gravel. The farmer grasped the door handle on the rear passenger-side door of the vehicle and yanked it open.

Albert placed a suitcase on the cloth-covered bench seat and retrieved another bag. Don picked up his wife's valise, the baby's diaper bag, his briefcase, and his wife's purse before regripping his crutches. He shuffled forward, stopped at the Oakland, and waited for his father-in-law.

"I'll take those, Son," Albert said, reaching out, the endearment catching Donald off-guard.

Don handed the bags to Albert, who wedged them into voids and spaces in the back seat. "There. All set," Albert said, retreating a few steps to admire his work.

"Nicely done."

Albert didn't reply. He beckoned the women to enter the car. Angeline pulled her skirt tight around her hips and slid onto the front seat while Albert moved toward the driver's door. When Don approached the car to open the rear driver's-side door for Bea and the child, Albert shook his head.

"They'll ride up front. Safer, given that the luggage might shift if we hit one of the million potholes between here and the farm."

Don nodded and escorted his wife and Marjorie to the front of the car. Leaning his crutches against the sedan, Don balanced on his good leg, took the baby from his wife, and watched Bea tuck her skirt beneath her rump and slide across burgundy velvet, the upholstery complimenting the sedan's blood-red exterior. Don handed Marjorie to his wife, reclaimed his crutches, and shut the car door. Retracing his steps, Don placed his crutches inside the car, folded his lengthy torso like a contortionist in circus side show, ducked into the rear of the sedan, and slammed the door.

Don appreciated that he would have to endure Albert Mondale's scrutiny. He made it his mission to manifest a hard-working persona, as Albert gave him—each morning at breakfast—a list of simple chores to accomplish. He shed his suit, tie, and spats for dungarees, woolen long johns, wool socks, a blue denim work shirt, a hand-me-down canvas work jacket, and a raggedy stocking hat. He wore a single Chippewa—one half of the new pair of boots Albert had purchased to prevent Don's right foot from freezing—while Donald's left leg remained casted. Properly clothed, the reporter negotiated the frozen ground of the Mondale farm on crutches, completing assigned chores as if he'd never left Oak Ridge.

In early April, Don visited a local doctor, and the plaster cast was removed. Restored to full mobility, Don fell back into farm life as if he'd never attended university, attained a degree, or worked as a reporter. Though Albert Mondale maintained a hesitant skepticism toward his son-in-law, his demarcation of Don as "Son" continued. Once the cast was removed, Albert handed his "good as new" son-in-law a backbreaking chore list, one that included mucking out the hog pen, feeding cattle, and repairing fencing.

Maybe I was too judgmental, Albert thought, as he watched Don hitch the farm's pair of big-framed, ebony Percherons to a hay wagon. It was near dawn. A late spring storm had dumped fresh powder snow across the monochromatic landscape. The sun rose as a mere suggestion behind the barn, its slow advance casting feeble shadows across the white pasture and the black wind-swept ice of East Chain Lake. The lake's shoreline was defined by leafless maples and willows, though stubborn, coppery leaves of occasional oaks remained firm against the omnipresent prairie wind. *Maybe there's more to the young man than I realized,* Albert concluded, as the hay wagon lumbered away with Donald riding on the seat, holding the reins.

Once Angeline learned Beatrice was again pregnant—the Swanson's second child destined to be born at Miller Hospital in St. Paul and not in the bed Beatrice and Donald shared on the second floor of the Mondale farmhouse—Angeline accepted Donald Swanson as family. *Despite whatever flaws there may be in his politics, his thinking, or his choice of vocations, Beatrice loves him. God has set them on a path, and it's my duty, as a mother and a grandmother, to support them on their journey as best I can.*

CHAPTER NINETEEN
St. Paul, Minnesota
May 1926

Don's first assignment at his new job—after leaving the Mondale Farm, moving to the Como Park neighborhood of St. Paul, and settling his family into a routine—was to learn the complex history of Minnesota's Farmer Labor Party (FLP). To this end, the young reporter poured over archival clippings maintained by his new employer, the *St. Paul Truthsayer*.

The Farmer Laborer Association (FLA) came into being in 1920 as an amalgamation of the Nonpartisan League (created by farmers seeking redress from high shipping, milling, and grain storage costs), and the Working People's Nonpartisan Political League (an analogous organization for labor unions). When the leaders of the two groups desired to stand candidates for political office, they formed the FLA. However, the Minnesota Attorney General (AG) opined that candidates running under the FLA banner needed to be sponsored by a registered political party. In response to the AG's edict, the leaders of the FLA formed the FLP.

As Don dug into the FLP's history, he learned that not all Nonpartisan Leaguers were happy with including urban workers in what had once been an agrarian movement. One of the chief dissenters was A.C. Townley, the founding father of the Nonpartisan League. Despite this philosophical rift within the new party, a handful of FLP endorsed candidates—including Sigurd Larson—achieved electoral success.

Sig Larson's ascension to power occurred despite rumors circulating that the new county attorney was not the fine upstanding young man he appeared to be. The gossip haunting Larson's meteoric rise was deemed by Donald Swanson's new boss—Everett Remington Cooper—worthy of inquiry. Cooper became convinced that Larson's past needed closer scrutiny than sycophantic mainstream newspapers in Minneapolis, St. Paul, and Duluth were willing to apply. After a few weeks on the job, Don's doggedness to task persuaded

Everett Cooper that his new reporter was the right man to investigate the Hennepin County Attorney.

Before digging into Larson's upbringing, youth, military service, and political connections, Don attained a basic understanding of the origination and makeup of the FLP. His parents—Gordon and Fawn—had been dues-paying, card-carrying members of the Nonpartisan League, and had, once the League lost its political muscle, transferred their allegiance to the FLA and the FLP. As a high school student, Donny had donned the mantle of a Nonpartisan Leaguer, an outlook that endeared him to his high school journalism teacher. While working for the *Brooklyn Observer,* Don attended debates and political events in and around the cooperative building his young family called home. Those outings altered his worldview. He avowed, though he did not belong to any official party or swear to a specific manifesto, Democratic Socialism. Even so, despite Don's leftward political migration, it wasn't difficult for him to shelve his deeply held views and inquire into the life, philosophy, and rise to power of Sigurd Thaddeus Larson with an open mind.

Donald scheduled a sit-down with Sigurd Larson upon hearing whispers that the county attorney, who'd been in office but a few months, was itching to seek loftier political peaks, most likely Minnesota's governorship.
    "It's a pleasure to meet you, Mr. Swanson," the war-hero-turned-prosecutor said, intercepting Don at the threshold to the county attorney's inner sanctum and offering an impressive right hand in greeting. "I've heard good things."
    Don, nearly the county attorney's equal in height but slighter of build, engaged in the obligatory handshake. "Thanks for seeing me."
    "Please," Larson said, pointing to a chair, resituating his cane, and adjusting his stance to address transitory pain, "take off your slicker, hang it and your hat on the coat rack, and have a seat."
    Don removed his coat and hat, hung them as instructed, sat on the appointed chair, opened his briefcase, removed a notebook and a stub of pencil, and closed the satchel as Larson struggled with an uncooperative prosthesis

to claim the chair behind his desk. Once Larson was settled in, Don began the interview. "So, how's it going, taking over the county attorney's office, after all that went on before you?"

Larson's predecessor had chosen to avoid the scrutiny of a reelection bid. Gossip had circulated. Hints of illegal kickbacks meant to profit friends and associates from South Minneapolis, the neighborhood where Edward Charles—the disgraced county attorney—had been raised. The gist of the whispering campaign against Charles was that the lawyer's old pals had made millions grifting the City of Minneapolis with Charles's benevolent assistance. Ledgers were obtained and scrutinized. Calculations were made. Those inquiries, conducted by reporters from the *Minnesota Leader,* the journalistic voice of the FLP, were so thorough that even the *Tribune* and the *Pioneer Dispatch* couldn't ignore the evident graft. Public entities had been charged double the going rate to replace roadways, sidewalks, curbs, and gutters. Materials provided by unscrupulous contractors were overpriced, undersupplied, and of poor quality, though the "official" bills submitted by Charles's cronies seemed in line with bids accepted by the involved public bodies. Free-flowing cash in large quantities had changed hands, some of which found its way into Charles's personal bank account. Don understood that Sigurd Larson was hot on the trail of Edward Charles, devoting much energy, staff time, and attention to investigating his predecessor's misdeeds.

"I've cleaned house, if that's what you're getting at. But then you already knew that. It's all over the papers."

"Three attorneys and four staffers sacked."

"More to follow. Can't have folks growing fat at the public trough."

Swanson scribbled notes.

"Rest assured: indictments will be pursued. Whether grand jurors agree with my perspective is another matter. But I'll make the effort."

"Does that include Charles?"

Larson nodded.

"That's a 'yes'?"

"It is."

Sig Larson reached across his desk, grasped the handle of a porcelain urn, lifted it, and filled two cups with coffee. "Sugar or cream?"

Don shook his head. "Just Black. I'm Norwegian, like yourself."

The attorney smiled and placed a brimming cup on a saucer and slid the cup and saucer toward Don. "My work is just beginning," Larson said, unsolicited.

"How so?"

"A particular passion of mine is investigating the prostitution of young women; girls forced into humiliation because few satisfactory options are available to them. I want to continue that work, charge those who do such loathsome things to the fairer gender with felonies where possible." Sig took a sip of coffee and reflected. "As a city prosecutor, the best I could do was charge purveyors of degradation and lust with misdemeanors. I hope to change that and to work with the feds in bringing scoundrels who debase young women to true justice."

"A noble cause."

Larson smiled. "I'm not doing it to be noble. I'm doing it because it's the right thing to do."

The men discussed the county attorney's upbringing, education, military service (though the veteran refused to discuss details of his injury or the medals he'd earned), and his work as an assistant city attorney. As the hour allotted for the interview neared its end, Don hadn't touched upon the real reason for the meeting. Drawing his breath and mounting his courage, he broached the two topics he'd been sent to inquire about.

"There's talk you'll run for governor . . ."

The county attorney displayed a poker face. "I haven't decided yet. But I should say: I'm perfectly content with my present situation."

"You're denying the rumor?"

Larson smiled but didn't answer. His face and demeanor appeared impenetrable.

Don took a breath, nodded, and moved on to another topic. "I know it's a delicate subject," he began, placing his pencil stub on his notebook, "but I must ask you about Councilman Miller's daughter."

Crimson flashed across Larson's face, but quickly waned. The attorney paused, blinked, and appeared engaged in marshalling a response. "Is there a question?" Larson finally asked.

Don took a deep breath before continuing. "Is it true Miss Miller died in an apartment owned by an associate of your friend, Mr. Rosenstein, and that the body was moved to avoid implicating that associate in her death?"

Where in fuck's sake did he come up with that? Larson thought. *Abram assured me Newhouse would bury the truth so deep it would never be uncovered by the most determined snoop. What the hell?*

Don kept his gaze fixed on Larson. He had more to ask, questions about Larson's past involving an attempted burglary, brawls at the behest of Kid Rose, and other minor scrapes and legal entanglements. But he'd voiced the most damning rumor, supplied to him by a reliable source inside the Minneapolis Police Department, a beat sergeant who was an ally of disgraced former County Attorney Charles and who could not abide Sigurd Larson being elected the county's chief prosecutor. Swanson hoped to learn something—anything—new concerning the circumstances of the girl's death, the supposed cover-up, and Larson's role in handling such a nefarious matter. But if Donald Swanson expected Sigurd Larson to reveal anything consequential about the death of Susanne Miller, he was mistaken.

"Sir, I must remind you: the young girl's tragic death was deemed accidental by the Hennepin County Coroner. No foul play was involved. It was, and is, a private matter: one I cannot comment on."

"But . . ."

Sigurd Larson gripped the edge of his desk with both hands and stood. "I think," the attorney said evenly, "this is a good place to end our discourse. I look forward to reading your profile regarding the good work I'm attempting here in the next issue of the *Truthsayer."* Larson suppressed internal disquietude and nodded toward the door. "Our time together is concluded. It was a pleasure to meet you, Mr. Swanson. Don't forget your slicker and your hat."

Don knew better than to protest. He would have to find answers concerning the governor's electoral intentions—and the man's role the cover-up of Susanne

Miller's demise—elsewhere. He stood, walked to the coat rack, slipped on his rain coat, settled it across his narrow shoulders, buttoned the slicker, removed his fedora from a hook, placed it on his head, opened the door, and stepped into the hallway.

"You can leave the door open," Larson said in a matter-of-fact voice as the muckraker retreated.

CHAPTER TWENTY
September 1926

Kid Rose considered the unpleasant news.

"The snoops at the *Truthsayer* somehow got wind of what happened to the Miller girl," Sig Larson had anxiously whispered as the two men sat at a table in the dining room of Abram Rosenstein's modest home.

Agnes Jacobson, Abram's common-law wife, bustled around the small, well-equipped kitchen, making sandwiches for the men. The woman's attitude was cheerful and upbeat. Her optimistic outlook came from two realities.

First, Kid Rose loved her, adored her, and was devoted to her. Their intimate connection was one Agnes Jacobson fortified with reciprocal passion. Additionally, and consequentially, Agnes no longer slept with strangers for money. These truths were more than enough to bring a smile to her face and lightness to her heart, despite the fact she was unable to have children and knew that Abram would never, given her past, propose marriage. She cut into a loaf of thick rye, slapped pastrami on the sliced bread, placed Swiss cheese atop the meat, lathered the sandwiches with mustard, and added homemade potato salad to the plates. She then removed two tumblers from a cabinet above the kitchen's gas range, wiped dust from the glasses with a towel, and filled them with iced tea. She carried the tumblers into the dining room, where the men were talking in low tones, and placed one glass in front of her beau and the other in front of Larson. Agnes retreated, retrieved plates of sandwiches and potato salad, grabbed forks from the counter, and returned to serve lunch.

"Thanks, doll," Kid Rose said, through a generous smile. "Could you scram, make yourself scarce, maybe take in a picture at the Palace while we hash things out?"

Agnes knew it wasn't a question, but a command. "I'll get my coat and purse and leave you two boys to your gabbing." She kissed Abram. "Just don't get yourself all worked up," she whispered. Agnes left the men, found her purse, coat, and black leather gloves, opened the door, and exited the house.

"You've got a good woman there," Sig Larson observed, between bites of sandwich. "You should marry that girl."

Abram shook his head as he sipped iced tea. "Not in the cards. Not gonna happen. Just can't do that to my folks," he said with lament, "even though they don't give two shits about me. Never have." He paused, placed his tumbler on the tablecloth, picked up his sandwich, and bit into it. "Really, it's more out of respect for my brothers and sisters, who are pretty rigid in their Judaism and morality, that I defer. No, there'll be no wedding bells in our future. I'm happy with things the way they are."

Larson finished his sandwich, stabbed potato salad with his fork, took a bite, and stared at his friend. "What do we do about the *Truthsayer*?" he finally asked. "If anything were to come out, well, that could destroy my chances of running for governor."

"Not satisfied to chase crooks and bootleggers?" Rosenstein asked through a broad smile.

The irony of the two men—one of them the chief law enforcement officer of Hennepin County and the other a rum-runner being investigated by the FBI and the Prohibition Bureau—sitting together and talking about scandal was not lost upon Larson. "Well," he said, "if I was actually interested in putting a stop to booze smuggling, I'd know where to start . . ."

"Ha!"

"Seriously, Abram. What are we supposed to do about this snoop from Cooper's rag digging into the Miller girl's death?"

Kid Rose pondered a moment before answering. "I think one of my associates needs to pay the newspaper's editor a visit and deliver the message that he needs to back off."

"For Christ's sake, Kid. I can't know about such things!"

Abram rose from the table, walked to a nearby buffet, removed the top of a slender cut-glass decanter, lifted the container, and poured whiskey into two glasses. The bootlegger capped the decanter, carried the glasses across the hardwood floor, and placed one glass in front of Larson and the other next to his own plate. The Kid sat heavily, situated himself, and raised whiskey to his lips. "You won't ever know the details," Kid Rose replied, taking a long draw from his glass. "This sort of business isn't something a lawman should be involved with." The Kid took another swig of booze. "I told you not to get personally involved in the Miller matter," he chided, after swallowing. "You contacting Newhouse wasn't smart. I had it covered."

"I needed to be sure, to be certain the girl's body was relocated. To protect Moe, which in turn protected you. I'd do it again, Abram," Larson answered with a shrug. "I'd do it again."

Kid Rose examined his friend's face. "I'm sure you meant well. But you need to avoid involving yourself in such things if you're serious about running for governor. Let me do what I do best: Let me take care of the dirty work."

Sigurd Larson, full in the knowledge that he'd made a mistake in contacting Newhouse, drained whiskey from his glass and nodded.

CHAPTER TWENTY-ONE
November 1926

The change came swiftly. The impetus behind the *Truthsayer's* severe divergence of course was not revealed to Donald Swanson. Everett Cooper's sudden insistence that no further inquiry into the actions—past or present—of Sigurd Thaddeus Larson would be undertaken by the newspaper was a sea change at the weekly that caused Don to doubt whether he'd made the right decision by casting his lot with the *Truthsayer*.

Jôhānān Epstein—aka "Johnny Finn"—Kid Rose's driver and right-hand man, was given free rein to deal with problems occasioned by the *Truthsayer's* persistence. Epstein, a short-statured, even tempered (but intimidating), black-haired, brown-eyed Jew had been born in Helsinki, where his father had been the rabbi of the local synagogue. Though Johnny was actually of Lithuanian descent, his friends, including Abram Rosenstein, considered him to be Finnish.

Johnny's parents, who'd been born and raised in Lithuania, emigrated to Helsinki in 1903 to escape yet another pogrom. Although both Finland and Lithuania were under Russian rule, religious and ethnic discrimination against Lithuanian Jews was far more severe than that experienced by their Finnish kindred. Johnny was born in Helsinki shortly after the family arrived. Eventually, the family left Finland, immigrated to the United States, and settled in North Minneapolis. As a youngster, Johnny Finn didn't run with Abram Rosenstein's gang, only falling in with the Kid after the delinquent was released from Red Wing.

For the better part of a week, a black Cadillac had been parked outside the modest home owned by Everett and Mary Cooper on Maryland Avenue in St. Paul. Johnny Finn sat behind the wheel of the sedan, noting the comings and goings of the childless couple and the antics of the family's black Labrador. He did not know the Lab's name. Finn only knew, from watching the dog squat to pee, it was likely female. For several days, the mobster watched Everett and Mary Cooper work on obedience training with the dog. Finn also observed that the couple relied on streetcars for transportation; the Coopers apparently not having the financial wherewithal to own an automobile. As he studied the situation, Johnny became convinced that the Labrador was the key to getting Everett Cooper's attention. Finn conveyed the results of his surveillance to Kid Rose and had received his boss's direction to "take care of it."

Johnny sat behind the wheel of the Fleetwood reading the *St. Paul Pioneer Press* sports page, a thermos of hot coffee on the bench seat next to him, the liquid so hot it would scald a lesser man's mouth. Movement on the Coopers' front stoop caught Johnny's eye. *She's finally going out,* he thought, watching Mrs. Cooper, her winter coat drawn tight around her short, rotund form, her hands gloved, and her feet booted against a snow squall arriving from the Dakotas. The woman called the Labrador into the house, locked the door, descended the front stairs, and slogged through shin-deep snow toward the nearest streetcar stop. *I'll give her time to catch the nine-thirty, and then I'll slip inside and do what needs doing,* Johnny thought in Finnish, the language he dreamed in and the language he used when conversing with his parents.

Things had not been easy for Isaac and Esther Epstein after the family arrived in Minnesota. There was no work for a rabbi who spoke sporadic English, fluent Lithuanian, and passable Finnish but had no ties to North Minneapolis and no relatives living nearby to assist in the family's assimilation. With no congregation to call his own, Isaac was forced to accept whatever work he was offered: enduring long hours at the end of a No. 2 shovel on construction sites or loading heavy cargo into horse-drawn wagons and trucks as a day laborer. Trapped by economic, ethnic, and religious prejudice, once the children—son Jôhānān and daughter Enni—were out of the house, Esther spent her days wandering the neighborhood begging for mending and darning work from the better-offs surrounding her family's poverty.

Enni was the only member of the Epstein clan to ascend to a life of prosperity. The girl married right out of high school and moved with her stern Orthodox husband—

Samuel Lehman—to Butte, Montana, where Samuel's family owned a dry goods store, a pharmacy, and a hotel; all of which profited from a copper mining boom that included the lynching of labor leader Frank Little from a railroad trestle as a warning to would-be union sympathizers. Johnny Finn didn't talk or write to his uppity sister but he knew he had three nieces living in Montana, kin he would never meet.

Finn's parents fretted, worried, and agonized over their son's chosen line of work, his abdication of religion, and his disdain for his family's heritage as he grew more and more distant. They had no direct knowledge of the nefarious activities that Jôhānān was involved with. His name, despite his close ties to an infamous gangster, didn't make the newspapers. But despite a lack of public shaming, Jôhānān's parents knew; there was no hiding the fall from grace that had claimed their son.

Familial history was of scant concern to Johnny Finn, as he waited for Mary Cooper to board her trolley. "I am who I am," he muttered in English, between sips of scalding coffee drawn directly from his glass-insulated Icy Hot bottle. "*Ollutta ja mennyttä*," Johnny whispered in Finnish, carefully sloshing coffee inside his mouth so as not to burn his tongue. "Over and done with," he repeated in English, as he watched heavy snow cover the neighborhood.

Once Mary Cooper boarded the nine-thirty, Finn moved the Cadillac onto a side street. Fresh snow clung to the Coopers' mauve-colored stucco two-story Tudor. Snow the size of corn flakes descended from a sullen sky as Johnny left the car, closed the driver's-side door, and walked confidently—as if he was a local and not a stranger—down the wintery sidewalk. Opening a gate leading to the Coopers' fenced backyard, Johnny glanced in both directions, noted that the adjacent street, alley, and sidewalk were deserted, and moved toward the house with purpose. Arriving on the back stoop, Finn opened the screen door, worked the entry door with a pick, unlocked it, opened the door, slid inside, and closed both doors behind him. Despite his stealth, the Labrador heard Finn's entry, leaped from her sleeping pad in the front hallway, assumed a defensive pose, and growled.

Johnny removed his gloves with deliberation, shoved them in a pocket of his pea coat, and raised bare, fight-gnarled hands in placation. The dog began barking. The unwelcome intruder pulled a hunk of roast beef from a pocket of his coat, displayed the treat, and cautiously advanced. "Easy girl," Finn whispered in thickly accented English. "I have something for you . . ."

He held the meat above the dog's nose. At first, the gesture had no effect. But canine nature overtook reticence, and in short order, the Labrador snatched the offering and swallowed it whole.

Johnny sat on a kitchen chair and waited. He felt little guilt as he studied the young Labrador—he guessed her to be five or six months old—as cyanide coursed through the dog's ebony body. Not long into the vigil, the dog collapsed onto the linoleum floor, foamed at the mouth, struggled for air, thrashed about, and died.

Finn removed a typewritten note from inside his coat and placed the message, which was folded in thirds and sealed in an unmarked envelope, on the dead dog. The intruder slipped out the back door, locked it, stood on the porch, and studied the neighborhood. The accelerating blizzard made Finn smile: Evidence of his visit would be obliterated by snow.

Mr. Cooper:
We are saddened to learn of the demise of your pet. But we are confident you will appreciate things will become immeasurably worse for you and your lovely wife if you do not heed this warning. By this, we mean to say that you and your staff at the Truthsayer *must immediately stop investigating the Hennepin County Attorney.*

Your attention to this request will ensure that your humble home is never again visited by our associates. Failure to adhere to this message will result in unfortunate consequences. Notifying the police will occasion severe retribution. We hope you take this message to heart and respond appropriately.
Concerned Friends

It was late afternoon. Everett Cooper stood in the kitchen of his St. Paul home. Diffuse wintery light illuminated the space. Lady, the family's six-month-old Labrador pup, lay at his feet, her body cold and her pink tongue twisted and distended from her mouth. He held the typewritten warning in his bare hands as he read it over and over and over again. Tears dripped onto the kitchen floor and joined snow melt pooling on the linoleum around his galoshes. Very shortly, Mary would arrive home. He had no idea what he would say to her or how he would explain Lady's death. But one thing was clear to Everett Remington Cooper, as he folded the warning, tucked it in its envelope, and hid the papers in a pocket of his overcoat. *I need to call off Swanson,* Everett thought, as he bent at the waist to embrace his beloved companion. *It's the only thing to be done.*

BOOK TWO: THE SWORD

"The sword is mightier than the pen."
Sajjad Hussain
(*The Nation*, 2017)

CHAPTER ONE
Minneapolis, Minnesota
1930

Donald Swanson adhered to Everett Cooper's admonition. The reporter confined his muckraking to grifters, petty politicians, and mobsters and did not reference Sigurd Larson disparagingly in print—though he wasn't completely compliant. In penning articles identifying Kid Rose as integral to the Irish mob's illegal bootlegging operation, Swanson could not refrain from including allusions to Rosenstein's connections to "powerful political figures"—unnamed elected officials who protected the crook from consequences.

The Volstead Act remained the law of the land: the manufacture and sale of beer, wine, and hard liquor—except for alcohol used for "medicinal and religious purposes"—remained federal offenses, investigated by the newly constituted FBI and the Prohibition Bureau (with assistance from local law enforcement), and prosecuted by the United States Attorney. Despite the involvement of the feds, Kid Rose remained—ironically, and in contrast to the nickname earned by Treasury Agent Elliot Ness and his Prohibition task force—*untouchable.*

Though the *Truthsayer* spent much column space highlighting the misdeeds of men like Abram Rosenstein, the newspaper's targets maintained collective silence. Johnny Finn begged Abram to respond, if not by deed, then in words—but the Kid demurred. "Never get in a pissing contest with a skunk," Abram would reply to Johnny's urgings. If Finn continued his entreaty, the Kid would deflect such pestering by calmly adding, "It doesn't pay to engage in a war of words with folks who buy paper by the ream and ink by the barrel."

As a result of Everett Cooper's "conversion," Sigurd Thaddeus Larson remained unblemished in print. But while Swanson bowed to his editor's demands "not to shake that tree"—meaning stay away from criticizing Larson—the reporter's curiosity was unmitigated. He could not cease and desist investigating the rumors and inuendo surrounding Larson's youth, his alleged connection to Kid

Rose, or his involvement in the coverup of Susanne Miller's death.

The muckraker amassed notebooks of handwritten off-the-record quotations, uncollaborated information concerning Larson's juvenile record, his propensity to engage in fisticuffs as a young man, details concerning an illicit involvement with an underage girl, and a smattering of other gossip. Additionally, whispered snippets suggested that the cover-up of the Miller girl's death involved a cop on the take, a tawdry house of ill repute, and a botched abortion, though such titillating leads went for naught.

"No, Don," Cooper would reiterate during the time Swanson worked under Cooper at the *Truthsayer*, "you cannot write anything remotely connected to Larson's past, his alleged involvement with the Miller girl's death, or his association with Abram Rosenstein."

When pressed as to why Larson—and Larson alone—was afforded such deference, Cooper would shake his head and reply: "Because I say so. I know the man, know his history, know his mettle."

The editor would invariably follow up his observations by asserting, "The man's a war hero, Don. A decorated soldier who paid a high price. He suffers daily from pain and disability attained in defense of this nation, and I'll not have you belittle his reputation."

"But . . ."

"There is no 'but'. No further discussion is required, regardless of what you may have heard about the man."

And that was how it went, as long as Everett Remington Cooper called the shots.

"I should just quit," Don bemoaned to Beatrice on a regular basis. "How can I look at myself in the mirror and claim to be a journalist when I'm prevented from exploring and writing about the biggest story in Minnesota?"

"There's a Depression on, love. Or have you forgotten that?"

Don would shake his head. "Oh, I'm well aware that my options are limited. If only I could find the money to buy Everett out . . ."

"Then what?" Bea would ask, feeding her husband's ego and his fantasy of becoming the owner of the *Truthsayer*.

"I'd print the goddamned truth about Larson," Don would mutter, sipping whiskey from a glass tumbler. "He's announced his intention to seek the governorship. Someone needs to let the voters of Minnesota know what their true choices are," he'd add after swallowing. "Give them the facts. Let them decide."

"But we haven't the resources to buy out Everett," Bea would observe. "My parents aren't an option, given how depressed beef prices are and how poorly my father's health is." She stopped and considered the difficulties confronting her father after a series of minor strokes had limited Albert Mondale's use of his dominant right arm. "He'll likely never be the same strong, upright man he once was. His affliction is putting a strain on not only him and my mother, but on their finances as well."

Don would nod and reach across the living room to pat his wife's hand. "I know, dear. I would never suppose that your parents could be our salvation."

In truth, Donald Swanson had a plan to buy the *Truthsayer*. Don had been spending his early morning hours—when Bea and the children, four-year-old Marjorie, and three-year-old Oscar, remained fast asleep—writing fiction. His manuscript, an epic novel along the lines of Rolvaag's *Giants in the Earth* but of an even darker mood and populated by sinister characters drawn from Don's prairie-influenced childhood, bore the working title, *This Troubled Land*. He'd finished a first draft while living in St. Paul. He'd found, through his connections in Brooklyn, a literary agent—Bruce Samskar of the Regency Agency—who'd fallen in love with the work's plot and characters, though in the agent's view, improvements were needed.

"You're a great storyteller, *Donny*, but the dialogue begs for help."

Given that Bruce was attempting to place the book with a major publisher, which Bruce assured would mean a four-figure advance against sales, the writer refrained from pointing out that he hadn't been known as "Donny" since high school and instead set about editing the manuscript.

Rent for the upstairs duplex owned by Mrs. Overstreet, a vacancy Don found in a want-ad posted in the very paper he worked for, was substantially less than what the family paid for their apartment in St. Paul, and, just before the Crash of '29, the Swansons packed up their belongings and moved from St. Paul to Minneapolis. The family's relocation to South Bloomington Avenue included the bonus of an unoccupied third bedroom, which Don turned into a home office: a space where he could edit *This Troubled Land* in undisturbed quiet.

The downside to the family's move was that Don's travel time to work in downtown St. Paul increased, so taking the streetcar was no longer an option. The new commute required expending the last of the family's savings on a cantankerous, undependable 1924 Oakland 6-54A coupe. But Don hoped to recover the cost of the car by completing *This Troubled Land* and placing the book with Bobbs-Merrill, a New York publisher expressing early interest in the novel.

"Fairy tales do come true, Donny," Samskar said over a long-distance telephone call one Saturday morning, a few months after Don had submitted the revised manuscript to his agent. "Not only will Bobbs-Merrill match the five-thousand-dollar advance I coaxed out of Harper on the heels of them buying Rolvaag's *Peder Victorious*," the agent said breathlessly, clearly excited at conveying good news, "but Bobbs will throw in an additional five if the book sells more than five thousand copies in the first month after publication. And that's on top of a five percent royalty!" Samskar said triumphantly.

"Let's do it, Bruce! Let's go with Bobbs!"

A deal was struck. The five-thousand-dollar advance was paid, less Samskar's ten percent. After depositing the advance in the family's savings account, Donald approached Everett, whose editorial skippering of the *Truthsayer* had—apart from his admonishments regarding Sigurd Larson—been nearly flawless. It wasn't Cooper's instincts as an editor that caused the newspaper to incur financial issues. It was Cooper's lack of business acumen that edged the *Truthsayer* toward bankruptcy, a circumstance that led Don to offer Cooper three thousand dollars for the weekly.

"I don't know," Everett mused, as the men nursed beer in a speakeasy a few doors down the street from the *Truthsayer's* offices. "The paper has been, with the exception of Mary, <u>the</u> love of my life."

"But you're nearly ruined. Alice has gone a month without pay and has given her two weeks. She's in bad straits, what with the Teamsters' strike putting her husband out of work," Don noted. "The bills are piling up. I can afford to take them on, buy you out, and right the ship, now that my novel has sold."

Everett Cooper leaned back from the bar and studied his young apprentice before staring at the golden lager in his glass. "You're right. Ever since Lady was murdered," he said quietly, revealing for the first time to Swanson the truth behind the event that caused the newsman to back off Sigurd Larson, "things have gone downhill."

"I thought your dog died from eating bad meat . . ."

"That's true."

"But there's more to it?"

Cooper sipped beer and stared at the shiny oak surface of the bar. "There is."

"Care to enlighten me?"

"I can't. No more than to say her death is directly related to me ordering you to back off from digging dirt on a certain politician."

"Larson intimidated you by having your dog poisoned?" Don asked incredulously.

"Not directly. But I've already said too much."

Don nodded. "Didn't mean to pry." He drained his beer and raised his glass in the smoky air of the crowded bar with his left hand. The bartender, a short, trim Irishman of indiscriminate age and scowling disposition, took the glass, filled it from the tap, and handed it back to Don. "About my proposal . . ."

Everett resituated his spectacles on his nose and considered Don with muted hazel eyes. "It's a fair offer. I've been thinking of trying my hand in San Francisco. Mary's father owns a piece of the *Examiner*. Has enough pull—though he's a banker, not a newspaper man—to get me in."

"Editor of the *Examiner*? Now that would be something . . ."

Cooper chortled. Beer dribbled down his bearded chin. "Don't I wish." Everett looked at Don with humility. "No, I'd be starting over, as a beat reporter covering the waterfront."

Don slapped his boss on the back. "Maybe I'm talking to the next Jack London, the working man's new beacon of truth!"

Cooper wagged his head, held his empty glass up for the barkeep, and continued. "I don't dabble in fiction, Don. I started as a lowly chronicler of man's condition, and such I shall remain," he added through a weary smile. The bartender took Everett's glass and filled it with lager before sliding it across the slippery bar.

Don slurped foam from his beer. "And my offer?"

Everett Cooper stroked his beard, white and gray infiltrating its native blackness—evidence of the stress and strain of trying to keep the *Truthsayer* afloat. "I accept."

CHAPTER TWO
August 1930

Governor Peder Lundquist's disdain for the working man, in distinct opposition to Sig Larson's "man of the people" approach, made him oppose the Teamsters' Strike with an iron fist. The walk-out by local truck drivers in July of 1930 caused Minnesota's unstable economy to slide further down the financial ladder. Lundquist's response? He sent in the National Guard, state troopers, and local lawmen to arrest the truckers and their supporters manning picket lines. "No quarter," was the Swede's mantra, as he sat behind an ornate teak desk in Minnesota's state capitol. "No negotiation. Let the trucking companies bring in strikebreakers, and I'll protect their right to do so. 'Might is right' is what I say!"

With Eddie Sullivan out on strike, Alice returned to the *Truthsayer*. She accepted her old position with the newspaper after Don bought out Everett Cooper's shares, and the former editor and his wife moved to San Francisco. Having reinvigorated the outspoken press with an injection of cash, Don had reached out to Mrs. Sullivan and rehired her as the *Truthsayer*'s office manager, bookkeeper, runner of errands, and maker of coffee.

It was a hot and humid Monday afternoon in August. The governor's race was in full swing; the candidates' rhetoric and disdain for each other was blaringly obvious as Larson and Lundquist dashed about Minnesota criticizing each other's integrity and intellect. Lundquist was desperate. Rumors flew that he'd already lost the Progressive wing of his own party to Larson, and that, come election day in November, the incumbent would be sent packing—back to the Lundquist family farm near Monticello to shovel cow shit.

The Teamsters' strike became entrenched. Men of dubious backgrounds piloted delivery trucks throughout Minneapolis and St. Paul as scab replacements for striking drivers. Teamsters—held at bay by Minnesota Army National Guard soldiers and assorted lawmen—picketed any business employing nonunion drivers. For the most part, the passions of the strikers—and those watching them with guns—were restrained. An uneasy truce existed until Kid Rose seized the opportunity to tip the electoral scales in Sigurd Larson's favor.

The riot commenced as a provocation between Johnny Finn, employed temporarily as a driver for Swenson's Produce—the family-owned company Eddie Sullivan had worked for prior to striking—and Eddie. The Irishman and his out-of-work mates crowded the sidewalk next to the gated yard leading to Swenson's warehouse, holding signs, milling about, generally behaving themselves as young baby-faced soldiers maintained order.

"Fair wages for a fair day's work!" Sullivan and his compatriots shouted as trucks came and went from the yard, raising and lowering their protest signs for effect. "Scabs, go home!"

Kid Rose calculated that sending Johnny Finn into the fray to seek out Eddie Sullivan, a man of slight build, distinctive scarlet hair, and a wildly untrimmed red beard, would stir things up enough to make Larson the logical electoral choice. Supporting an old friend's political ambition was one reason behind Kid Rose's decision to become involved in the Teamsters' strike. But Abram Rosenstein had another, more personal agenda in mind when he again called upon Finn to do his bidding.

The Depression had hit the Rosenstein family hard. When the Crash came, Amos, Abram's younger brother, was employed as the manager of a grocery store. Due to the store's financial instability, Amos, two years Abram's junior with a wife and three small children to provide for, lost his position. Though Abram was estranged from his family, when Amos came to him, hat in hand, and asked if there "Wasn't some work I can do?", the request had touched Abram.

Fully cognizant that political forces were gathering to repeal the Volstead Act, Kid Rose developed a two-pronged approach to protect his pocketbook. He used illicit cash to target small, financially distraught, legitimate businesses. One of the enterprises Kid Rose acquired for less-than-fair-market value was Swenson's Produce. Additional purchases of struggling operations at bargain-basement prices allowed the bootlegger to protect his financial standing through diversification.

In addition, a future, as-yet-unscripted political campaign piqued Abram's interest. Electing Larson as Governor of Minnesota was but an interim step in attaining a more valuable prize. Kid Rose's real goal was gaining Larson a seat at the table in Washington, D.C. to decide the fate of Prohibition. The Kid's end game didn't culminate with Sigurd Larson becoming governor: that office was but a placeholder on Rosenstein's calculated path for Larson, a path that included the Kid's old friend being elected to the United States Senate.

To satisfy his first goal, economic diversification, Abram purchased Swenson's Produce, and with full and complete understanding that Abram called the shots, he'd installed Amos as the company's operational manager. As to Abram Rosenstein's second objective—ensuring Sigurd Larson's elevation to the U.S. Senate—winning that lofty prize would require time, money, skill, luck, and the patience of a rabbi.

When the strikers commenced shouting and raising signs and middle fingers at the rickety old delivery truck Johnny Finn was driving out of the Swenson yard, the bed was filled with sacks of potatoes from Minnesota's Red River valley bound for local grocery stores. Instead of cautiously weaving the truck through the crowd, Johnny stopped the vehicle in the midst of the angry throng. He knew the risks, knew he was outnumbered, but Kid Rose had made it clear: "Get Sullivan."

After unexpectedly stopping the vehicle, Johnny grabbed a baseball bat from beneath the truck's front seat, opened the door, and exited the flatbed.

"Hold on there!" a barely-old-enough-to-shave guardsman, a staff sergeant, called out as Finn exited the truck. "We've got the situation under control," the soldier added.

Come on, boys. Where are you? Finn knew that Rosenstein had seeded a dozen roustabouts—men loyal to the rum-runner—in the crowd. *Now's the time!*

As guardsmen nervously watched the gathering storm, insults were hurled at Johnny Finn by the strikers. Without warning, Rosenstein's men emerged from the crowd to scream, "Get the scab!" and other inflammatory insults at Johnny Finn.

"Move in!" the boy-sergeant commanded. "Separate the parties!"

A phalanx of soldiers wheeled, bayonets drawn on their Enfield rifles—leftovers from the Great War and fully loaded—and advanced. But the maneuver came too late. Kid Rose's men clambered onto the truck, brandishing pocketknives, and tore into the sacks of potatoes.

"See here!" the sergeant implored. "Get off that truck!"

Kid Rose's thugs kept at it until every man held a fist-sized spud. Potatoes were launched. The shower of vegetables was accompanied by epithets and slurs. Johnny Finn dodged the fiercely hurled vegetables as he searched the crowd. Finn found his man and came at Eddie Sullivan with purpose. Once inside the milling mob, Johnny raised and swung his baseball bat. But instead of striking Sullivan, the cudgel connected with another man's head. Blood spattered bystanders. The unfortunate striker crumpled. A scrum ensued and the sergeant gave a fateful command.

Johnny Finn was shot twice, though neither wound proved fatal. An errant bullet blew out the back of a picketer's skull: the man was dead before he hit the curb. Another Teamster perished when a bullet penetrated his heart. At the sound of gunfire, cadres of Minneapolis cops, clusters of Hennepin County deputies, and a contingent of state troopers rushed toward the fracas. It took the assembled force an hour to restore order.

Twenty-nine strikers, guardsmen, instigators, and innocent bystanders—including five women and two children—required hospitalization. One of the children, a ten-year-old girl, was shot in the back, the bullet entering her spine and paralyzing her from the waist down. A woman drawn to the confrontation by curiosity sustained a wound to her left thigh. The bullet severed the femoral artery, although her life and her left leg were spared by the quick application of a tourniquet.

The ugly melee was a horrific circumstance orchestrated, in large part, by Kid Rose. "But," Abram observed as he listened to Governor Lundquist's half-hearted radio plea to "obey the law" on WCCO, "sending Johnny in to stir things up was what was needed to cast Lundquist as an inept, out-of-touch Hoover man."

Shortly after the riot subsided, Simon Caine made his way to the *Truthsayer's* office. The Minneapolis police sergeant had previously visited the Minnesota Building to apprise Donald Swanson of details concerning Susanne Miller's demise. To his surprise, Caine had read nothing about his bombshell revelations in the *Truthsayer*. But during subsequent conversations, Don assured Caine that he hadn't forgotten what he'd been told, even going so far as to guarantee that eventually, Sigurd Larson's secrets would be revealed in print.

"Mrs. Sullivan?" Caine asked, wearing a smartly pressed blue uniform, his brimmed blue patrolman's cap turning nervously in thick fingers, his face expressing empathy.

"Yes?"

"Your husband's Eddie Sullivan?"

"He is."

Caine noted the woman's expectant expression and sought a genteel, tactful route for his disclosure. *There is none.* "I hate to be the bearer of bad news, Ma'am," Caine said bluntly, "but your husband's been shot."

Alice stood up from her desk, clasped her face in trembling hands, and cried out, "Oh my God!"

The cop waited for the woman to calm down, but she remained inconsolable. Unable to find a more compassionate path to relay what he knew, Caine plunged ahead.

"Unfortunately, Ma'am, that's only part of the bad news . . ."

CHAPTER THREE
January 1931

Governor Larson twirled, dipped, and glided across the polished-to-sheen floor with his wife despite the fact he was dancing on one good leg and a prosthesis.

Wearing the mantle of brotherhood and benevolence, promising economic assistance, political reform, and social justice for the downtrodden while protecting Capitalism, Sigurd Larson bested Governor Peder Lundquist, a taciturn, no-nonsense, no-more-spending, anti-labor Conservative aligned with President Herbert Hoover. Larson's war record, his reduction of vice in Hennepin County during his brief tenure as county attorney—and the support he garnered from Liberals and Negroes—led to the Minnesota Democratic Party's hesitancy to endorse a candidate for governor. Democratic dithering—before finally naming an anemic, unknown as its gubernatorial challenger—allowed the FLP to hit the ground running, concentrate its fire on Lundquist, and use the man's indifference toward labor unrest and economic catastrophe as a cudgel to dislodge Republicans from political power in the state.

Amelia Salveson Larson's girlish figure had been reclaimed after the birth of the couple's only child. Michael Marcus Larson—now five years old—was fast asleep in his bedroom at the governor's unofficial residence, a dreary mansion the Larsons were leasing on Grand Avenue. Consequently, the child was missing the Governor's Inaugural Ball in the St. Paul Hotel's opulent ballroom. The band, an ensemble from the St. Paul Orchestra joined by horn players hand-selected for the event, played waltzes and traditional numbers, mixing in an occasional popular tune so attendees could "let their hair down."

    "You're divine," Sigurd said as he clutched the slender form of his beloved to his chest and dipped her, a trumpet trill signaling the end of the song.

    "You're not half bad either, Mr. Governor! Why don't we dance more often?" Am' asked.

"Time, my dear—the lack of it," Sig lied, pain caused by his artificial limb constituting the real reason ballroom dancing was a rare event for the couple.

They separated. Sig retrieved his cane. Though the governor's freshly pressed white shirt under his black tuxedo jacket was sodden from sweat, the First Lady looked no worse for the effort. Amelia's face, neck, and arms bore no trace of perspiration, her fresh appearance belying the pace of the fox trot the couple had just concluded. Despite the governor's shortness of breath and his use of the cane, the pair moved with grace through an admiring crowd of FLA members, politicians, and men and women of power and wealth. Sigurd Larson's supporters had gathered to dine at the elaborate buffet and to drink ice-cold punch, hot tea, and scalding coffee in honor of the war hero's electoral victory.

Sig leaned his cane against the table, pulled out a chair for Amelia, and helped her settle with ladylike poise. The orchestra struck up another number, but the governor was too spent to take up the challenge. Couples danced, whirled, and spun beneath ornate chandeliers as the Sig took stock of his good fortune. But his's smile turned to a frown when Sig caught sight of Abram Rosenstein and Agnes Jacobson entering the room. "Shit," he muttered, knowing as he did that Abram would never attend such an event simply to enjoy music, food, and good company. *With that man, there's always an agenda.*

"What?" Am' asked.

"Nothing," Sigurd lied. "Just thinking."

"Well, stop that!" she teased. "Today is your big day. Today is about smiles and laughter and pats on the back for a journey well made," she added, before kissing her husband coquettishly on his right ear lobe. "Later, we can celebrate in a more *private* fashion . . ."

"Aren't you the dickens . . ." he whispered.

Abram remained occupied, talking to other folks, which eased Sig's concern. The music swelled. Notes rose to collide with the distant ceiling of the large, open space as men and women worked their arms feverishly, dancing the Charleston and then, without a break, the Black Bottom. The tempo and texture of the music brought frowns to the faces of Pastor and Mrs. Salveson, Amelia's parents, who were seated next to Sig's parents across the table.

"Demon music," Uriah Salveson said in a stage whisper. "Heathen paganism!"

"Mother!"

Sigurd patted his wife's pale white hand. "It's all right," he said quietly. "Jazz isn't everyone's cup of tea."

"It's absolutely sinful and suggestive, is what it is," Pastor Salveson opined.

"Father!" Am' hissed. "You promised—knowing the sort of music we'd have at this event, the best day in my husband's life, the pinnacle of his career—that you'd not make a scene. You said you'd refrain from casting aspersions and recriminations on our celebration. You promised," she continued, her mouth curled in such a way as to make her repaired cleft more visible, "and yet, here we are."

The pastor took a deep breath, sighed, and nodded. "Perhaps it's time for us to go."

"Father, don't do this," Amelia pleaded. "Don't ruin Sigurd's big night by acting like a child." She eased her condemnation and continued. "I want you here. We want you here. Can't you withhold judgment for one damn minute and simply enjoy our triumph?"

"Amelia!" her mother gasped, placing her right hand over her mouth. "Such language . . ."

Unspoken was the likelihood that both Elliot and Uriah Salveson had voted for Governor Lundquist, whose politics and rigid Puritanism aligned more closely with their own worldview. Larson had won the three-way race for governor handily (though the Johnny-come-lately Democratic candidate hardly mattered) and the Republicans had been ousted from power. Like Herbert Hoover, Governor Lundquist had insisted upon a laissez-faire approach to the state's economic tailspin and, in a supreme misjudgment, chose to use violence rather than negotiation to deal with union protests, picket lines, and strikes occasioned by the Great Depression. In evangelical and politically conservative circles, Sigurd Larson was seen as something of a Socialist: a harbinger of the End Times. This, Amelia and Sigurd knew, was why the Salvesons, despite their familial ties to the new governor, were uncomfortable celebrating their son-in-law's triumph.

"Pardon me, Governor," a familiar voice said, as Sigurd wrangled to find a path, a means, to keep peace in his family. "Might I have a word?"

Damn.

Larson set his half-empty coffee cup in its saucer, placed his white linen napkin on the tablecloth, and stood. "What is it, Abram?" There was anxiousness behind the governor's question. Sig looked at the Kid while noting that the gangster's live-in was engaged in conversation elsewhere. *Damn him! He brings a former prostitute to this event? Does his hubris know no bounds?*

"What I need to tell you is best said in private," Abram whispered. "Is there someplace we can chat?"

Rosenstein was not dressed as a gangster but as a prosperous businessman. He was an invited guest, having donated a thousand dollars to Sig Larson's campaign.

"Might I have the pleasure of an introduction?" Reverend Salveson asked, leaving his chair, and moving toward the conversation.

"Abram Rosenstein," the Kid said, extending his right hand. "Old friend of the governor."

Elliot Salveson returned the gesture. "How so?"

Sigurd remained mute.

"Grew up together. A Norwegian Lutheran and a Ukrainian Jew end up being lifelong pals," Abram added. "Go figure!"

The reverend smiled. "My wife, Uriah," he said, nodding toward the seated woman. "And Amelia," he added, placing an affectionate hand on his daughter's bare shoulder, "our only child and the governor's wife."

Sigurd's parents remained mute, as if trying to avoid being seen or heard. Their silence worked: Kid Rose ignored their presence, and the governor, knowing his parents' desperate need to remain inconspicuous, didn't draw them into the conversation.

"Ah, Mrs. Larson—The First Lady! We've met before," Abram said. "Nice to see you again, ma'am." It was then Abram realized he'd failed to acknowledge Mrs. Salveson's presence. "And you, ma'am, as well," he said through an intoxicating smile. "Governor, is there a place we could talk?" Kid Rose asked again.

"What the hell is so important that you'd crash my inaugural ball?"

They were standing in the hotel's Palm Room, the space empty save for the two men in conversation.

"We've got a problem," Kid Rose explained. "And I didn't crash your party, Siggy," the Kid corrected. "As a contributor—a hefty one I might add—I was invited by your inaugural committee."

Sigurd's face reddened. His stump ached, and he leaned heavily on his cane. "Fine. You were invited. But you didn't have to come." The governor paused to reflect. "You said there's a problem of some sort?"

"Like a dog with a bone, Swanson—that goddamned reporter—won't let things go."

Sigurd studied Kid Rose's darkly featured face. Abram's demeanor hadn't altered. There hadn't been, despite the gravity of the news, any change in the Kid's inflection. "In what way?"

"Well, you know we were able, when Cooper was running things, to convince him to stay out of our business."

Larson blew air through his lips and looked at the ceiling. "I don't want to know about that," the governor said quietly.

"Understood. My methods are mine and mine alone."

"Go on," Larson said impatiently. Though he didn't relish returning to the ballroom to deal with his in-laws, he was hopeful that he and Am' could take a few more turns around the dance floor before the gala concluded.

"Swanson's poking his nose into the Miller affair with help from a Minneapolis P.D. sergeant. Guy by the name of 'Caine'."

"Simon Caine?"

"You know him?"

"Of him. He's a pal of Ed Charles." The governor paused to consider how much information he wished to share. *What the hell.* "I investigated connections between Caine and the money trail involving Charles and illegal contracts. Tried to find something to tie Caine to the corruption that undid Charles."

"And?"

"Never got the goods on him," Larson said with regret.

"Well, he's a carbuncle on your ass, at least when it comes to Swanson. The word is he has information on you, including the fact that the girl's death involved a cover-up, as well as details concerning the botched abortion. Seems Caine is, when he wants to be, a pretty good sleuth. Found the doctor who did the deed and has the guy in his pocket. Saving him for just the right moment."

"Christ!"

"Don't know about that, being Jewish. But hey, I guess He was too, right?"

"Cut the clowning."

Rosenstein studied an ornate tapestry hanging on a wall. "Nice digs. Must be rough, being able to afford a party in the swankiest joint in St. Paul." Abram paused and waited for the governor to calm. He knew Larson would never raise a hand against him; they had too much history for that. He watched Sig's face relax. "Remember our little burglary?"

Larson again blew air through his lips. "How could I forget?"

"Caine's on that trail, too."

"Christ!"

"You already said that."

"Get on with it, would you?"

"And that incident with my cousin ..."

"You mean Helen. Helen Golden?"

"The very same."

Images of a lovely, brown-haired, brown-eyed girl spilled across Sig's memory. They were together. The girl's mohair sweater and silk camisole were raised to expose her youthful bosom. Her skirt and underwear rested on the dewy lawn. His trousers were down, his uncircumcised manhood seeking, then finding, a place of warmth and fulfillment. They came together figuratively, and literally, Helen's bare bottom slapping the top of a wooden picnic table in a neighbor's backyard, the event, a felonious crime, taking place two blocks from the Larson home. *It was a wonder,* the newly-elected governor thought as images of that night flooded his consciousness, *she didn't get splinters in that tender, beautiful ass . . .*

"I thought she moved to Chicago."

"Oak Park. A suburb."

"How the hell did Caine get to her?"

Abram shrugged and placed a firm hand on his companion's tuxedoed shoulder. "I only know he's been snooping around, asking about Helen because she called me. I hadn't talked to her in years, so the call threw me for a loop." He paused to study the governor's face, searching for a reaction. "She's not out for vengeance or retribution or looking for a payoff or anything like that," Abram added. "She simply wants that long-ago incident to be kept quiet, out of the papers, and away from her family, including her husband, who, get this, is a cop!"

"Christ!"

Abram shook his head. "You're repeating yourself." Kid Rose released the governor's shoulder and stood back to take stock. *He's trembling. The war hero is afraid of what might happen if this stuff gets out. Gotta help him through this. Gotta come up with something to keep his past in the past. He's no good to me if he goes down because of scandal.* "Siggy," Abram said quietly, "I've told you everything I know. The question is: what should we do about it?"

CHAPTER FOUR
April 1931

The Twin Ports were bustling. Vessels crowding the docks and wharves of Duluth, Minnesota, and Superior, Wisconsin, were demarcated "boats"—not ships—because only intra-lake carriers plied the waters from the western end of the Great Lakes—where Duluth and Superior are located—to Buffalo, New York. Until the St. Lawrence Seaway was completed in the 1950s, ocean-going vessels ended their journeys at Lake Ontario because the route west was too shallow and too narrow to accommodate bluewater ships. Before the completion of the Seaway, freshwater boats were limited to plying the lower Great Lakes and delivering iron ore, cement, coal, grain, flour, and copper, as well as packaged goods to cities—major and minor—along the shores of Lake Superior, Lake Michigan, Lake Huron, and Lake Erie.

In addition, passenger boats, sleek of beam and powered by sail, coal, or oil, delivered mail and passengers to Port Arthur, Sault Ste Marie, Milwaukee, Chicago, Detroit, Cleveland, Buffalo, and innumerable smaller ports in between. Though the United States went "dry" with the passage of Prohibition, Canada remained "wet," and the U.S.'s northern border, including the Great Lakes, became a porous entry point for smuggled booze.

There were fewer than seventy local, county, state, and federal lawmen patrolling northeastern Minnesota when the Volstead Act took effect; there were simply too many crooks and not enough cops to suppress the importation of illegal alcohol. Lawmen patrolling border country rarely—if ever—made a "big score" by taking down major bootleggers. Local cops, county deputies, and federal agents working in Outstate Minnesota had to be content with incremental success—including dismantling backyard stills. Additionally, dishonest lawmen looked the other way when it came to organized crime. Officers, deputies, and agents filled their pockets with bootleggers' gold, ignoring major smuggling operations to allow the unimpeded flow of clandestine spirits.

"Damn it," Ian "Stuffy" McNulty said, sitting with Kid Rose at a table in the Green Lantern on Wabasha Street in downtown St. Paul, sipping Canadian rye, "we lost John Murphy. Now we've lost his cousin too."

John Murphy had been Duluth's chief of police. Long before Kid Rose fell in with the Irish mob, Murphy was arrested as the ringleader of a gang distributing Canadian whiskey, English gin, and Cuban rum throughout northern Minnesota. Unfortunately for Prohibitionists, the case against Murphy, filed in Federal District Court and assigned to Judge Page Morris, fell apart.

Judge Morris had postponed Murphy's jury trial, stating plainly, "This defendant is a man of high moral standing. I'm exhausted from a continuous stream of contests involving illegal liquor and must refrain from a rush to judgment. The Murphy matter needs to be delayed to ensure fairness."

When the case finally came before a jury, McNulty made certain that the government's coop of stoolpigeons was empty. Additionally, Murphy's defense that he'd accidentally stumbled upon a large cache of liquor in rural St. Louis County and that he'd secreted bottles of the best stuff in the basement of his Duluth home "as evidence" earned John Murphy a "not guilty" verdict. Despite the acquittal, the jury's decision wasn't universally seen as reflecting the man's innocence. By unanimous vote of the Duluth City Council, Murphy was denied reinstatement to his former position and banned from seeking *any* employment with the City of Duluth.

"Patrick Murphy?" Stuffy asked, staring hard at the Kid. McNulty's nickname stemmed from his habit of stuffing C-notes in the pockets of anyone he believed could be "enlightened" to see things his way—including cops, judges, bailiffs, and, on occasion, Roman Catholic priests. "I thought he was doing what we'd asked him to do: skippering the boat and moving cargo from the Sault to Duluth."

Voyages of the *Nautilus*, a steel hulled blue-water boat boasting twin V-8s that could outrun anything the United

States or Canadian Coast Guards possessed, began at a secluded pier in Sault Ste. Marie, Ontario. The trawler crossed the oft-tempestuous waters of the Big Lake under the cover of darkness before docking in Superior. Once the contraband was off-loaded, it was organized for distribution in a warehouse owned by McNulty. The water route worked well from late April until freeze-up. During the winter months, the deluge of whiskey, rye, and gin carried by the *Nautilus* was replaced by a trickle of booze trucked into the U.S. through Fort Francis and Fort William, the main points of land entry along the Minnesota/Ontario border.

Abram Rosenstein considered his partner's question.

For five years, Patrick Murphy's luck had held—until it didn't. Someone in Sault St. Marie spilled the beans. One moonless night, as the *Nautilus* settled against its dock in Superior, Prohibition Bureau agents, local cops, and county deputies hit the lights on a dozen squad cars to illuminate the trawler.

"Murphy tried to make a run for it," Abram noted, emptying his glass. "But the goddamned Coast Guard had a cutter lying in wait with its lights out and its guns ready. By the time Murphy restarted his engines, it was too late."

"How much did we lose?"

"Two hundred cases."

"Lord."

"And don't forget," Kid Rose added, waving to the bartender, gaining the man's attention, and raising his glass in the muggy air of the saloon to order another double shot of rye. "The feds took our boat."

The St. Paul speakeasy the smugglers were sitting in—the Green Lantern—was a gangster's hideaway. Under the protection of Dan Hogan, widely known as "Dapper Dan," visiting mobsters, including the likes of John Dillinger, Baby Face Nelson, and the Barker Gang, fell under Hogan's protection. As long as visiting guests agreed to commit no crimes within fifty miles of the Twin Cities, lawmen didn't harass the patrons of the speakeasy, no matter how infamous or high up on the FBI's Most Wanted list a man or woman might be. The protection afforded under this "Layover Agreement" required criminals to check in with

Reddy Griffin, the man assigned by Hogan to administer the "arrangement" between Dapper Dan and John O'Connor, St. Paul's Chief of Police. As part of an informal registration process, visiting "dignitaries" were required to provide nonrefundable "security deposits" to Griffin, who in turn slipped cash to lawmen on the take.

As McNulty and Kid Rose drank in the dimly lighted saloon, there were no other men or women of infamy visiting the place, just the two bootleggers, a bartender, a bouncer, and a couple of locals minding their own business.

"They make bail?" Stuffy asked.

The Kid nodded and sipped from his refilled glass. "Took care of it through a local lawyer. Cost an extra two hundred—beyond the five for the lawyer—to get a federal magistrate out of bed in Madison to set bail by telephone. I paid a hundred apiece, cash bail, for the captain and his crew." Abram explained. "Cost us an even grand to get Murphy and his boys out of the Superior calaboose."

"Where're they now?" McNulty asked.

Abram smiled. "Bought 'em three tickets on the first train out of Duluth." He paused. "More cash down the toilet," he added as an afterthought. "I have contacts on the West Coast who can use their talents. More importantly, their vanishing act means they're not here for court."

"Smart. You're a smart man, Abram."

The unspoken import of McNulty's compliment was one Kid Rose knew by heart from years of working with the Irish. Theirs was a clan that, no matter how effective, efficient, and intelligent he might be, he could never join. *For a Jew, you mean. Smart for a Jew.* It would do no good for Abram to point out the prejudice ingrained in McNulty's stilted praise. "Thanks. I try," the Kid replied.

"The boys in Chi-Town ain't gonna like it," McNulty continued, indifferent to his friend's vexation. "The fact we lost an entire shipment is bad enough. But losing the *Nautilus* and having its crew arrested? Well, that's a real pisser . . ."

The bootlegger's reference was to Irish mobsters in Chicago who financed, protected, and oversaw Stuffy McNulty's operation in return for a share of the profits. The North Siders—the Irish Catholic gang financing Stuffy—had once been run by Dean O'Banion. Shortly before his death, the Irishman's operation was placed under the control of Italian mobsters. Despite being irritated at the new hierarchy, O'Banion reached an accord with his new masters and pocketed more than a million dollars a year running booze. But the truce—arranged by Mafia kingpin Johnny Torrio—fell apart. Bad blood simmered between O'Banion and a Torrio underboss, Angelo Genna, leading to a feud that eventually turned violent.

Shortly after meeting with Frank Nitti and Al Capone in an attempt to smooth things over, O'Banion was gunned down in his flower shop, a front for the Irishman's illegal activities. Torrio had tried to placate O'Banion by suggesting that the Irish mob partner with South Side Italians engaging in prostitution. Being a devout Catholic, O'Banion rejected any involvement in the sex trade. His position in this regard doomed any chance for reconciliation. The Irishman's murder by Genna's goons diminished the Irish mob's influence in Chicago. By the time Kid Rose joined McNulty's smuggling ring, George "Bugs" Moran, a non-Irishman born to French Catholic parents, had succeeded O'Banion as the head of the North Siders. Moran held his nose, his tongue, and his desire for retribution to regain a small piece of the bootlegging operation for himself and his Irish compatriots.

Bugs was not only Catholic like McNulty: he was also Minnesota born, having spent his childhood in St. Paul, where he attended Cretin High School—a private Catholic military academy. But in his teens, Bugs fell in with a bad crowd and decided a life of criminality exceeded the rewards a high school diploma could offer. As a result of their delinquent behavior, both Bugs Moran and Stuffy McNulty spent time at the Red Wing Reformatory—the same institution where Abram Rosenstein would, a few years later, contemplate his sinful ways.

Moran was sent to Red Wing for thievery. Ian McNulty did his stint for beating a St. Paul patrolman into a coma when the cop, a German immigrant, called Stuffy "a dirty little Mick." After testing each other's mettle at the reformatory, Moran and McNulty became friends. Despite

Moran moving to Chicago upon his release from Red Wing, and McNulty returning to St. Paul upon completing his sentence, the two maintained their friendship. When Prohibition created the need for a steady hand to control bootlegging in Minnesota, Moran offered McNulty a position of authority within his organization.

The 1929 St. Valentine's Day Massacre—the mass extermination of Bugs Moran's top lieutenants by Al Capone—temporarily diminished Bugs's importance. But, after escaping the assassination attempt (Moran wasn't present when fake cops lined up his capos and executed them), Bugs used fear, chicanery, and wads of cash to reclaim a place in Chicago's criminal hierarchy. Moran's resurrection allowed him to finance Stuffy McNulty and Kid Rose's smuggling ring, including the purchase and operation of the *Nautilus.*

"What're we supposed to do now?" Stuffy finally asked, after a lengthy lull in the bootleggers' conversation.

"Simple," Kid Rose answered with a grin. "We buy another boat!"

CHAPTER FIVE
April 1931

Donald Swanson stepped off the *Empire Builder*, the Great Northern Railway's passenger train running from Chicago to Seattle and back. It was a gamble for the reporter to purchase a ticket to Chicago. There was no way of knowing whether the target of his interest, a young mother living in Oak Park in a modest domicile shared with two kids and her policeman husband, would speak to him, much less give him the goods on Sigurd Larson. He had nothing more to go on than rumors dredged up by Sergeant Caine—rumors concerning an underage affair between the former Helen Golden, now Helen Ginsburg, and Minnesota's governor.

    Caine had used guile to connect with a detective he knew in Oak Park, fabricating a tale that Caine was investigating a prostitution ring. Caine was so credible in his plea that, in the end, despite the detective being friends with the woman's husband, Caine's contact confirmed that, yes indeed, he'd heard gossip regarding Helen's past, including allusions to an illicit liaison between a youthful Miss Golden and some bigshot Minnesota politician. But no details were provided as to who the man might be, which meant Don Swanson, before he wrote one word about Sig Larson's supposed connection to the woman, needed confirmation of the alleged indiscretion. The only way Don could see that happening was to meet with and ask Mrs. Ginsburg directly about an event over a decade old.

Though Don was determined to get to the bottom of the innuendo concerning the Left's new hero, there was an element of hesitation in his quest. Governor Larson was rolling up his sleeves and making the settlement of the Teamster's strike his number one priority. To this end, Larson had toned back the violence and the rhetoric and made it clear to the commander of the Minnesota National Guard that citizen-soldiers were forbidden to fire upon unarmed picketers who were peacefully exercising their rights of free speech and assembly. There was a positive outlook regarding the new regime being fostered in

Minnesota's mainstream newspapers, which had made Don pause his inquiry into the governor. But Eddie Sullivan's death compelled him to renew his quest for the truth regarding Sigurd Larson's connection to Abram Rosenstein, the man alleged to have caused the riot that claimed Eddie Sullivan's life. After consoling Alice Sullivan, hearing Simon Caine out, and uncovering Kid Rose's involvement in the altercation at Swenson's Warehouse, Don was determined to shed light on the untoward relationship between Larson and Rosenstein.

"What a pickle," Don muttered, as he carried his briefcase by its shoulder strap out of Chicago's Grand Central Station. He was traveling light. He hadn't brought so much as a change of boxer shorts with him. He hadn't booked a hotel room, thinking that once he would met up with Mrs. Ginsburg and either been shown the door or obtained a glorious scoop, he'd catch the next train back to St. Paul. "This whole exercise might be a colossal waste of time," he muttered, as he waited for a streetcar.

  The ride to Oak Park was long. But the commute gave Don a chance to review questions he'd scribbled in his reporter's notebook. "I can assure you, Ma'am, that I'll keep your name confidential," he'd practiced in his head until the line was memorized. "All I'm after is information. I'm not here to ruin your life."

  As the trolley clacked along, Swanson recounted the times he'd attempted to forego a trip to Illinois by telephoning the woman long distance. He'd obtained the Ginsburgs' home number through Sergeant Caine, but his calls were unproductive. Mrs. Ginsburg refused to discuss anything of substance over the telephone. Ultimately, he'd yielded to Mrs. Ginsburg's recalcitrance, while maintaining hope that maybe, just maybe, she'd be more forthcoming during an in-person conversation.

  Still, he thought, as the streetcar rolled to a stop at the corner of South Boulevard Street and Oak Park Avenue, *it's a long shot*. He waved to the conductor, stepped off the car, and began walking.

  Don was unaware that his path through Oak Park took him past the birthplace of a man who would become a celebrated author. As he walked through the suburban landscape, Swanson had no way of knowing that the man, a graduate of the local high school, would one day win both a Pulitzer and a Nobel. At the time of Don's visit, Ernest Hemingway was known chiefly as a war correspondent—for the *Toronto Star* and the *Cooperative Commonwealth*—and as a short-story writer. However, Hemingway's second foray into long fiction—a recounting of his exploits as an ambulance driver in Italy during the Great War—had created a sensation. Don's copy of *A Farewell to Arms*, a gift from Beatrice, sat unread on a nightstand in the master bedroom of the family's South Minneapolis apartment, as the reporter walked unsuspectingly through a neighbor that had birthed literary genius.

Don turned east on Superior Street and crossed the avenue. He timed his arrival, such that Mrs. Ginsburg would be alone. Her husband was at work, engaged in his duties with the Oak Park Police Department. As Swanson stopped in front of a modest two-story home, he began to perspire. *I'm not sure about this . . .*

He climbed a wooden staircase onto a covered front porch. Swaying like a gangly, nervous giraffe, he opened the screen door and rapped on the home's entry door. His subtle knocking caused a young woman to appear. Given Mrs. Ginsburg's full figure, deep chestnut eyes, and look of intelligent suspicion on her face, Don surmised the rumors were true. *How could Larson not fall for such glory? How could he withstand such charms, even if she was only a teenager at the time of their meeting?*

"How may I help you?"

While Helen Ginsburg scrutinized Don Swanson, two toddlers, a boy, and a girl, peeked out from behind their mother to stare wide-eyed at the lanky stranger. The reporter smiled at the kids, cleared his throat, and cast fate to the wind.

Don's return trip was as uneventful as the interview had been.

"No, Mr. Swanson, I do not wish to speak to you on or off the record."

"It would be best if I heard the truth of the matter from you, Mrs. Ginsburg."

"I thought I made my position clear when you telephoned me," was her curt reply. "There is nothing for me to say and hence, nothing for you to hear." Those words had been accompanied by the slamming of the front door and the click of a deadbolt.

"Shit," Don muttered, as the Great Northern train he'd boarded for his return to Minnesota eased away from Chicago's Grand Central Station. "That was an utter waste of time."

Urban bustle gave way to tidy farms, newly planted fields, leafing trees, and a greening countryside. As the locomotive belched coal smoke and steam to claim speed, the repetitive clickety-clack of steel wheels over rails and ties lulled the reporter into slumber. As he slept, Don experienced unsettling dreams. In his fanciful ruminations, it was he, not Sigurd Thaddeus Larson, who had encountered Helen as a fetching teenager. Despite Don's love for Beatrice, his fidelity could not forestall images of a younger version of Helen Ginsburg in the altogether intruding upon his nap.

The train slowed to enter St. Paul's Union Depot. The change in speed roused the reporter from a dreamscape filled with longing that, until he'd spoken with Helen in person, he hadn't believed possible. And yet, as Swanson wiped drool from his mouth and patted sweat from his face with a white linen handkerchief, that truth was evident.

She was and is a beauty, Don thought, as he rose from his seat, picked up his briefcase, slid the strap over his slender shoulder, and headed toward the exit. *Though I have no confirmation of the affair, there's not a doubt in my mind that our governor did what he's rumored to have done.*

CHAPTER SIX
May 1931

"The Cadillac blew a head gasket," Johnny Finn lamented as he stood in the front entry of Abram Rosenstein's and Agnes Jacobsen's home in Highland Park. "I had the beast towed to Plunket's Garage. Gabby says it'll be out of commission for a week," Johnny continued. "Sorry, Boss, but you'll need to call a cab to make your dinner engagement.'"

"Shit," Abram muttered, helping Agnes into her coat. "I don't much like being in public without that car. Or you."

Agnes pinched the Kid's right cheek. "It'll be fine, dear. The Lex's quiet and refined as speakeasies go. And," she added, buttoning her red, wool coat, and grabbing a matching leather purse from a bench in the foyer, "you do so love their T-bone!"

Abram grinned. "That's true. Still, I don't like being out and about without Johnny along for backup."

"I could ride along in the cab and hang out in the kitchen while you kids enjoy yourselves."

Rosenstein shook his head. "No, you were supposed to have the night off until this last-minute meeting with Moe came up," Abram said. "He wants to go over some news he thinks is important—too important to share on the phone, which means I can't beg off." The Kid opened the front door, and the trio ventured outside. "We'll take a cab, and you, my friend—you go and have yourself some fun," Abram said with finality as he shut and locked the door.

The Lexington—located at the corner of Lexington and Grand—would, after Prohibition's repeal, become a legitimate restaurant. But in 1931, the place operated outside of the law as a speakeasy and purveyor of decent meals. As with most such establishments, the owners paid a monthly fee to the local constabulary to ensure that the place wasn't raided. The same chief of police, John O'Connor, who worked with the underworld to provide sanctuary for visiting mobsters upheld a similar under-the-table arrangement between the city's speakeasies and its coppers.

Barry "Babe" Reardon (so nicknamed because he was a dead ringer for the legendary baseball slugger), the owner of the Lexington, paid his "dues" on time and, with his connection to Abram Rosenstein and Stuffy McNulty, was assured of a constant flow of whiskey, rye, gin, and rum. Beer was homebrewed in the Lex's basement, but given that it wasn't much good, it didn't really factor into Reardon's profit margin.

Abram and Agnes exited a taxi idling in front of the speakeasy, the Kid generously tipping the driver and asking him to return at eleven. The late spring sky was overcast, threatening rain. The cab departed, and the couple walked with verve toward a dazzlingly obvious neon sign announcing the Lex's illegality to the world.

"Good evening, Mr. Rosenstein, Mrs. Rosenstein," "Handsome" Harry Halom, the bouncer, said, greeting the couple with a smile as they entered the eatery.

Harry was a tall, angular Irishman with hands like bear paws who'd once played professional football for the Duluth Eskimos. When the team folded in '27, Harry found himself unemployed. Uncle Babe installed his out-of-work nephew as a bouncer at the Lexington, a job that paid well and allowed Harry no end of opportunity to flirt with shapely ladies frequenting the establishment. Given his blond hair, chiseled jaw, angled chin, and athletic build, Harry was always getting into jams involving "dates" considered to be the property of mobsters patronizing the place. But Babe had enough clout (and money) to smooth over most situations in which his none-too-bright nephew became entangled. "It's worth it to me," Babe had once confided to Abram, "to maintain peace with my sister by tamping down problems the boy causes and keeping him on the payroll."

That said, Harry had once come close to winding up in the Ramsey County Morgue. The bouncer had taken a fancy to a moll who'd entered the Lex on the arm of a Dillinger associate. When Harry's interest in the girl was returned in spades, the pair vanished, only to be surprised when the Dillinger man discovered them partially disrobed and headed toward bliss in a secret passageway behind the Lex's coatroom. The gangster encountered the lovers, lifted his .45 semi-automatic Browning from its holster, and pressed the business end of the pistol into Harry's left cheek with every intention of disrupting the bouncer's handsome smile. But Babe, who'd heard the woman's screams, opened the door to the passageway, found his nephew half-dressed with one foot in the grave, and smoothed things over.

After his near-death experience, Harry seemed, despite the dullness of his intellect, to have learned his lesson. In line with his reformation, the bouncer did not flirt with Kid Rose's woman—despite Agnes Jacobsen's exuded sensuality—as he greeted the couple.

Inside the Lex, the pungency of cigar and cigarette smoke, accented by the faint odor of marijuana, filled the dining room. Babe saw Abram and Agnes enter, smiled, waved, walked over, and ushered the couple to a corner booth occupied by Moe Feldman and a fetching companion. The Kid had not yet met Moe's new girlfriend, but he knew that Louise Gregorson, Moe's longtime squeeze, had succumbed—not to alcoholism as had been expected—but to tuberculosis. He'd heard that Moe had taken up with another working girl but the Kid had not, until that moment, met Lou's replacement.

"Good to see you, Kid," Moe said brightly, standing up and offering his right hand. The men exchanged a vigorous handshake. Feldman winked at Abram's companion. "And so nice to see you again, Agnes. You never age!"

"You're such a liar, Mr. Feldman!" Agnes replied through a bright smile. "But thanks all the same."

Abram and Agnes removed their coats, hung them on nearby hooks, and claimed seats in the booth across from their host. Moe filled four glasses with whiskey, neat, no ice, from a bottle sitting atop a white linen tablecloth. A waiter—dressed head to toe in white—appeared. "Anything other than the whiskey and ice water to drink?" he asked.

Moe looked at Abram, who shook his head. "We're fine. Give us a few minutes," Moe replied, before remembering he'd failed to introduce his escort. "This is Miss Melody Chastain," he said, turning to Abram after the waiter retreated. "And these fine folks are Mr. and Mrs.

Rosenstein," the brothel owner added, asserting the lie that protected Agnes from public scrutiny.

Kid Rose inventoried Miss Chastain, noting her flaming red hair, pale white skin interrupted by myriad freckles, and her generously proportioned body, before addressing her. "Call me Abram or Abe or Kid. They all work."

"Pleased to meet you, Kid," Melody said, her reply tinged with coquettishness.

"You can call me Agnes," the Kid's live-in urged, with an edge meant to solidify her standing.

"Pleased to meet you as well, Agnes," Melody replied, taking the hint and backing off.

Silence ensued as the couples studied menus. The waiter reappeared. Dinner was ordered, and more whiskey was poured. After making small talk, the food arrived, and the couples began to eat.

"So, Moe, what's on your mind?"

"It's not about business, Kid. At least directly."

Abram looked puzzled.

"I see you don't catch my drift," the older man observed. "What I mean to say is: I've heard tell you are urging Governor Larson to consider a run against Shipstead."

"How in the world . . .?

Moe chewed steak, swallowed, and cleared his throat. The brothel owner set down his fork and pointed to his right ear with his right index finger. "See this? Doesn't miss much!"

Abram guffawed, causing him to gag on a chunk of T-bone.

"Careful, love," Agnes whispered. "I don't want you choking to death."

Kid Rose swallowed and regained his composure. "I'm fine." He looked straight into the deep brown—nearly black—eyes of the bald man seated across the table. "OK. I get that. And yes, I've talked to Siggy about running for the Senate. Seems to me that with everyone's dander up about Prohibition, it's inevitable folks in Washington start pushing for repeal."

Moe Feldman nodded, took a swig of whiskey, put down the glass, and stroked his narrow hairless chin with his right hand. "That would not be good for your bottom line."

Abram stabbed a slice of cooked carrot, brought it to his mouth, and took it in. "True," he admitted after swallowing.

"Makes sense to send Larson to Washington to help out an old friend."

Kid Rose studied Moe. "Somethin' else eatin' you?"

Feldman tidied his napkin. The women continued chatting. Moe looked up from his lap and spoke in a soft, low tone. "I know you're not a religious man."

"That's obvious."

Moe smiled, but to Abram, the older man's reaction appeared defeated. "Well, you might think, given what I do for a living ...," he paused, and looked at Melody, but the girl was deep in conversation with Agnes and didn't acknowledge his glance, "... that I too avoid the Synagogue. But that's not the case. I attend services and try, as best as a fallen man can, to live a devout life."

"I know. But what does that have to do with Larson running for Senate?"

Silence ensued as a busboy removed dirty dishes. Once the table was cleared, the waiter returned, and Moe ordered chocolate cake and vanilla ice cream for the table. In a matter of minutes, the waiter reappeared from the kitchen and placed four desserts on the table.

"Another bottle of the Canadian blend," Abram said to the young waiter. "Put it on my tab."

"Very well, Mr. Rosenstein."

The men ate ice cream and cake and remained mute while waiting for the second bottle of whiskey. Agnes and Melody talked between bites of dessert, chatting about the latest fashion trends, and, obliquely, about leaving "the life," something Agnes had successfully accomplished and something Melody was hoping to do. "You keep giving Moe what he wants," Agnes whispered, "and he'll fall head-over-heels for you. This is your chance to get out, to start over."

Melody smiled but didn't reply.

The waiter brought another quart of Canadian. Abram poured whiskey into the four empty glasses. The women sipped liquor between bites of cake and ice cream, while the men returned to their discussion.

"Are you up on what's going on in Germany?" Moe finally asked, answering Abram's question with a question.

"Whatdaya mean?"

"Hitler and the laws he's putting in place to degrade our people."

"I know Hitler's no lover of the Star of David."

Moe averted his eyes to study the restaurant's pressed-tin ceiling. "It's getting worse," he finally said, returning his gaze to Abram. "Family over there—uncles and aunts and cousins—are anxious."

Kid Rose shrugged his shoulders. "So? Tell them to leave." Before Moe could respond, the Kid added: "What's this got to do with Larson?"

"I need to visit the powder room," Agnes interrupted. "Melody?"

The younger woman shook her head.

"Be right back," Agnes said, rising from the table and heading toward the lavatory.

"About Larson," the Kid repeated. "How's he connected to your German problem?"

"Family's too big to get them all out. Borders are closed to Jews unless you bribe the thugs running the show. It's gotten so expensive, even I can't afford to buy their exit." Moe paused to collect his thoughts. "Their only hope is America, seeing what's going on, and doing something about it." The phrase was delivered with what seemed to Kid Rose to be a hint of acceptance—or worse, a tacit admission that Feldman's relatives were doomed. "Shipstead is an antisemite. He won't be of any use. Electing Larson to Shipstead's seat would be of great benefit," Feldman added, inserting a hint of optimism into an otherwise dismal scenario.

Abram nodded. "I get your drift. With Siggy in Washington, he might be able to help."

"Exactly."

Agnes was returning from the lavatory when a ham-fisted knuckle breaker—a man Abram knew to be trouble—grabbed Agnes as she tried to pass his table and dragged her onto his lap.

"What in God's name do you think you're doing?" she screamed.

"Ain't you a fine one, acting all righteous and saintly when you's nothin' but a Jewman's whore."

Though Agnes's former profession remained safely concealed from her Highland Park neighbors, the man in question, Emil O'Connell, had frequented the brothel owned by Moe Feldman, where Kid Rose had worked as a bouncer and Agnes had plied her trade. And while Mrs. Agnes Rosenstein had elevated her appearance, manners, and poise since those untoward days, her high cheekbones were a dead giveaway to someone who'd frequented her former place of business. Though O'Connell had never been one of Agnes's customers, he'd been in and out of the building enough times to recognize the woman and announce her nefarious past to the world.

Agnes struggled to break free, but O'Connell, drunk and seeing the need to degrade the woman further, held Agnes fast while groping her right breast through her blouse and brassiere.

Abram was out of his seat in a flash. Handsome Harry was in the men's john, unable to address the mobster's transgression. O'Connell saw Abram coming, knew the Kid's reputation—as a hothead who could outfight men twice his size—and discarded Agnes like an unwanted ragdoll. In the process, O'Connell tore buttons from the front of Agnes's blouse, exposing her silk brassiere. Agnes clutched her chest and sobbed as she rocked back and forth on the floor. Melody gasped. Moe, transfixed by the chaos, remained silent until he saw O'Connell reach into his waistband.

"Gun!"

O'Connell pointed the business end of a .38 snub-nose at Rosenstein, but before the Irishman could pull the trigger, the Kid hit the man square on the chin with a solid right. The blow surprised O'Connell and caused him to drop the handgun. O'Connell regained his composure and balled his hands into fists. But there would be no bar-room brawl, as Kid Rose kneeled, retrieved the .38, aimed the revolver at the Irishman, and pulled the trigger.

CHAPTER SEVEN
May 1931

"What are you talking about, Don?"
  The conversation between Sergeant Simon Caine, newly retired from the Minneapolis Police Department, and Donald Emerson Swanson, the owner, editor, and chief reporter for the *St. Paul Truthsayer*—the muckraker's middle name given him by his mother as a bow to Ralph Waldo Emerson, the writer and thinker she admired most—took place in the Forum Café. The cavernous eatery on 7th Street South in downtown Minneapolis was frequented by blue-collar workers, professionals, and powerbrokers. The diner's interior, an array of Art Deco posh—boasting a stylized Viking motif, chrome walls, and glass tile—was a favorite of Don's. Caine was large of girth and short of stature, sporting a gray beard, muttonchops, and unruly, shoulder-length graying hair now that he was no longer a cop. Don, still mostly blond despite the rigors of running a newspaper on a shoestring budget and as lanky and thin as he'd been during his high school days, sat next to Caine at the lunch counter. Both men were perched on vinyl-covered stools, sipping hot coffee and eating cold sandwiches.
  "I told you I'd dig up more on the Golden girl, or Mrs. Ginsburg—however you wish to address her—than mere rumor."

Don had, upon his return to St. Paul from Oak Park with an empty notebook, gone to the *Truthsayer's* offices and telephoned Caine to grouse.
  "I never said you should march off on your own and interview her," Caine remonstrated during the call. "In fact, I told you I had another angle."
  Don argued with the cop, clear-minded and stubborn in his belief that Caine had said no such thing.
  "Check your notes from the last time we met. You'll find it there."
  After hanging up in a huff, Don had scurried about his office, tossing notebooks hither and yon, looking for the scribbles he'd written during his last in-person visit with

Caine. The two of them had met at the Marjorie McNeely Conservatory in Como Park. They'd sat on a stone wall near a gurgling fountain in the glass-domed paradise as Caine revealed details concerning Sigurd Larson's sordid past. Swanson took notes, all the while sensing that the illumination of truth and justice was nearly in his grasp. But somehow, the information Caine had conveyed had been misplaced and, as Don Swanson studied his notes on the train to Chicago, was nowhere to be found.

"Look for the name 'Fay Goldfine.' She's a friend of Ginsburg's and another gal I was going to interview."

That segment of the conversation in the conservatory, reduced to scrawls across white, lined notebook paper, was what Don was searching for as he tore apart his office. In the end, he'd found the missing notes, not at work but in a stack of papers on his desk at home.

"How'd I miss this?" Swanson lamented as he held up the missing notebook for Caine to see as they ate. "This would have been something to look into when I was in Chicago."

"For certain."

"Where do I find this 'Miss Goldfine'?"

"Mrs. Patchett. She's married, no kids, living a couple of doors down from Ginsburg."

"You mean ...?

The former cop nodded. "Yup. Could've killed two birds with one stone. You could've met with both Ginsburg and Patchett in one trip."

"Shit."

Caine smirked. "After you tore me a new one—without justification I might add—I knew you wouldn't want to take another ride to Chicago. So, I got Mrs. Patchett on the line and coaxed her to tell me what she knew." The ex-sergeant paused to gather his thoughts. "She was reluctant to break a confidence. But I impressed upon her how the guy who did the crime was now the governor of Minnesota and shouldn't, just because of his office and power, get away with abusing a young girl." Caine sipped ice water to clear his throat.

"The story is pretty simple. Being statutorily raped by a guy who was once the Hennepin County Attorney and is now Minnesota's governor isn't something a gal keeps to herself." Caine stopped talking, took a bite of his Denver sandwich, and swallowed. "Especially when confiding to your best friend, someone you've known since high school." Caine swigged cold milk from a glass and wiped froth from his whiskers with the back of a hand.

Don became edgy. "Get to the point, will you?"

"All right already." The cop shook his head. "I thought reporters were patient."

Don didn't reply. Caine continued.

"Apparently, Mrs. Ginsburg related the details of her one-night stand with Larson to Mrs. Patchett. Spilled the beans multiple times. Each version was consistent: Larson and Golden—now Ginsburg—got it on like goddamned bunnies when he was eighteen and she was only fifteen, still in junior high."

"For real?"

Cain watched an attractive waitress working the counter bend over, the movement exposing cleavage that brought a smile to the twice-divorced cop's face. "For real," Caine added, returning his attention to the conversation. "But here's the kicker. The guy who introduced Larson to the girl?"

"Yeah?" Don said tersely, impatience returning.

"Kid Rose."

"Holy shit!"

"Holy shit, indeed. Ginsberg is Rose's first cousin."

Don considered his ham-salad-on-rye sandwich. "Will Patchett talk?"

Caine smiled, exposing big, unruly front teeth. "Aren't you listening? Already has. But off the record: I couldn't take a formal statement. She won't repeat it to you—if that's what you're askin'. All we have is my word as to what she said."

The reporter put down the remainder of his sandwich and picked up his pencil. "She say anything else?"

Caine nodded and provided additional information—as related to him by Mrs. Fay Goldfine Patchett—concerning the night Sigurd Larson and an underaged Helen Golden Ginsburg made love on a picnic table.

CHAPTER EIGHT
June 1931

Abram Rosenstein admitted shooting Emile O'Connell to the homicide detectives interviewing him.

"I did it, gentlemen. But it was self-defense."

The problem for Kid Rose was that eyewitnesses confirmed he'd disarmed the Irishman, knocking the .38 out of O'Connell's hand before picking it up, aiming the pistol at the man, and pulling the trigger.

"No need to do that," was the refrain St. Paul Police Department detectives heard from folks who'd witnessed the altercation.

Given that most of the patrons in the Lex were of Irish heritage and given that the two detectives who whisked Abram away from the crime scene were also Irish, Kid Rose's claim fell on deaf ears.

"Get bail money, Moe," Abram had shouted as he was shoved into the back of an unmarked squad after shooting O'Connell in the face. "They'll arraign me in the morning."

"Consider it done!" Moe Feldman yelled from the sidewalk outside the Lex.

A burly homicide detective had swung in behind the steering wheel of the unmarked squad. His razor-thin partner slid onto the front bench seat of the Ford Model A. The cops shut their doors. The black sedan roared to life, pulled away from the curb, and vanished.

Agnes Jacobsen stood outside the speakeasy and watched the Ford squeal its tires and leave. She sobbed and shook with concern over what might happen to her common-law husband.

Melody Chastain enveloped Agnes in a hug. "It'll be fine," the redhead said quietly. "Moe says he's got a good lawyer on retainer for such situations."

Agnes shook her head and created distance. "I can't bear to think of Abram in jail for one minute, much less one night. He spent time at Red Wing and still has nightmares about the place."

"Moe will make sure he's taken care of."

Agnes shook her head again. "The fucking Irish. I don't trust them: no matter what Moe says. Abe killed one of their own. In this town," Agnes had continued, her tears finally abating, anger surpassing fear, "where the Micks control everything."

Moe had overheard Agnes, stepped up to the distraught woman, and offered her a clean white monogrammed handkerchief. "I play poker with Reddy Griffin," Feldman said quietly. Agnes accepted the square of starched linen and dabbed her cheeks. "He's the go-between between Dapper Dan and Chief O' Connor. Already called Reddy. He's got men working in the lockup. They'll put Abram in solitary, out of the general population: keep him away from anyone connected to O'Connell. He'll be safe until morning, when I'll attend his arraignment and post bail."

"Thank you, Moe."

The story presented to jurors during Kid Rose's manslaughter trial in June of 1931 was a fable.

In the version of the shooting Moe Feldman related to Bill O'Malley—the attorney hired to defend Abram Rosenstein—during trial preparation and again under oath to jurors in front of Judge George Manion—another Irishman and the former Ramsey County Attorney—was that O'Connor's revolver had discharged when it was knocked out of the mobster's hand by an irate, yet justified, Mr. Rosenstein.

"An accident, plain and simple?" O'Malley asked Feldman when Moe took the witness stand at trial.

"Objection, Your Honor!" said Stephen Bailey, the Assistant Ramsey County Attorney presenting the state's case, rising to his feet. "Calls for a legal conclusion."

"Sustained. The jury will disregard the question."

But Moe was not about to have his response, an answer that could save his friend, curtailed. "Yes. An accident. Mr. Rosenstein, in coming to the defense of Mrs. Rosenstein, merely intended to disarm the brute who had dishonored her."

"Your Honor!" Bailey bellowed, his face flashing anger. "I move for an immediate mistrial."

Judge Manion glowered at Feldman. But the judge's scrutiny softened when he noted Mrs. Rosenstein's blond-headed, androgenous presence weeping softly in the pew behind the attorneys and the defendant.

What the judge did not appreciate—and what even the prosecutor did not know—was that Abram and Agnes were not married. Bill O'Malley was, however, privy to that truth and, consequently, was in a pickle when it came to Agnes's presence during the trial.

"I can't assert spousal privilege directly," O'Malley had told Abram during a conference where Kid Rose revealed the lie he and Agnes were living. "If I claim you're married, I'm defrauding the court. I could be disbarred," the lawyer murmured, turning toward Moe Feldman, a man he'd represented regarding disorderly house, prostitution, and white slavery charges for more than a decade. "What the hell have you gotten me into, Moe?"

Feldman had pondered the situation. "What about Miss Chastain and I setting the scene as to why Abram went after O'Connell. We were eyewitnesses to O'Connell's assault on Agnes. That way, we keep her out of it."

O'Malley mulled over the suggestion. "But what if Baily tries to call Agnes as *his* witness?"

Abram had considered the dilemma. "Can't you simply say, 'Your Honor, given the marital privilege . . .'?"

Moe smiled. "Brilliant, Kid. That way, Bill, you're not *directly* claiming they're married. You're only making an insinuation, a *suggestion*, of such being the case."

O'Malley sipped coffee, swallowed, and nodded. "That could work. Provided, when I say the words, and Bailey tries to press the issue, the good judge shuts him down."

"You know Manion. Is that likely?"

O'Malley had considered the point and nodded. "It is. He's no-nonsense, loves to drive the train. I think it'll work."

The scenario played out exactly as Bill O'Malley hoped. When Bailey attempted to call and examine Agnes as a hostile witness, and O'Malley insinuated that marital privilege—a legal precept preventing one spouse from testifying against the other spouse—*might* apply, Judge Manion raised his hand and silenced the prosecutor. The good jurist, without hearing Bailey's argument, had then ruled that Mrs. Rosenstein could not be compelled to take the witness stand, thereby disposing of the issue.

The ruling regarding Agnes's status was foremost in Judge Manion's mind as he studied the anguished woman crying in the front row of the courtroom gallery. *I've been around long enough to know real tears when I see them,* Manion thought, mindful that he needed to make a ruling concerning Feldman's outburst. He cataloged his options, including granting the state's motion for a mistrial, before rendering his decision.

"Motion denied. The jury is ordered to disregard anything Mr. Feldman uttered after I sustained the state's objection. You are not to consider Mr. Feldman's opinion, his belief that the shooting was accidental, including any implied reference to the defendant's state of mind. That is the ruling of the Court."

The judge ignored the ire on Stephen Bailey's face, knowing full well that his admonition had, in fact, highlighted Moe Feldman's opinion that the shooting was accidental. "Anything further, Counselor?"

"The defense rests, Your Honor," Bill O'Malley said, suppressing a smile.

Rebuttal witnesses called by the state could not unring the bell. The jury deliberated for ten minutes—foregoing the free lunch promised by the bailiff—and found Abram Rosenstein not guilty of manslaughter.

A just result, Judge Manion thought, after thanking the jurors for their service, banging his gavel, smiling at the woman he believed to be Mrs. Abram Rosenstein, rising from his chair, and exiting the courtroom.

CHAPTER NINE
November 1931

Sigurd Larson lay atop Amelia. His eyes were closed. He was still. His prosthesis and cane leaned against a bedroom wall. His breathing was steady and calm. His heartbeat had slowed. He opened his eyes to find his wife's lovely cocoa-brown eyes inventorying him, a slight smile dimpling her flushed cheeks.

Her cleft is almost invisible, he thought, as he studied her face. *The work those surgeons did is amazing.*

He knew, from the one time he and Amelia—early on during their courtship—had discussed her condition, that his wife, despite the minimal scar left by two surgeries, considered herself blessed.

"In ancient Sparta," Am' had said, on that singular occasion, "newborns with clefts were left to die of exposure on Mount Tagete. In Rome, babies with cleft lips or palates were thrown into the Tiber. Even Plato went along with such purges, believing—as many did—the condition to be a sign of an evil spirit."

"That's awful," Sig had mumbled, trying not to envision such a fate befalling the woman he loved, "not to mention barbaric."

She had nodded, smiled, and kissed him. "'Twas. But thankfully, I was born into a different time . . ."

"That was astounding . . ." Amelia whispered.

Sigurd rolled off his wife. Free of Sig's weight, Am' breathed normally.

"It certainly was," he agreed.

Sig relished the intensity of their couplings because such unions masked a new, intrusive pain in his low back: a recently manifested annoyance that Sig ascribed to his wartime injuries.

Just that morning, he'd brought a load of maple firewood into the family's rented mansion on Crocus Hill and had, in the process of dumping logs into a copper hopper next to the fireplace, felt a twinge in his low back. Sig had doctored himself by taking two aspirins, followed by a shot of gin, which dulled the agony. But when he and Am' had moved together in bed, Sig's backache had returned, dissipating only when carnal pleasure overwhelmed all other sensations.

"How's your back?"

"Fine. Seems whatever we did set things right."

Am' drew the bedsheet over her small brown-nippled breasts, her bosom having returned to its natural curvature after she'd finished nursing their son. Birthing Michael had been arduously long, painful, and ultimately destructive. Amelia was—at thirty-two—the victim of a hysterectomy and no longer able to conceive: a circumstance she once viewed as tragic but, given the renewed vigor of their love life, came to realize was a blessing. *No more worrying about pregnancy ...*

"I wonder how Michael is doing?" Sigurd asked.

Amelia playfully tugged her husband's right earlobe, ignored stickiness on her thigh, and whispered: "He's fine. Spending the week with my parents will do the child some good." Her deep-set eyes scrutinized Sig's face, taking in its handsome Nordic lines, before she wiggled out of the sheet, left his side, and floated naked across the bedroom toward the master bath. "After that," she said impishly, "I need a nice, long, hot soak."

"We still driving to Stillwater to pick Michael up?" Sig asked. "Spending Thanksgiving Day and staying overnight with your parents?"

"As we agreed. Why?" Amelia asked, looking back at Sig while holding a terrycloth robe in her left hand.

Sigurd, spent as he was, could not help admiring his wife's intimacies. The scar that faintly creased her firm tummy, rather than disfiguring and troubling, reinforced the sacrifice Amelia had made by giving birth to their son. "Oh, nothing important. Just trying to make sure I understand the schedule."

She nodded, stepped into the lavatory, and closed the door. Sig heard water gush from the bathtub's taps. He lay in silence, considering his good fortune, and, after a few minutes, heard his wife slide into water.

The Teamsters' strike had ended in an amicable negotiated settlement. Shortly after the agreement between the truckers and the owners was announced, another union dispute, one involving a meat packing plant in Worthington, required the governor's attention. Larson mediated a common-sense approach to resolving the meat packers' demands for shorter hours and higher pay by getting American Packing to agree to limit mandatory overtime and increase the hourly wage—not quite as generously as union leadership hoped, but enough to gain approval from their membership. However, continued financial instability, unprecedented bank failures, and resultant poverty solidified angry distrust between working men and women and farmers on one side of the economic divide and the owners of factories, banks, railroads, grain mills, and iron ore mines on the other.

As Minnesota's economy faltered in the grasp of the Great Depression, farmers attempted Farm Holidays—boycotts whereby farmers refused to bring crops or livestock to market and, in the case of dairy farmers, dumped tons of milk on the ground to protest low prices. Such Holidays caused no real changes to be enacted by the legislature to protect family farms; in fact, they resulted in a surge of foreclosures due to striking farmers being unable to meet their mortgage obligations.

County sheriffs sent deputies to monitor the auctioning of livestock, tractors, and farm implements that were subject to bank loans once a farm was emptied of the family's meager personal possessions—the farmer, his wife, and their children taking with them their clothing, furniture, toys, books, cookware, and hand tools. The remaining items—all of which were subject to bank liens—were offered for sale to the public. After encumbered moveable property was sold, the involved lender would then sell the land and its structures to the highest bidder. These auctions, where the lifeblood of rural Minnesota was being snatched up for pennies on the dollar by greedy, unscrupulous speculators, caused a rift between Governor Larson and rural members of his own party.

Each Farmer Labor Club—local units of the FLA and the backbone of the FLP—notified its membership when farm auctions were scheduled. On the appointed day, club members would show up at the affected farm. Neighbors in attendance remained orderly, not because they were intimidated by the deputies supervising the sale, but because violence was not the goal of the FL'ers in attendance.

"What's the bid for this fine Holstein?" an auctioneer might bellow out. "Starting value's twenty dollars."

"Ten cents," an FLA man or woman in the crowd might say.

"That's outlandish!" the auctioneer would retort. "Why, she's a fine milk producer and, if even only bought to butcher, the twenty-dollar starting point is too low!"

"My offer's still ten cents," the bidder would repeat.

If an outsider, a stranger, or anyone dressed in a business suit attempted to voice a competing bid, FLA'ers would surround the interloper and make it clear that his or her participation in the auction was not welcome—not welcome at all.

Offering up a like-new Allis Chalmers narrow-front tractor would garner a dollar bid; announcing a hay mow for purchase prompted someone to offer a quarter; displaying a sow and her ten suckling piglets drew a bid of a nickel. In frustration, the auctioneer would look to the banker for direction. The money man would shrug, make a cutting motion across his throat, and put an end to the farce. The intent of the FL'ers in attendance was to buy back a farm's assets—piece by piece for pittances—and then gift the retrieved property to the farm's former owners. Though the FLA's tactics only delayed the inevitable, they were effective enough to put Governor Larson in a bind.

By overwhelmingly winning the gubernatorial race in 1930 under the All-Party banner, Larson compromised the ideals and principles of the FLP. By relying upon the support of Progressive Republicans, disgruntled mainstream Conservatives, and disaffected Democrats—Larson attained the governorship but lost a defined platform from which to move the state forward. By engaging in boycotts and protests that delayed farm foreclosures, Larson's fellow FL'ers were at odds with small business owners and local bankers who, though they'd grown tired of do-nothing Hooverism sufficiently to support Larson, weren't willing to forego their legal rights, including the right to collect on overdue debts.

"Damn it, Sig . . ." Larson muttered to himself. "What are you going to do?" The tall, stately man cursed as he left his marital bed, shifting his internal rumination from intraparty difficulties to a proposal Abram Rosenstein had advanced while they lunched at the University Club.

"You need to run against Shipstead," Kid Rose had suggested, as they ate corned beef and cabbage stew in the elegant private club on St. Paul's Crocus Hill.

"He's an FL'er. I'd have to take him on in the '34 primary."

"So?"

Sigurd finished eating before answering. "I'm not interested in fighting with my own party."

Abram looked around, determined no one else was listening, and muttered, "Bullshit. Henrik Shipstead is no more an FL'er than Old Lindbergh was."

Larson understood the reference. "I'll grant you that the Flyboy's father bent himself into a pretzel trying to get elected as a Nonpartisan Leaguer and then, before he died in the middle of the '24 campaign, as an FL'er," Sig admitted. "I'll also grant you that Henrik Shipstead is less of an FL'er and more of a Republican't than most."

Abram laughed. "Republican't! I like that one!"

"I *can't* take credit for the term," Larson said, smiling broadly. "Am' came up with that gem when talking to the press about the failures of Hoover to lift folks out of despair and poverty."

"It fits."

"I'm not so sure it fits Shipstead. Jury's still out on his true heart. I'm willing to give him the benefit of the doubt."

"Don't. Listen, my old friend: I'm needing some help here, and Henrik Shipstead isn't about to listen to a Jewish bootlegger from North Minneapolis."

"*Alleged* bootlegger. I can't be seen in public with a *convicted* criminal."

"The jury acquitted me of the shooting, you know."

"I *do* know."

"So other than some nasty rumors and some dicey juvenile, shall we say, *circumstances*, I'm as clean as a new born babe."

"Right . . ."

"You seem skeptical."

"Now who's full of bullshit?" Sig whispered, ensuring his expletive wouldn't be overheard.

"Think about it."

"What?"

"Challenging Shipstead."

"Why?"

"Prohibition will soon be on the table," Abram said, taking a long draw of hot coffee from his cup.

"And?"

The Kid narrowed his eyes. "I'll need your help."

The governor looked at the ceiling, thought a moment, and resumed scrutinizing his childhood friend. "That's a heavy lift."

"You're a strong man," Abram rejoined. "Besides, opposing repeal would endear you to your in-laws."

Larson chuckled. "You've been talking to Pastor Salveson and his good wife?"

"Don't need to. They're all over the papers, with their letters to the editor in opposition to repeal. Hurts my feelings, of course, to know Amelia's parents think I'm a crook."

"Ha!"

"But, back to '34. Think about challenging that *Republican't* hiding inside your party, Mister Governor."

Sigurd Thaddeus Larson had nodded but made no promises.

"I'm going down to the kitchen," Sig called out to his wife after strapping his prosthesis onto the stump of his left leg, putting on fresh boxers, and dressing for the day. "Am'?"

"I'll meet you downstairs," Amelia replied from her bath, her attention fixed on shaving her legs with a straight razor. "Make something dreamy for breakfast, would you, dear?"

"Eggs, toast, bacon, and American fries?"

"I'm more in the mood for pancakes. With some of that pure maple syrup your farmer friend from Hill City sent us. But yes: bacon, toast, and potatoes of some sort as well. I'm famished," Am' added, hinting at their recent encounter.

"As you wish, my queen," Sig replied, leaving his wife to her privacy. The governor picked up his cane, exited the bedroom, descended the staircase, entered the home's expansive kitchen, and began making a mess—one Amelia would eventually have to clean up.

CHAPTER TEN
November 1931

Otis Lathrop sat at the bar of Casey's Saloon—the watering hole being one of the most decadent places in Minneapolis to wet one's whistle. The good doctor—the adjective being somewhat inflated when it came to a former surgeon who had, due to alcohol abuse and extramarital affairs, lost his medical license, his surgical practice, an academic appointment at the University of Minnesota, and his family—was pie-eyed. He'd had more than his fill of cheap English gin, as he sat by himself in the dark and musty tavern.

A large man, his face marred from departed acne, his hair thick, black, and greasy, opened the saloon's front door and entered the establishment, accompanied by another impressive figure—a gentleman of lesser height but more heavily muscled. A bouncer sitting on a stool near the door eyeballed the two men, nodded, and let them pass.

"Beers," said the shorter, more bullishly configured newcomer to the barkeep as the men selected stools next to the disgraced doctor.

The bartender grunted, picked up two glasses, wiped dust from the rims, and poured beer from a tap.

"Nasty weather we're having, eh?"

Doc Lathrop didn't realize the shorter of the two strangers was addressing him.

"Cat got your tongue, Mister? Or are you just being unsociable?"

"You talkin' to me?"

"I am."

"Oh. Sorry. Didn't know you were. How's that again?"

The bartender finished his pours and slid two glasses of foamy draft lager, the beer made in the speakeasy's basement, placed in kegs, and hooked to the establishment's refrigeration system to provide cold beverages to thirsty working men in front of the new customers. The taller man picked up his glass and slurped foam as he scrutinized—like a wolf scanning a sheepfold—other patrons in the saloon.

"I said: 'The weather's for shit today.'"

"'Tis."

The shorter of the two men extended a world-weary right hand. "John Epstein," he said. "But you can call me 'Johnny Finn.' Everyone does. Right, Burt?"

Burt nodded but said nothing.

"Twenty cents," the barkeep said, holding out his left palm.

Burt snorted, pulled two dimes from the front pocket of his dungarees, and placed them in the man's hand. The bartender returned Burt's unsociable look and retreated to the till.

Lathrop reciprocated Finn's handshake. "What do you fellows do for work?"

"Who wants to know?" Burt said curtly.

Johnny, who'd recovered from the wounds he'd received during the Teamsters' strike, slapped his companion on the back. "Cut the animosity, Burt. Doctor Lathrop is just interested in what we do for a living. Am I right, Doc?"

Lathrop winced, as if stung by a wasp. "How is it you know my name? And that I'm a doctor?"

Johnny smiled, exposing teeth yellowed from coffee and chewing tobacco. "Relax. Don't everyone 'round here know who 'Doc Lathrop' is?" Finn's genteel manner eased Lathrop's alarm.

"I guess so."

"But you asked a question . . ."

Lathrop nodded.

"We're out-of-work plumbers, looking for leaks," Johnny said through a wry smile.

Burt guffawed. "Yeah, that's us. Two plumbers looking to <u>plug</u> leaks!"

Johnny Finn glared at his companion. He was concerned that Burt might unintentionally reveal their purpose in stalking, finding, and ultimately dealing with the abortionist. But Burt had returned to eyeballing other patrons and didn't detect Johnny's change in demeanor.

"Need to use the facilities," Lathrop said, after finishing his drink. "Watch my spot, will you, boys?" he asked, sliding off the barstool and staggering toward the lavatory.

"Sure thing," Finn replied. "I'll order you one on Burt," he quipped, gesturing to the barkeep to refill Lathrop's glass.

The bartender poured. Burt paid. The restroom door opened. Doc Lathrop entered the lavatory. The door slammed behind him. Johnny reached into a pocket of his Pendleton shirt, removed a glass vial filled with white powder, and emptied the vial's contents into the abortionist's drink.

"Took care of our little *plumbing* problem," Johnny said, sitting on a chair in front of Abram Rosenstein's cluttered desk. The Kid's office was in what had once been the dining room of an elegant home. The old building—rundown, needing paint, cleaning, and tender loving care—housed one of Moe Feldman's brothels.

Abram frowned. "Don't want to know the details."

Johnny removed a tin of chewing tobacco from a shirt pocket, opened it, took out a pinch, wedged it between teeth and gums, and grinned. "They'll never find the baby killer."

"I said," Abram repeated with edge, "I don't want to know the 'how' or the 'where', only that the authorities won't be parading that damn quack in front of a grand jury."

Finn nodded. His role was to clean up messes, not to pontificate as to his methods. But he couldn't resist having the final say on the matter: "He went quietly. No fuss. No muss. That Micky Finn," Johnny said, smiling at the nickname of the powerful sedative he'd slipped into Doc Lathrop's gin, "did the trick."

Kid Rose said nothing.

"About Chicago . . ." Johnny finally asked.

"Yes?"

"How you gonna handle your cousin's friend?"

Rosenstein stared hard at his sergeant-at-arms. "McNulty made a call for me."

"Nice."

Kid Rose looked at his hands, noted that his fingernails needed trimming, and asked, "Anything else?"

Finn shook his head. "No, Boss."

Abram stared out a window. "It's snowing again. Maybe time to put chains on the Caddie."

"Sure thing, Boss."

When Helen called a few days later, Abram feigned a consoling tone.

"Did you hear?"

"What?"

"About my neighbor, my best friend from high school, Fay Patchett."

"Don't think I've met her."

Abram's cousin began to cry, emitting guttural, animal-like sounds akin to the whimpering of a puppy looking for its mother's teat. "Helen?"

"No, you haven't. But we were as close as sisters," she whispered through sobs.

The Kid let his cousin have her cry. *It had to be done. You blabbed, even though I told you not to talk about that night. With anyone. Not with your rabbi, your husband, or God forbid, to some Oak Park housewife. But you didn't listen, did you?* As the woman wept, Kid Rose suppressed an urge to explain, in no uncertain terms, that the car crash that claimed Fay Patchett's life was Helen's doing. But he couldn't reveal his hand behind the unfortunate woman's end. "Cousin . . ."

Helen found a snippet of composure and calmed. "Yes?"

"What happened?"

The distraught woman took a breath and told the story.

On the way to see friends in Milwaukee, a jallopified 1924 Buick roadster driven by Mrs. Patchett went off the road and struck a tree. According to the coroner, the woman died of a broken neck. Racine cops examining the car's brake lines discovered a small leak had allowed the car to brake normally until it didn't. That was the *official* cause of Fay Patchett's untimely death: accidental brake line failure.

The North Siders behind the hole in the line, easily accomplished at night as the Buick sat on the street in front of the Patchetts' modest home, had followed Fay north in a Ford Model A. But the *whole* truth, unknown even to

Abram Rosenstein, was that, after hitting the tree, Fay Patchett was not dead. A gangster in the surveilling Ford exited the car, walked to the disabled Buick, and discovered Mrs. Patchett slumped over the steering wheel, unconscious but still breathing. It was a simple matter for the nameless assassin to snap Fay's flaccid neck before she came to.

"I'm sorry," Abram said, when Helen was done relating what she knew. He waited for his words to sink in before proceeding. *I am truly sorry to order the execution of a young woman,* he thought. "But," Abram's voice turned sharp, "sometimes things happen to innocent people when they know too much."

"What are you saying?" Helen gasped.

He was not about to spell it out for her. Helen was a smart, modern young woman who had given up dreams of college to settle down with a cop and raise a family. He let the innuendo sink in. "You know very well what I'm saying."

"You had my best friend killed?"

Abram didn't consider himself to be coldblooded. He was simply a practical man living in an impractical world. He regretted being placed in a position to ask McNulty, who in turn asked Bugs Moran for a favor. But he couldn't admit his part in Fay Patchett's death—not even to his cousin. "I never said that."

Helen became upset. "You certainly inferred it! And you also inferred that her death was somehow my fault!"

"I'm not God. I won't postulate as to why some folks live and some folks die. Save that for the synagogue."

Helen grew exasperated. "You bastard!"

Perhaps. But unpleasant things do, from time to time, need to be done. Even to a nice, goodly, honorable young woman who could, if allowed to talk to muckraking reporters, end a friend's political career. "I think you know what you need to do, Cousin, so that no further *accidents* occur."

Helen slammed the telephone's receiver down without responding. But Abram Rosenstein knew his message had been received. Despite Helen Ginsburg being married to a cop, she would never reveal her suspicions to her husband. Kid Rose was also certain that Cousin Helen would never again relate the details of the night she spent with Governor Sigurd Thaddeus Larson to anyone, including her rabbi.

CHAPTER ELEVEN
November 1931

***You** pull on a loose thread,* Johnny Finn thought, watching the tenement building at the corner of Plymouth and DuPont, *and the whole damn coat falls apart.* It was a saying his father had oft repeated to Jôhānān Epstein during Jôhānān's childhood. As he surveilled a whorehouse owned by Moe Feldman, waiting for a signal from Gretchen Holmgren that Detective Derrick Newhouse was asleep, the thought of the last loose thread threatening the fabric of Governor Larson's future being mended made Johnny smile. *I'm a tailor—a tradesman—something Father and Mother can be proud of!*

Sigurd Larson had considered making an announcement—after consulting his wife and supporters within the FLP, and after taking stock of Henrik Shipstead's record in the United States Senate—that he'd run for one additional term as governor, and then seek Shipstead's post. Gubernatorial terms were two years. Sigurd had been elected governor in 1930, meaning he would, if he was returned to office in 1932, serve four years as the state's chief executive. Larson's plan was to announce a challenge to Shipstead in late 1931, while still gathering support for a second gubernatorial bid. He would oppose the sitting senator in the 1934 FLP primary—regardless of whether he was endorsed by the party or not. An announcement of his intentions two years ahead of an intraparty challenge would give Larson time to muster support for his coup. Having reached a conclusion on the point, Sigurd Larson delayed making any public pronouncements regarding his ambitions, waiting, as a prairie farmer does, to harvest his wheat only when it's ripe.

The Kid is right, Sig had ultimately concluded. *I need to give it a go.* Larson wasn't concerned that if he ran against Shipstead, won the FLP endorsement—or the primary—but lost the general election, he'd be labeled a has-been. *Got more gasoline in the tank than that*, he thought. *I'm only thirty years old: A youngster in terms of political life. The world is my oyster. I can do anything I set my mind to.* The real question in Sigurd's mind was whether—if he became a United States Senator—he could repay Abram Rosenstein's loyalty. *Blocking the repeal of Prohibition is an iffy proposition.*

He'd met clandestinely with Abram Rosenstein and Moe Feldman. Moe made his pitch concerning the Jewish situation in Germany, and after dutifully listening and promising to take the plight of the Jews to heart, Larson was assured of Moe's full support. Left unsaid, but understood by the governor, was that Abram Rosenstein, Larson's old friend and a man who kept close the governor's secrets—things even Amelia knew nothing about—would take care of business. No details were shared between Kid Rose and Sigurd Larson, and yet the state's chief executive instinctively knew the extent to which the bootlegger would go to ensure Larson's success.

In keeping with their understanding, Abram did not discuss with the governor another extremely delicate matter requiring Johnny Finn's considerable talents. *Mending a loose thread before the whole coat unravels!* he thought, chuckling to himself at Johnny's cleverness. *I like it!*

Gretchen Holmgren had been sleeping with Derrick Newhouse for several months when she was approached by Moe Feldman to "Have a drink with Johnny Finn—no hanky-panky required."

Johnny and Gretchen had met at the Blue Heron, a neighborhood speakeasy down the street from the whorehouse where Gretchen lived and worked. After exchanging pleasantries, the pair talked in hushed tones over glasses of bootlegged Canadian. As the conversation drew to a close, Johnny had slipped the whore a twenty—her normal nightly rate—plus an additional two hundred in "traveling money" before asking her to share the pattern of Detective Newhouse's comings and goings.

"Thursday night, he'll be here," the girl said. "He gets off shift at five. We'll have a bite to eat at the Heron and then head back to my room."

"Perfect," Johnny had whispered, before adding, "Thanks a lot, hon."

Gretchen knew better than to question why the brooding, scary man with the unique accent was asking about the cop. *None of my business,* she told herself as the gangster gave her simple instructions concerning Thursday evening, stood up, donned his four-square cap and coat, and left her to finish her drink. *What Moe wants done, I'll do and not ask questions.*

"I need a bath," the prostitute said, after she and Newhouse finished their Thursday night tryst. "You wore me out," Gretchen added, pecking Newhouse on the cheek as she left her bed, grabbed a silk robe, covered up, and headed toward the bathroom shared by the girls on her floor. The door to the hallway opened. The whore's departure caused Newhouse to sit up, grin, and watch his lover bounce away.

Down the hall, Gretchen closed and locked the bathroom door, drew her bath, disrobed, and slid into an ornate porcelain tub. Moe had spared no expense in refurbishing the lavatories of the brothel. Plumbers, tile layers, carpenters, and electricians had ensured that the community powder rooms in the building were exquisitely appointed. Gretchen luxuriated in hot, soapy water, scrubbing away untoward memories. The girl attacked her sins with a bar of Ivory soap and a washcloth while humming a tune her mother had sung during Gretchen's childhood baths.

As the prostitute soaked, Newhouse swallowed the last bit of laudanum in his flask, turned out the light, and fell asleep.

This isn't my end game, Gretchen thought as she stepped out of the tub, pulled the black rubber stopper free of the drain, and dried off. Wrapping a towel around her wet, shoulder-length blond hair, Gretchen studied her body in the full-length mirror Moe's remodelers had installed. The working girls were unaware that their boss spent much of his time flitting from one floor to another in the whorehouse, watching naked women take care of all manner of personal hygiene through one-way glass the girls believed to be a mirror. What Moe did as he watched, only he can say. In any event, as Gretchen scrutinized her reflection, the brothel owner was not behind the mirror. *I'll use the money to vamoose. Time to get the hell out of this town,* she concluded before sliding her damp body into the scarlet, silk robe adorned with white lotus flowers—a birthday gift from Moe—and exiting the steamy room.

How Gretchen Holmgren would survive unskilled, uneducated, twenty years old, and alone in the world without a mother or a father—her parents having died from the Influenza—she had no earthly idea. As the girl walked back to her room in bare feet, her soles chilled by the hardwood floor, she was confident of one thing and one thing only: whatever the big Finlander had in store for Newhouse wasn't something she wanted—or needed—to know.

Gretchen opened the door, entered her room, closed the door, crossed carpeting, stepped up to a window, raised the shade, and peered outside. A black Cadillac, one she'd seen Johnny Finn park in front of the Blue Heron, was idling on the street below. *Time to scram,* Gretchen thought. She dressed in a flurry, not bothering to rouge her cheeks, brush her hair, or draw lipstick across her precocious lips. As she packed her things, the girl cast intermittent, furtive glances toward Newhouse, who slumbered sonorously in her bed.

Goodbye, the girl thought, picking up a cloth valise containing the entirety of her worldly belongings. *I can't say it's been a pleasure.* Gretchen Holmgren walked to the light switch and, as per prearrangement with Johnny Finn, flicked it three times before leaving her room—and her past—behind.

CHAPTER TWELVE

Governor Larson to Run For Second Term: May Challenge Shipstead in '34
(*Farmer Laborer Leader*, December 20, 1931)

Shit, Donald Swanson thought, as he put down the paper printed by his competition. *Scooped again.*

"I tried to reach out to Fay Goldfine like you asked," Simon Caine had related during a telephone conversation earlier that day. The ex-cop's inflection had been a dead giveaway that something was amiss. "Tried to set up a meeting with her in Oak Park and take her statement about Helen Ginsburg's one-night stand with that piece-of-shit who calls himself 'Governor'."

"And?"

"Got her husband instead. He was a basket case, given his wife had just been killed in a car accident."

"She's dead?"

"Yessiree Bob."

"Goddamn it!" As Don had paused to collect his thoughts, it dawned on him that Fay Patchett's demise might be more than mere coincidence. Why his mind wandered down such a twisted path, he had no idea. It was just a hunch, a suspicion, that made him consider the notion that, perhaps, just perhaps, Mrs. Patchett's death might somehow be tied to Kid Rose. "You sure it was an accident?"

The retired cop didn't answer.

"Simon?"

"The investigation by Racine PD turned up 'brake failure' as the cause."

"So, an accident?"

More silence.

"Sergeant?"

Caine mulled over a response. "Sure. Unless you take the train to Racine, spend time inspecting the brake line, and find a very suspicious hole—one that slowly leaked fluid, which caused the brakes to fail."

"You did that?"

"Yes, sir."

"Out with it: What's your thinking?"

"Someone tampered with the line. Made it look like fluid leaked out due to ordinary wear and tear. It was very professionally done, which is why the Racine cops, who were perfunctory in their examination, thought the woman's death was accidental."

"Shit."

Caine had continued. "I can't say who did the deed. But I have a pretty good guess."

"Kid Rose?"

"Not directly."

"But you have a theory?"

"I do."

"Damn it, Simon. Out with it!"

"Rosenstein is connected—through Stuffy McNulty—to the North Side Gang in Chicago. Bugs Moran and the like. Know of them?"

"Heard of them."

"They supply McNulty and Rosenstein with booze. That's likely to change, given the Italians are taking over. But for now, there's a direct link, a link that both Chicago PD and Agent Ness of the Prohibition Bureau confirm, between Kid Rose and Bugs Moran."

"What does that have to do with an Oak Park housewife dying in a car crash?"

There had been another pause. "I have no proof, you understand, only a theory," Caine finally admitted.

"Go on."

"Seems to me that, with you getting closer and closer to unraveling Larson's past, including whatever it was that Mrs. Patchett might have known about the statutory rape of an underage Helen Golden Ginsburg, along with the rumor that Larson will challenge Shipstead, a move that would, if the asshole wins, give Rosenstein and McNulty a voice in the upcoming Prohibition fight . . . well, it doesn't take much of a genius to figure out who's behind the 'accident'."

"Makes sense. But her death leaves me with no way to confirm the rumor that Larson slept with a fifteen-year-old girl."

"True."

The conversation stalled as the ex-cop determined how best to let the other shoes—plural—drop.

"Something else you want to tell me?"

The cop cleared his throat.

Don Swanson heard traffic, the honking of horns, the whirling of motors, the sounds of a city at work behind Simon Caine. "Get to it, man. I haven't all day."

"There are two other incidents that support my theory."

"OK . . ."

"Newhouse, the detective who investigated the death of Councilman Miller's daughter, a guy I've been trying to get a sit-down with . . ."

"Yes?"

"He's also dead."

That news so shocked Swanson, it brought bile to his mouth. "Shit." He paused to swallow, regain his composure, and push on. "How?"

"Overdose. Heroin. Died in a whorehouse on DuPont, in a building owned by Moe Feldman."

"The Kid's benefactor?"

"The very same."

"I take it you have suspicions concerning his death as well?"

"Doesn't take much imagination to figure out who's behind it." Simon Caine had glanced out a window to witness snow cloaking the adjoining street. Passersby on snow-drifted sidewalks, surprised by the sudden shift in weather, struggled forward—hatless, bootless, and gloveless—as powdery flakes propelled by a Dakotan wind brought Minneapolis to a standstill.

"Rosenstein and Feldman?"

"Yup."

"I'm guessing Newhouse's death was also ruled an 'accident'?"

"Yup. Newhouse was an addict. But he was a laudanum man—not a heroin mainliner. That's what makes his death curious, to say the least, given he died with a syringe by his side. Looking at pictures taken by the police photographer it appears Newhouse had bruising on his wrists: as if someone held him down. But the coroner was vehement in his opinion, and, because Newhouse wasn't particularly liked by other cops, his death was classified as an 'accidental overdose'."

"Christ." Again, there had been silence. "Oh, for Pete's sake, Caine. You're not telling me . . ."

"'Fraid so," Simon Caine said apologetically. "There's more bad news."

"Can't get much worse. Let's hear it."

"Doc Lathrop has vanished."

"The abortionist?"

"Yes."

"When you say 'vanished' . . ."

"As in gone. Off the map. Can't be found."

"Dead?"

"Don't know for sure. But he was last seen drinking in a rattletrap bar with Johnny Finn—Kid Rose's driver and fixer."

"You wanna hazard a guess?"

"His body hasn't been found. But the Mississippi isn't far from the bar. Doc Lathrop was a little guy, out of shape, and a habitual drunk. It'd be easy for a thug like Finn to make a drunken old man take an unintended dip in the river. At any rate, Lathrop didn't show for Sunday dinner with his daughter. They'd been estranged but were reconciling. With nothing more to go on, the cops ruled it a 'missing person' case and put it on the back burner."

Silence.

"Anything I can do, Don, for you at this point?"

Don had muttered, "No. Thanks for all you've done," and hung up the receiver.

Don Swanson thought long and hard about where his investigation stood following Caine's disclosures. The fact the man he'd wanted to unmask had been elected governor, was seeking re-election—and had higher political aspirations—caused Don renewed distress.

Compounding Don's upset was the reality that the *Truthsayer* was nearly insolvent. Readership had surged when he'd taken control of the paper but, as the Great

Depression intensified, subscriptions fell away and newsstand purchases declined to the point where the paper's survival was problematic. *Despite my meager purse and the likelihood the* Truthsayer *has maybe five or six more weeks before creditors seize its presses, furniture, and equipment—after garnishing my bank accounts—I can't stand by and allow Larson a free pass. He must be held accountable.* Don stood up, approached a window overlooking Minnesota Avenue, and watched pedestrians waddle across snowy sidewalks. No cars, buses, or trolleys moved. The city's vehicles remained tucked against curbs, immobilized by the storm.

Swanson consulted Beckett after the unsettling conversation with Caine.

"I'm not sure going into a gunfight with a pencil is the smartest move," Ellis Beckett warned, nervous about his future and cognizant the newspaper was on the verge of folding. "Larson has some pretty nasty pals."

Don was operating the paper on a shoestring. The mortar that held the operation together, Alice Sullivan, had left again—this time for good. The office manager had never recovered from her husband's death and, one Friday, without giving her two weeks' notice, she had simply walked into Don's office and said "I'm done, Mr. Swanson. I can't do this anymore."

Don's attempts to reason with the woman, to get her to stay on until he closed up shop, had fallen on deaf ears. In the end, despite shaky finances, Don had given Alice two week's severance, hugged the woman, and seen her to the door.

Beckett, who was as bald as a goose egg, with a face afflicted with unshaven stubble, and who dressed in a ratty, rumpled three-piece-suit that likely came from a St. Vincent de Paul second-hand-store, had tried his best when his boss had proposed running a piece on the governor's past indiscretions supported only by rumor, to dissuade Don from plunging into such shark-infested waters. It was no use. Donald Swanson's fixation on Sigurd Larson's past edged Don, as the paper's editor and owner, closer and closer to journalistic suicide.

Ellis Beckett stammered objections. The man's natural stutter rendered his halting pleas for caution abysmally ineffective. Beckett felt he had two choices: stay on and see things through or quit. Despite his better judgment, Ellis Beckett was a loyal man. He decided to stand by his boss.

"Well," Don finally said, after weighing his options aloud. "If this paper is sinking, it might as well plummet straight to the bottom like the *Titanic*."

He mulled over his options before deciding to pay the governor an unannounced visit. As a muckraker, Don knew it was unlikely Larson would reveal anything incriminating during their meeting. "Still, I have to try," he said, as he left Beckett's office to call Beatrice and warn her that he'd be late for dinner. "If Sig Larson wins a senate seat," Don muttered, as he dialed his home number, "he'll eventually run for president. And that—given his ties to Kid Rose and a checkered past—is not something I'm about to let happen."

CHAPTER THIRTEEN
December 23, 1931

"**What** the hell?"

Governor Larson sat in the splendor of his capitol office, haranguing Kid Rose over the telephone after enduring an unpleasant visit from Donald Swanson. "The man is like an incessant mosquito!"

"What's got you so upset?" Abram asked.

"Swanson. He came by to see me while I was working on the farm relief bill."

"And?"

A stab of pain crippled the governor as he reached for a humidor across the desk. *Damn, it's getting worse,* Larson thought, as he waited for the spasm to relent. When the pain finally ebbed, Sig ignored his longing for a cigar and drew a deep, cleansing breath. "He claims three dead bodies are on me, Abram. Three!"

"What, exactly, did he say?"

"He talked nonsense about a woman being killed in an automobile accident in Wisconsin. Claims the police got it wrong, that it was murder!"

"What does that have to do with *you*?" Abram asked, wanting to add *or me,* but exercised restraint.

"That little . . ."

Abram could tell, from the forestalled curse—something Sigurd rarely engaged in—the governor was becoming unhinged. "Yes?"

". . . claims you had something to do with it. Says he has 'evidence' that the Chicago North Siders, the Irish mob, supply you and Ian McNulty with booze, and that you called in a favor."

"Did Swanson say how this unfortunate woman is tied to either of us?"

"He did," the governor replied, his voice becoming steady. "He claims she was the best friend of your cousin."

"Helen Ginsburg?"

"I knew her by another name," Larson said.

"Golden. Her maiden name."

"Right," the governor agreed, collecting his thoughts. "Anyway. Swanson claims your cousin told this Mrs.

Patchett, the dead woman, about that night, that unfortunate—for me—night I spent with your fifteen-year-old cousin. Swanson mumbled something about 'statutory rape', which, as a former prosecutor, I clearly understand his insinuation."

Abram Rosenstein pulled a pint bottle of Canadian whiskey from a desk drawer, uncapped it, poured himself a drink, and fortified himself by draining the booze in one swallow. "I have no idea what he's talking about. I haven't," he lied, "talked to Helen in months. And I certainly don't believe, given the caution I urged upon her when last we spoke about that night—as I recall, right after you were elected—she'd say anything to anyone."

Spasmodic pain stabbed the governor. "So, you had nothing . . ." Sigurd whispered through grimaced teeth.

"You sound miserable. Back bothering you again?"

"Yes." What he didn't add was that, in addition to the spinal pain, his normal routine at the toilet had become an irregular, difficult chore punctuated by black stools. He'd kept the latter symptom from his physician, his staff, and the public, chalking it up to a change in beverage habits as he'd increased his early morning coffee routine from one cup to three. Only Amelia knew about the tarry stools.

"You need to see a doctor."

"I will."

"Siggy . . ." There was a pause as the Kid pursued a thought. "You said the police ruled the woman's death an accident?"

"Yes."

"What proof did this little pipsqueak offer that goes against the position of the authorities?"

"Claims he had someone, he didn't say who, go over it all. Said it was clearly *not* an accident."

Damn it to hell. I have no idea who's been poking around our business. It'll take some digging to figure out. But, in the meantime, I need to know what that fucking reporter suspects. Suspicion can be as bad as fact in such cases. "Well, that's unlikely, isn't it? I mean, he's here in St. Paul writing his little bullshit articles, and the poor lady died an entire state away. Best to disregard his tales as mere fables invented by a desperate man."

The phone line crackled. The back pain dissipated. "OK. I'll consider his claims to be the ramblings of a man whose paper, by all accounts, is headed for receivership."

"Things are that bad?"

"So I've heard. But . . ."

"Yes?"

"He also accused you of orchestrating the deaths of two other folks."

"What in the Sam Hill are you talking about?"

"A doctor disappeared."

Rosenstein maintained composure. "Who?"

"The guy involved in the death of that Miller girl, the abortionist: he's missing."

Abram considered a response. "I hear that butcher's a drunk, a real piece of work. Wouldn't surprise me if he turns up dead in a ditch."

"Don't know about that. Don't know anything about the man. I'll take your word for it." Sigurd Larson stood up from his desk. "But here's the damnable piece of it," he whispered. "Swanson claims your man, Johnny Finn, had something to do with the doctor's disappearance."

Shit. Whomever the reporter has digging up dirt has some skill. Likely a cop. Or a private dick. Still, there's nothing out there that can come back to hurt Siggy or me. Nothing. "Johnny is a hardworking man. He's no thug."

"Look, Kid, I've heard things, things about you and Finn that aren't in the best light."

Abram poured more whiskey, raised the glass to his lips, sipped, and put the heels of his black dress shoes atop his desk. "Rumors, Siggy. Ignore them."

"About the doctor . . ."

"I'll talk to Johnny. But I can assure you: I had nothing to do with whatever happened to the man," Abram lied. "Besides," he added slyly, "one might argue the world is better off without him."

"Maybe. Though I understand he has family, a daughter frantic to find him. So there's that." Sigurd looked at the ceiling. "But thank you, Kid, for taking my concerns seriously."

"Always."

Sigurd Larson gathered up the gumption to deal with the final supposition Swanson had raised during their short and very unpleasant interaction earlier that evening. "The death of Newhouse, the cop who investigated Susanne Miller's death: Swanson brought that up, too."

"He died of a drug overdose. You know that, right?".

"I do." There was a pause. "You remember I made the unfortunate mistake of calling Newhouse after the Miller girl died?" Another break in the conversation. "I'm not worried about the call," the governor added. "But I'm concerned by Swanson's suggestion that I had something to do with the man's death."

"That's not on you."

"But I can see where Swanson might put two and two together and allege a connection between me and Newhouse's overdose."

He's nervous. I can hear it in his voice. "Hogwash. Whatever you did or didn't do concerning the covering up of the Miller girl's death died with Newhouse."

"I guess that's true," the governor admitted, with hesitancy.

"There's more you wish to say?"

"He brought up our old burglary," Sigurd continued. Feeling the onset of another spasm, Larson struggled to remain focused. "Went on and on about how you and I were involved in other 'illicit, youthful activities'."

"So? Those records are sealed. I have the original hearing transcript, the original police reports, and the original court file. They're in a safety deposit box for my eyes and my eyes only."

"Why haven't you just burned those damned papers?"

Rosenstein grinned. "Leverage. Insurance that friends remain friends."

"You don't trust me?"

"Oh, I do. Until something comes along and forces you to abandon an old pal who helped you along the way. Keeping those records assures I'll never be a casualty of changing whims. Friendship can be a fickle union."

Sigurd sighed. "Maybe so."

"Siggy ..."

"Yes?"

"I'll have a chat with Swanson and try to make him see the error of his ways." *He's had his warning,* Abram recalled, considering a prior incident the governor had no knowledge of. *It's time I dealt with the asshole personally.*

The governor took another deep breath. "He also said that, regardless of what I acknowledge or don't acknowledge in public, he's going to assert his theories as 'editorial opinion' in that damnable paper he runs." Larson paused. "He sounded like a defeated man who wants to go out with a splash."

A cornered rat is dangerous, Kid Rose thought. *Time to put the rodent out of its misery.* "Like I said, I'll talk to Mr. Swanson. Make him see the light. When do you suppose he'll publish?"

"It'll take a day or two to write up whatever he thinks deserves ink. Plus, the next issue doesn't hit the streets until Tuesday," Sigurd said, renewed pain and numbness in his right foot making it difficult to concentrate.

"I'll see him tomorrow."

"On Christmas Eve?" the governor asked, his voice weak, his mind disturbed by agony, the words expelled as mere habit.

"I'm Jewish. What the hell do I care about Christmas?"

CHAPTER FOURTEEN
Minneapolis, Minnesota
December 24, 1931

Marjorie didn't appreciate that her mother had joined her on the covered front porch. When the machine gun stopped its horrific rat-a-tat-tat and Donald Swanson crumpled into a ball, Marjorie uncupped her hands from her ears and dove atop her father. The five-year-old sought to shield the stricken man from further harm, as blood leaked from bullet holes to pool around his twitching form like oil spilled on a garage floor from an overturned can.

"Daddy, Daddy!" Marjorie screamed as she fixed her eyes on a departing automobile. Marjorie saw—despite the darkness of the night, the meager light of the streetlamps, her tears, and her agitated state—the face of the man holding the gun, but was unable to see the car's driver with similar exactitude.

"Oh my God!" Bea screamed. The distraught woman opened the duplex's screen door, crossed the threshold, and fell to her knees while fixing her gaze on a retreating Cadillac. *B, as in "Boy". B as in "Boy". Year '31. Year '31. 417 098, 417 098* Bea repeated in her mind, shielding her trembling daughter and her fading-from-life husband with her pregnant body. Beatrice grasped Donald's left wrist. Nothing. She touched recently shaved skin beneath his nostrils. Nothing. "He's gone, Marjorie. Daddy's gone."

The fetus in Beatrice Swanson's womb was not yet active. But as the mother of two—soon to be three—came to grips with her new reality, she retched. After expelling morning coffee, breakfast, and lunch, and after wiping spittle from her lips with the sleeve of her white blouse, Bea pried Marjorie off Donald's corpse.

"Daddy's gone," Beatrice repeated, placing the child in a seated position against the clapboarded wall of the duplex, the girl's hands covering her eyes, sobs racking her meager body like an internal earthquake. In shock, Bea didn't think to search for Oscar, her four-year-old son, or consider what this day, this loss, might mean to the boy.

Marjorie cried and shook like an aspen leaf in an autumn wind as she cowered. Beatrice avoided engaging her daughter's pitiful eyes, leaned over Don's chilling corpse, slid her hands beneath his winter coat, and lifted her lover and best friend into her arms.

"What happened?" Agnes Overstreet asked, startling Beatrice by appearing from inside the duplex without warning. Agnes, a robust, white-haired, perpetually cheerful widow in her mid-eighties, was the building's owner and downstairs tenant.

Bea did not speak. Marjorie stared at Mrs. Overstreet through blood-stained fingers and whispered, "Someone shot Daddy."

"God!" Agnes cursed as she walked across the porch in felt slippers, carefully selecting a path that avoided the bloody pool. "What has this world come to!" The expression came out as an exclamation and not as a question.

Oscar Swanson, a tow-headed child possessing his father's build and his mother's eyes, appeared behind the screen door. He'd been playing with Lincoln Logs—a toy invented by John Lloyd Wright, the famed architect's son—in his bedroom and had not heard the gunfire. It was only after he noticed his mother and sister were missing that Oscar ventured onto the porch. "Momma," the boy whispered, "what happened to Daddy?"

Bea sobbed. Her head rested on Don's chest as she clung to him in despair. She cradled her husband's stiffening body and ignored the streaks of red staining her blouse. She did not answer the boy. Snowflakes were falling, their steady, slow, downward descent creating a pastoral backdrop to tragedy.

"I heard gunshots and called the police," Widow Overstreet said, placing a hand on Beatrice's right shoulder.

Though Beatrice heard the high-pitched scream of distant sirens, her eyes never left Donald's face. She held the dead man tightly—like a child embracing a favorite teddy bear—ignoring the approaching police cruisers and her children's upset while whispering to no one in particular, "Those bastards! Their goddamned war on truth murdered my husband . . ."

BOOK THREE: THE AFTERMATH

And if you wrong us, do we not revenge?
William Shakespeare

CHAPTER ONE
December 26, 1931

"**What** did you see, ma'am?"

The question was posed to Beatrice Swanson as she huddled with her children in an interrogation room of police headquarters in downtown Minneapolis.

It was a question Detective Marty Aronson had tried to get an answer to while standing outside the Swanson home. Given the shock to Beatrice's system and the fact she had two bawling, out-of-control children attached to her blood-soaked blouse and skirt like frightened kittens, Aronson had received only a blank stare in response to his on-the-scene questioning. Stonewalled by silence, Aronson had made no further inquiry at the time. Instead, he had escorted Beatrice and the children to an idling police cruiser, helped them in, shut the door, and followed the squad car to the station. Other officers had remained on scene to collect evidence, including shell casings and spent cartridges that appeared to be consistent with rounds fired by a Thompson submachine gun.

Uniformed cops canvased the neighborhood and found two witnesses who described the getaway car: a black Cadillac Fleetwood bearing Minnesota plates. But those witnesses had not been able to clearly see the plate number as the car rumbled away.

Stephen Weatherby, a Negro in his nineties, a veteran of the Civil War, and a former high school janitor living in a four-plex two doors down from the Swansons, had rushed outside at the sound of gunfire. The old man wasn't wearing his eyeglasses but claimed to have seen a white man in the rear driver's-side seat holding "One of them there Tommy guns." Beyond observing that generality, the elderly man provided little additional information. Mr. Weatherby told the uniformed officer that it was unlikely he could identify either the gunman or the driver, the only two people he had observed in the Cadillac.

The other witness was Joyce Big Eyes, an Ojibwe woman employed by Greene's Butcher Shop—the neighborhood grocer Don Swanson had visited minutes before his death. She was home when the reporter pulled up in his Oakland motorcar, outside her modest bungalow with her back to the street, sweeping snow off the front porch, when she heard a noise that caused her to spin on her heels. "Sounded like popcorn popping," she reported to the investigating officer. More importantly, the Native woman volunteered that she'd seen the man holding the gun and recognized him.

"I seen his picture in the paper. He's the man they call 'Kid Rose'."

"Abram Rosenstein?" the uniformed cop had asked.

"Don't know his real name. But there was an article in the *Star* a while back, including his picture, that talked about him being a big-shot bootlegger."

"That's Rosenstein." The cop had paused, looked at the short, stout Native woman, her eyes clear, her affect very matter-of-fact. *The best kind of witness. No guesses. No embellishments. Just the straight skinny.* "Can you describe him, ma'am?"

Joyce described the man sitting in the rear driver's-side seat holding the gun, beginning with his face, completing the portrait by saying, "He looked to be shorter than the driver, but well built, muscular. Not fat. Wearing an overcoat, sports jacket, shirt, and tie. No hat. Couldn't see his shoes."

Detective Sparks, a tall, narrow-chested Negro, had approached and, after conferring with the uniformed cop, had taken over. "You see the driver?" Sparks asked.

The Native woman shook her head. "Not really. Only that he was a man, wearing a hat: a four-square. Can't tell you what color. Can't describe his clothes. But he was taller than the guy in the back seat."

"Anything else you can tell me?"

"No, sir."

"Thank you, ma'am," Sparks had said, handing Joyce his business card. "We may want you to come in and look at a lineup at some point," he said. "Meanwhile, if anything comes to mind, give me a call."

"I will."

Sparks had also interviewed Mrs. Overstreet. Other than confirming she'd heard gunshots in rapid succession, suggesting a machine gun was indeed the murder weapon, the landlady had nothing else to offer in terms of specifics.

"Ma'am?"

"B 417 098. 1931 Minnesota plates," Beatrice Swanson whispered, holding her children tight to her bosom. Her stomach rolled over. *The baby will never know his or her father.*

"You got the entire plate number?" Detective Aronson asked incredulously. "You wrote it down?"

Bea shook her head. "Memorized it."

"With all that was going on?"

She nodded.

"Can you describe the car?"

"Cadillac four door. Black. A Fleetwood."

"Could you see inside?"

Bea released her grip on Marjorie to itch her chin, but continued hugging Oscar. "I saw a man with a gun."

"Anyone else?"

"There was a driver, another man, I believe. Can't give you details. But the passenger holding the machine gun, him, I saw quite plainly."

"The man with the gun ... have you ever seen him before?"

"Only in the newspapers."

"How's that?"

"I've seen him on the front page. He was involved in an altercation where a man died at the Lexington."

"Remember his name?"

"Only his nickname."

"And?"

"Paper called him 'Kid Rose.' Said he was mixed up in organized crime."

The children fidgeted. Detective Aronson picked up the receiver of a telephone sitting on the table and dialed. A uniformed female cop opened the door to the interrogation room and entered. "Come on, kids. Let's go get sodas," she said.

"Mommy?" Marjorie asked, as if being separated from Beatrice might cause her mother to disappear from her life as her father had.

"It's OK, sweetie. Take Oscar by the hand, and follow the nice lady."

The patrolwoman led the children out of the room. The door shut, trapping moist, warm air in the small space. Marty Aronson stared at his notes, looked into Beatrice Swanson's gunmetal eyes, placed his pencil on his notepad, and rubbed his jaw. "You have any idea why Abram Rosenstein—that's Kid Rose's real name—would want to kill your husband?"

Bea returned the cop's gaze, straightened, folded her hands, and nodded. "Donald was investigating ties between Kid Rose and Governor Larson. Stories about the governor having an affair with an underage girl, his involvement in criminal matters, and a cover-up regarding the death of a city councilman's daughter."

"Susanne Miller?"

Bea thought for a moment. "Yes, I believe that's the name of the unfortunate child."

Marty Aronson was Jewish. He'd been born and raised in Minneapolis. In his youth, he'd experienced run-ins with Kid Rose and the Kid's "associates," including Sigurd Larson. The detective nodded, picked up his pencil, and jotted additional notes. "Do you think you could pick the man holding the gun out of a lineup?"

Beatrice studied her fingers. The momentary distraction ended, and the widow focused on Marty Aronson's question. "Yes," Bea answered quietly. "I believe I could." The widow paused a bit before volunteering, "And so could Marjorie."

CHAPTER TWO
December 30, 1931

"**You** got the wrong man, Pal," Kid Rose said from the rear seat of an unmarked squad car—a Model A sedan—as it rumbled over icy streets. "I was at the barber when you say the ink bleeder bit the dust."

Marty Aronson sat in the front passenger seat of the Ford. Detective Sparks was driving. Aronson didn't turn his head to respond. "Save it for the station."

"I'm just telling you you're making a big mistake, friend."

"I'm not your friend."

The Ford slammed to a stop, narrowly missing the rear end of a delivery truck that had braked for a stop sign.

Benny Madsen will lie through his teeth, Rosenstein thought, *and say that I was in his chair, getting a haircut and a shave at the time of the shooting.* The bootlegger smiled in recognition of the protection friendship, a common heritage, and wads of cash could buy. *And Moe will back him up.*

As for Johnny Finn, the Kid had arranged for Johnny's gal of the moment, Gertie Gustafson—a big-boned, platinum-headed stripper—to affirm that she and Johnny were "otherwise engaged" at the hour of Swanson's death. Johnny Finn's neighbor, Bartholomew Richards, the owner of a chain of shoe stores that laundered cash for Rosenstein and Stuffy McNulty, would collaborate the lie, claiming he saw the couple enter Johnny's apartment around the time of the shooting and affirm that the lovebirds never left their flat.

Iron clad, Abram Rosenstein thought, as the squad coasted to a stop outside police headquarters. *You boys got nothin' on us.*

Beatrice Swanson had been—in the opinion of Mrs. Overstreet—hysterical after the shooting. Even so, Bea's recitation of the license plate number and her identification of Kid Rose were solid. The chief difficulty confronting Abner James—the Assistant Hennepin County Attorney assigned to the case—was that the only eyewitness to the shooting itself was a five-year-old child. The key to the state's case was whether Marjorie Taylor Swanson was competent to testify. *I have no idea what Judge Reilly, newly appointed to replace Judge Dubus—who died unexpectedly—will make of testimony from a traumatized young girl.*

James worked the case up, reviewing statements collected by the police and re-interviewing key players on the state's side of the ledger, including Marjorie. James also met with Moe Feldman, Gertie Gustafson, Bartholomew Richards, and the Kid's barber, Benny Madsen, in hopes of challenging their collective story—a story that Abner James feared could result in Abram Rosenstein and Jôhānān Epstein walking away from a murder trial as free men. But Abner's efforts—including threats of prosecution for perjury during sit-downs with the defense witnesses—netted him nothing but scorn and derision from the men and the woman duty-bound to protect their friends. Still, the murder of an investigative journalist, one digging into the sordid past of a sitting governor, could not be swept under the rug. And so, Abner James moved forward with the case.

"Too bad Minnesota doesn't have the death penalty," Abner lamented, as he sat in the Blue Heron, a familiar haunt for not only the morally corrupt but also for men and women working for the justice system, sipping whiskey, the booze strong, warm, and lacking ice. "When they botched the hanging of Willie Williams, that ended capital punishment in the state."

Marty Aronson sat next to Abner James at the bar, staring into a glass filled with gin and tonic—the clear liquid reflecting the low light of the speakeasy—and nodded. "You got that right, Big Ab'."

"Big Ab" fit a man topping the scale at over three hundred and fifty pounds. The lawyer was tall, six-one, and yet, despite his height, he was the fattest man Marty Aronson knew.

Aronson had started his career in uniform—walking a beat—but soon made detective. True to his Jewish heritage, in that he married a Jew, routinely attended synagogue, and was raising three children—two girls and a boy—in the faith, Marty Aronson was God-fearing, righteous, and disarmingly honest.

Abner James, a veteran of the Great War who, unlike Sigurd Larson, did not see combat, had worked in the Minneapolis City Attorney's Office with Larson. The lawyers had become friends, with Larson serving as James's mentor. As prosecutors, they had encountered Marty Aronson as a detective investigating prostitution and white slavery cases. Given the limitations of the city attorney's authority, such matters were routinely referred up the legal food chain to the county attorney or the United States District Attorney. When Sig Larson was elected Hennepin County Attorney, he offered Abner James the position of chief prosecutor—the attorney in charge of serious criminal cases—an offer James readily accepted. Inevitably, Assistant County Attorney Abner James heard whispers concerning Larson's supposedly untoward past, including allegations of an inappropriate relationship with Kid Rose. Absent anything concrete indicting his friend's character, James ignored the gossip as unverified slander. However, the murder of Donald Swanson impacted James's view. The statements of the witnesses and the way the investigative reporter had been gunned down—gangland style—opened the lawyer's eyes to the possibility that his friend, now Minnesota's governor, either had something to do with Swanson's death or, at the very least, knew something about Abram Rosenstein's intentions before the muckraker died in a hail of bullets.

James was not certain as to the extent or nature of Larson's relationship with Rosenstein. He'd heard the rumors, the whispers, but such meager inuendo did not, when weighed against Larson's seemingly unimpeachable character, convince Big Ab' that Sig was in cahoots with gangsters until the reporter's bloody demise. *It's a possibility,* James thought as he downed the last of his whiskey, slammed his glass against the bar, and shouted, "Barkeep, another for me and my friend!"

Aronson shook his head. "No, thanks. Gotta drive home."

Both men understood that they were violating federal law by buying and consuming "non-medicinal" alcohol. But the cop and the prosecutor were immune from being pinched, given the Blue Heron was "off limits" to raids conducted by local cops, sheriff's deputies, and federal agents.

"What're you gonna do about the girl testifying?" the cop finally asked.

James shrugged, as the barkeep placed another whiskey in front of him. "Fucking Reilly. One would think, given the time he spent in juvie, he'd be amenable to letting a little girl have her say. But nothing's guaranteed with that ignoramus." Big Ab' looked at Marty and sneered. "He's an empty suit when it comes to the law."

Aronson smiled, tipped his glass to his lips and drank greedily. "I was surprised when Larson appointed him."

"You and me both. If Sig had called me up and asked me what I thought of making Reilly a district court judge, I would have told the governor he was off his nut." The lawyer paused. "But I guess a generous campaign contribution trumps smarts when we're talking judicial appointments."

"Thanks for the drink. If there's anything else I can do, let me know," Aronson said, as he climbed off the barstool.

"It's not your job to educate a judge who has his head up his ass," Abner mumbled, as the cop walked across the floor, opened the front door, and exited the bar.

Big Ab' reflected on judicial ignorance for a few moments before draining his second whiskey. "I gotta visit Sig," the lawyer muttered, setting the empty glass on the bar and following Marty Aronson outside.

CHAPTER THREE
February 1932

Sigurd Larson and Abner James walked side by side on St. Paul's Kellogg Boulevard. "It's good you called. Been too long since we got together," the governor said.

James—his black, wool coat buttoned tight against a March zephyr, an out-of-style black bowler pulled down on his head so tightly it tortured his ears—felt burdened by the death of an innocent newspaper man that might, just might, be tied to his friend's political ambitions, and did not immediately respond. Despite the wind threatening to unseat his hat, James kept his gloved hands in his coat pockets as he pondered a reply. "The inaugural ball," James finally answered. "That was the last time we spoke. I took a spin around the dance floor with the First Lady."

"Amelia's a better dancer than me. Or you, for that matter!" the governor teased, the metal joints of his artificial left leg clicking in the cold as he relied upon his cane for balance. In addition to the difficulty of walking in freezing weather with a prosthesis, the governor's low back pain was reasserting itself, causing bolts of sharp, unrelenting agony to shoot down his right leg.

"You got that right."

Sigurd opened the door to Frederick's Diner and bade Abner enter.

"Governor!" Pete Frederick, the delicate, nattily attired, carefully groomed restauranteur sporting a prim bow tie, said after seeing Larson and his rotund companion enter the eatery. "Nice of you to stop in."

Sigurd and Abner hung their coats and hats on a wrought iron coat rack.

"Pete, this is my friend, Abner James," the governor said, as the café's proprietor ushered the men to a booth. "He's with the Hennepin County Attorney's Office."

Frederick wiped a greasy right hand on his mostly clean white apron and extended it to James. "Pleased to make your acquaintance."

"Likewise," Abner replied, completing the gesture before taking a seat in the booth.

Sig also shook Pete's hand before claiming a seat on the vinyl-covered bench across from Abner. Settling in, the governor leaned his cane against the wall. "What's good today?" the governor asked, accepting two menus from the owner, keeping one and handing the other to James.

Pete glanced at a blackboard hanging behind the lunch counter. "The special: sliced ham, two eggs, a side of American fries, and toast. Three bits. The chicken noodle soup with two slices of homemade rye is also popular. Just two bits."

"Still make that cold meatloaf sandwich with a boatload of green pepper and onion?"

"Yup. Side salad or fries comes with it. That'll set you back a buck."

Sigurd put down his menu. "I'll go with my tried and true. Meatloaf sandwich with fries and a cup of black coffee. And give me the bill."

Abner placed his menu on the table. "I'll try the special," he said. "And coffee. With cream and sugar."

Frederick nodded, retrieved the menus, replaced them in a wire holder affixed to the spotless wall, and walked toward a stainless-steel percolator. "Two cups of coffee, one black, one with cream and sugar, coming right up," he said casually, never looking back at the booth as he filled one mug, then another, with steaming coffee.

Abner's girth pressed against the table's harsh edge. *I need to lose weight*, the prosecutor thought. *Maybe if I had a wife . . . But the divorce did a number on me. Evangeline's still running around with that mortician: God, how could she? That was the end of us. I need a reason to stop eating. When I was courting Evie, I got down under three hundred, kept it off too—until I found out about Stephen Bonafice. Not so much found out, as caught the asshole in <u>my</u> bed with his head between <u>my</u> wife's tits.* Abner James recalled the moment he'd pulled a .45 Browning semi-automatic out of his underwear drawer and nearly ended the fornicator's life. But as angry as James had been, he'd let the sniveling, apologetic worm flee naked from the James's marital bed— the frightened cuckolder gathering his slacks, shirt, and jacket as he scampered off—without so much as a scratch. *Maybe she would have stayed with me had I shown any balls that night. But I didn't. I let Bonafice off the hook,* *tossed my pistol on the bed, closed the door, and wandered off to get drunk.*

That night had been a doozy—epic really. When Abner James had finally stumbled home, disheveled and reeling from booze and betrayal, the house was empty. Evangeline had gathered up her clothes, jewelry, and cosmetics, tossed her worldly possessions into two suitcases, and left a curt, unsigned note in dainty handwriting alongside the Browning on the unmade bed. Her goodbye wasn't profound or apologetic. Evie's neatly penned and unsigned message simply read: *It's over.*

Those were the personal memories that intruded as Abner James sought a path, a means, to talk to his friend about some very unseemly rumors. In the end, as the two men sipped coffee and ate, Abner decided upon a direct approach.

"You hear about the murder of Donald Swanson, the reporter?"

Larson didn't look up from his meal to reply. "Who hasn't?"

"We're bringing Rosenstein in for a lineup." Abner realized that if, as had been alleged, the gangster still maintained a close—perhaps nefarious, perhaps innocent—relationship with the governor, Larson likely already knew a lineup was in the works. As he waited for a reply, Abner surveyed Sig's demeanor for any clues that the information conveyed was unsettling. The governor continued eating as if nothing in the world could disturb his meal—a sign, Abner James knew, that meant just the opposite. Sigurd Larson's tell in such circumstances was feigned nonchalance.

Visions of Kid Rose's wet, bone-chilled body gasping and coughing and rolling about on precarious ice, Sigurd nearby, soaked to the bone, hypothermia raging inside him, the Norwegian gasping as he sought to breathe, interrupted Sig's contemplation. The governor bit the inside of his cheek to forestall displaying emotion. "That's not news. Heard that was in the works." There was a break in the conversation as the men ate. "What's that got to do with me?" Larson finally asked.

Before Abner James dove deeper into any possible connection between Sigurd Larson and Donald Swanson's murder, he wanted to explore less onerous matters. "I read about your intentions with respect to Shipstead," Abner said matter-of-factly.

Sig displayed placidity. "Again, not really news. It's been in all the papers," the governor said evenly.

Abner finished mopping egg yolk with his toast before placing dirty utensils and a soiled napkin on the table. "I've heard something else: a rumor I don't put any weight behind. But one heard nonetheless."

Larson finished his sandwich, left his French fries untouched, reached across the table, lifted a stainless-steel urn, poured himself another cup of coffee, and returned the urn to its place of rest. "Such as?"

"That Swanson's death is tied to an exposé he was gonna publish about your past," Abner said in a low tone. "Something about your knowledge of the death of Susanne Miller, a juvenile burglary, and a tryst with an underage girl. Old gossip, but saucy and salacious enough for Swanson to see value in dredging it up."

Sigurd's right foot went numb as pain shot from his beltline through his hamstring, into his calf, and across his toes.

"You alright?"

"Goddamned back's giving me fits again."

"Sorry to hear it." Abner maintained a respectful silence until he felt it seemed appropriate to press the issue. "Swanson: Did you know he was after you?"

Sig Larson considered his options. The ledger listing visitors to Minnesota's capitol was public information. Swanson's unexpected visit the evening before his murder was recorded. Lying about the man's presence would only add to the governor's troubles. *Besides, there's nothing linking me to that unfortunate man's death. Sure, I suspected the Kid as soon as I read the headline. A logical conclusion given Abram told me—on the night preceding the reporter's murder—that he was going to confront the man.* The governor mulled over a response. "Mr. Swanson came to see me at the capitol. He wanted answers to questions regarding the topics you've raised. But I had nothing to do with that man's murder. Nothing."

Abner James eyed his former boss. "You sure about that?"

Larson rose. The abruptness of the movement and the instability of the governor's prosthesis caused him to wobble, though he quickly regained his balance. "Goddamn it," Sigurd whispered angrily before slamming a ham-sized right fist down on the table. "I told you: I had nothing to do with that man's death!"

The vitriolic escalation caught Abner James off guard. James was still collecting his thoughts when Governor Larson snatched his cane, limped toward the exit, grabbed his overcoat and fedora from the coat rack, and left the eatery without dressing for the weather or paying for the meals.

He knew. Or should have known, Abner James thought. *Now, what the hell am I supposed to do?*

CHAPTER FOUR
March 1932

"The lineup was tainted," Bill O'Malley argued, as he stood behind a counsel table, his clients seated next to him, in a Hennepin County courtroom presided over by Judge Edmund Reilly. "The men selected to stand beside Mr. Rosenstein looked nothing like him."

Bill O'Malley and Abner James were arguing the merits of motions brought by O'Malley on behalf of Kid Rose and Johnny Finn. The hearing was held in advance of the jury trial at the end of a very busy day for Judge Reilly: a "call of the calendar" consisting of numerous, serious, and unrelated felony cases heard sequentially. Most were procedural matters—requests for bail reduction and the like. But at the end of a trying afternoon, the jurist was confronted by two motions challenging the judge's legal acumen and—given the late hour—his patience.

The first matter raised by O'Malley concerned the men selected to appear with Abram Rosenstein during his lineup. None of the men standing behind one-way glass, as five-year-old Marjorie Swanson, her mother, and Joyce Big Eyes scrutinized them, looked anything like Kid Rose. In fact, one of the lineup participants had been a Negro, which caused O'Malley to complain on the spot. Despite O'Malley's protest, Abner James had not been moved.

"If you don't like it, file a motion," the prosecutor had retorted.

In truth, the lineup had been rushed. Word made its way to James that the suspects were close to making bail, which had been set at $100,000, cash or bond—meaning the gangsters had to come up with a bail bondsman and ten percent down: $10,000 each—to be released on bond, or fork over $100,000 in cash. The alleged co-conspirators had been lodged in the Hennepin County Jail on second degree murder charges pending a grand jury indicting them for first degree murder. "Get me six men—guys from off the street, cops—I don't care who," James had said over the telephone to Marty Aronson. "I want to be able to argue that our witnesses picked those bastards out of separate lineups and ask for increased bail from Judge Reilly <u>before</u> the grand jury comes back."

"Got it, Big Ab'," Marty had replied.

Aronson had thrown together a lineup of six men that included two vice detectives, three drunks off the street, and a Negro mechanic working in the police garage.

"A Colored man? Christ, what the hell were you thinking?" James had lamented. O'Malley was talking to his clients in lockup and was not present when Kid Rose's lineup had been assembled.

"It was the best I could do on short notice."

"I hope to hell Judge Reilly doesn't toss the whole mess in the shitter."

"I wouldn't worry about that. He's not about to let Kid Rose skate on this one. They have history, you know," Aronson had replied.

James did know. He'd done his homework and learned that once upon a time, Abram Rosenstein and the current governor had appeared together before Judge Reilly in juvenile court. Though records concerning the boys' arrests and appearances had mysteriously vanished, there were men and women working in the Minneapolis Police Department with long institutional memories.

"The way I heard the tale," James had said, killing time while waiting for O'Malley and Kid Rose to come over from holding, Marjorie Swanson, Beatrice Swanson, and Joyce Big Eyes sequestered and out of hearing, "is Rosenstein went to Red Wing and Larson went to war."

"I wasn't on the force yet," Marty had said, "but that's the history that pops up anytime Kid Rose's connection to the governor becomes a topic of conversation around the water cooler." Aronson paused. "Usually something to do with how different men take different paths. One falls into a life of crime; the other becomes a war hero, a prosecutor, and a politician."

The door had opened. Bill O'Malley entered the viewing room. On the other side of the glass, Kid Rose was placed in the lineup. "Hello, Bill," Abner had said. "You ready to do this?"

Abram Rosenstein stood between a detective and the Negro in the lineup. Kid Rose was a head shorter than the two men, making him stand out like a sore thumb.

"Lord!" O'Malley had complained. "Why don't you just send him to the electric chair without the charade of a trial?"

James smiled. "Minnesota doesn't have the death penalty, Bill. But then you knew that."

The curtain had closed, and Marjorie Swanson had been escorted into the viewing room by a female cop. The curtain opened, and the child, who stood on a four-legged stool peering over the window ledge, studied the lineup. The seven participants in the lineup held cardboard placards displaying numbers, as the girl viewed them through one-way glass.

"Take your time, child," Abner said kindly. "A person we think was involved in your father's death may or may not be in the lineup. If you see him, tell me the number of the man you believe was present when your father was killed."

Marjorie's face had turned deadly serious. "Number four," she said, pointing her right index finger at Abram Rosenstein.

"Where do you recognize No. 4 from?" James asked.

"He shot Daddy."

"What else do you remember?"

"He was in a big black car on the street outside our house. He pointed a gun at Daddy and shot him."

"Are you certain?"

Marjorie had turned toward Big Ab' and nodded, tears flowing down her cheeks and wetting the collar of her jumper. "That's the man," she'd repeated in a whisper, her tiny body trembling in fear.

Abner James had closed the curtain and nodded to Marty Aronson. The detective left the viewing room. Within seconds, the detective returned with Beatrice Swanson, who, seeing her daughter in distress, immediately took the child into her arms. Once Marjorie's tears abated, a female officer escorted the child from the room so that Bea could make her own identification. She had been confident, as confident as her daughter, that No. 4 was the person she saw in the back seat of the Cadillac holding a machine gun and leaving the scene of her husband's murder.

Joyce Big Eyes had viewed the same lineup and collaborated that Kid Rose was in the rear seat of the Cadillac, holding a Tommy gun as it drove away from the crime scene.

When Johnny Finn appeared in a separate lineup standing alongside six different men, Joyce Big Eyes had been unable to identify Finn as the driver of the getaway car.

Beatrice Swanson and Stephen Weatherby had not been asked to participate in Finn's lineup, since they had related only vague descriptions of the driver to officers on the scene. Only Marjorie Swanson, the last person to view Johnny's lineup once she had calmed from her earlier ordeal, *thought* Finn was the man driving the "big black car" away from the murder.

After completing the lineups, Abner James had convinced Judge Reilly to increase bail for Rosenstein and Finn to one million dollars—cash or bond—apiece. With the alleged killers behind bars, James then secured grand jury indictments against the two gangsters for first degree, premeditated murder.

Following the indictments, Abner James had asked for another increase in bail, but Reilly refused the state's request, indicating that the bail amount he'd previously set was reasonable "under the circumstances."

The judge had been right on that point. As well-heeled as Kid Rose was, he didn't have a million in cash to gain his freedom. Nor did he have a hundred thousand on hand, the amount needed to secure a bond, to facilitate his release from jail. The same was true for Johnny Finn. And while Kid Rose might have reached out to McNulty or Feldman, given the notoriety of the hit on Swanson, something Kid Rose hadn't—but should have—anticipated was akin to kicking a hornet's nest, Abram had known better than to expect outside financial assistance. *I'll get myself out of this pickle,* the gangster had thought as he sat in a grimy, odiferous cell, eating the county's idea of dinner, *and come out of this shithole smelling like a rose—pun intended—without anyone's help.*

Abner James stood at the conclusion of Bill O'Malley's argument.

"Your Honor . . ."

"Take your seat, Mr. James. I don't need to hear from you," Judge Reilly said, through pursed lips. "The lineups stand. The court is convinced that, despite the child's young age, she saw what she saw. In addition, her version of events has been corroborated by adults. Motion denied."

"But Your Honor . . ." O'Malley interjected.

The judge flashed temper. "Sir, the issue has been decided. The Supreme Court can review any and all of my rulings once the trial is concluded. Proceed."

Bill O'Malley cursed beneath his breath.

"What was that, Counselor?"

"Nothing, Your Honor."

"I thought not. Proceed."

The second issue raised by O'Malley was more complex. It involved a legal challenge to Marjorie Swanson's ability to testify. In essence, because Marjorie was of "tender age," her ability to appreciate the difference between reality and fiction—her ability to discern truth—was at issue.

The child was escorted into the courtroom by a uniformed policewoman. Beatrice Swanson trailed her daughter and the cop, nervous and fraught that her five-year-old daughter was being placed under a microscope. Judge Reilly had deemed it to be in the public's interest that all hearings, including his inquiry into Marjorie's competency, be open to the public. Uncharacteristically for such a high-stakes matter, the judge's departure from decorum did not elicit objections from either attorney.

Beatrice sat in a wooden pew behind Abner James. As she settled in, she avoided eye contact with Johnny Finn and Abram Rosenstein. But both defendants—wearing jail stripes, handcuffs, and leg shackles—turned in their chairs to eyeball Mrs. Swanson, whereupon Kid Rose caught the widow's gaze and winked.

Judge Reilly, accustomed to dealing with children from his days as a county court judge, bade Marjorie to take a seat in the witness stand. Reporters and the curious crowded the courtroom. Murmuring swept over the proceedings like a tornado racing over the Great Plains.

"Pipe down," Reilly said firmly. "Or I'll have Deputy Vincent here," the jurist continued, pointing to an armed and uniformed deputy serving as his bailiff, "toss you out on your collective behinds."

The female cop who'd accompanied Marjorie to the witness stand poured the child a glass of water from a pitcher, nodded at the judge, turned, walked toward the rear of the courtroom, and took up a post at the exit.

"Hello, Miss Swanson," Judge Reilly said, his admonition to the crowd having taken effect, the room so quiet that you could hear the squeaking of fidgety shoes against the floor. "How are you?"

"Fine," she whispered.

Reilly looked at Marjorie over the frame of his eyeglasses. "You'll have to speak loudly so that Mr. Robertson over there, who's writing down everything we say, can hear you. OK?"

"OK!" the child replied vigorously.

"That's better!" Judge Reilly said through a broad smile. "Do you know the difference between the truth and a lie?"

Marjorie nodded.

"Again, you need to answer aloud and not use nods or shakes of the head."

"OK!"

"So, do you know the difference?"

"Sure. A lie is something that's not real. The truth is what's real."

Folks in the gallery sniggered. Reilly glared. The spectators quieted, and consequentially, the judge issued no admonition. "Let me ask it this way . . ." Reilly pulled out an empty sheet of paper and held it up. "If I told you this paper was full of words, would that be the truth or a lie?"

The child giggled. "A lie, of course, Judge. There's nothing on it!"

Reilly smiled and nodded. "Right." The judge picked up a pen, dipped it in the ink well, put nib to paper, and drew a cartoon duck. The judge, who considered himself a fine doodler, let the ink dry before showing his creation to the child. "If I said that this was an elephant, would that be the truth or a lie?"

The girl giggled again. "I think it's duck—or maybe a chicken. But it's no elephant!"

The gallery roared. Reilly ignored the commotion. "Do you go to church, Marjorie?"

"I do."

"Sunday school?"

"Oh, yes."

"And your teacher, has he or she talked about sins and such?"

"Mrs. Anderson—she's my teacher—she's told us about the Ten Commandments."

"So, you've heard the phrase, 'Thou shalt not bear false witness'?"

The child struggled to remember. "Sure. That means it's wrong to lie about someone else."

"That's right, young lady. That's right." Judge Reilly glanced at the attorneys and defendants. "You know that we are going to, sometime soon, ask you to talk about things you saw, things involving other people, including your father," Reilly said, after refocusing on the child.

The girl's eyes teared. It seemed that the child might, despite displaying maturity beyond her tender years, fall apart. But Marjorie Swanson recovered, drew a deep breath, wiped her cheek with the sleeve of her one-piece corduroy jumper, and replied, "I know."

"And when you're asked questions about other folks, can you promise me you won't 'bear false witness against them'?"

She nodded, and then, remembering the Court's prior instructions, answered, "I promise."

In advance of Marjorie's appearance, the judge had made it clear that he and he alone would ask questions concerning competency. Once Reilly finished his inquiry, the child was escorted from the witness stand, rejoined her mother, and exited the courtroom, holding her mother's hand. The door closed. Judge Reilly looked up from his notebook, glared at the defendants, and delivered his decision.

"This court is satisfied that, despite Miss Swanson's age, she is aware of the difference between telling the truth and telling a lie. She will be allowed, for better or worse, and subject to legitimate objections and cross-examination, to tell the jury what she knows." Edmund Reilly took a deep breath, surveyed the gallery, and continued. "I believe that addresses the matters on my docket. As such, court is adjourned!" Reilly proclaimed, banging his gavel.

Abner James smiled. He was surprised by the clarity of the magistrate's decision. *Maybe he won't make a mess of things, after all.*

Spectators moved toward the door. The prosecutor collected handwritten notes and typed pleadings and stuffed them in his briefcase. As departing spectators chatted, Abner James stood up, snatched his coat from the back of a chair, found his bowler on the empty seat next to him, and dressed for the thunderstorm he knew was raging outside. As the prosecutor reached for his briefcase, his attention was drawn to an animated conversation between Kid Rose, Johnny Finn, and their lawyer. The discussion ended when the men discovered Abner eavesdropping. Uncomfortable silence ensued before Kid Rose's face erupted in a wicked, knowing Cheshire smile: a gesture that seemed presciently out of place given the judge's rulings.

CHAPTER FIVE
June 1932

"**Friends**," Governor Sigurd Larson said in a clangorous voice, "it is time that the man serving as our United States Senator fully and completely adopts and embraces the values of the Farmer Labor philosophy or faces the consequences!"

Despite a constant, near stabbing pain in his low back, a pain that Amelia Larson had grown increasingly concerned about given its unrelenting nature and its impact upon her husband's steady, stoic demeanor, Sigurd stood tall, his artificial leg braced against the speaker's podium to provide stability, his omnipresent cane hidden behind him, as he addressed a perspiring crowd on a hot and humid June afternoon. The governor spoke from a makeshift stage located near the pitcher's mound of Nicollet Park, the home field of the Millers, Minneapolis's beloved minor league baseball team.

Just one more term in St. Paul, Larson thought, as he looked out over the packed ballpark. *And then, if I can best Shipstead, we're off to Washington!*

All 4,000 seats in the venue were occupied. At the urging of the still jailed and awaiting trial Abram Rosenstein, Moe Feldman had bought up every unsold ticket for the game scheduled to follow the governor's address and passed them out to the citizenry. The contest between the Millers and their archrival, the St. Paul Saints, would pit future Hall of Famer George "High Pockets" Kelly—the hard-hitting, slick-fielding Miller first baseman—against the Saints' starting pitcher and future reliever for the World Series Champion New York Yankees, Johnny Murphy. It was the anticipation of the game—where Kelly, leading his team in home runs and batting average, would duel the crafty Saints' hurler—not the genius of Governor Larson's oration that enticed a standing-room-only-crowd into the bleachers of Nicollet Field to endure temperatures topping ninety degrees.

Senator Shipstead had followed a moderate, if uninspired, middle-of-the-road course in the Senate. He was a Farmer

Laborite in name only, having metaphorized from Republican conservativism to pledging fealty to the progressivism of the FLP.

Sigurd Larson believed his quick resolution of the Teamster's Strike, his careful and thoughtful solution to the meatpacker's walkout in Worthington, his steady support for Prohibition, and his ability to garner votes in the legislature to enact a mortgage foreclosure moratorium and a civilian conservation corps would give him a leg up on the incumbent if both men sought the FLP's endorsement for Shipstead's senate seat in 1934.

Though the governor's position on Prohibition enthused his mother-in-law, Uriah Salveson, an ardent member in—and vice president of—the Minnesota Woman's Christian Temperance Union, Sigurd's father-in-law, Pastor Elliot Salveson, and the Conservatives within Larson's All-Party coalition, the governor knew political reality was at odds with his announced views regarding the Volstead Act. As Sigurd launched his gubernatorial reelection campaign, he understood his unspoken opinion—that Prohibition was a failure, and that its repeal was inevitable—was one shared by future president Franklin Roosevelt and the Democrats controlling Congress. Despite this inevitability, Larson felt duty bound, given his history with Abram Rosenstein, to oppose any attempt to undermine the Volstead Act.

"Senator Shipstead has been, throughout his public life, certain about one thing and one thing only: his flexibility—his ability to change political beliefs as a chameleon changes color." Feeling the heat, the governor removed his black felt fedora, placed it on the podium, and picked up a warm glass of water. After sipping greedily, Larson set the glass down, wiped sweat from his brows with a white handkerchief, returned the damp linen to a front pocket of his vest, and continued. "More succinctly, my good friends, Senator Shipstead is fully consistent in a singular attribute, that being his inconsistency. The man's views on everything, from labor unions to farm moratoriums to price setting to government assistance to the unemployed, blow hither and yon like an aimless prairie wind."

The governor stopped and allowed applause to thunder across the stadium. *These are my people,* Sigurd thought, his chest puffing out in pride at his ability to turn a disinterested crowd sitting on its collective hands into a gallery of support. But as he studied the ocean of faces before him, the audience constituting a cross-section of the income levels, ethnicities, political ideologies, and religions forming his All-Party coalition, pain sliced through the man's body like a blaze of high-voltage electricity and dropped the governor to his knees. Only an iron-like grasp on the podium prevented Sigurd Larson from toppling face first onto the stage.

Two state troopers providing security—and Emmitt Eldridge, the governor's chief of staff—rushed to the governor's side. "Get a doctor!" Eldridge shouted at a trooper—a man nearly as big and brawny Eldridge. "Now!"

Audience members stood to see what was happening. Concern hubbubbed. A well-dressed man of indeterminable age, short of stature but thin and fit, a handlebar mustache drooping from his beaky nose across crimson cheeks, appeared on stage.

"Doc Olmstead works with the Millers. Found him in the locker room," the trooper who'd retrieved the doctor told Eldridge.

Olmstead kneeled next to the stricken man, opened a black leather medical bag, pulled out a stethoscope, inserted the ends of the device into his ears, and applied the business end of the instrument to Larson's neck. "Pulse is strong. Heart's good." The doctor pulled up Larson's white dress shirt and placed the instrument over Sig's heart. "All seems normal. Governor, can you hear me?"

Sig Larson's eyes had closed when the spasm dropped him to his knees, but as the doctor addressed him, the patient's eyelids jetted open. "Yes," he whispered. "But this goddamn back pain is killing me. Can you give me something for it, Doc?"

Olmstead nodded, reached into his bag, and found a vial of morphine and a syringe. "Sir," he said, addressing Eldridge, who was cradling the governor's head in his hands. "Can you remove his suitcoat and roll up the left sleeve of his shirt?"

Eldridge removed Larson's suitcoat, rolled it in a ball, and tucked it under Sig's head as a pillow. The crowd grew nervously insistent as Eldridge pulled up the right sleeve of the governor's white dress shirt to expose his skin. The doctor loaded the syringe with morphine and injected the narcotic. "Goddamn it, Doc," Sig muttered, battling incalculable pain. "I have never felt anything like this; not even when I was hit in France."

Amelia Larson made her way through the crowd. She'd been sitting behind home plate, listening to her husband's speech, and anticipating a fine example of minor league baseball when Sigurd collapsed. "Oh my God!" Amelia cried out as she stumbled onto the stage. "I knew he needed to see a doctor," she whispered as she kneeled next to Olmstead, grasped her husband's clammy, wet-with-sweat right hand, and placed it against her left cheek. "What happened, my love?"

Sig opened his eyes. "I don't know. I was getting ready to leave off bashing Shipstead and talk about my reelection campaign when the lights went out."

Olmstead inventoried the teary, earthen eyes of the First Lady. "How long has this been going on?"

Amelia stroked Sig's cheek as his eyelids closed. "A year."

"Any other symptoms?"

Amelia hesitated. She did not relish revealing the secret Sig was hiding. "He's had black stools for several months."

The doctor blew air over his teeth. "Has he been seen for that? Had X-rays taken of his low back, stomach, and bowels?"

The First Lady shook her head. A siren blared. Groundskeepers opened a gate to allow an ambulance onto the field. "What do you think is wrong with him?" Amelia asked.

"I'd be guessing."

Emmitt Eldridge stood up and looked with intensity at the physician. "But you have an idea what it might be?"

"I'd hate to be wrong."

"Damn it, Doc. What the hell do you think is ailing the governor?"

"It'd be one possibility of many until radiographic studies and bloodwork are completed."

Amelia held her husband's head to her bosom. "He's sweating like a Finn in a sauna."

"That would be consistent."

"Out with it, Sawbones!" Eldridge's tone turned threatening.

Amelia looked up with pleading, pitiful, tearful eyes. "Please?"

The doctor surveyed the anxious crowd before returning his attention to Amelia. "If I had to guess," Olmstead said quietly, "it's likely he has an abdominal tumor, possibly in the colon."

Olmstead did not use the word "cancer." But from his halting, hesitant manner, Doctor Charles Olmstead revealed his opinion, and adding such detail was unnecessary.

CHAPTER SIX

Governor Larson Stricken While Giving Major Address

Governor Larson took ill yesterday during a speech before a standing-room-only-crowd preceding a contest between the Minneapolis Millers and the St. Paul Saints at Nicollet Field. While addressing his supporters, the governor collapsed onto a temporary stage erected in the infield.

Medical attention was immediately provided, and Governor Larson was taken to the University of Minnesota Hospital by ambulance. No further information is available concerning the governor's condition. The game between the hometown Millers and the visiting Saints was canceled and will be rescheduled.

According to the sources within the Millers' organization, tickets for yesterday's contest will be honored at the rescheduled game.

(Minneapolis Star)

It was cancer. But not just of the colon. X-rays taken at the University of Minnesota Hospital revealed a large, though operable, tumor in Sigurd Larson's colon and smaller tumors on his liver, kidneys, and lumbar spine.

"We can remove the blockage, the one causing him the most difficulty," Dr. George Armstrong Cyrus—unfortunately named by his parents in honor of the infamous general killed at the Little Big Horn—said to Amelia Larson in the lobby of the hospital's emergency room as nurses attended their celebrity patient behind closed doors. "We can attack the others with radiation.

"Will that heal the governor?" Amelia asked, her hands wringing, her heart seeking reassurance that all would be well, her mind knowing—given the dire aspect of the doctor's demeanor—that wasn't the case.

"Unfortunately, no. The cancer is too advanced." Dr. Cyrus sat on the empty chair next to Amelia and placed his right hand atop the small elegant fingers of Amelia's left hand, covering the modest diamond engagement ring and wedding band she wore. "The best we can hope for is that the radiation arrests the secondary tumors."

"How long?" She was alone in her conversation with the physician. She had sent Emmitt and the troopers and Sigurd's other staff away. Michael was staying with her parents in Stillwater for the weekend, so Sig could concentrate on the successful launch of his reelection bid. *It's a blessing that Michael isn't here to see his father, a man he thinks is invincible, in such a state.*

"These things are unique to each body," Dr. Cyrus whispered, clearly not wanting to share the awful truth of what he surmised.

"Doctor! I am not," Am' continued, wiping away a migrant tear with a dainty lace handkerchief before slipping it into the wrist of her yellow cotton blouse, "some delicate flower that cannot bear up under a hard rain."

Cyrus nodded. "Maybe a year. Maybe less," he said. "Certainly not more."

Amelia's mouth opened, but no words came out. The news stunned her, despite her protestations of strength and will, and dragged her into a premature well of loss and sadness. "Oh my God!" she finally gasped.

"I am so sorry," the doctor said. "Voted for him in '30 and I'd do so again." Dr. Cyrus removed his hand from Am's wrist and stood. "I need to see about getting the operating room ready for surgery." He watched the woman's eyes widen and cascade renewed tears. "Don't worry. The resection will not be difficult, and, despite the overall prognosis, will provide him with respite from his pain."

Amelia nodded, removed the handkerchief from her sleeve, and dabbed tears. Cyrus turned and began walking away. "Doctor!"

George Armstrong Cyrus stopped, turned, and faced the distraught woman. "Yes?"

The First Lady returned the handkerchief to her sleeve, stood up, and walked up to the physician. She stopped in front of Dr. Cyrus, absently noting, despite her trauma, that he was tall, nearly as tall as her husband. By contrast, Amelia was petite, which required her to crane her neck to consider the healer's muted blue-green eyes. "I have a favor to ask."

"Yes?"

"I want you to keep the ultimate prognosis from the governor. Can you do that?"

Cyrus frowned. "Why so? I mean, he won't be in any shape to continue campaigning. The radiation will sap every ounce of his stamina and strength."

Amelia nodded. "I understand. I'll work with his staff to put out an announcement. We'll say that the campaign is 'temporarily suspended.' I can sell that to Sigurd."

"But ..."

"Please hear me out." She gathered gumption and pressed on. "He doesn't need to know that things are hopeless. That will do his attitude, his outlook, his readiness to comply with treatment, no good. Better, since I know the man more intimately than anyone else, to keep the true prognosis from him."

George Armstrong Cyrus considered the request. "All right, Mrs. Larson. I'll tell him, when he wakes up from surgery, that a tumor in his colon was successfully removed and that he'll require a course of precautionary radiation to prevent that tumor's recurrence."

Amelia grasped the physician's right hand and squeezed. "Thank you, Doctor. It will mean all the difference going forward." She thought, as she let go of the man's hand, that the conversation was over and that the doctor would leave. But George Cyrus didn't move.

"At some point, he will have to be told. So he can be prepared, I mean," the physician said in an even, comforting tone.

Amelia nodded.

The physician turned on his heels, walked to a door leading to the hospital's emergency room, opened it, and disappeared.

CHAPTER SEVEN
July 20, 1932

Four women and ten men were selected to hear the case against Abram Rosenstein and Jôhānān Epstein. Two citizen jurors were selected as alternates: folks who would hear evidence but would be released before deliberations began, unless other jurors took ill or were otherwise unable to serve.

Judge Reilly had allowed both sides to conduct *voir dire*—the questioning of potential jurors—the judge refraining, due to his inexperience in such weighty matters, from making inquiries. There were no folks of color selected. Among the *white* folks picked to hear the case, five were unemployed men, two were single women who worked—one as a waitress, and one as a kindergarten teacher—and two were married women staying home to raise children. The other five jurors were all employed men. One worked for a railroad, one was a restaurant cook, one was a professor of ethics at Augsburg Lutheran College, one was a high school history teacher and football coach at Minneapolis Washburn High School, and the last man on the panel was a retired St. Louis County Sheriff who'd worked in Duluth before moving to Hennepin County to be closer to his grandchildren. The ex-deputy and the railroad worker were the last two jurors selected and, unbeknownst to them, the alternates.

"This is a case of eyewitness testimony," Abner James said, as he stood in the well of the courtroom in front of the jury and delivered his opening statement. James didn't use the podium or notes to address his audience. "The defendants were identified in separate lineups by witnesses whose collective testimony will be that the gentleman seated to the left of Defense Counsel, the man known as 'Kid Rose'— whose real name is Abram Rosenstein—did, on Christmas Eve last, use a Thompson submachine gun to murder Donald Swanson in cold blood." The attorney stopped, engaged his audience with a serious aspect, and went on. "Eyewitness testimony will also confirm that the man seated to the right of Defense Attorney O'Malley, a man known as 'Johnny Finn'—whose given name is Jôhānān Epstein—was the driver of Mr. Rosenstein's Cadillac on that fateful day."

Abner knew he needed to add pazazz to his opening. Fully understanding the court's ruling, one that allowed the state to refer to the defendants as "gangsters," the prosecutor dove in. "And this gangland slaying . . ."

"Objection, Your Honor," Bill O'Malley said, rising to his feet. "The use of such a pejorative adjective is prejudicial."

"But Your Honor," James interjected, attempting to assert that the issue had been covered in pretrial motions, wherein the court opined the use of "gangsters," "gangland," and "gangland slaying" was permissible. But Abner James's attempt to call this truth to Judge Reilly's attention drew an unexpected and immediate rebuke from the jurist.

"NOT IN MY COURTOOM, COUNSELOR!" Judge Reilly boomed indignantly. "The jury is ordered to disregard the state's use of the term 'gangland slaying.' And you sir," Reilly added in a less-onerous voice, as he stared at Abner James with fierce coal-black eyes, "are advised that any further use of that term, or any similar slander, will result in an immediate mistrial." After unloading his ire on the prosecutor, the judge resumed his former calm. "Are we clear, Mr. James?"

Abner mulled over whether to ask for a sidebar: a conference out of the jury's hearing. But the prosecutor thought better of requesting a private audience with the judge. *I don't need to call this a 'gangland slaying' or the defendants 'gangsters' to prove my case. Better to simply move on.* "A misstep, Your Honor. I apologize. It won't happen again."

The judge nodded. James continued.

"In addition, you'll hear from an agent with the Federal Bureau of Investigation, a man recognized as an expert in fingerprint analysis. His name is Willis Rhodes. He's been with the Bureau since its creation and is, in fact, a preeminent authority on that aspect of forensic science." Abner, who had regained his confidence, plunged ahead. "What Special Agent Rhodes will tell you, ladies and gentlemen, is that fingerprints recovered from the steering wheel of Mr. Rosenstein's Cadillac—the automobile described by witnesses as the getaway vehicle—are consistent with Mr. Epstein's."

O'Malley conceded the point. He didn't raise a fuss because Johnny Finn was Kid Rose's driver: it would only be natural to find Finn's fingerprints on the Cadillac's steering wheel.

"In addition, a Thompson submachine gun was found in a storage locker at one of Mr. Rosenstein's businesses." The use of the word "submachine gun" grabbed the attention of the jurors and the standing-room-only gallery of the courtroom, such that one could hear the wall clock above the judge's bench tick with each passing second. James waited for the import of his disclosure to sink in. "Upon finding the Tommy gun, ladies and gentlemen, Special Agent Rhodes will testify that he noted two things of importance. First, he will testify that the gun had fresh powder residue on the barrel, indicating it had recently been fired. And second . . ."

"Your Honor!" O'Malley interrupted with vigor, again rising to his feet from behind the counsel table where he and his clients were seated. "A sidebar, please!"

Abner James turned to face the opposing attorney, his mouth agape. *What the fuck? Judge Reilly conducted an offer-of-proof hearing on the "novel" science of fingerprint analysis. He required me to bring Agent Rhodes to court for an evidentiary hearing and to be cross-examined by Bill. Bill asked his questions and tried to knock Rhodes off his game. But in the end, the judge ruled in my favor. The Kid's prints on the murder weapon are "in." What the fuck is going on?*

"Approach."

The attorneys walked up to the judge's bench and stood in front of Reilly. "Is there an objection, Counselor?" the judge whispered.

"There is," O'Malley replied quietly. "I know you ruled before trial that the fingerprints are 'in'. But, given the novelty of fingerprint analysis, and given that no one from local law enforcement will testify in support of Agent Rhodes's *theories*, I urge you to reconsider."

James fumed. "Judge, fingerprinting isn't some novel *theory*. It's based upon *scientific* principles that've been around since the 1860s. It's settled law that if a man is certified and qualified to conduct fingerprint comparisons, his testimony, subject to other foundational aspects and cross-examination, comes in." Abner stopped, controlled his breathing, contained his outrage, and concluded. "We went through a two-hour offer-of-proof hearing on this very subject, after which you ruled that Special Agent Rhodes's testimony on this point could be introduced at trial."

"That's true," Reilly admitted.

"But if you allow such evidence in, when the only eyewitness who can put the Tommy gun in Mr. Rosenstein's hands *at the time Swanson was murdered* is the dead man's five-year-old daughter, you severely prejudice the defendants," O'Malley argued.

"Come on, Bill . . ."

"Enough, Mr. James. I've heard enough." The jurist looked over the frame of his glasses. "Judges sometimes error, Counselor. It seems that's the case here. The analysis done by Mr. Rhodes," the judge said tersely, avoiding the honorific 'special agent' when referring to the FBI man, "is out. I'll advise the jury accordingly."

"Jesus fucking Christ, Ed . . ." James blurted out in a voice loud enough for everyone in the courtroom to hear.

"Lower your voice," Reilly admonished with inexplicable calm. "Finish your opening so we can hear from Bill and get this case moving," the judge added, through a troubling smirk.

Bill O'Malley's opening statement was a predictable attack on the state's evidence and witnesses.

First, O'Malley challenged the ability of Mr. Weatherby, who wasn't wearing his eyeglasses when he viewed the retreating Cadillac, to add much of anything to the state's case.

Then, the defense lawyer questioned Joyce Big Eyes's statement—that the man in the back seat of the car was Kid Rose—by advancing the subtle supposition that the Minneapolis police, in not more closely scrutinizing Joyce's sobriety on the evening in question, may well have taken a statement from an Indian woman under the influence of alcohol. Without a hint of shame, O'Malley played to likely, though undisclosed, prejudices held by the jurors.

But Bill O'Malley reserved his most vociferous skepticism for the anticipated testimony of Beatrice and Marjorie Swanson.

"Can you imagine what went through the mind of a five-year-old, a child innocent in the ways of the world, who witnessed the assassination of her father?" O'Malley paused. "Or the thoughts of a wife cradling her dying husband in her arms? I can't." Another pause. "But when young Marjorie and her mother take the stand, you will hear their versions of what they *claim* they saw. And you will also hear about police lineups involving my clients."

"What I ask, as you listen to this sad business—as reported by a frightened little girl and her distraught mother—is that you follow the jury instructions Judge Reilly will give you concerning witness testimony. He'll provide guidelines in this regard both *before* the trial begins and later, at the *conclusion* of the evidence." O'Malley paused again—looking confident behind the wooden lectern—reviewed his notes, took a swig of water from a glass, returned the glass to its perch, and continued.

"And what do those instructions from His Honor say? They tell you to consider a witness's 'age, experience, and education' as you weigh testimony. Keep the court's instructions in mind as you listen to young Marjorie Swanson."

O'Malley looked at the jury, detected a frown or two from its members, but remained confident in his ability to persuade and went on. "As far as Mrs. Swanson is concerned, obviously her statements and observations must be viewed in context. She will tell you that she did not see who fired the machine gun—and we concede that, in fact, it was a deadly Thompson submachine gun that took Donald Swanson's life—but that she arrived on the porch to find her husband gasping his last, earthly breath after the fatal shots were fired. You'll be asked to apply the same guidelines to evaluate Mrs. Swanson's claim that she saw my client holding a gun on the day in question." O'Malley took a cleansing breath. "Pay close attention to the instructions the judge gives and the ways in which you are to evaluate Mrs. Swanson's perceptions in the context of her having just stumbled upon the brutal murder of her husband."

Defense counsel made similar statements regarding the evidence against Johnny Finn, finished his outline of the case, and sat down. Judge Reilly, as Bill O'Malley had predicted, then provided the jurors with preliminary instructions of law, including guidelines as to how to evaluate witness testimony. At the conclusion of the jury instructions, gavel banged wood, and court was adjourned.

The room cleared. Abner James looked up from a legal pad full of neatly scripted notes, his hands clenched, his anger nearly uncontrollable. It took every fiber of the Assistant County Attorney's resolve to refrain from screaming out, "I see the fix is in!". The prosecutor watched in disgust as Judge Reilly rose from his perch, opened a door behind the bench, and vanished. *Shit,* Abner James thought as he placed his notepad and pencil in his briefcase, closed the satchel, stood up, and walked toward the exit. *It looks like Judge Reilly has already decided this case.*

CHAPTER EIGHT

Governor Ill: Suspends Campaign

Following Governor Larson's recent collapse before a crowd at Nicollet Field, a large tumor was removed from the governor's colon by University of Minnesota Hospital physicians. The governor's office announced that Governor Larson will undergo a course of "precautionary radiation treatment" at the Mayo Clinic in Rochester, and that the governor's re-election campaign has been "temporarily suspended." No further information was provided by the governor's spokesman regarding the severity of Governor Larson's illness, the extent of the radiation treatment, whether the diagnosis is one of cancer or non-malignancy, or the expected duration of the campaign's hiatus.
   (St. Paul Pioneer Press, July 21, 1932)

On the cusp of having to face Kid Rose and Johnny Finn in open court and being close to birthing her third child—feeling the weight of the fetus, as well as the reality of widowhood and the burden of raising three small children alone—Beatrice Mondale Swanson was forced to make decisions concerning her dead husband's newspaper.

Subscriptions to—and advertisements in—the *Truthsayer* had fallen to levels that made the enterprise unsustainable. As the reluctant new owner of the *Truthsayer*, Bea was forced to release the lone remaining employee—reporter and office administrator, editor, and circulation manager Ellis Beckett—from service.

Alice Sullivan had departed the *Truthsayer* before Don's murder, accepting a job with the *St. Paul Pioneer Press* as a proofreader. Due to Eddie Sullivan's tragic death during the Teamster's Strike, Alice knew firsthand the grief, loss, and darkness threatening to overwhelm Beatrice. Consequently, Alice approached Bea at Don's funeral—a small, private affair despite the notoriety surrounding the reporter's murder—embraced the widow, whispered consoling words, and handed the devastated woman a scrap of paper containing her telephone number before departing.

Following a private internment on the Oak Ridge farm owned by Don's parents—an occasion attended by immediate family and the local Missouri Synod Lutheran pastor—Bea and Alice began regular weekly conversations over the telephone and, when their schedules allowed, met at neighborhood eateries for lunch. As the birth of Bea's third child loomed, Alice drove Eddie's rusty, held-together-by-bailing-wire 1928 Chevrolet flatbed truck—the only significant asset Eddie had left Alice—from her apartment in East St. Paul to diners and greasy spoons near Bea's Bloomington Avenue duplex, keeping the luncheon outings within minutes of Abbot Hospital's Janney Children's Pavilion where Bea's third child was to be born.

In addition to dressing Marjorie and Oscar for the day, feeding them, making sure they played safely and innocently with neighborhood children, reading to them, preparing Marjorie for kindergarten, and readying the children for bed—to include reciting the Lord's Prayer before the lights went out—cleaning house, doing dishes, and chatting and dining with Mrs. Sullivan, it fell upon Beatrice to sell off the furniture, presses, typewriters, and other equipment owned by the *Truthsayer.*

The proceeds from such sales—once the newspaper's offices were empty and its lease in the Minnesota Building was canceled (the termination of which required Beatrice to pay a penalty)—equaled half the amount loaned to Donald by Bea's parents to keep the paper afloat. After a desperate call from Beatrice just weeks before Donald's death, the Mondales had advanced sorely needed funds in an ill-fated, last-ditch attempt to keep the *Truthsayer* in operation.

The nest egg Don accumulated when his novel, *This Troubled Land,* was snapped up by Bobbs-Merrill, had sustained the paper through lean times. But as the book's popularity waned, as subscriptions to the *Truthsayer* dried up, and as sales of the paper stalled at local newsstands, Bea had swallowed her pride and asked her parents for assistance. Loan documents were drafted by an attorney and signed by the parties. But with Donald dead and Bea struggling to liquidate the newspaper's assets, her folks understood that the cash Bea handed them after the sale of the newspaper's physical assets was all they'd ever receive as repayment for an improvident act of parental love.

The murder trial was a terrible ordeal for the widow and her daughter to endure.

"Now, Marjorie, where were you when you say you saw the man you *claim* shot your father?" Bill O'Malley asked when he was allowed to cross-examine the child.

The five-year-old had been poised and succinct when answering questions posed by Abner James on direct examination. She bravely recounted standing on the front porch of the family home on Bloomington Avenue and was unhesitatingly detailed in her description of her father's appearance, the paper sacks he'd been carrying up the stairs, the sudden appearance of the "big black car," and the unexpected burst of gunfire that startled her.

"That's him," Marjorie had said, pointing directly at Kid Rose when asked if the man who pulled the trigger was in the courtroom. "He shot Daddy."

Spectators gasped. The gallery's expression of surprise was followed by shouts of "Fry the bastard!" and "Hang the Kike!"

"Officer!" Judge Reilly demanded, his dander up, his temper at a fever pitch. "Remove that man!" the jurist hollered, pointing at a disheveled man sitting in a wooden pew. The spectator who'd uttered the slur wore a filthy shirt, grease-stained dungarees, and unpolished work boots. His hair was uncombed, his haggard face was emaciated and displayed a week's worth of whiskers, and he was as thin as a rail, as if he hadn't eaten a decent meal in months. The rabble-rouser looked to be another casualty of the Great Depression and, perhaps, an ardent reader of the *Truthsayer* who viewed the murder of his muckraking hero akin to the way devout Catholics cherish martyred saints.

A Hennepin County deputy grabbed the troublemaker by the collar and lifted the offender from his seat.

"Thirty days for contempt," the judge said, as the deputy dragged the heckler from the courtroom. "Now, where were we?" Judge Reilly asked, looking to the attorneys for guidance.

Abner James had continued his questioning. The child methodically recounted the lineup process at

Hennepin County Jail. The prosecutor concluded his examination by having Marjorie identify Johnny Finn, who was seated with his lawyer and Kid Rose at the defense counsel table, as the man she believed was driving the Cadillac when her father was gunned down.

When cross-examined by Bill O'Malley as to where Marjorie had been when her father was shot, the girl seemed puzzled.

"Minneapolis . . . ?"

The gallery tittered. The judge cracked a smile but did not interrupt the cross-examination to quiet the audience. Reilly's failure to admonish the crowd evinced a blasé attitude that puzzled Abner James. The prosecutor had tried, by enlisting Minneapolis cops and Hennepin County deputies—men whose integrity he trusted—to discover the source, the reason—and perhaps the leverage—behind the judge's peculiar rulings. But the lawmen had been unable to find any link between Abram Rosenstein and the judge's erratic decision making.

"I understand. But I'm asking about exactly where, *in* Minneapolis, you were when your father was shot," O'Malley continued once the laughter dissipated.

"Oh. Sorry," the girl said, looking flustered. "I was on our front porch watching Daddy come up the stairs."

"And how far, in terms of feet or any other measure of distance, including an object in this courtroom, were you from the car that drove past?"

"Mmm . . ." The child considered the question for a moment before answering. "From here to the tables, where you and the other men are sitting."

"Your Honor, let the record reflect that, having made measurements before the trial began, the distance from the witness stand to the counsel tables is exactly thirty-five feet."

"So noted."

"This was at night?"

"Yes."

"There was a streetlamp, as the policemen have said, on the corner?"

"That's right."

"Any lights on the porch?"

"Yes."
"Were they on?"
"No."
Any lights inside the house?"
"Yes."
"Those on?"
"The one inside the door was on."
"It was night. There were no lights on the porch. The nearest streetlamp was a half-block away. And there was one light on in the hallway inside the house?"
"Yes."
"The front door. Was it open or shut?"
"Open." The child turned shy and admitted, "I forgot to close it."
"That's fine. Was the screen door open or closed?"
"Closed."
"But light could shine through the screen, onto the porch, from the hallway?"
"That's right."
"I assume the street was somewhat dark?"
The child considered the question. "Yes," she finally said.
"Shadows here and there?"
"Yes."
"But you say you were able to see the shooter?"
She nodded.
"Marjorie," Judge Reilly interjected, "my court reporter, Mr. Robertson over there with the big book and the pen, needs your answers to be said out loud."
The girl nodded again.
Judge Reilly smiled. "Your answer aloud, please?" He stopped, studied the child's innocent face, and asked, "Do you need the question asked again?"
She shook her head.
"Marjorie . . ."
"Oh, sorry. No, I remember it. Yes, there were shadows."
"Fine. Thank you." O'Malley paused. "And you have told the police, Mr. James, and the jury here that, while you *believe* Mr. Rosenstein was the man holding the gun, you only *think* Mr. Epstein was driving the car. Do I have that right?"

Abner James rose to his feet. "Objection, Your Honor. Counsel's use of the words 'believe' and 'think' misstates the testimony."

"But . . ." O'Malley began.

"Save it, Counselor," Reilly said, raising his right palm like a traffic cop. "The objection is overruled."

"Exception," an exasperated Abner James said.

"Noted."

If that was all the judge had said, Abner could've lived with the ruling and made his arguments about the child's certainty of mind at the close of the case. But Judge Edmund Reilly wasn't finished.

"Ladies and gentlemen of the jury," Reilly said tersely. "I will remind you of the instructions I gave you before testimony began regarding how you are to weigh and gauge the validity of a person's sworn affirmations. Here, you are dealing with a young child. Granted, I've allowed her to testify because she knows the difference between the truth and a lie," Reilly added, taking a swig from the mug resting on his bench.

It was assumed by observers that the cup contained only black coffee. In truth, the coffee had been fortified with whiskey. After enjoying the slow, calming embrace of alcohol, the judge returned the cup to its leather coaster and continued.

"My allowance of the child's testimony should, in no way, be viewed as an endorsement of her recounting of events. In fact, as you deliberate the evidence at the end of this trial, be mindful that you are to evaluate a person's under-oath recollections in the context of the witness's age, experience, and education.

"Here, you are confronted with the *perceptions* of a child too young for school, a youthful soul just beginning to read, whose world experiences are limited. You must give her view of things enhanced scrutiny because, as we all know, young children—especially young girls—live inside their heads in a world populated by fancy, fantasy, and fairies. Gauge her testimony carefully, and remember: her words alone should never carry the day."

"YOUR HONOR! SIDEBAR!" Abner James shot out of his chair, claimed his feet, and screamed at the judge before he realized what he was doing.

Edmund Reilly shook his head and, despite the disrespect evident in the prosecutor's eruption, modeled serenity. "No, sir, I will not entertain further discussion on the point." The judge nodded. This, to Abner, seemed to be a gesture of satisfaction that Reilly had fulfilled his part in an unsavory bargain. "Mr. O'Malley, you may continue."

"Ma'am, you were asked to participate in lineups regarding my clients, correct?" Bill O'Malley asked Beatrice Swanson when it was the widow's turn for cross-examination.

"Yes."

"It's true, is it not," the defense lawyer continued, "that, while you and other eyewitnesses gave the police general descriptions of the person *alleged* to be the driver, only your daughter *thought* Mr. Epstein was the person driving the car?"

Clever, Abner James mused. *He's using words like "alleged" and "thought" to create a sliver of uncertainty, which, of course, is all he needs for an acquittal. He's also asking her to recount the statements and opinions of others. I need to object ...*

"Objection, Your Honor," James said, rising to his feet.

"State your objection."

"Cumulative and asks this witness to vouch for other witnesses."

When Bill O'Malley attempted to respond, the judge bade him to remain seated and O'Malley complied. "No, Counselor. What is being asked is whether this witness knows what the jury already knows: that none of the *supposed* eyewitnesses, with the sole exception of a five-year-old child, have identified Mr. Epstein as the person who *allegedly* drove the black car on the night in question. Overruled."

"Exception."

"Noted."

Christ! "Supposed eyewitnesses"? "Supposed?" Despite his upset, knowing which way the wind was blowing, Abner James realized that if the judge made mistakes as to law and procedure that prejudiced the state's case, unless it could be proven that the court's errors were products of a bribe or something similarly nefarious, double jeopardy would preclude retrying the defendants upon acquittal. *Absent illegal conduct by the judge, an appeal by the state—at best—secures only an admonishment from the Minnesota Supreme Court regarding Reilly's ineptitude, not a second swing at the ball.*

"Do you recall my question?" Bill O'Malley asked.

"Yes."

"Can you answer it?"

"Only Marjorie picked Mr. Epstein out of the lineup as the driver."

"And it's also true that, while you picked Mr. Rosenstein out of a lineup as the man you say was holding a machine gun on the evening at issue, neither you nor the other *adult* witnesses saw the actual shooting?"

"That's true."

"Thank you." O'Malley then produced an eight-inch by twelve-inch glossy black and white photograph, vacated his seat, and handed the picture to the court reporter. The photo was marked as an exhibit and returned. "Defense Exhibit A, Your Honor," O'Malley said.

"Show it to opposing counsel."

Bill O'Malley walked up to Abner James and handed him the photo.

Oh, shit. "Your Honor, may we approach?"

Judge Reilly shook his head. "Counselor, if I let you come up here any old time you want, these fine ladies and gentlemen," the judge said, gesturing toward the jury with an open hand, "will be spending Labor Day inside this courtroom. No, you may not conference at the bench. But you may state your objection."

"The photograph is irrelevant," James said weakly, unwilling to telegraph to the jurors what he suspected was in store.

"Overruled. You can examine *your* witness on the exhibit's merits during redirect."

After the bomb has exploded, you mean . . . James held his tongue, failed to note an exception to the ruling, and sat down, disgust evident on his large, oval-shaped face.

"May I approach the witness, Your Honor?" O'Malley asked.

"You may."

O'Malley walked up to Bea Swanson and handed her the photograph. "Please take a look at this picture, ma'am."

Bea complied. "OK," she said, after scrutiny.

"Who do you think is depicted by this photo?"

"YOUR HONOR!" James screamed, leaping to his feet.

"SIT DOWN, COUNSELOR!" the judge spit out. "I've had just about enough of you! One more outburst and you'll face not only a mistrial, but a finding of contempt and you'll be able to consider your sins alongside that unruly spectator I sent to the Hennepin County Jail." The judge paused, sought to reign in his temper, and asked evenly, "Do I make myself clear?"

Fuck. I'm fucked. My case is fucked. "Yes, Your Honor. It won't happen again."

"It best not . . ."

Abner James's outburst was supported by institutional knowledge.

Early in the investigation of Donald Swanson's murder, Moe Feldman had planted seeds of doubt as to who pulled the trigger. Minneapolis cops friendly to Feldman and Rosenstein brought Moe's theory of an alternative perpetrator to Marty Aronson, the lead detective on the case, who then brought Moe's unsupported hypothesis to Abner James. The theory floated by Feldman and relayed to Abner was that, because Kid Rose was in a barber's chair at the time of the murder, and because Mr. Rosenstein bore an uncanny likeness to Gilbert "Gunner" Halloran—a contract killer affiliated with the Chicago North Siders—Halloran, not Kid Rose, was the killer.

Feldman's fable included a supposition that Swanson's investigation of Rosenstein's suggested connections to Irish mobsters, coupled with the reporter's delving into Governor Larson's past, troubled Bugs Moran—the Chicago gangster fronting Kid Rose's bootlegging operation—such that Bugs put out a contract on Don Swanson's life—a contract Gunner Halloran had accepted.

This false narrative, one Abner James had dismissed out of hand as fiction, occupied the prosecutor's thoughts as he sat behind a mountain of file folders, his eyes downcast, his will to fight near an end.

"The photograph?"

Beatrice nodded, set the picture down on the oak surface of the witness stand, before replying: "Why, that's Mr. Rosenstein, of course!"

"Thank you, ma'am. No further questions."

An identical exchange took place with Joyce Big Eyes. The Ojibwe woman had been certain, on direct exam, that the man in the rear passenger's seat of the Cadillac holding a Thompson submachine gun was Kid Rose. And when presented with Defense Exhibit A during O'Malley's cross, Miss Big Eyes was just as certain, as Bea Swanson had been, that the person depicted in the photo was Abram Rosenstein.

Despite all the setbacks experienced by the state, when Bill O'Malley sought directed verdicts in favor of his clients, Judge Reilly denied the motion with respect to Kid Rose. But, as to Johnny Finn, the judge concurred with O'Malley's position. The case against Finn, a case based on the hesitant words of a five-year-old child, had not been made. The charges against Johnny Finn were dismissed, and Kid Rose's most trusted associate was released from custody a free man.

Reilly granted O'Malley's motion for a directed verdict regarding Finn but left the Kid's case for the jury to decide, likely to make it seem he was being "fair," James thought. *Fuck that shit. The little weasel should have never been appointed to the District Court, and if it is the last thing I do, I'll figure out what Kid Rose has on the man—or promised the man—that compelled Reilly to tank my case.*

The defense brought in liars, cheats, and misfits to provide an alibi for Abram Rosenstein. That Moe Feldman and the others stood by their stories supporting Kid Rose's innocence didn't shock Abner James. What caught the prosecutor off guard was the testimony of Herbert Mullen.

"Sir, could you tell the ladies and gentlemen what it is you do for a living?"

"I'm a crime photographer for the *Chicago Daily Times.*"

"How long have you been doing that work?"

"Ten years."

Bill O'Malley left his seat, collected Defense Exhibit A, and stood in the well of the courtroom. "Your Honor, may I approach?"

"You may."

O'Malley walked up to the witness and handed the photograph to Mullen.

"Do you recognize Defense Exhibit A?"

"I do."

"What is it?"

"It's a picture I took. Date's on the back," he said, turning the photograph over. "June 13th, 1928."

"Who's depicted?"

"Gilbert "Gunner" Halloran."

"Do you know Mr. Halloran?"

"Only by reputation, and through my work as a crime photographer. I don't know him socially, though I've met him a half-dozen times."

"What occasioned the taking of this photograph?"

O'Malley's inquiry piqued Abner James's curiosity, but given the court's prior rulings, he remained mute.

"I took this when Halloran was waiting in the hallway of the Cook County Courthouse in the custody of deputies. He was about to enter a courtroom."

"Do you remember why Halloran was there?"

James rose hesitantly, his enthusiasm and vigor bested by the court's disdain. "Objection. Relevance," he said without conviction.

Judge Reilly pondered the issue. "Oh, yes, Mr. O'Malley. Can you identify where this line of questioning is headed."

"But Your Honor, if Mr. O'Malley does that in open court, he may well prejudice the state in that he'll be talking about issues better heard at sidebar or in chambers."

Reilly waved off the prosecutor with a dainty, never-worked-at-labor right hand. "Oh, I'm certain it will be fine, Counselor. After all, Mr. O'Malley is an officer of the court. Proceed, *Bill*," the judge added, emphasizing defense counsel's first name as if they were bosom pals.

"I'm prepared to provide certified court documents that outline and, indeed, support charges made against Mr. Halloran. Charges that ended not with a verdict, but in a mistrial when a key witness—Mr. Halloran's mistress—disappeared."

"Well then," Judge Reilly said with satisfaction, "I'm certain such a discussion will be extremely valuable to this jury. Objection overruled. Proceed with your questioning."

Abner held his breath and stared at his hands. "Exception," he muttered.

"Noted. Continue, Mr. O'Malley."

"Mr. Mullen?"

"Gunner was there for a trial concerning the contract murder of a policeman: a death penalty crime in Illinois. But without the mistress—Halloran's getaway driver who'd fingered Halloran as the triggerman in return for leniency—the case fell apart."

"Does Mr. Halloran have any connection to Minnesota?"

"Objection. Foundation. The question is also vague as to the term 'connection'," Abner James said quietly.

"The objections are overruled. You may answer."

James was so embittered by the judge's demeanor and prior rulings that he again failed to note an exception to Reilly's decision.

"He does. He's associated with Irish mobsters engaged in bootlegging here. There's talk he was hired to 'take care' of a reporter who was poking his nose where it doesn't belong ..."

James, who had remained on his feet, addressed the judge with rekindled outrage. "For Pete's sake, Your Honor . . ."

"Counselor, I understand your objection and your concerns," the judge said. Reilly frowned at Bill O'Malley before addressing the jury. "Ladies and Gentlemen: The witness's last statement, that Mr. Halloran killed Mr. Swanson because Mr. Swanson was poking his nose 'where it doesn't belong' is stricken. That statement should not be considered by you during your deliberations."

You can't make something like that vanish from people's minds, Abner James thought as he watched the judge feign removing his thumb from the scales of justice. *Jurors don't ignore words once spoken. I haven't the balls to ask for a mistrial, and given the judge's evident bias, he'd never grant one anyway. It would also be a waste of time to voice an exception to his ruling.*

"How did this happen?" a distraught, tearful, uncomfortably pregnant Beatrice Swanson asked as she stood next to Abner James outside the courthouse. The sun was bright, the sky cloudless, with late July heat radiating off concrete and asphalt and a blanket of humidity making the day feel ten degrees warmer than the eighty-five degrees registering on a nearby pharmacy's outdoor thermometer. "I am certain, one hundred percent, that it was Kid Rose, not some thug from Chicago, who killed my husband."

Abner looked at the pregnant, stoutly configured woman. Beatrice wore her thick, glorious, blond hair pinned in a tight bun atop her head. Moisture leaked from her hairline and slid down her face.

The underarms of James's dress shirt and the belly of his vest were soaked from perspiration. His wrinkled, blue pinstriped suit jacket was thrown casually over his right shoulder. His eyes expressed defeat. His large, oval, face oozed sweat. The attorney appeared to be exhausted from the day's heat and the jury's rejection of his cause.

Well, for one thing, Kid Rose, dressed to the nines, his hair slicked back, his manner poised and confident, charmed the pants off the jury. I tried to create cracks in his story to tarnish the shine. But it was useless. He couldn't be moved, Abner thought. *The man jurors heard and saw was so polished, so business-like, there was no way, in their minds, he was capable of murder. And, of course, when asked, he denied everything. That alone, without all the other issues in the case, probably sank our ship.*

"I am too. But the judge . . ." Abner chose not to mince words. *There's no reason to soften what happened. She deserves to know the full extent of the jurist's untoward behavior and the impact of his god-awful rulings, rulings that trampled justice.* "Judge Reilly . . . tanked the case. Pure and simple. He caused this unfortunate and unfair result."

"Are you certain I couldn't have done more? Or Marjorie? Or Miss Big Eyes? Or the other witnesses? Maybe we could have done more . . ." Beatrice broke into a body-wrenching sob that left her gasping for breath.

The lawyer embraced the woman with his corpulent body, holding her so tightly sweat wicked from his clothing onto her pregnancy smock. "No, Mrs. Swanson. You and your daughter and all the rest of the folks who testified—including the police—did the best they could. It was the judge, plain and simple, who did us in."

Bea's cerulean eyes met Abner's gaze. "Are you certain?"

"I am."

She withdrew to create space. "And you, Mr. James, you too did everything you could to seek justice for Donald. For that, I'm eternally grateful."

"*I* could've done more. *I* wanted to remove the pipsqueak as our judge, but *I* could never get the goods on him. Rosenstein got to Reilly. Somehow. Someway. But even the full weight of the Minneapolis Police Department and the Hennepin County Sheriff's Office couldn't solve that puzzle."

Alice Sullivan pulled up in her rickety flatbed truck. She'd been working, unable to attend the proceedings, but had been fully apprised of the trial's result during a telephone call from Bea after the verdict was returned.

Alice leaned across the front seat and rolled down the passenger-side window. "Sorry it turned out this way. Let's get you home so you and the kids can start to heal."

Beatrice nodded, retrieved her purse from the sidewalk, made herself as tall as she could, pecked Abner James on the cheek, and lowered herself again. She walked to the truck, opened the door, slid onto the bench seat, closed the door, and waved to the lawyer.

Alice worked the clutch, shifted the Chevy into gear, and pulled away from the curb.

"Mrs. Sullivan is a good friend and a smart woman," Abner mumbled as he picked up his battered briefcase and walked toward a streetcar stop, "but she's dead wrong: Mrs. Swanson and her children will never heal from their loss."

CHAPTER NINE
August 1932

"**It** isn't like I relished gunning down a husband and a father in front of his family," Abram Rosenstein said to Moe Feldman. "That wasn't something I wanted to happen," Kid Rose added, as the pair sipped rot-gut whiskey from water glasses while sitting at a table in the Pelican's Roost, a speakeasy owned by the Kid's Irish cohorts. "But the asshole ignored my warnings, including the setup in Duluth."

Moe nodded. "You tried to warn the man, just like you did with Cooper."

"Dispatching that asshole's dog," Abram noted after draining his glass, "was an unpleasant necessity required to get Cooper to back off." He looked at his large hands and shook his head. "If only Swanson had been as smart."

In May 1931, an FLP statewide organizing meeting had been held at the Curling Club in Duluth. Donald Swanson and Ellis Beckett had attended the event in hopes of cornering party officials about news that was unsettling party unity, the rumor that Sigurd Larson would serve one additional term as governor and then oppose incumbent Senator Henrik Shipstead during the FLP's 1934 nominating convention.

The reporters had, despite the newspaper being near impoverishment, booked rooms at Duluth's Spalding Hotel. The hostelry was located on Superior Street, across from the Lyceum Theater, an opulent venue towering over the cityscape where vaudeville acts, plays, and talking pictures filled the theater's main floor and three balconies with patrons for nearly every performance.

At the Curling Club, the reporters spent their time trying to pigeonhole party bigwigs and chasing after the governor (who was the event's keynote speaker) and Senator Shipstead, to no avail. Scoop-less, Swanson and Beckett found themselves in a ramshackle saloon located beneath the Lake Avenue boardwalk sipping bootlegged gin and lamenting failure.

"That was a waste," said Beckett, a descendent of Welsh immigrants on both sides of his ancestry who, besides lacking hair, had been shorter, thicker of girth, and darker in complexion than his boss. He raised an empty glass to attract the attention of the barkeep.

"And it's no secret," Don had bemoaned, "what with Alice leaving, and our cash flow in decline, that we can ill-afford this trip. Coming up with absolutely nothing concerning the party's discord? Well, that, my friend, is an unsettling coda to a fool's errand."

The bartender had filled Beckett's glass. The reporters sat side by side on stools, studying their drinks, silent in defeat. Two young women stepped into the tavern. Late spring chill and the clatter of a downpour followed the women inside the bar. The bouncer, a burly out-of-work stevedore—his hands as large as his head—nodded to the newcomers and allowed them to pass without interrogation. In a manner that seemed brazen for their youth, the girls had avoided myriad empty tables to claim seats alongside the reporters.

"Buy a gal a drink, Mister?" the young lady next to Swanson had asked, her face made up in garish adornment. The girl, who seemed far too young to be patronizing such a place, wore her flapper-style dress immodestly short, though the attention her bare thighs, garters, and silk stockings attracted did not appear to bother her.

"How old are you anyway?" Don asked, while thinking, *You have no business talking to this tart while your wife is at home caring for your children.* Still, attention from a pretty girl, even one likely to be a professional "date," was consoling against the disappointment of the day.

"Old enough to be here," she had answered confidently, engaging Don with deep brown, nearly sable eyes. "Elsie," she said, extending a tiny right hand to the reporter. "Elsie Givings."

"Don," he'd replied, returning the handshake. "Barkeep, two of whatever the young ladies desire."

The bartender, a short stout man displaying thick black muttonchops and a matching mustache, nodded and went to work, obviously familiar with the girls and their preferences.

"Who's your friend?" Emmitt had asked, leaning in to address the fetching, if slightly world-weary, girls.

"I'm Rose. Rose Watkins," the taller girl said, batting amber eyes at Beckett, who, given he was nervous around women unless three sheets to the wind (which he was at that moment) had never been married and, in fact, had not been laid in a month of Sundays.

"Emmitt," the reporter had said shyly.

The party of four had talked, laughed, and flirted as Don battled guilt over his not-so-innocent betrayal of his marriage. After spending every bill in Don's wallet, the group left the speakeasy and stumbled back to the Spalding.

Had Don been sober, he would have examined Elsie's claim—that the girls were also staying at Duluth's most expensive hotel—with a reporter's unclouded lens. But he was so addled from gin that he didn't scrutinize the girls' disclosure.

It turned out the young ladies weren't staying at the Spalding but, in fact, were hoping to find comfort, lodging, and recompence with their new friends. As the four drunks staggered onto one of the hotel's elevators, Don's grasp on right and wrong, on fidelity and honesty, had fallen by the wayside. He ushered the fetching Miss Givings into the waiting car, the elevator operated by a smartly dressed, crisply uniformed teenage boy. "Four please," Don said. The operator nodded. Doors closed. After a slow ascent, the car stopped, the doors opened, and Don tipped the boy his last Morgan half-dollar before exiting the elevator.

"I was sure," the Kid said, "when snapshots from that night were placed in front of Swanson—pictures taken by a man I hired to get the goods once the sedative took effect—the fucking louse would give it up to Johnny rather than have his precious wife see him preserved for eternity in his birthday suit next to an underaged whore."

"Me too," Moe concurred. "It was genius having a private dick and a photographer trail those two rubes and pay the bartender to doctor their drinks." Feldman took a sip of whiskey. "Masterful play, Kid."

Abram shook his head. "I wasn't sure they'd bite. But the sob story the girls told—that they were runaways with no place to stay on a rainy, cold night in Duluth, worked. Beckett, of course, did more than just give up his bed to 'Rose.' Things happened, given she's only fifteen, that violate the law." Rosenstein looked pensive, paused, and then continued. "But I wasn't after Beckett: I wanted Swanson. And I thought, after he let 'Elsie' sleep in his room, he'd eventually take the bait."

"But . . ."

"My fucking bad luck he was a Boy Scout. Photographer and private dick showed up to find Swanson passed out on the floor, a pillow under his head, fully clothed, covered in a bedspread. The girl was passed out in Swanson's bed, still wearing all her clothes. Had to be roused by my guys. The private dick undressed the mark, while the girl stripped down to her skivvies to stage the scenes."

"That should have been enough, right? I mean, you show him the pictures, he folds, and promises to stop investigating Larson."

Rosenstein raised his glass. The barkeep wandered over, snatched the empty, and walked away. "Thing is, when I had Johnny confront the nitwit with the photos, he just laughed."

"'What the hell do I care if you send those to the other papers?' he says to Finn. '*Truthsayer* is about to fold. I have no money. The girl can't extort anything from me. Plus, my wife already knows.' Turns out, he'd made a full confession to the mother of his kids, who, after a month of giving him the cold shoulder, let him back into her good graces." He paused. "I doubt whether Agnes would buy such bullshit . . ."

The barkeep slid a glass across the polished surface of the bar. Abram grabbed it, raised it to his lips, and gulped. "This is absolute crap; the worst we've ever brought in."

Moe nodded. "You're right about that. But back to your play. You still had Beckett on the hook for fucking an underage girl. Couldn't you use that as leverage?"

Abram shook his head. "The problem with runaways, Moe, is just that: they run away. Both girls vamoosed once they got paid. Last I heard, they were in Vegas, screwing gamblers and living the high life. But Nevada's too damn far to chase after them just to prove a point."

"With the girls gone, you had no one to support the lie that Swanson had done the nasty with an underage girl in a rented room in Duluth . . ."

Rosenstein nodded. "That left me with only one option."

"You could've asked McNulty or Moran to handle it. Maybe get them to bring in Halloran or some other trigger man."

Abram shook his head. "Couldn't, Moe. See: Donald Swanson made it personal. He laughed at Johnny, which is the same thing as laughing at me. And being laughed at, my friend, is not something a man in my position can abide."

CHAPTER TEN

Sigurd Larson died on November 12, 1932. As summer meandered toward autumn, it became evident the governor could not continue his bid for re-election. Lieutenant Governor E. Talmadge Hunter became the FLP's standard bearer in Larson's stead and easily won the state's top political office just days before the governor's death.

Once the ailing governor was told his true prognosis, Larson summoned Nordic resolve and refused recommended radiation treatments and additional palliative surgeries. The governor spent his final days in a Lake Minnetonka cottage—a quaint log cabin with a quintessential stone fireplace—purchased for the governor by wealthy anonymous supporters. In a rented hospital bed overlooking the frozen lake, the war hero battled excruciating pain unmitigated by morphine. As he drew his last breath, Sigurd Thaddeus Larson was not surrounded by sycophants, staff, or advisors; only his wife, his son, his parents, and his in-laws were present as the governor's spirit faded from this life into the next.

Larson's funeral, held at the Minneapolis Armory and conducted by a Norwegian Lutheran bishop, was a standing-room-only affair. Thousands of mourners, unable to find seats in the Armory, stood outside in the freezing cold, listening over loudspeakers as President-elect Roosevelt, Ethel Ray, Governor-Elect Hunter, and other dignitaries eulogized a beloved man and political icon. Larson's body was interred at the Fort Snelling Military Cemetery, overlooking the confluence of the Mississippi and Minnesota Rivers. His simple white unadorned marble tombstone bore the epitaph, "On the contrary . . .", the last words uttered by Norwegian playwright Henrik Ibsen.

Sigurd Larson was the first of four Farmer Laborite governors elected in Minnesota. Larson's successor, E. Talmadge Hunter, died in an automobile accident just days after being inaugurated and was succeeded in office by Lieutenant Governor Floyd B. Olson, who was in turn followed by hapless Elmer Benson. Benson was defeated by Republican Harold Stassen after Stassen pledged to end patronage jobs (state positions handed out as "spoils" to supporters of victorious candidates) and institute a merit-based civil service system. Benson's fate was sealed not so much by Stassen's bold proclamation to end patronage but by Benson's inability to control Communists agitating within Larson's All-Party coalition.

After once again securing the FLP's endorsement, Henrik Shipstead was reelected to the United States Senate. In 1940, the senator upset Minnesota politics by rejoining the Republican Party. Despite this philosophical sleight-of-hand, Shipstead was reelected to yet another term. An ardent isolationist and antisemite, the senator allied himself with Charles Lindbergh, Jr., and Henry Ford to oppose America's entry into World War II, and later, the formation of the United Nations: unpopular stances that led to the senator's undoing. In 1946, Shipstead was defeated by John Thye in the Republican primary. Thye went on to win Shipstead's senate seat, ending the turncoat's political career.

Amelia Larson and son Michael fled Minnesota and relocated to Oregon, where the widow married a local surgeon and became immersed in Liberal causes. She died at the ripe old age of eighty-nine, venerated in the press for her lifelong support of women's suffrage, civil rights for Negroes, and natural resource conservation and preservation.

Prohibition's end was finalized when Utah—home to teetotalling Mormons—voted for repeal, which led to the passage of the Twenty-First Amendment. The demise of the Volstead Act ended the lucrative business arrangement between Abram Rosenstein and his Irish partners.

But Kid Rose did not walk the straight and narrow once his bootlegging days were over. With cash to burn, he acquired antiquated rolling stock from the Minneapolis Street Railway Authority—public assets that should have been sold to the highest bidder but were instead purchased by the Kid for a song. With Moe Feldman's financial support, Abram Rosenstein ensured—with carefully placed and generously proportioned bribes—that his bid, which was by no means the highest submitted, was selected. The profit reaped by the Kid from selling steel salvaged from the rolling stock he acquired from the transit authority made him a very wealthy man.

Abram and his common-law wife continued to reside in their modest Highland Park bungalow until, as World War II ended, Agnes was diagnosed with the same mysterious degenerative condition that had claimed baseball great Lou Gehrig. Agnes's end, only three months after her diagnosis, was blessedly swift but devastatingly abrupt.

Hoping to find distraction from grief through activity, Abram Rosenstein partnered with Moe Feldman to purchase dozens of decrepit, failing, nearly-bankrupt taverns, bars, saloons, and supper clubs struggling to survive in a post-Prohibition world. The two former rum-runners refurbished their newly acquired watering holes and eateries and recruited young women, employees whose occupational talents induced patrons to pay top-dollar for "services rendered." The partnership between Moe and Abram flourished because the Minneapolis mob atrophied after Prohibition's repeal and Catholic piety prevented the idled Irish gangsters from operating houses of ill-repute. The resulting void in Minnesota's underworld freed Feldman and Rosenstein to build an uncontested and lucrative monopoly on the backs of unfortunate women.

"Goddamn it, Kid," Moe lamented after reading a headline from the *Minneapolis Star* as he and Abram ate lunch at the Forum. "You told me there was no way Humphrey would become mayor."

"Well," the Kid said, carefully placing his soup spoon on a napkin, chicken soup dribbling down the goatee he'd grown to look the part of a legitimate businessman, "since '20, all you've had over here is Republican mayors. Except for Anderson and Latimer—faggotty FL'ers who snuck into office on Larson's coattails." Abram paused and let history sink in. "The last Democratic mayor elected in this town served three decades ago. So, pardon me if my hunch wasn't spot on."

Moe bit off a hunk of an egg salad sandwich on oat bread, chewed, and thought through the point being made. "The FLA is gone. The Commies did them in. Good riddance, I say. But now, Humphrey and his gang of Irish, Italian, and Nigger Democrats have taken over." Moe chomped down on his sandwich, bit, chewed, and finished his thought. "Damn Democrats will probably win the governorship. Given their 'law and order' mantra, them being in charge of things isn't good for business."

"It's because of that import from South Dakota," Abram said, referencing Hubert Humphrey as he lifted a spoon filled with broth, noodles, and chunks of chicken, opened his mouth, and slurped. "There hasn't been but one Democratic governor since statehood," he added. "But I think you're right: the new 'DFL'—as it calls itself—has more power and more support than the old Democrats ever did."

Feldman nodded. "Humphrey put the only supervisor in Minneapolis P.D. not on our payroll in charge. Plucked Ed Ryan from internal affairs and made him chief. The guy's cleaner than Elliot Ness: the prick who did in Capone." Moe stopped his diatribe long enough to sip coffee.

"Got that right," Kid Rose agreed. "Putting Ryan—a choirboy if there ever was one—in charge makes things harder, what with the feds keeping an eye on us in terms of the Mann Act and all."

Moe nodded. "Make sure you recruit only good, wholesome Minnesota girls for our houses. No Bucky Badgers or Iowa Hawkeyes. Only Grade-A Gopher girls for us!"

"That's what I love about you, Moe: smarts. If our girls don't cross state lines, the feds don't give a shit what we're into."

"That's the way it's gotta be."

Rosenstein grew reflective. "You hear about Chickie Berman's meeting with the new mayor?"

Moe shook his head.

"Humphrey said he was open to talkin' to folks like us, folks, who operate 'alternative' businesses." The Kid finished his soup, put the spoon back on the linen napkin, raised a glass, took a long draw of ice water, set the glass on the table, and lowered his voice. "When Chickie asked 'What'll it take to stay in business, Mr. Mayor?', Humphrey grinned and said, 'Seventy-percent.'"

Moe shook his narrow, bald head. "For such a little man, you gotta hand it to the pharmacist. He's got a pair on him!"

Despite having killed two men, Abram Rosenstein had never been convicted of a crime as an adult. That changed when he took an ill-advised road trip to Hudson, Wisconsin.

Her name was Wilma Richards. She was eighteen years old and living on her own, having fled the family farm outside Black River Falls after her father tried to advance from fondling her breasts to sleeping with her.

Anne Richards was out of town when her husband—and Wilma's father—Bill Richards, made his move. The teenager, being strong, fierce, and tough, kicked her old man in the balls, dropping him to the floor of her bedroom. Before he'd tried to bed his daughter, Bill had downed a quart of Old Crow, rendering him incapable of responding—other than wailing and rolling around like a harpooned seal—to his daughter's well-aimed blow. With her father out of commission, Wilma packed a suitcase, stole the hundred bucks Anne kept hidden in her underwear drawer, and fled.

Wilma's best friend, Nora Bates, had run off a year earlier. After Nora ended Uncle Burt's attempts to molest her by stabbing him in the chest with scissors and telling her parents what had happened, a Jackson County deputy showed up to investigate the fracas. Based upon Burt's claim that "The crazy bitch attacked me for no reason," and Nora's hesitant revelations as to her uncle's intentions, the wet-behind-the-ears deputy chalked up the dispute to a "misunderstanding" driven by "female hormones" and declined to arrest Uncle Burt for attempted rape or Nora for assault. Nora's mother believed her brother's version of events. Nora's father remained silent on the matter: as silent as the corn standing in his field.

Nora Bates fled the farm and found a position at the Green Light supper club as a waitress. One night, after getting drunk and flirting shamelessly with Moe—the club's manager—she lost her virginity. Following their tryst, Moe continued grooming the girl for her new occupation, and within months, Nora was sleeping with strangers for money.

She wrote to Wilma regarding her transition from waitress to working girl in vague terms, but was clear as to one key point: as long as she was three sheets to the wind, she didn't find her new "position" at the Green Light objectionable. Details concerning patrons who caused Nora disgust, alarm, or concern were not shared. That information would, if Wilma decided to cast her lot with the Green Light, be something she discovered on her own.

"You're a friend of Nora's?" Abram asked in a fatherly voice, as he sat across from a young lady at a table in a Hudson greasy spoon.

He bought dinner: two plates brimming with flat iron steaks, potatoes, gravy, carrots, homemade wheat bread, and peach cobbler for dessert. They finished their meals, Wilma trying not to show that she was—after living on her own for four months—famished. Her attempts to take dainty, lady-like bites were poorly orchestrated, such that Kid Rose knew she was ripe for suggestion.

"I am."
"She's written?"
"A few times."
"Told you that she works for me?"
"Not you. A guy named 'Moe'."

Abram smiled, picked up his water glass, and slurped. "My partner. We own the Green Light together."

"Oh. I didn't know that."

She's a bit unkept, Abram thought. *But she's got good teeth and clear skin. A serviceable figure, though a bit skinny. No tits to speak of. But hey, that's not a dealbreaker. Get her started as a waitress, and then either Moe or I can show her the ropes. Likely a virgin, so that must be done kindly, gently, and on her terms. Or at least let her think that's the case.* "You lookin' for work?"

Wilma drew back. "Not the sort of work Nora is doing!"

Abram's smile widened. "I'm not sure what you mean by that. But I'm talking about waitressing at the Green Light. We serve booze and food. Ever waitressed?"

She shook her head.

"Think you could learn?"

Wilma pressed her hands to her lips, her stomach churning due to its emptiness having been unexpectedly filled. She couldn't forestall a belch. "I'm sorry. That was rude."

"Not to worry. It happens." The Kid studied her, his gaze conveying paternal kindness. "Have you been getting enough to eat? Do you have enough money?"

"'No' to both. I'm down to my last twenty and won't make rent."

Kid Rose nodded. "How about it, young lady? Starting pay for a waitress is two bits an hour plus tips. You don't share tips with the bartender, the dishwashers, or the busboys. You keep every cent you earn."

She looked at her hands, which she'd removed from her face and placed in her lap, noting her untrimmed, unadorned, and dirty fingernails. The dress she wore was haggard and unwashed. The soles of her shoes were nearly worn through. When Wilma finally returned Abram's gaze, her fawn-colored eyes were clear, honest, and open. "Where would I live?"

Kid Rose removed a paper napkin from its holder, touched it to his lips, crumpled it, and laid it on his empty plate. "There are rooms above the bar. Every floor has a shared bathroom. All remodeled and clean. Rent for employees is on a sliding scale, based upon your first month's wages and renegotiated after a year."

Wilma nodded. "OK. I'll take the job."

Abram enticed Wilma into his arms. Their "sessions" awakened the girl in unexpected ways and made her envious of the money Nora was making—nearly four times what a waitress earned. Having lost her pride and virginity to a man who was old enough to be her grandfather, Wilma cast her caution and her morality to the wind—after succumbing to a routine of drinking four whiskeys neat after each waitressing shift. Wilma Richards became a filly in Moe's and Abram's stable, a fresh, young, innocent, yet enthusiastic enigma who drove customers wild.

"That Badger girl you brought in is a real moneymaker," Moe said more than once with envy.

"Yup."

Neither man was concerned about the fact that Abram had violated their business plan by transporting Wilma from Wisconsin to Minnesota in his yellow 1945 Cadillac convertible to work in the world's oldest profession. Abram's spur-of-the-moment decision, an inspiration that came to him after spending time "getting to know" Nora Bates, only became problematic when Wilma's mother came to grips with what her husband had tried to do, tossed Bill Richards out the door, and filed for divorce.

Once the farm was empty of Bill's unsavory predilections, Anne Richards interrogated Wilma's friends and learned that her daughter was living in Minneapolis. Through Nora Bates's family, Anne discovered that Wilma was working and living at the Green Light. With a farm to run, it was impossible for Anne Richards to leave Black River Falls to retrieve her daughter. So, cognizant of the anti-crime mindset of Minneapolis's new mayor, Anne wrote to Humphrey. She didn't expect to hear back from the man. She believed her petition, a plea from a non-constituent living a state away—to find and save a young woman—would be ignored.

Mayor Hubert Humphrey called Ed Ryan into his office after receiving, reading, and considering Anne Richards's letter.

"I've a favor to ask," said the short, precise man with rapid speech and thinning hair from behind his desk.

"How's that, Mr. Mayor?" the lanky, narrow-faced, wavy-haired chief of police asked as he claimed an empty seat across from his boss.

"Take a look at this," Humphrey said, handing the cop Anne Richards's letter.

Ryan reached across a stack of precisely typed city council minutes to accept the document and read it. "You're kidding me, right?"

Humphrey smiled. "We got the SOB, Ed. After skating on that manslaughter case in St. Paul, after his acquittal in the Swanson murder—a travesty that should've never, in a million years, happened—we've finally got Kid Rose!"

"By the short hairs, I'd wager," Ryan whispered. "I'll get right on this. It's a Mann Act case, federal jurisdiction," he added. "But we can assist the FBI in finding the girl and backing them up when they put the cuffs on that little Himey."

"Ed!", Humphrey said curtly, "I don't want to hear any of that antisemitic crap. Not after what our Jewish brothers and sisters went through in Europe. Plus, you need to appreciate that Jewish support was crucial to me being elected mayor."

"Sorry, Boss," Ryan mumbled. "Old habits die hard. I grew up across the street from the Bernsteins." The cop stopped and recalled childhood interactions with his Jewish neighbors. "They called me 'a stupid Mick' and I returned the favor. But it was never done with malice. Just kids being kids."

"Well," the mayor said, tapping a finger on an ink blotter, "you're not a kid anymore. Time to put childish slurs behind you. You're my chief of police. I expect better."

Ryan nodded. "Got it. Will do."

Humphrey pointed to the letter Ryan still clutched. "About the young lady's situation ..."

"I've got this, Boss. I'll clear my calendar, head over to the FBI, and work up a plan as to how we get Wilma Richards home."

The raid caught Abram Rosenstein and Mosiah Feldman flat-footed. They no longer had "ears" in the Minneapolis Police Department and had no "eyes" in the FBI's Minneapolis field office to portend a platoon of special agents, vice detectives, and uniformed cops storming the Green Light on a Tuesday evening.

Wilma was working, chatting up a businessman from Des Moines—a man twice her age—at the bar. Chief Ryan accompanied the raid and spotted Wilma dressed in a fashion that would make her mother blush, walked across the saloon, put cuffs on the erstwhile John, took the girl into protective custody, and, with great relish, watched FBI special agents arrest the owners of the whorehouse.

Kid Rose did not escape justice. The case against him was prosecuted by the United States Attorney for the District of Minnesota: not by the Hennepin County Attorney's Office, where Feldman and Rosenstein still maintained connections. The jury trial was held in the federal courthouse in Minneapolis before United States District Court Judge Robert Cook Bell. Bell, a no-nonsense former lawyer from Detroit Lakes, had been appointed by FDR to replace Duluthian William Cant. Prior to ascending to the bench, Bell had been the chief attorney for the Pillager and Red Lake Bands of Ojibwe. From his tribal work, Bell knew the devasting impact prostitution had on Native women; a background that made Bell the perfect choice to hear the government's Mann Act case against the owners of the Green Light.

"Ten years, Mr. Rosenstein," Judge Bell had pronounced at the end of a short and uneventful trial.

There had been no witnesses to support Kid Rose's alternative world view: no alibis, no tricks up Bill O'Malley's sleeve. Twelve jurors, six men and six women, listened intently to a young girl, who, having been reunited with her mother, had reclaimed her old life in Black River Falls. She had also returned to the local Methodist church in search of solace and healing and, within weeks of her repatriation, Wilma Richards began waitressing at a local eatery managed by a maternal great aunt. Around coffee klatches in Black River Falls, Anne defended Wilma's honor with the protectiveness of a mother grizzly guarding her cub, dressing down anyone who attempted to slander her child. By the time the trial was held, the garishly adorned and scandalously dressed hussy who'd briefly earned money for sex was replaced by a church-going, soft-spoken, trim, lovely brunette farm girl: the sort of young woman every juror wanted to adopt and take home.

"That's the maximum sentence allowed and that's the sentence you'll serve," Judge Bell continued. "Marshal, take Mr. Rosenstein to holding to await transfer to a federal penal institution; his ultimate destination to be determined by the Bureau of Prisons."

Moe Feldman—who'd not been involved in transporting Wilma Richards across state lines—was also convicted. Despite his protestations that Abram Rosenstein had violated the Mann Act without his prior approval or knowledge, the jury found Moe to be Abram's co-conspirator. Feldman received a five-year sentence, and

Judge Bell made it a point to instruct the Bureau of Prisons to incarcerate the former business partners in separate correctional facilities.

Mosiah Feldman didn't serve out his term. Housed at the federal penitentiary in Lewisburg, Pennsylvania, Moe died of a massive "widow maker" heart attack in his cell during the early evening hours of October 1, 1951, just three months ahead of his scheduled release.

    Abram Rosenstein served the entirety of his sentence at the federal lockup in Leavenworth, Kansas. A model inmate, Kid Rose completed correspondence courses through the mail, earning certificates of competency in bookkeeping and accounting. After being released and completing parole, Abram moved to Miami, where he changed his name to Elmore Lockett and reinvented himself as an Anglo-Saxon-Presbyterian unlicensed accountant, thereby shedding his Jewish heritage once and for all.

    Despite Abram changing his identity, the notorious gangster Meyer Lansky reached out to the former bootlegger and convinced him to oversee the financial affairs of hotels Lansky owned in Miami Beach and Las Vegas. Most importantly, for Lockett *nee* Rosenstein, Lansky entered into an arrangement with Cuban dictator Fulgencio Batista to develop the Hotel Rivera—a destination resort in Havana. Because Cuba did not have an extradition treaty with the United States, the Rivera became a safe haven for mainland mobsters. Elmore Lockett spent considerable time at the new hotel, working to ensure Lansky's share of the take was accounted for and was sufficiently laundered to avoid scrutiny. Days before Fidel Castro toppled Batista, Lockett fled Cuba, making it off the island one step ahead of the new dictator's *soldados*. Shortly before departing, Myron Lansky's moneyman transferred his personal fortune to a handful of community banks in Florida. Millions were deposited in accounts bearing assumed names, successfully hiding Lockett's ill-gotten gains from the prying eyes and subpoenas of United States Treasury agents.

    Settling into a new life free of criminality, the man formerly known as Abram Rosenstein became beloved by St. Petersburg residents as wealthy, philanthropically inclined, church-going, retired accountant Elmore Lockett.

CHAPTER ELEVEN

The verdict in the murder trial devastated Beatrice Mondale Swanson. After returning to the family farm, Bea tried, as best she could, to put the trial behind her. There was no question in her mind that, but for a corrupt judge, the jury would have followed Abner James's lead and convicted Abram Rosenstein and Jôhānān Epstein of murder. Living in southern Minnesota with her parents and her three children (daughter Millicent having been born after Donald's death), Beatrice sought to reclaim her life—a life devoid of her beloved—though that goal proved elusive.

Bea never remarried. She remained a grieving widow, spending her time assisting her aging parents on the family farm and raising her children. A lump on Bea's left breast became painful to the slightest touch during the summer of 1941—when Marjorie was a sophomore at Elmore High, Oscar was a freshman, and Millie was but nine years old. A radical mastectomy, and the radiation treatment Bea received at the Mayo Clinic in Rochester, her stroke-addled, elderly father driving her to and from appointments in the family's Dodge sedan, arrested the disease long enough for Bea to see Marjorie graduate from high school. But eventually, the widow and mother lost her battle against the out-of-control cells crowding her body. After the obligatory Lutheran funeral, Beatrice's remains were interred alongside Donald's in the Swanson family graveyard overlooking the Pomme de Terre River.

Bea's death sent Marjorie, a bright and precociously serious young lady, into a downward spiral. She was—when home and not enjoying the taverns of nearby towns; haunts where she found solace in the arms of itinerant field hands, tractor mechanics, vagabond threshers, and assorted bad boys—constantly bemoaning the hand Judge Reilly had dealt her family. She routinely bent the ears of her brother and little sister as to how, someday, somehow, she would avenge their father's death by hunting down and killing Judge Reilly, Johnny Finn, and Kid Rose.

Years after being elevated to the Minnesota Supreme Court by Sig Larson—Reilly's appointment emanating from the governor's death bed overlooking Lake Minnetonka—Associate Justice Edmund Ignatius Reilly died of a brain hemorrhage, having issued a catalog of forgettable decisions while sitting on the state's highest court.

"Damn it," Marjorie had muttered when she read the news announcing Reilly's demise in the *Pioneer Press,* "that only leaves Johnny Finn and Kid Rose. I've no idea where those bastards are or whether they're even still alive."

Though Justice Reilly's passing denied Marjorie complete retribution for her father's death, the jurist's demise had, for a time, allowed the eldest child of Donald and Beatrice Swanson a modicum of peace. During her hiatus from hate, Marjorie managed to find and retain, despite a lack of enthusiasm for work, a position with Northwestern Bell as a switchboard operator—a job that barely allowed her to make ends meet.

It was evening. The eldest child of Donald and Beatrice Swanson was sitting on a coffee-stained sofa in the living room of her flat in St. Paul's Midway neighborhood, staring out grease-coated windows. Her life, a life that she once believed would see her graduate from St. Olaf College in Northfield with a degree in biology and grades sufficient to land her in medical school, had taken unexpected turns.

No specific triggers prompted her disquieting reflections, memories that brought Marjorie, or at least the five-year-old version of the hopeless woman she'd become, to a familiar front porch on a long-ago Christmas Eve. As untoward images overtook her rational mind, Marjorie sipped Merlot she couldn't afford from a long-stemmed glass to forestall anxiety, but the imported Italian wine proved ineffectual against the trauma permanently imprinted upon her psyche. As an oh-so-familiar scene emerged in her minds' eye, Marjorie began to shake and to cry.

Father is smiling, carrying paper sacks, his open black galoshes flapping as he climbs the front stairs. A streetcar passes, revealing a slow-moving black car. The car's driver's-side passenger window opens. A gun barrel appears. Rat-a-tat-tat. Cacophony splits the quiet of early evening like a hammer striking glass, the noise shattering her family's life—and Marjorie's future—into a million shards of loss and grief. The gun barrel retracts. The window rolls up. The Cadillac creeps by; the driver seemingly unconcerned that a five-year-old girl has just witnessed her father's murder.

Marjorie wiped tears with the sleeve of her blouse, placed the empty glass on a dusty end table, rose from the couch, and disrobed as she walked toward her apartment's filthy, cockroach-infested kitchen. Her rumpled blouse billowed and fell to the floor. She unhooked her skirt. The garment descended and came to rest atop the blouse. She removed her slip, bra, and girdle, the undergarments drifting toward the hardwood like parachutes. Marjorie stood naked in the kitchen, her body and spirit abused and worn thin by nights spent with men she did not know and did not care to remember. She opened a cupboard and removed a bottle of Finnish vodka from a shelf. She did not bother with a glass. Carrying the bottle in her right hand, her eyes still tearing, her body still shaking, she made her way into the bathroom. She set the vodka on the tile floor, filled the bathtub with hot water, turned off the spigots, and walked to a medicine cabinet above the sink.

"Fuck," Marjorie whispered. "Fuck it all."

She'd explained, in no uncertain terms, to Oscar and Millie what needed to be done. But Oscar was not interested in finding and killing Johnny Finn and Kid Rose. Her brother had completed high school and a course of study at Dunwoody Institute that landed him a good-paying job as a union electrician. Though their grandfather had wanted Oscar to take over the Mondale farm, once Bea passed, Oscar fled Elmore like an armed robber running from a crime scene. He found solace in forgetting, not remembering. He did not dwell upon the men who had murdered his father. He had, once he met Nellie Thomas, a waitress in an Uptown eatery he frequented, fallen in love. The couple had married and were expecting their first baby, and Marjorie could not persuade her younger brother to join her quest for retribution.

Millie was another matter. Though young—only twenty—she was sympathetic to Marjorie's pleas. *Millie gets* it. *She really does. She's the one, not me—and certainly not Oscar—who'll see this through.*

Despite finding comfort in her supposition, Marjorie's emotional turmoil would not abate.

"Daddy," she whispered, reaching into the medicine cabinet, removing a bottle of sleeping pills, closing the cabinet door, and padding across chilly tile to the waiting tub and the vodka, "show me the way. I want to come home."

EPILOGUE

CARIBBEAN SEA
1975

A warm wind caressed the woman's face as her left hand grasped the teak wheel of the Alden cutter to subtly turn the bow of the fifty-seven-footer and catch a breeze blowing in from Puerto Rico. *Bountiful Bea* was a sleek, well-preserved old girl with good bones. The woman secured the wheel, ducked under the boom, scampered to the front of the sailboat, unfurled the spinnaker, returned to the helm, and took advantage of the wind.

Time to start over, she thought. Hidden in the anonymity of the Caribbean, the woman hoped to find a place of seclusion, rest, and renewal. *I've been enthralled with Dominica ever since discovering Jean Rhys.*

The name she'd requested, after paying Mexican emigre Eduardo Zapata three hundred dollars to forge a Canadian passport, was "Monica Rhys," an homage to both her dead mother (whose middle name had been Monica) and the famed novelist. The voyage from Key West, where her boat had been berthed, to Dominica—using Cuba, Espanola, and other Caribbean islands as cover against the prying eyes of the American, British, and French Coast Guards—would prove, despite much of the journey being accomplished at night, uneventful. She had learned to navigate by the stars—and by the big brass compass affixed to the helm of the sailboat—during a torrid affair with a yachtsman—a man she would have married had he not already had a wife. Their passionate couplings had ended not because of guilt but because she'd aged out of the role of mistress. She'd entered menopause and the wealthy real estate developer had severed their relationship in favor of a younger lover. *'Twas for the best,* she thought as the sailboat plowed through the blue-green sea. *I'd grown tired of trading sex for isolated moments of affection.*

It puzzled her, as the *Bea* negotiated the channels of the Virgin Islands, that she felt only release, not guilt. She was not prone to evil. She was not a woman absent of morality. That was not how she was constituted or how she'd been raised on her grandparents' farm. And yet, as the stars and the waning crescent moon—in its final phase—emerged to shine weakly against the night sky, it intrigued her that she could be so easily free of remorse. It had been a tedious exercise, one involving years of sleuthing and patience, to locate Elmore Lockett—*aka* Abram Rosenstein—in an assisted living facility in Fort Myers. The fact that the old man's death and the beginning of her voyage had taken place on Christmas Eve was not coincidental.

Forty-three years old, she mused, adjusting her grip on the wheel. *No children. Never married. No lover. Both parents gone. My sister dead by her own hand. My brother estranged and unwilling to join me in the task bequeathed to us by Marjorie.*

Too bad it took so long to track Epstein down. He was living under an assumed name in that little mining town. What was the town's name again? Ah, yes, Gilbert ... Gilbert, Minnesota. But he was already gone! Stabbed to death in his own bar, The Thirsty Finn, *when he tried to stop a fight between two iron ore miners. I'd worked it all out, how I'd confront Johnny Finn out at his place on Embarrass Lake and end his putrid existence. But God, whoever or whatever She is, stole that from me. Damn. I so wanted to see the man's eyes when he realized who I was and what was going to happen. Water under the bridge, as they say ...*

When she placed extract of wolfsbane into the intravenous line affixed to Elliot Lockett's left arm—the old man, his breathing hesitant and halting due to an inoperable, nonmalignant tumor on his brainstem, the former gangster staring up at her from his nursing home bed with cloudy, cataracted eyes—she knew she'd entered a domain, a place, from whence she could not return. Her years of work as a registered nurse, as a healer, were rendered morally insignificant when she injected poison into the intravenous line running into the old man's left hand; the vein distended and bluer than the water she now sailed upon.

It was worth it, she thought as the Caribbean turned choppy. A fresh wind swept in from the south, requiring her to leave the helm to adjust the spinnaker. *I wish I'd had the opportunity to tell him who I was—why his death was necessary. But there was no time for revelation. There was only time to inject the wolfsbane, leave the man to his fate, and vanish.*

She'd learned wolfsbane's deadly secret from her grandmother. "Don't touch that plant, child!" Grandmother Angeline had said the very first time the girl worked alongside the old woman in the flower garden bordering the back porch of the Mondale farmhouse. The curious girl had reached towards a beauteous purple blossom, intending to pluck a petal and smell it. "That's wolfsbane. Though useful as a healing herb, it's poisonous, even to the touch." The old woman had stopped, studied her granddaughter, and smiled. "You know what 'poisonous' means, don't you?"

The child, four years old at the time, had nodded and replied, "Yes, Grammy."

Though her grandmother's lesson highlighting the deadly propensities of wolfsbane had been brief and occurred years before the girl was charged by her older sister with setting things right, it was a lesson the girl, grown to womanhood, never forgot.

Elmore Beckett had been gifted a death that was, in her view of things, too generous. She'd used an amount of poison that granted its victim a foreshadowing of impending death. The wolfsbane's effect had begun as slight, uncomfortable numbness in Beckett's cheeks. As the toxin affixed itself to the old man's facial nerves, he'd likely noticed something metabolically different transpiring. *And Monica thought, once his limbs began to tingle, followed by heart palpitations, chest pain, nausea, and the loss of bowel control, he'd have known that something was amiss.* She stopped, reflected on her actions, and looked out over the unfathomably vast sea. *It's even possible he could have remembered a kindly smiling nurse injecting something into his IV. But he likely had no idea why the person he referred to only as "Doll" would do such a thing.*

Beckett's passing would appear natural, as if the tumor had done him in, an illusion, a sleight of hand that allowed Monica to exit the nursing home, drive to Key West, ditch her car, walk to the marina, untie the *Bountiful Bea's* lines, fire up the boat's ancient flathead Gray Marine six, and motor away.

As the boat sailed on, the woman also considered what she'd learned about Governor Sigurd Larson, a man she'd never met, a man who'd died before she was born.

Amelia Larson agreed to see me after I'd completed my three-year registered nursing course at St. Luke's Hospital in Duluth and took a job in Seattle. When I knocked on the front door of her oceanside bungalow, intending to confront her about her husband's role in Daddy's murder, the woman was disarmingly candid.

"No," *the governor's widow had said as we sat at the kitchen table. Michael—her son—had grown and moved away, and her second husband—the doctor—was long dead. The room was bathed in sunlight beaming through windows overlooking the little harbor town of Seaside, Oregon.* "No," *she said again,* "Sig never knew. I asked him, after he made that absurd appointment of that judge . . ." *The widow had stopped to remember the jurist's name but couldn't.*

"Edmund Reilly . . ."

"Yes, Reilly. Anyway, I asked him, 'Darling, did you know what your friend Rosenstein—I never called him 'Kid Rose'—was up to?' I never did like that man. There was an aura about him I couldn't abide. But they were lifelong friends, you know? Anyway, Sig assured me that he would not have been a party to the intimidation—much less the death—of a newspaper man. Still . . ." *Amelia stopped, seemingly hesitant to say more.*

"Yes?"

The widow's face tightened. "Well, I know what happened during the trial. Criticism of the judge's rulings made national news. And yet, right after the verdict, Sig appointed Reilly to the Supreme Court." *The old woman stopped to sip hot tea from an English teacup, an act that appeared to ease her nerves.* "I don't think Sigurd was in his right mind when he did that. It was out of character for my husband to do something like that, something that might be seen as a quid pro quo for Judge Reilly tipping the scales of justice in favor of an old friend."

"That's my feeling too."

"I don't believe, knowing my husband's character, he had anything to do with your father's death."

The visitor had accepted the widow's view of things, finished her tea, and departed, leaving the old woman to wrestle specters epiphanized by the past.

Kid Rose deserved a crueler death, the murderess thought, as she steadied the sailboat's wheel. Hesitant stars and the departing moon lost vibrance against advancing dawn. Guadeloupe rose to the east, its coastline demarcating the last island the boat would sail past before reaching its destination. *If I spoke French,* Monica mused, *Guadeloupe would be a good place to hide. But I don't. Plus, I like the symbolism, the symmetry, of starting over on Jean Rhys's island.*

She had no grand plan, no design beyond her leaving and her arriving. She would sell the *Bea*, which, given the plethora of wealthy Brits lounging about Dominica, would net her a tidy sum. That nest egg would be enough, until she found work as a nurse's aide—her professional credentials having vanished with her identity—to see her through. There would be a lover, perhaps a dark-featured islander, perhaps a tan and lean and educated Brit, to amuse her. Maybe even a succession of men, there being no reason to be cautious, given she was no longer able to become pregnant. *Not becoming a mother,* she considered as waves lapped the yacht's wooden hull, *is my one regret.*

She'd been pregnant twice. Her foresight had been bested by poorly made, spur-of-the-moment carelessness. The results had been predictable, and being a medical person, she knew people who could take care of such things. Those decisions were agonizing, because she so wanted children. But not that way; not without love and respect and all the other things necessary to forge a family, a level of domestic stability she never attained. She'd undergone two abortions by two different practitioners. *It was necessary,* she reminded herself, as the sun crept over the eastern horizon to bathe Basse Terré in gauzy, early morning light, *but I paid a price.*

The boat sailed true as the woman lifted the world-weary briefcase her father had once toted to work, placed it on the steering console, and opened it.

The first book she removed from the satchel was a distressed, yellow-with-age-paperback copy of Jean Rhys's

Wide Sargasso Sea. The woman had read and reread the novel many times. Her copy was dog-eared, had a broken spine and a torn cover, and held no value beyond the story it told.

Setting the paperback aside, she retrieved a hardcover copy of *This Troubled Land* from the briefcase. She'd never read the book; she had never even seen it until she stumbled upon the copy she was holding during a visit to Powell's Bookstore in Portland. Discovering the rare, out-of-print novel in a locked glass bookcase, she'd wept. The price, one hundred and fifty dollars, was outrageous. *But I'd pay ten times that to own a signed copy of Daddy's only published book,* she had thought, when the store manager unlocked the cabinet, removed the novel, and placed the book in the woman's unsteady hands.

She'd resisted reading the novel, saving that pleasure for a sultry day when she was reposed on a Caribbean beach enjoying a piña colada. *I never knew him;* she lamented as she held the book—the dust jacket's colorful imagery of Norwegian settlers struggling to survive a Minnesota winter still crisp and pristine—and opened it. Her copy of *This Troubled Land* bore an inscription to a woman, likely a stranger who'd stood in line, wide-eyed and nervous, with other admirers at a book signing:

> *To Madeline Campbell:*
> *Remember what Norman Rockwell said: "The story is the first thing and the only thing."*
> *Keep writing!*
> *Fondly,*
> *Donald Emerson Swanson*
> *May 1, 1931*

"I wish I'd known him," she said softly, closing the novel, replacing *This Troubled Land* and *Wide Sargasso Sea* in the briefcase, closing the satchel, and reclaiming the wheel.

As the *Bea* neared landfall, the youngest child of Donald and Beatrice Swanson steered her melancholia toward optimism. She vowed—as an honorarium to her parents—to embrace and flourish in her new life on Dominica: a life destined to be filled with hard work, desolate beaches, plentiful rum, passionate trysts, pastoral dreams, seasonal storms, and—perhaps—atonement.

The End

AUTHOR'S NOTE

As a high school student, I believed the great stories of the world were imagined from whole cloth like extended fairy tales. Only after reading Hemingway and *about* Hemingway in my late twenties did it dawn upon me that the best works of fiction contain elements of history and truth. The trick, then, is to find something from one's own life—or the life of another—and twist it, turn it, mold it, and fabricate it into fable. To that end, each story, whether short fiction or a novel, needs a start. Maybe you don't care from whence authorial inspiration arises. That's a legitimate position: one I won't challenge here. But, given that the story you just read incorporates the lives and experiences of real human beings into a fictional tale, I think I owe you (and the kin of the departed) an explanation.

For the past quarter-century, my mornings have included listening to Garrison Keillor's *The Writer's Almanac* (*TWA*).

Walter Liggett

Garrison is not above repeating an item from a prior broadcast. Twice on *TWA*—first on December 9, 2014, and then again on December 9, 2020—Mr. Keillor included a synopsis of the life, career, and death of muckraking Minnesota journalist Walter Liggett. I adore Garrison's effort to educate through *TWA*, and as an author, I find great value in making his musings part of my writerly ritual. That's a long-winded way of saying the inspiration for this story came from Garrison Keillor.

Kid Cann

Evidence points to Liggett having been gunned down by Minneapolis gangster Isadore Blumenfeld, otherwise known as "Kid Cann." Pundits have speculated that Cann, a friend of Minnesota Governor Floyd B. Olson, killed Liggett because the journalist was investigating ties between Cann and Olson. Though that allegation was never proven (and, in fact, was discredited by Liggett's daughter, Marda Woodbury), it persists. That being said, this novel is not an attempt to solve the riddle of Walter Liggett's death: it's a work of entertainment concocted and created from the mists of history.

Many details behind my invented character Abram Rosenstein (*aka* "Kid Rose") are drawn from the life of Kid Cann, including the fact that Cann was—despite five eyewitnesses fingering him as the triggerman—acquitted of Liggett's murder. And in another bow to Kid Cann's biography, my gangster-antagonist ends up in prison for other misadventures, and later, like Cann, spends time in Florida. The rest of Kid Rose's story, including his ultimate demise? Pure fabrication.

Governor Floyd B. Olson

The third key figure in my story, Sigurd Thaddeus Larson, is again, fictional. To flesh out *my* governor, I assigned attributes, quirks, and bits of biography to Governor Larson that have their genesis in the lives of Governor Floyd B. Olson and his successor, Governor Elmer Benson. In making Governor Larson a war hero, I "borrowed" Elmer Benson's service in the Great War. However, Larson's rapid ascent and his rise from prosecutor to governor to candidate for the United States Senate roughly mirrors Floyd B. Olson's ascension in Minnesota politics. How deep the connections between Governor Olson and Kid Cann went, including whether Olson had any foreshadowing of what was in store for Walter Liggett, we'll never know.

One thing is certain: Floyd B. Olson remains a titanic figure. My uncle, State Representative Willard Munger, the last Farmer Laborite to hold office (he died of colon cancer in 1999) deified Olson. Like Donald Swanson in the novel, Uncle Willard grew up steeped in Nonpartisan League and FLA politics, eventually becoming a regional worker in, and manager of, Floyd B. Olson's campaigns. To Minnesotans who lived through the Great Depression, labor strife, Farm Holidays, farm auctions, and the troubled times depicted in this novel, Olson was and is a political saint. As a descendent of Farmer Labor Party loyalists, I grew up believing Floyd B. Olson to be a good man and an astute politician. Researching and writing this book did not change my opinion of him.

I should add that, if one reads the honorific biography of Governor Olson (*The Political Career of Floyd B. Olson*), you won't find any mention of Kid Cann or Walter Liggett's murder in that tome. I guess heroes, at least as rendered by their biographers, are most often memorialized as flawless, untarnished role models for children.

The depiction of Donald Swanson dabbling in novel writing is drawn from Walter Liggett's life. I own a signed copy of one of Liggett's fictional works, *The River Riders.* Though Liggett's career as a writer of pulp action-driven stories does not mirror the success of Donald Swanson's *This Lonely Land* depicted in my tale, as a failed journalist, I was intrigued to discover that even investigative reporters sometimes feel the need to flex their novelistic muscles!

Finally, I confess that—like Millie Swanson—I've not yet read *my* muckraker's novel. But I intend to.

Mark Munger
Duluth, Minnesota
September 15, 2023

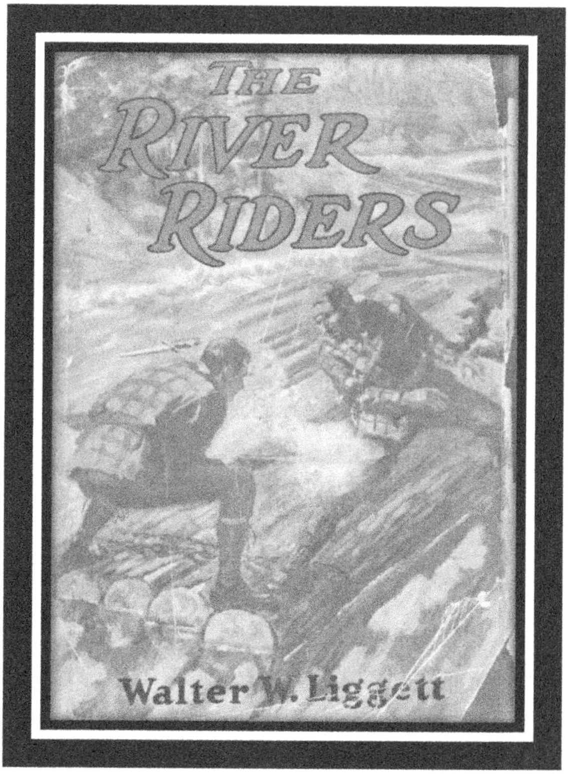
THE
RIVER
RIDERS
Walter W. Liggett

Resources

Books

Mr. Environment: The Willard Munger Story by Mark Munger (2009. Cloquet River Press. 978-0979217524)

Muckrakers by Ann Bausum (2007. National Geographic. ISBN978-1-45966-718-1)

The Political Career of Floyd B. Olson by George H. Mayer (1951. University of Minnesota. ISBN 978-087351206-0)

Stopping the Presses: The Murder of Walter Liggett by Marda Liggett Woodbury (1998. University of Minnesota. ISBN 978-081662929-90

The River Riders by Walter W. Liggett (1928. Macaulay)

The Jungle by Upton Sinclair (2003. BN Books. ISBN 978-1-59308-008)

Music

"The Walls of Red Wing" by Bob Dylan
https://www.youtube.com/watch?v=zCzn532kltk

Websites

"Abbot Hospital"
https://en.wikipedia.org/wiki/Abbott_Hospital

"Aconitine" https://en.wikipedia.org/wiki/Aconitine

"Amputations and Prosthetic Limbs in the First World War" by Alex Purcell https://throughveteranseyes.ca/2017/09/18/amputations-prosthetic-limbs-in-the-first-world-war/

"Andrew Volstead" https://en.wikipedia.org/wiki/Andrew_Volstead
"Bill Terry" https://en.wikipedia.org/wiki/Bill_Terry

"Battle of the Canal du Nord" https://en.wikipedia.org/wiki/Battle_of_the_Canal_du_Nord

"The Birth of Lincoln Logs" https://www.history.com/news/the-birth-of-lincoln-logs

"Blumenfeld, Isadore 'Kid Cann' (1900-1981)" by Paul Nelson https://www.mnopedia.org/person/blumenfeld-isadore-kid-cann-1900-1981

"Brooklyn" https://en.wikipedia.org/wiki/Brooklyn

"Brooklyn's First Voluntary Hospital" https://www.tbh.org/about-us/history
"Brooklyn Bridge Trolley" https://en.wikipedia.org/wiki/Brooklyn_Bridge_trolleys

"Blue Earth River State Water Trail" https://www.dnr.state.mn.us/watertrails/blueearthriver/index.html

"Capital Punishment in Minnesota" https://en.wikipedia.org/wiki/Capital_punishment_in_Minnesota

"Carl Panzram" https://en.wikipedia.org/wiki/Carl_Panzram

"Charles August Lindbergh" https://en.wikipedia.org/wiki/Charles_August_Lindbergh

"Chicago City Railway"
https://en.wikipedia.org/wiki/Chicago_City_Railway

"Chicago, St. Paul, Minneapolis and Omaha Railway"
https://en.wikipedia.org/wiki/Chicago,_St._Paul,_Minneapolis_and_Omaha_Railway

"Cleft Lip: The Historical Perspective" by S. Bhattacharya, V. Khanna, and R. Kohli
https://www.ncbi.nlm.nih.gov/pmc/articles/PMC2825059/

"Committee Makes Report (Red Wing)
https//corpun.com/red_wing

"The Dakota 400" https://www.american-rails.com/dkta.html

"David Graham Phillips"
https://en.wikipedia.org/wiki/David_Graham_Phillips

"Dean O'Banion"
https://en.wikipedia.org/wiki/Dean_O%27Banion

"Duluth Eskimos"
https://en.wikipedia.org/wiki/Duluth_Eskimos

"Ebbits Field" https://en.wikipedia.org/wiki/Ebbets_Field

"Empire Builder"
https://en.wikipedia.org/wiki/Empire_Builder

"Ethel Ray Nance"
https://www.mnopedia.org/person/nance-ethel-ray-1899-1992

"Ether in Surgery" by Josh Bicker
https://histmed.collegeofphysicians.org/ether-in-surgery/

"The Farmer-Labor Association: Minnesota's Party Within a Party" by Paul S. Holbo
https://collections.mnhs.org/mnhistorymagazine/articles/38/v38i07p301-309.pdf

"The Forgotten Crime Boss" by Brian P. Rubin
https://archives.lib.umn.edu/repositories/15/archival_objects/1177260

"Forum Cafeteria"
https://en.wikipedia.org/wiki/Forum_Cafeteria_(Minneapolis)

"George Kelly (Bascball)
https://en.wikipedia.org/wiki/George_Kelly_(baseball)

"The Great Depression"
https://en.wikipedia.org/wiki/Great_Depression

"The Green Lantern Saloon" by Owen Forsyth
https://theirishmob.com/the-green-lantern-saloon-st-paul-minnesota/

"Herbert Hoover"
https://en.wikipedia.org/wiki/Herbert_Hoover

"History of the Brooklyn Dodgers"
https://en.wikipedia.org/wiki/Brooklyn_Dodgers

"History of Jews in Finland"
https://en.wikipedia.org/wiki/History_of_the_Jews_in_Finland

"How Near North Came To Be …"
https://www.minnpost.com/mnopedia/2020/01/how-near-north-came-to-be-one-of-minneapolis-largest-black-communities/

"Jazz" https://en.wikipedia.org/wiki/Jazz

"Jean Rhys" https://en.wikipedia.org/wiki/Jean_Rhys

"John Francis Hylan"
https://en.wikipedia.org/wiki/John_Francis_Hylan

"Kid Cann and the Blumenfeld Family"
http://slphistory.org/kidcann/

"Kid Cann" https://en.wikipedia.org/wiki/Kid_Cann

"Kid Cann: The Kingpin of Minneapolis"
http://millcitytimes.com/news/kid-cann-the-kingpin-of-minneapolis.html

"Kiss Off Minneapolis-Following the Mob to Tropical Paradise" by Tony Randgaard
http://minnesotaconnected.com/news/local-happenings/kiss-off-minneapolis-following-the-mob-to-tropical-paradise_1312733/

"Lincoln Steffens"
https://en.wikipedia.org/wiki/Lincoln_Steffens

"List of Mayors of Minneapolis"
https://en.wikipedia.org/wiki/List_of_mayors_of_Minneapolist

"Lucky Strike History"
https://antiqueadvertising.com/lucky-strike-history/

"Mafia Stories"
https://mafiasome.blogspot.com/2015/05/white-hand-gang.html

"Marjorie McNelly Conservatory"
https://www.mnopedia.org/structure/marjorie-mcneely-conservatory-como-park-conservatory

"Minneapolis General Strike of 1934"
https://en.wikipedia.org/wiki/Minneapolis_general_strike_of_1934

"Minneapolis and St. Louis Railway"
https://en.wikipedia.org/wiki/Minneapolis_and_St._Louis_Railway

"The Minnesota Building"
https://en.wikipedia.org/wiki/Minnesota_Building

"Minnesotan" https://en.wikipedia.org/wiki/Minnesotan

"Minnesota Farmer Labor Party, 1924-1944"
https://www.mnopedia.org/minnesota-farmer-labor-party-1924-1944

"Minnesota's 'Godfather'"
https//www.tcdailyplnaet.net/Minnesota-godfather-kid-cacc-had-northeast-liquor-interests

"Moonshine Poured Across the Border" by Tom Olsen
https://www.parkrapidsenterprise.com/news/the-vault/moonshine-poured-across-canadian-border-during-prohibition-overwhelming-authorities-in-the-northland

"Nicollet Island"
https://en.wikipedia.org/wiki/Nicollet_Island

"Nicollet Park" https://en.wikipedia.org/wiki/Nicollet_Park

"1924 Oakland 6-54A"
https://auto.howstuffworks.com/1924-oakland-6-54a.htm

"1925 Brooklyn Robins" https://www.baseball-reference.com/teams/BRO/1925.shtml

"1931 Miller Statistics" https://www.baseball-reference.com/register/team.cgi?id=e5ac1fed

"Not Like Mother Used to Spank" https//corpun.com/red_wing

"Organized Crime in Minneapolis" https://en.wikipedia.org/wiki/Organized_crime_in_Minneapolis

"Oscar R. Dahlgren WW I Journals" https://libguides.mnhs.org/ww1/abroad

"Passenger Trains in Minnesota" https://www.allaboardmn.org/riding-on-a-train/case-for-trains-history/history-of-passenger-trains-in-mn/

"Phyllis Wheatley House, Minneapolis" https://www.mnopedia.org/place/phyllis-wheatley-house-minneapolis

"Polo Grounds" https://en.wikipedia.org/wiki/Polo_Grounds

"Red Wing State Training School" https://collections.mnhs.org/

"Repeal of Prohibition in the United States" https://en.wikipedia.org/wiki/Repeal_of_Prohibition_in_the_United_States

"The St. Paul Hotel" https://www.saintpaulhotel.com/
"St. Paul Saints 91901-1960)" https://en.wikipedia.org/wiki/St._Paul_Saints

"Second Battle of the Somme"
https://en.wikipedia.org/wiki/Second_Battle_of_the_Somme

"Sunset Park, Brooklyn"
https://en.wikipedia.org/wiki/Sunset_Park,_Brooklyn

"Teamsters Strike of 1934"
https://teamsters464.org/remember-1934/strike-history

"349th Infantry Regiment"
https://en.wikipedia.org/wiki/349th_Infantry_Regiment_(United_States)

"Trinity Brooklyn" https://www.trinitybrooklyn.org/trinity-history

"Twin Cities Assembly Plant"
https://en.wikipedia.org/wiki/Twin_Cities_Assembly_Plant

"Upton Sinclair"
https://en.wikipedia.org/wiki/Upton_Sinclair

"Volstead Act" https://en.wikipedia.org/wiki/Volstead_Act

"The Walls of Red Wing" by Brad Zeller
https//citypages.com/the_walls_of_red_wing/

"Walter Liggett"
https://en.wikipedia.org/wiki/Walter_Liggett

"War and Prosthetics" by Hunter Oatman-Stanford
https://www.collectorsweekly.com/articles/war-and-prosthetics/

"What is the Mann Act?"
https://www.findlaw.com/criminal/criminal-charges/what-is-the-mann-act.html

"White Hand Gang"
https://en.wikipedia.org/wiki/White_Hand_Gang

"Why Did Roosevelt Beat Hoover?"
https://www.markedbyteachers.com/gcse/history/why-did-roosevelt-defeat-hoover-in-the-1932-presidential-election.html

"Winchester Model 1897"
https://en.wikipedia.org/wiki/Winchester_Model_1897

Writer's Almanac for Wednesday, December 9, 2020
https://www.garrisonkeillor.com/radio/twa-the-writers-almanac-for-december-9-2020/

"Zach Wheat" https://www.baseball-reference.com/players/w/wheatza01.shtml

About the Author

Mark Munger, a former trial attorney and District Court Judge, is a lifelong resident of Northeastern Minnesota. Mark and his wife, René, live on the banks of the wild and scenic Cloquet River north of Duluth. When not writing and editing, Mark enjoys hunting, fishing, skiing, and reading excellent stories.

Other Works by the Author

The Legacy
(ISBN 0972005080 and eBook in all formats)
Set against the backdrop of WWII Yugoslavia and present-day Minnesota, this debut novel combines elements of military history, romance, thriller, and mystery. Rated 3 and 1/2 daggers out of 4 by *The Mystery Review Quarterly*.

Ordinary Lives
(ISBN 97809792717517 and eBook in all formats)
Creative fiction from one of Northern Minnesota's newest writers, these stories touch upon all elements of the human condition and leave the reader asking for more.

Pigs, a Trial Lawyer's Story
(ISBN 097200503x and eBook in all formats)

A story of a young trial attorney, a giant corporation, marital infidelity, moral conflict, and choices made, *Pigs* takes place against the backdrop of Western Minnesota's beautiful Smoky Hills. This tale is being compared by reviewers to Grisham's best.

Suomalaiset: People of the Marsh
(ISBN 0972005064 and eBook in all formats)

A dockworker is found hanging from a rope in a city park. How is his death tied to the turbulence of the times? A masterful novel of compelling history and emotion, *Suomalaiset* has been hailed by reviewers as a "must read."

Esther's Race
(ISBN 9780972005098 and eBook in all formats)

The story of an African American registered nurse who confronts race, religion, and tragedy in her quest for love, this novel is set against the stark and vivid beauty of Wisconsin's Apostle Islands, the pastoral landscape of Central Iowa, and the steel and glass of Minneapolis. A great read soon to be a favorite of book clubs across America.

Mr. Environment: The Willard Munger Story
(ISBN 9780979217524: Trade paperback only)

A detailed and moving biography of Minnesota's leading environmental champion and longest serving member of the Minnesota House of Representatives, *Mr. Environment* is destined to become a book every Minnesotan has on his or her bookshelf.

Black Water: Stories from the Cloquet River
(ISBN 9780979217548 and eBook in all formats)

Essays about ordinary and extraordinary events in the life of an American family living in the wilds of northeastern Minnesota, these tales first appeared separately in two volumes, *River Stories* and *Doc the Bunny*. Re-edited and compiled into one volume, these are stories to read on the deer stand, at the campsite, or late at night for peace of mind.

Laman's River
(ISBN 9780979217531 and eBook in all formats)

A beautiful newspaper reporter is found bound, gagged, and dead. A Duluth judge conceals secrets that may end her career. A reclusive community of religious zealots seeks to protect its view of the hereafter by unleashing an avenging angel upon the world. Mormons. Murder. Minnesota. Montana. Reprising two of your favorite characters from *The Legacy*, Deb Slater and Herb Whitefeather. Buy it now in print or on all major eBook platforms!

Sukulaiset: The Kindred
(ISBN 9780979217562 and eBook in all formats)

The long-awaited sequel to Suomalaiset: People of the Marsh, Mark Munger's epic novel of Finnish immigration to the United States and Canada, *Sukulaiset* portrays the journey of Elin Gustafson from the shores of Lake Superior to the shores of Lake Onega in the Soviet Republic of Karelia during the Great Depression. The story unfolds during Stalin's reign of terror and depicts the interwoven lives of Elin, her daughter Alexis, an American logger, and two Estonians wrapped up in the brutal conflict between Nazi Germany and Communist Russia. A page- turning historical novel of epic proportions.

Boomtown
(ISBN 978-0979217593 and eBook in all formats)

An explosion rocks the site of a new copper/nickel mine in northeastern Minnesota. Two young workers are dead. The Lindahl family turns to trial attorney Dee Dee Hernesman for justice. A shadowy eco-terrorist lurks in the background as Hernesman and Sheriff Deb Slater investigate the tragedy. Are the deaths the result of accident or murder? Equal parts legal thriller and literary fiction, this novel reprises many characters from Munger's prior novels. A page turner of a tale.

Kotimaa: Homeland
(ISBN 978-1-7324434-0-2 and eBook in all formats)

Wondering why Anders Alhomäki, the protagonist in *Suomalaiset* left Finland as a young man? How does the historic migration of Finns from Nordic Europe tie into the present-day immigration of Muslim refugees to Finland? Is a terrorist's threat on the cusp of Finland's centennial real or imagined? Part historical novel, part contemporary thriller, this book is the culmination of more than fourteen years' research. The final chapter in Munger's Finnish trilogy, *Kotimaa* is certain to challenge and entertain!

Kulkuri (Vagabond) and Other Short Stories
(ISBN 978-1-7324434-1-9 and Kindle eBook)

Mark's second collection of short fiction includes award- winning stories and the new novella, "The Angle," as well as a handful of other, brand new gems. Tales from Minnesota to Estonia to Hawaii will engage and enlighten and entertain readers who love short-form fiction.

Duck and Cover: Things Learned Waiting for the Bomb
(ISBN 978-1-7324434-2-6 and Kindle eBook)

A coming-of-age memoir set in northern Minnesota during the Cold War, this collection of candid and humorous essays will cause readers to consider their own personal histories.

Visit us at:
www.cloquetriverpress.com
Shop at our online store!

SmileTrain

Changing The World One Smile At A Time.

10% of all gross sales of CRP books are donated by CRP to SmileTrain in hopes of helping children born with cleft lips and palates across the world. Learn more about SmileTrain at http://www.smiletrain.org/.

Made in the USA
Monee, IL
22 September 2023